Books by
Elaine Stienon

Lightning in the Fog

Utah Spring

The Light of the Morning

In Clouds of Fire

The Way to the Shining City

Children of a Northern Kingdom

a story of the Strangite Mormons in Wisconsin
and on Beaver Island, Michigan

Elaine Stienon

authorHOUSE®

AuthorHouse™
1663 Liberty Drive
Bloomington, IN 47403
www.authorhouse.com
Phone: 1 (800) 839-8640

Published by AuthorHouse 09/08/2017

ISBN: 978-1-5462-0334-6 (sc)
ISBN: 978-1-5462-0333-9 (e)

Library of Congress Control Number: 2017912420

1

THE ONLY THING RUSTY Manning knew for certain was the year: 1846. Late spring already. Time to put crops in the ground. And here he was, walking beside a carriage somewhere in northern Illinois. Twenty-seven, big-boned, large in stature, he had strong arms and shoulders from years of work in a blacksmith shop. He strode now through tall grass as they followed a wagon trace to the north.

The carriage itself, once one of the finest rigs money could buy, now looked ancient, its colors faded. Rusty tried not to think of how their small procession must appear to the outside world. Even the horses looked old, matched bays with their muzzles graying. A younger horse, a grey speckled gelding, plodded behind the carriage.

Adriel, whose name meant 'beaver' in his native language, sat in the driver's seat with the reins in his hands. He was a man of indeterminate age, his features strong and impassive. His jet black hair, tied loosely at the nape of his neck, hung down his back. His skin, bronzed and weathered by the sun, hinted at his native American parentage. His ragged clothes and the droop of his shoulders gave the impression of tiredness. Like all of us now, Rusty thought.

A third man walked on the other side of the carriage, brushing away gnats from around his face. He appeared to be a mixture of many races, native American, European, even a trace of what might have been African ancestry. He had the look of a pirate about him, and a way of drawing his black brows together and glaring at people. This characteristic, along with others, had earned him the name 'Crazy

Charley.' Rusty knew that Charley was not crazy, but very wise and shrewd. And in his hands the expedition lay.

Behind the carriage, a pair of young oxen trudged, their coats encrusted with mud from the journey. The wagon they pulled had seen numerous repairs, maybe one too many. The wheels creaked in protest at each bump, each rock or fallen tree limb. Eb Wanfield, once a slave, drove the ox team. He sat hunched in the front seat, his hair untrimmed, shaggy, a blacksmith like Rusty. In the wagon, packed alongside clothing, dishes, and bedding, rode most of the tools they would need to establish a blacksmith shop.

They were refugees, these four, fleeing from trouble and persecution. Their clothes were unwashed and shabby, their faces lined with dirt. Toughened by the journey, they looked warily about, uneasiness in their eyes. For they were Mormons, driven out of their city of Nauvoo with what little they could salvage. With their leader Joseph Smith assassinated, their charter revoked and mobs descending on them, they had little choice but to leave the city.

What united this particular group was the belief that another prophet and leader had come forth, a man by the name of James J. Strang, who claimed to have been appointed by Joseph Smith to gather and lead the people. It was to this gathering that they were headed, Voree on the White River in Wisconsin Territory. Voree, the 'Garden of Peace.'

May it be so, Rusty thought as he put his hand on the carriage. Freedom, the speckled horse walking just behind them, gave a snort and shook his head.

"Whatsa matter, fella?" Adriel looked back over his shoulder. "You see something we don't?"

Charley spoke from the other side of the carriage. "Deer, most likely. Some wild critter."

"It lunch time yet?" Rusty asked hopefully. The other two exchanged glances, and Rusty figured the answer was no.

"Let's get closer to the river first," Charley said.

They had a deadline to meet. Before they struck a northeasterly course for Voree, they had to pick up the rest of the family. Rusty thought with longing of his young wife Marie-Françoise, and how he had missed her these past four weeks. Now that the time of reunion was almost upon them, he could hardly believe it.

Gabriel Romain, the leader of their group, had decided that since Marie and Eb's wife Jess were both expectant mothers, it was wisest for them to travel most of the way by boat and join the teams at Dubuque for the overland trip across Wisconsin. Rusty protested at being parted from Marie, but since Gabe was not only Marie's brother but a medical doctor as well, his decision prevailed. At least Marie would have a doctor with her at all times. The task of the team-drivers was to be waiting when the steamboat docked. "Even if you have to camp out there and bide a spell," Gabe had said, "do it."

If Gabe had calculated things right, they had three days to be at the rendez-vous point. When Rusty fretted about getting there too late, Adriel only grunted.

"We know this river, inside and out," Charley told him. "I reckon we be right on course."

Rusty nodded. *Should've known better.* Long before Rusty and his co-religionists had settled in Illinois, Adriel and Charley had been on the Mississippi. 'River rats,' some had called them. New converts to Mormonism, they had joined Gabe's group once they heard he was headed for Voree. And Rusty, for one, was glad for their expertise.

"We'll stop here for some grub," Charley said. "Over by that stand of trees. River's right there, and we'll fill up our jugs."

Soon they were sitting cross-legged in the shade of the trees. Eb sliced bread and cheese, which he passed around. "We be runnin' low again."

"Seems like we just bought victuals in the last town." Rusty wiped his mouth on his sleeve.

"That were two towns ago," Charley said.

They leaned back against the tree trunks. Adriel took a swig of water and passed the jug to Charley. "At least the water's free."

Charley tipped up the jug and drank. "That be right good." He passed it to Rusty. "All I need now is someone to read to me so's I can take a nap."

"I reckon you'll get plenty of that when you get to Voree," Adriel said. "Preachin', and what not."

"Last thing I read was that newspaper. The *Voree Herald*," Eb said. "Gabe made us all read it, but I'm not sure why."

Rusty put down the jug. "Don't you 'member? The letter of appointment was in it. You know—the one saying James Strang was to be our new leader. Joseph wrote to him from Nauvoo, and he got it after the prophet was kilt."

Charley nodded. "It's hard to forget them things. Why, Strang wrote in the newspaper that he was anointed at the hands of an angel. Derned if the angel didn't come to him at 5:30, the afternoon of the assassination. Ordained him ruler of God's people. And here he was in Wisconsin, miles away."

"If that don't beat all," Eb said.

"What's important is what the angel said to him." Rusty gestured as he passed the water jug to Eb. "'Thou shalt save his people from their enemies. While the day of the wicked abideth, thou shalt prepare a refuge for the oppressed and for the poor and needy.'"

"That be us, all right," Eb said. "Ain't nobody poorer and more needy that I can see."

"And them plates," Adriel said.

"Ah, yes." Charley wiped his hands on his trousers. "The Plates of Voree. It told about how he said where to dig, and the fellers that dug them up couldn't see that the ground was disturbed in any way."

Adriel smiled. "Sounds like the kind of prophet for my money."

"Blame it." Charley gave a short laugh. "You don't even have any."

They decided that since they would need food for the ones who were joining them, Rusty would stop at the next farmhouse and offer to split wood for some provisions.

"But why me?"

"Why, yer the prettiest," Charley told him. "If I did it, or Adriel, they'd most likely run screaming. Or take a shotgun after us. Eb can help you with the wood, if they're agreeable."

So Rusty prepared to hike to the nearest farmhouse and offer his services. Eb walked with him, leaving the others with the teams. Eb paused when they reached the front gate. "I'll just wait here till you gets things settled."

While they worked splitting logs, Rusty thought of the others that would be arriving by boat. Besides his own Marie, and Eb's wife Jess, there was the twelve-year-old daughter of Eb and Jess—Turah, whom Gabe and Eb had bought out of slavery. There was Gabe himself, quick and wiry, his mop of black hair shaggy about his ears and neck. He had a wisp of a black moustache on his upper lip, which made him look even more like Rusty's idea of a French *voyageur*. Gabe's wife Bethia, once pretty, now looked dumpy and cross most of the time—cross mainly at Gabriel and his escapades. Then Rusty's father, Calvin Manning, and Sarah, his outspoken second wife. Rusty wondered if she was done protesting about the loss of the two black mares. "Such a right smart team." His father had traded them for the oxen.

"Horses can't haul all them tools up to Wisconsin. It be a long, hard pull."

Gabe had agreed. Since the group now considered him their leader and advisor, the matter was settled. Rusty collected the split pieces and put them on the pile. An image rose in his mind—his friend Gabe Romain, called Dr. Gabriel by most of his patients. Shorter than most men, slender, Gabe had a quickness to his step, a way of slipping through woods in silence. This skill had helped him lead countless runaway slaves to safe houses in southern Ohio. If there was such a thing as a passionate abolitionist, Gabe was it. He was twenty-nine, a few years older than Rusty and Marie. Rusty marveled at how Gabe had been his close comrade during the growing-up years in Kirtland. It was there that Gabe had studied medicine, and later, in Nauvoo, he had worked to teach them all the trade of blacksmithing, which he had learned in his youth. Now, finally, he had assumed the leadership of their little group and was determined to get them to Voree. Rusty leaned his ax against the fence post.

"What? You're gonna let me chop the rest of this by myself?" Eb's voice jarred him back to the present.

"No—I was just resting a spell, is all. I was minded of Gabe, and—and all he's been through. And now he's responsible for all those women and—and such like." *Bethia,* his mind said, but he didn't go on.

"You worried about Marie? I reckon she's in pretty good hands."

"I wasn't thinking of Marie. I was thinking more like—well, Bethia wants a child more than anybody. And the rest of them are going to be mothers, and she isn't."

Eb put up another chunk of wood and swung at it. "It's too bad. I reckon life ain't fair. Like as not, Gabe will find a child for them to adopt."

"In the meantime, I don't guess she's making life any easier for him."

Eb put down the ax and looked at him. "I be minded of the time when you wanted to marry her yourself."

"Thank goodness I didn't. I was luckier than I knew. Finding Marie was the best thing ever happened to me."

Eb let out his breath and nodded. "Well, Bethia was fine when Gabe married her. She changed—something happened to her. Gabe says she's fragile—kind of a sickness of the mind. We all have to take care of her."

They carried the provisions they had earned—a slab of bacon, a pail of fresh eggs and a loaf of new bread. Rusty sniffed at the sack of bread. "Corey Langdon, now. Marie and Jess kept sayin' what a fine wife she would've made for Gabe."

Eb stopped. "Now, hang it all. That's all in the past. Whatever Gabe might have thought about Corey—and God knows he didn't do nuthin' about it—she be long gone. Her father has taken her and her sister west, with Brigham Young's group. They be halfway across Iowa by this time, I reckon. And, in case you forgot, we don't hold with plural marriage."

"I know all that." He'd said too much. What he'd forgotten was that Eb was Gabe's best friend, quick to defend him. "I only meant—"

"Whatever you meant, it's best you don't speak of it again. Say what you want to Marie, but keep mum in front of the others. Especially Bethia. You want to bring all hell down around Gabe's head?"

"He tried to get them to come with us."

"And they didn't. I reckon it's for the best. The farther away Corey gets, the better. Now, let's have no more such talk."

Rusty sighed. Ahead of them he could see the horses and oxen, with

Charley napping under the wagon. Beyond that, the sun glittered on the river in patches of light.

A wind blew at their backs. It was not a cold wind, but it was fresh, full of the faint scent of fish from the river. Eb said to Gabriel, "If'n we had sails, it could blow us to Voree."

Bethia sat beside Sarah in the carriage. Sarah, stout and middle-aged, had frizzy gray hair framing her roundish face. She wore a critical expression most of the time. Bethia counted Sarah as her nearest relative, in a way, since Sarah had been married to Bethia's Uncle Jake. Jake had died in Kirtland, and later Sarah had married the widower Calvin Manning, father of Rusty. He was also the father of Hannah, married to Nat Givens, their former leader. Nat had elected to stay near Nauvoo, on the Iowa side of the river.

"I wouldn't worry about him none," Charley had said. "All them cabins he's got hid. If'n they burn one, he just finds another."

Bethia was trying to overcome her dislike of Charley and Adriel. Gabriel had told her more than once how much they knew about the territory and how useful they were. He liked them both, she knew, but it was hard to see why. Now they were her brothers in the faith. She drew a deep breath and let it out again. Easy to accept them when they weren't around her. But now, on this journey east, they lived in such close quarters that avoiding them was impossible.

She sighed again. She'd been on countless journeys—from New York to Kirtland, Ohio, from Kirtland to Far West, Missouri, back across Missouri to Illinois, a brief stay near Montrose, Iowa, and then to Nauvoo. This one to Voree should be no different.

"What is it, honey?" Sarah turned to look at her. "You be feelin' poorly again?"

"No. Just tired of riding, is all."

"Next time we stop, I reckon you c'n walk a spell. That's what I aim to do."

In fact, the main trouble was that she felt just fine. Here she'd planned for a child, had wanted one since she'd been married. But no blessed event had come her way. Instead she'd had to watch while Marie and Jess went through the first months of pregnancy. They'd shared together the times of nausea and weakness, and now, both in their fourth month, they slept nestled together in the wagon.

Bethia ran the ends of her shawl through her fingers. She wanted to weep, but then Sarah would know—most likely suspected already. Bethia had tried to like Marie, her own sister-in-law. For her, Marie was too energetic, even frolicsome—one of those people who seemed to live twice as fast as anyone else. But Rusty loved her. And this was another sore spot. She could have married Rusty—could have had him instead of Gabriel. Maybe then she would have been a mother.

Gabriel, riding ahead on the speckled horse Freedom, doubled back and looked in the carriage. "I reckon we'll stop for the noonday meal. Time for us to eat a bit."

What he meant, thought Bethia bitterly—it was time for the expectant mothers to eat.

"We have the makings of soup," Sarah said. "Carrots and potatoes." She nudged Bethia. "We'll get them in the pot right away."

Gabriel said a few words to Calvin, who was driving the carriage. Then he turned the horse back beside the wagon and spoke to Eb. In a short time they stopped in the shade of the trees. Rusty and Adriel got a fire going, and Sarah hauled out potatoes and carrots.

"Here," she said to Bethia. "You get these peeled. I'll look for that turnip we saved. Charley, we need you to go for water."

"Creek's right yonder." He took the pail and sauntered off.

Bethia allowed herself a few tears as she dropped the peeled potatoes into the pot. Marie and Jess were not expected to work—Gabriel saw to that.

"You be slow." Sarah's voice spoke at her shoulder. Then Sarah took over the making of the soup, pouring water over the vegetables and hanging the pot over the fire. She stood stirring it, adding salt from their supply. Bethia was wiping her eyes with her apron when she sensed someone beside her.

"How're you makin' it, Bethy?" It was Calvin; she looked up. His thick eyebrows drew together, the same shade as his graying hair. Of stocky build, he had a broad nose and wide mouth. His eyes crinkled at the corners as he smiled.

"I—all right, I reckon." She was touched by his kindness, his obvious concern for her.

"I'm glad to hear it. This ain't the easiest part of the journey. But it's less'n seventy miles now, if we figured right. Maybe another week."

She smiled at him. He went on. "I reckon yer missin' yer friend Corey. I know Marie and Jess do. Too bad she had to go with her father."

Bethia felt her smile fading. "Excuse me. I think I'll go set a spell."

She went to sit on one of the fallen logs. *Corey indeed.* All she needed. She tried not to recall how glad she thought she'd be without Corey around. Jess and Marie had really taken to Corey; they'd been close friends. Now she was long gone, and Bethia was still unhappy.

Sarah ladled out soup and Rusty carried the first bowls of it to the women in the wagon. Bethia hunched over and began to weep.

<hr>

They reached Voree in the mid-afternoon. Gabriel, walking beside the wagon, caught Eb's eye and pointed. Eb slowed the oxen to a stop.

A river made a slight bend in front of them. On either side grew cattails and marsh weeds, with a clump of vegetation, like an island, in the middle.

"A pretty place," Eb said.

On their side of the river stood a group of houses, plain dwellings, some half-finished. Tents and covered wagons dotted the area, and board shanties hastily erected.

"Looks like an encampment," Charley remarked. "But, like as not, it's the town."

Marie and Jess were sitting up in the wagon, with Turah holding up the edge of the tarp so they could all peer out—two black faces, one pink, their eyes alight with hope and wonder. Gabriel smiled at the sight of them and moved closer. "My friends, I reckon we've found it. Fair Voree."

Eb clicked to the oxen and they moved on. A murmur of voices came from the carriage, Sarah and Bethia discussing something, Calvin joining in.

Gabriel tried to think if everything was in order. His mind went over every detail. The animals all in good shape. The people—a bit tired, but otherwise provided for. The mothers-to-be both healthy. Marie all right in her first pregnancy. He'd worried about Jess because she was older—no one knew her exact age because she'd escaped out of slavery. And she was not a big woman—both she and Turah seemed small, delicate to the point of fragility. But they held their own. Like as not, if Jess could have Turah, she'd give birth to this second one without difficulty.

The tools for the shop. All secure. And tools to build cabins—everything they would need. Even the steamboat voyage—uneventful, a calm ride for the women, as he'd hoped. He began to relax, reassured, his burden lifting. He'd brought them through at last. Nat, their former leader, couldn't have done better. He stepped up beside the lead ox and strode into the little settlement.

People hurried out of the ramshackle houses and advanced toward Gabriel and his caravan.

"If it ain't Dr. Gabriel!"

"And his family of blacksmiths! The Lord be praised!"

Gabriel recognized men he'd remembered from Nauvoo—some he hadn't known were supporters of Strang. Many had kept quiet about it in Nauvoo, for fear of threats from the Brighamite faction, the followers of Brigham Young and the Twelve. One of the men shook his hand.

"Well, I reckon we don't have to worry about Aunt Peggy no more."

Gabriel laughed. "I'll wager she's long gone."

"Gone west," another man said. "And good riddance."

'Aunt Peggy,' their term for a whipping, had been promised to anyone in Nauvoo caught listening to the Strangite missionaries. "Them days are over," one man said. "We can worship as we please, now."

Rusty dismounted from Freedom and stood holding the reins. Just then the crowd parted, and a lone figure walked toward them. All voices stilled. The man was not tall, but he moved with grace and authority. Slender, he looked to be in his mid-thirties. He had an arresting appearance—a high, bulging forehead, reddish hair and a full beard. He wore a blue shirt and black-and-white checked trousers, and he carried a straw hat. Gabriel stared, mesmerized by the forceful glint in the other's eyes.

"Uh—Brother Strang?"

"Yes, brother. Welcome to Voree." They shook hands. "And you are—"

"Gabriel Romain, sir. And this be my brother-in-law Rusty Manning, and my friend Eb Wanfield. I'm a physician, but the rest be blacksmiths and farmers." He introduced them all, even the women. Strang nodded, listening gravely.

"Well, you be right welcome. I suggest you find a place to camp for the night—anywhere here along the river is good. Then, when you're ready, we can talk about lots—we have one–quarter of an acre lots and whole acres available for fifty dollars each. Then there're smaller ones for twelve fifty each. We don't have exposure to those river fevers—I know you'll miss them. Here our industry is rewarded, our rights respected. The only thing we insist upon is that there be no spirituous liquor."

"We didn't bring any," Gabriel said.

"Charley already drank it all," a voice said from behind the carriage. The crowd began to laugh.

Brother Strang paused, then continued. "No spirituous liquor."

Gabriel spoke quickly. "Of course, sir. We'll get set up—we have several small tents, and the women can sleep in the wagon. The sooner we can get a place built, the sooner we can set up a forge for the smithy."

"That will be very welcome, I'm sure. We'll give you all the help you need. Right, boys?" Strang looked around at the crowd. "First priority is getting this blacksmith shop set up."

They prepared to camp in the bend of the river. Jess and Turah would stay in the wagon with Eb and the tools. Sarah and Calvin had the carriage, which Gabriel covered with a piece of canvas. Gabriel helped Rusty put up two small tents, one for Rusty and Marie, the second for himself and Bethia. Come dark, Charley and Adriel would walk off into the woods with their bedrolls, which they had done all during the journey. "That way, we won't crowd you none," Charley had said.

With the camp complete and the bedding in place, Gabriel looked around. Calvin and Eb had the fire going, and Sarah had a mess of beans cooking in the pot with a little salt pork.

"You figure there be fish here?" Adriel asked.

"Well, of course there be fish," Charley replied. "That heron ain't gonna stand out there for nothin'."

"I don't mean minnows and such-like. I mean real fish, like trout."

"Why don't you fellers go see?" Gabriel said. "Catch some, we'll have a mess."

Charley and Adriel walked down to the river with their improvised fish hooks and poles. Gabriel noticed Bethia sitting alone on a log. Downcast, as usual. She'd acted angry at him for days, although he couldn't think why. Maybe she needed some attention. He went to sit beside her, wondering if he would be rebuffed.

"It's a right pretty place, isn't it?" he remarked.

She turned to look at him. "You call this pretty? All these shacks and tents?"

"Kind of like Far West, isn't it?"

"They—they had cabins."

He shrugged. "Well—there're some here."

She lifted her hands in a gesture of hopelessness, then let them fall in her lap. "Gabriel—you brought us all the way on the boat, and across the prairie, for *this*?"

He gave a little laugh. "Well, I didn't know what was here. I didn't expect golden towers and flags flying—not in this wild country. But we're gonna build us a city. You heard him say they'd help with putting up a shop. And I reckon you'll have that house you wanted, before the snow flies."

She let out her breath. "Like as not, we'll have to crowd in with everybody else."

"If we do, it'll only be for one season. Come on, Bethia—look at the good things. We be safe here. No one's chasing us, threatening to drive us out. That means a lot." He reached for her hand. She jerked it away. He tried to keep his voice pleasant. "I reckon you'll feel better after we've eaten."

She made no reply. He sat for a moment, looking at the preparations for dinner. Then he sighed and got to his feet. *"Eh bien.* I expect I'd better go see to the animals."

2

IN TWO WEEKS THEY had the shop building up and one of the cabins started. Gabriel not only had help from his crew of friends, but five other men from the community as well. They all had different ideas about where to put the chimney for the forge.

"At this end. Look—you just walk in and the forge is right there."

"You don't want to trip over it," one of the men said. "You fall into that, it be a mighty hot surprise."

"T'other end be further away from them trees, I reckon," Eb said.

Gabriel made the final decision and sent Rusty and Eb out to gather stones for the chimney.

"There be plenty of them over in old Elmer's field," someone said. "He can't even plow the ground for all the rocks. He'll thank you if you take 'em."

Gabriel nodded. "I'd be beholden if you showed 'em where to look."

The rest, under Calvin's direction, continued work on the cabin. Gabriel went to stand beside Calvin. "How's it going?"

"It'll be up in no time, most like. Tomorrow afternoon, if'n we're lucky. I reckon this one better be for you and Bethia. She's so skittery-like, and it might calm her down some."

They planned to build a cabin for Eb and his family, and a bigger one with two sleeping rooms to house Calvin and Sarah, and Rusty and Marie. Charley and Adriel would have a room behind the smithy. Calvin and Gabriel had chipped in together to buy one of the large lots and intended to plant crops on the back portion.

"And don't forget the animals," someone said. "Less'n you want 'em all in the common stable."

"That'll do for a while." Gabriel picked up one end of a squared-off log.

"Sure be plenty of wood to work with," Calvin said. "Mostly pine, from what I see."

As they worked, they talked about the news of the community.

"I hear tell that Brother Strang sent a message to Nauvoo," a bearded man said. "He ordered Brigham Young and the Twelve to appear in Voree. Can you imagine—*here*—to be tried for usurping authority."

"What'd they do?" Calvin asked.

"Well, they ignored it, of course. You think old Brigham would come here and be excommunicated?"

Charley lifted a log in place. "I reckon he's got enough on his mind—leading all them folks west."

"In fact," the bearded man said, "he allowed he'd excommunicate any folks listening to Strangite missionaries. That's what they be calling us now. Strangites."

An older man with whitish blond hair handed up another log. "I hear Brother Strang went and converted at least three hundred from that group. He was debating a feller named Reuben Miller, down around St. Charles. Derned if Miller warn't convinced also."

Gabriel gave a laugh. "I reckon Brother Strang can be pretty persuasive."

The blond man went on. "Just afore you got here, we had a conference. We sustained Brother James and his counselors. But Brigham Young and most of the apostles got excommunicated anyway. And they weren't even here."

"Seems kind of silly," Charley remarked. "I mean, now everyone be excommunicated."

Gabriel shrugged. "Gives 'em something to do." He felt a hand on his shoulder. Startled, he turned. Turah stood beside him.

"Oh, Dr. Gabriel. I be so sorry to disturb you." She stood on one foot, then the other. "Sarah done sent me."

Instantly alert. "What is it? Your momma doing all right?"

"Oh, momma's fine."

"Marie, then. Anything wrong with Marie?"

The girl's eyes widened and her words tumbled over each other. "No, no—Marie—she be all right. Oh, sir, it's—it's Bethia. She done run off."

"Run off?"

"They can't find her anywhere. Sarah's looked all afternoon. Even my momma and Marie—they be out looking. They looked in the wagon, the carriage, the tents. They went to all the neighbor folks—"

"Excuse me," Gabriel said to the men. They nodded and kept working. He walked with Turah down toward their camp by the river. "I can't believe she'd just go off into the woods alone. These are wild places, full of bears and such-like."

Turah was breathing fast. "I know. I wouldn't go in there by myself, no, sirree."

"Well, you have more sense." He glanced at her—she looked to be taller than her mother now, not as scrawny as when he'd first met her. He tried to speak calmly, not wanting to upset her even more. "In fact, you be growing up just fine. But you should be keeping on with your lessons—we've neglected them, with all the traveling. I thought Bethia was teaching you."

"My father helps me with the reading now. Most every night we read together. And momma's learning too."

"That's fine." Gabriel brushed away a gnat. "Soon as the cabins are up, we'll do even better than that. We'll have a regular school—for everybody."

Sarah met them in front of the carriage. She wiped her eyes with the hem of her apron. "It's all true—like Turah said. We've looked high and low—simply everywhere. Talked to all the neighbors. They—"

"*Eh bien*. Now, listen. First I want you to find Marie and Jess. Make them stop looking—they need to rest. Now, where's Adriel? Him and Charley—why, they can track most anything."

"Adriel be off fishing. He said he'd have a mess for dinner."

Gabriel looked at Turah. "Go see if you can find him along the river bank. And then get Charley—he's up working. Don't go into the woods."

"I won't, sir."

"All we need is two folks lost. Now—when did you last see her?"

Sarah wrung her hands and gave a little hopeless gesture. Turah said, "'Bout mid-morning. Up by the new cabins. See them trees right there? She went up to watch the men work."

Gabriel nodded and started back up toward the cabins. He passed the crew of workmen and entered the woods. He moved silently, alert for any noises. The faint sounds of hammering came to him, and chickadees high in the pines. Somewhere a crow gave its raucous cry.

What was the matter with her? He had asked himself the question time and again. To change from someone who was dependable to a person who had to be watched, like a young child. He felt the frustration of not being able to help her, of not having enough competence to fix whatever was wrong. For a physician, trained to discover the cause of the ailment and try to make it better, it was doubly hard. He gave a deep sigh and brushed aside the low-hanging branches.

For the first time in many weeks, he allowed himself to think of Corey. *Memories coming with a rush—meeting her on the road out of Far West after her father had fallen from the front seat of the wagon. Rushing to her aid. Finding Jubal Langdon uninjured, but suffering from a severe cold. Talking with Corey, instructing her in the care of her father, telling her to make a place in the back of the wagon for him.*

What he remembered most—Corey's steadfast, earnest look, her strong features, the resolute set to her jaw. Whatever happened, he had the feeling she would get her family out of Far West to a place of safety, both her sick father and her younger sister who could not speak but only make singing noises. Somehow they would reach their relatives in the next county.

Which they did, and Gabriel's own expedition stopped at that very farmhouse as they fled Far West. There Hannah had given birth to her second child, a daughter. After that, the three Langdons had become part of their lives—the widower Jubal and his daughters Casey and Corey. *Especially Corey.* If he'd had any sense, he would have married Corey. But he was already promised to Bethia, and the art of seeing the future had been denied him.

Remembering—saying good-bye to her the morning the people in his charge had boarded the steamboat. Knowing he would never see her again. Even while everything within him was urging him to take her and run away, begin again somewhere else, he knew his duty lay with shepherding his community north and making a new start in Wisconsin Territory.

Now—where was he? Somewhere in the wilds of Wisconsin, with a shop building erected and a cabin almost finished. And a wife missing— one with very little sense, it seemed— lost in a trackless wilderness. *Had he made the right decision?* Better, maybe, if they'd stayed in Nauvoo— they would have been safe across the river, on Nat Givens' farm. Or gone west with the main group of refugees.

He stopped, and his mouth tightened. They were here now, and he had to make the best of it. Angry that the memory of Corey seemed so fresh, as if her very spirit was with him in the pine-scented air. *Your past goes with you,* he decided. *Always part of you.* But now he had to think in the present. If he were Bethia, where would he have gone?

Somewhere to the west, crows were calling. He heard the faint alarm-bark of a squirrel. Moving silently, he made his way toward the sounds. A sick feeling gnawed in the pit of his stomach. What if they couldn't find her before nightfall? Or what if something else got to her first—bear or catamount, or unfriendly Indians? And once he did find her, how could he keep her from wandering off again? He crossed a clearing, a meadow full of high grass, and entered the forest again. Trees grew thicker here, pines taller—not much light. Like as not, she wouldn't have come this way. The squirrel barks rang out just ahead; he would investigate and then turn back.

He thrust aside a pine branch and saw her sitting on a log not ten feet away. A little creek ran beside rocks and clumps of underbrush. Tiny, delicate ferns poked out from beside its bank. Bethia was gazing at the water, a fern frond in her hand. Not wanting to startle her, he shuffled his feet in the dry leaves. She looked around.

He stepped toward her. "Ah, there you are."

Her whole body seemed to stiffen. "How—how did you find me?"

"The birds and squirrels told me where to look. Don't get up. I see you've found a pretty place." He sat down beside her on the log. Already he could sense her moving away from him. "I take it you did want to be found."

She didn't answer. He waited, wondering what to do next. Finally he said, "When you go off like this, Bethia, I reckon you know you're alarming a whole community. Adriel and Charley—they be looking for you too."

"I didn't figure anyone would care."

"Of course they care. And they're taking time from their work to go and find you. Here our cabin's almost built, and Charley had to stop work..." He trailed off, not wanting to sound accusatory. "Well, I guess a few day's delay won't matter none. Two more nights in the tent."

She looked down at the bit of fern in her hand. "I—I reckon I didn't see it that way."

He tried not to sound insistent. "Bethia, why did you run off?"

She waited before she spoke. "I used to go sit by the river in Nauvoo—just watch the water—the birds and such-like. I just wanted to be by myself for a spell."

"I see. Well, there's a perfectly good river there by the settlement. You don't have to go off into the woods."

She didn't look at him. Time for the heavy artillery. "You know, going off alone like this—it's not a good idea. I don't mean to frighten you, but these are not the banks of the Mississippi. This—" He waved his hands. "—it's wilderness. Not only can you get lost, but there's bears—"

"Bears? *Here?*"

"And catamounts. Wildcats, lynx, badgers—what else? Wolves, most like. And some Indians who may not be too friendly."

She stared at him, her eyes as wide as Turah's. He shrugged. "I mean, if you don't care about meeting up with critters—"

"Oh, I do. I do."

He pressed his advantage. "And there's even snakes—Charley told me. A rattler that lives in boggy places like this. Now, most snakes, they rattle before they bite you. But this one—it bites you first and then it rattles."

A tear spilled out of one eye and slid down her cheek. He went on.

"Yes—once one of them bites you, it's all over. Forget about anything else."

She shuddered. He reached for her hand, and this time she let him take it. He helped her to her feet. "I reckon we'd best go back and tell the others. They'll want to know you're safe."

She stepped beside him into the thicket of forestland, then across the meadow. Shadows fell on the high grass. "I reckon Sarah's started cooking supper by this time," he said.

At the edge of the clearing, before they entered the woods again, she burst out, "Oh, Gabriel—I'm right sorry. I'll stay out of the woods from now on."

"It's all right," he said gently. "I reckon you didn't know about how wild it is in these parts."

"The thing is—I don't feel at home here. I miss Nauvoo—the big houses, and the river so close and beautiful."

"I think we all do. No one likes to pick up and leave such a pretty place. But what else could we do? They were hunting us like rabbits. Here we can make a new start—build up another town. I don't know—I reckon I'd rather deal with a bunch of wild critters than folks so riled at us."

She looked at him, and the lines around her mouth seemed to relax. For a moment she looked like the young girl he had courted and hoped to marry, back in the Far West days. He pressed her hand. "Things will be all right. Trust me. Soon our cabin will be ready, and we'll have a home again."

"I reckon what I really want is—is a child. A baby of my own."

He tried to think what to say. "I know you do. And maybe here—after we get settled some—it'll happen. It can still happen—there's lots of time."

She sniffed. "That's what you always say."

"I happen to believe it."

They walked hand in hand under the trees. Suddenly she stiffened; a wary, tense expression rushed over her face. Gabriel saw Charley tramping toward them from the direction of the river.

"I found her!" Gabriel called out. "She's safe."

"I—I thought it was a bear," Bethia said.

Gabriel laughed. "Just Charley. He may smell like a bear, but he's a good sight to see if you're ever lost."

"Adriel's just behind," Charley said when he had reached them.

They heard something moving in the dried leaves, and Adriel appeared between two large pines. He looked at Bethia without smiling. "I'm right glad you turned up."

She did not reply. Gabriel sensed she was offended, but Adriel had not intended any disrespect; it was just his way. *A man of few words.* They started back toward Voree. Gabriel could feel Bethia slipping away from him—it was like a curtain coming down between them. By the time they reached the river, it seemed as if the woman he had known so briefly had disappeared, and in her place walked a tight-lipped, disapproving stranger.

⸺⸻⸺

Rusty's wife Marie had not yet joined the Mormon Church; she had remained Catholic. Every week he drove the carriage to Burlington, a two-mile trip, where she attended mass. He waited for her, and sometimes attended with her. He enjoyed these times with her—enjoyed the closeness they had in the last months of her pregnancy. And in spite of what his Huguenot ancestors might have said, he even enjoyed the mass itself, a time to reflect and relax from his labors at home.

On a morning in late July, they prepared for the usual pilgrimage. He clicked to the horses and they left the tiny settlement of Voree, the encampment of shacks and cabins, of tents and covered wagons.

"More folks comin' in all the time," Rusty remarked.

Marie smoothed back her long, black hair, which hung about her shoulders in natural ringlets. "You know what Gabriel told me? He said there be gentile folks who meet the Mormons and try to keep them from comin' in. They tell 'em Voree's a bad place, full of scoundrels."

"I heard, but I didn't pay it no mind. Doesn't seem to stop 'em any."

Marie paused, then turned her gray eyes on him. "Oh, Rusty. What is Gabriel so upset about?"

Rusty considered before he answered. "I reckon he figured Voree was going to be a new start—a fresh place where we wouldn't have all the old troubles we had in Nauvoo. But now, it looks like Brother Strang is bringing in some of the very folks that was causing the troubles."

"Why is he doing that?"

"Well, he probably figures he can use anybody he can get. I mean, he needs men who can go out and persuade folks to join us. But these fellers—why, talk about scoundrels. I hear Brother Strang feels they've repented of their misdeeds. And folks like Gabriel—why, I don't reckon Gabe'd trust Dr. John C. Bennett any further than he can throw 'em."

Marie's eyes widened. "Seems like he's more bothered than he should be."

Rusty went on. "The thing is, Bennett made a lot of trouble for the Saints in Nauvoo. Word got out that the good doctor had abandoned a wife and children back in Ohio. He pretended he was a single man, and even said that promiscuous behavior was part of our belief. When Joseph finally excommunicated him, he spread lies about us all up and down that side of Illinois. Some think that what he did even helped cause the deaths of Joseph and Hyrum. And now, here he is. General-in-Chief to our own James Strang."

Marie nodded, looking out over the prairie. Rusty said, "And George Adams—he's not much better. Charged with adultery back in 1843— he returned from his British mission with a wife and child. The thing was, he already had a wife and child in Nauvoo. They excommunicated him. For that, and embezzling church funds."

"So now he wants to come back?"

"Oh, he's back, all right. Brother James has forgiven him for his past behavior, and his alleged drunkenness. He's just not to do it again— now, that's like asking a skunk to change his stripes."

Marie looked shaken. "Anything else I should know?"

"Well, William Smith, even though he's Joseph's younger brother, isn't exactly a paragon of virtue either. He got caught up in the plural marriage business—even teaching it, so people say. And he has a temper that'd make a bear beg for mercy. He once beat up his brother Joseph so bad the poor man could hardly walk."

Marie nodded. "So that's why Gabriel—"

"I reckon Gabe's advice is very good. We're to wait and see what happens, and not get mixed up in anything."

Marie looked amused. "Like what?"

"Like, for instance, whether the folks comin' to us should be re-baptized, or accepted on their original baptism. Brother Strang thinks the original should be sufficient. But others disagree."

"And how do you feel?"

Rusty chewed his lower lip. "I don't reckon it matters that much. The original baptism is fine. I'm with Brother James on that one."

She nestled against him. He kissed her forehead as they made the turn toward the little church built of logs. He jumped down, tied the reins to the fence post, and lifted her down. They walked inside holding hands.

He hadn't told her the worst part. She'd find out soon enough.

Shortly after John C. Bennett had come to join them, Brother Strang had a revelation instructing the Saints to build a home for Strang and his family. They were also told to begin construction of a temple. Nothing amiss about that, Rusty thought. Joseph had done much the same thing. It was the Halcyon Order of the Illuminati which had Gabriel really riled.

Bennett had moved the two miles into Burlington and set himself up as 'professor of the principles and Practice of Midwifery and the Diseases of Women,' according to the flyers he had distributed. Gabe was pretty sure that Bennett had thought up the Illuminati, a secret society which had an imperial primate, a grand council, noblemen, viceroys—designed to be a governing council of the 'Strangite Kingdom of God on earth.' Rusty's father Calvin, the senior member of their little family, had been invited to join the Society. Gabe had declined his own invitation.

"If it's something Bennett cooked up, I want nothing to do with it."

This he said in private to Rusty and Calvin. Calvin had compromised his own vows of secrecy to relate to Gabe the details of the July 6 meeting of the order, and the meetings which followed. These Rusty had learned from Gabe as they prepared for a morning's work in the shop.

"So—according to Bennett, Joseph Smith received a revelation for this Illuminati business back in 1841. We're supposed to believe that he left instructions for Bennett to establish it to 'perpetuate the Kingdom of God.' Like those ceremonies they were doing back in Nauvoo in the Red Brick Store—the sealings and anointings."

What had happened at the meetings?

"*Eh bien*—the first thing they did was confirm Brother Strang as Imperial Primate. And guess who was appointed General-in-Chief of this so-called kingdom? John C. Bennett himself. Then they started initiating folks to be chevaliers, marshals, earls, and I don't know what all."

Rusty drew on his gloves and picked up the hammer. "That's it! I want to be a chevalier. I always knew that was my calling."

"Wait till you hear the rest. What they do is, they place their right hand on a cross on top of a table, and Bennett says, 'Receive thou the accolade by which I now create thee an Illuminatus, in the name of the Father, and of the Son, and of the Holy Ghost, and by the authority of the Holy Priesthood, and the special edict of the Imperial Primate, our absolute monarch.'"

Rusty tried not to laugh. "They couldn't a had more authority less'n they'd had Joseph Smith himself. Or the Pope."

Gabe did not smile. "Be serious, now. This is serious business. Bennett says something like, 'In behalf of the true, holy, catholic and apostolic Church of Jesus Christ of Latter Day Saints, by an edict of the Imperial Primate, I now extend to thee the right hand of fellowship on the five points.' And then he gives them the secret handshakes, signs and code words so they can know who's a member and who isn't. Old Calvin's supposed to 'conceal and never reveal' any of this stuff, so you're not to tell anyone."

"Secret handshake?"

"Oh—like what they had in Nauvoo. Here—take off that glove." Gabe grabbed Rusty's right hand, three fingers within three.

"That's it?"

"That's not all. They swear to obey all the edicts, decrees and commands of the General-in-Chief—that's you-know-who—and pledge what amounts to total obedience to the 'Imperial Primate and Absolute Sovereign.' In other words, Brother James. This is supposed to take precedence over any other law, obligation or mandate of anyone else you can think of. Can you beat that?"

Rusty could only stare, open-mouthed.

"Then they had to sign their names in a record book. Your father said some even signed in their own blood."

"My God!" Rusty shook his head as he drew his glove back on.

"*Mon Dieu* is right. Now I hear that Bennett's trying to get up membership diplomas or certificates that tell everything about the person—age, height, hair color, eyes—even what tribe they're from. I take it they mean what tribe of Israel."

Rusty looked at Gabe. "What've we got ourselves into?"

"Nothing, yet. It's Calvin who's in it. He'll keep us informed. In the meantime, let's hope it doesn't go much further. All we need is more nonsense like this."

Rusty, sitting beside Marie in the little church in Burlington, decided that she didn't need to know any of it. The most important thing was that she would remain untroubled and at peace long enough to give birth. And maybe—by that time—the whole business would have been forgotten, along with Bennett himself.

Rusty thought it strange that Gabe, reckless and defiant most of his life, now urged caution about rebelling in any form. When men came into the shop complaining about the new order, and the pledge everyone was supposed to sign, Rusty noticed how Gabe acknowledged the reputed injustices, but made no comment of his own.

"We can't just up and leave," he told Rusty. "We be settled here now. If they throw us out, we've no place to go. Best not to make any trouble—for the moment."

But there were those who railed against Brother Strang, and some who advocated apostasy because of the actions of John C. Bennett. Before Strang left on a two-month mission in August, he preached for three hours, warning about the rebellion in his community. The dissenters he called 'pseudo-Saints,' or 'pseudos.'

"Be you one of them pseudos?" Eb asked Gabe.

"No, and neither are you, if you know what's good for you. Just keep yer mouth shut and tend to your business."

In an atmosphere of distrust and uneasiness, the summer drew to a close. They heard that one hundred and seventeen members at Voree had already taken the covenant, as the oath was known. Gabriel refused to sign the pledge. Rusty followed his lead; so did Eb, Charley and Adriel. The little group headed by Gabriel remained steadfast and silent, even when Aaron Smith, after learning about the Illuminati and the covenant in September, declared that he knew by revelation that "it was not of God." Not content with that, he and other dissidents put John C. Bennett on trial and voted to expel him from the church.

Another dissident, Reuben Miller, president of the Voree Stake, challenged Strang's claim to leadership and his assertion that an angel had anointed him after the death of Joseph Smith. In September, Miller published his pamphlet, *James J. Strang, Weighed in the Balance of Truth, and Found Wanting.'*

Rusty, not considering himself overly religious, wondered at his own sense of confusion. Like most male Mormons, he held a priesthood office. He was an Aaronic priest, whose duty was to provide ministry to families. Before the troubles in Nauvoo, he had been called to the office of elder, but in the chaotic days before they left the city, he had not yet been ordained. He had intended to mention it to Brother Strang. Then he realized that the longer he put it off, the less work he would have to do, since elders had more duties and responsibilities than priests.

Now, working in the shop beside Eb and Gabriel, he wondered how he could possibly know what was true and what wasn't. He thought of the advice in James 1:5, and wondered if it would work for him the way it had for the young Joseph Smith.

'If any of you lack wisdom, let him ask of God...'

When he mentioned it to the others, Gabe looked at him a moment before he answered.

"Pray all you want. But don't jump to any conclusions before Brother Strang gets back."

When Strang did return, Charley hurried into the shop with news.

"He's fixin' to bring folks to trial for misdeeds against the church. All those pseudos, the one who wrote that pamphlet and the man that excommunicated Bennett—"

"Aaron Smith." Adriel had entered just behind Charley.

Gabriel laid down the hammer. "*Eh bien.* I thought as much."

Charley looked at Gabe. "I got to hand it to you. You knew which way the wind was blowing."

Gabe sighed. "Well, don't think it's over just yet. Just tend to your business, and be careful what you say."

This was so unlike Gabe that Rusty frankly stared. Was the man ill? Charley went on.

"They be sayin' that missionary tour was a great success. Scores of folks listened to him in Kirtland—they say once he preached for eight hours straight. That conference upheld him as prophet, and Strangites— that's us—now have legal possession of the temple at Kirtland."

Adriel said, "They say he went to Pittsburgh and Philadelphia. Where else? New York, Boston. Convincing folks everywhere he went. They be saying that Lucy Smith and the whole Smith family is supportin' him. And the Brighamites didn't even want to debate him."

Charley gave a laugh. "They didn't dare. The plural marriage issue would sink their ship."

"Speakin' of ships," Adriel said. "On the way home, they stopped off at this island in the middle of Lake Michigan—"

"Now, that's enough!" Gabe waved his arms. "We got to get some work done here. Put on the apron, Adriel. It's time for some apprentice work. We'll have you knock out a few hinges for our barn doors."

3

"It's about the postmark," Charley was saying as Rusty built up the fire. "There it was, plain as day, in red ink just as it should have been. The Brighamites said the postmark was black and too large. Also, they found a dot at the top of the J in June. But derned if Strang didn't find other letters from the same day—mailed from Nauvoo on June 19. The same dot was there. Like Strang said, how could any forger know that on that particular day, a little splinter would get into the mailing stamp and mark every letter with a dot?"

Eb shook his head. "If that don't beat all."

Gabe stamped in rubbing his hands together. "You talking about the letter of appointment? Getting downright cold out there." He looked at Rusty. "How's Marie this morning?"

"'Bout the same," Rusty replied. "Kind of tired-like. Big as a house."

Eb laughed. "Jess, too. There's hardly room for both of us in that cabin."

Gabe blew on his hands as he looked at the forge. "Well, I reckon that'll change."

"You think it'll be soon?" Rusty tried not to sound anxious as he drew on his gloves.

Gabe gave him a long look. "All I can say is, if you haven't got that cradle built yet, you'd better start."

"Mine's all built," Eb said. "She nagged me till I got it done."

"My father's helpin' with mine." Rusty picked up the hammer and shifted it from one hand to another. They began work.

"Where's Adriel?" Gabe asked. "He's supposed to be learnin' his trade."

"He went out hunting early this morning," Charley replied. "Said he had a dream about a big buck north of here."

Someone pounded on the large pine door—sharp, staccato beats. Gabriel hurried to open it.

"Like as not, it's him," Charley said. "Couldn't find no buck."

Turah rushed into the room. She waved her hands in little agitated circles. "Oh, Dr. Gabriel!"

Gabe stood holding the door. "What's wrong?"

"It's Momma!" Her eyes widened. "Oh, come quick! She wants you—and Marie!"

Gabe drew off his blacksmith's apron and hung it on a peg. "Now, child. I'll come. But stay calm. If she's in labor, that's good. Things don't usually happen as fast as you think."

Eb spoke just behind him. "According to my reckoning, it's a mite early."

"Mine, too. Maybe it's a false alarm." Gabe stepped toward the door with Eb and Turah following.

Rusty felt a sudden urge to run up to the main cabin and look in on his wife. "Maybe I'd better see if Marie is all right."

Gabe eyed him, amusement in his look. "I reckon she's fine. You just said so. Don't you remember?"

"Yes, but—"

"You'd best stay here. Sarah will tell us if we're needed." Gabe closed the door behind him.

Rusty sighed and turned back to his work. Charley put another log on the fire. Rusty looked at him. "You were saying—about that postmark, and folks thinkin' it were a forgery."

Charley began to talk, and Rusty tried not to think of Marie and Jess, and the babies waiting to be born.

Too soon. Gabriel tried to keep the apprehension out of his mind.

As he tramped over the uneven ground, strewn with roots and fallen branches, he thought of what he would need. "Turah, run up to my cabin and tell Bethia. Bid her come, and to bring my leather knapsack. She'll know the one I mean."

"Yes, sir."

He'd worked to train Bethia as a midwife. Maybe her assisting at this birth would help lift her out of the gloom she was in. He waited as Eb opened the door to his cabin.

It was a tight little cabin, solidly built. Turah's paintings and sketches hung on the pine logs. The bedstead, made of pine like the table and benches, stood in the corner. Jess lay on it, covered in blankets.

"Why don't you build up the fire?" Gabriel said to Eb. "And set some water to heat."

Eb bent over his wife. "How you makin' it?"

"Not good."

"Well, Dr. Gabriel be here now. He'll take care of you."

"Marie," she said in a weak voice. "I want Marie."

Eb went to put logs on the fire. Gabriel placed a hand on Jess' forehead. "When did the pains begin?"

She spoke with an effort. "Long about sunrise. They getting bad now." She paused, panting. "Can you find Marie? She said she be with me."

He considered. "I think it's best if Marie doesn't come right now. Maybe later. But Bethia'll be here. She knows how to help."

"I don't want Bethia. I want Marie."

Eb had the fire blazing brightly as Turah came in, followed by Bethia. Gabriel gave her a brief smile as he reached for the knapsack. He was met by a stony stare. *Something wrong.* She looked sullen, unresponsive.

He tried again. "Glad to see you. We're going to need your help in just a little while."

She looked at him then. He saw that she'd been crying; her eyes were red, her cheeks still streaked with tears. "Not well today?"

"No. But I don't expect you to care. Oh!" The knapsack slipped from her grasp. He managed to grab it before it hit the floor. Her mouth sagged suddenly, and she gave a strange little laugh. "I can't even take a nap without being bothered by somebody."

He spoke quietly. "Bethia. Jess is about ready to have her child."

"What is that to me? She can go ahead and have it for all I care. You don't care at all about how I feel."

Gabriel stood stunned as the realization hit him. Bethia was not able to help. While he could deliver a baby by himself, it was good to have someone else there. Especially with it coming so early. He drew in his breath and made a quick decision.

"All right, Bethia. Turah, run up and fetch Sarah. Bring Marie too, if she'll come. Tell them to bring all the clean towels they can find."

When Turah had left, Gabriel turned to Eb. "I reckon you'd best help Bethia back to her cabin. She's not well this morning. Then you can go up to the shop. I'll take care of things here. And nothing will happen for a while."

Bethia protested. "Buh—buh—"

"Go with Eb. He'll see you get home. We don't need you for this one."

Nor any one, he thought. Eb took her elbow and escorted her out the door. Alone with Jess, Gabriel had just a few moments to wonder at his lack of insight. Thinking that Bethia would be able to assist him, as she had before. One of the few things they had done together. Now the confirmation of her deteriorating condition was complete. Sick at heart, he bent over the slight form on the bed.

"Jess?"

"The pains are bad, doctor. This one—"

"It's all right. Take little breaths."

Sarah and Turah came in, their arms full of towels.

"Marie be coming, soon as she can." Sarah handed him the towels. "What else can I do, doctor?"

He spread some of the towels out on the bed. "Just stand by, for now. Make sure the fire doesn't go out. That water hot?" He washed and dried his hands.

Just before the birth, Marie entered and sat by the side of the bed.

She took Jess' hand and held it, patting it gently. Gabriel, watching, thought *She's the one I should train as a midwife.*

The child was born in the early afternoon, an undersized boy. Gabriel, holding him up by the heels, prayed that this one would live. So many births he had seen, so many babies—some born way too soon, some never drawing breath. This, the son of his best friend, born into freedom—this one had to survive. One sharp slap, and the babe cried lustily.

"There we are," Gabriel said. "Music to my ears."

Sarah blinked. "My, but he's little."

"Bathe him very gently—keep him warm. I'll see to momma, here. Turah, I reckon you can run up and fetch your Papa. Watch about opening the door, now. We must be careful of draughts with this one."

When Eb saw his son, he could not contain his delight. "He be a wiry little cuss. Look at 'em wriggle."

Gabriel tried to emphasize the rest Jess would need, and the special care they must give the tiny boy. "Keep him warm—keep that fire going."

The parents looked at him with glazed eyes, as if they were too distracted to take his words seriously. But Turah listened and nodded gravely.

Gabriel kept a strict watch over the child, looking in on him every few hours. To Gabriel's relief, the baby hung on for the first days of life and began to grow. Sarah and Marie, along with the other neighbors, brought dishes of food for Jess and Eb. Adriel, who had found the buck he had seen in his dream, kept the family supplied with venison.

They named the boy James Joseph Wanfield, familiarly known as J. J. That ought to do it, Gabriel thought. Anyone named for two prophets of the Lord had a good chance of survival.

Three weeks later. Marie wondering if her child is ever going to be born. Lying now in her bed, looking out the one window in the early morning. Trees moving, branches trembling in the slight wind. Most of the leaves gone now.

Then she feels it—a pain gripping her midsection. She has been feeling contractions for days, none of which she would call painful. But this one is, and she puts her hand on her abdomen, wondering if it is time to tell Rusty. He has gone to bring in more wood. If she tells him while he is carrying it, he will most likely drop it and make a mess. She decides to wait. If it comes again, she will let him know.

She hears him in the main room, carrying the wood. Sarah says something to him; she can't hear what it is. Then the pain grips her. She cries out. Sure enough, she hears the wood hitting the floor. Both Sarah and Rusty rush into the room. Rusty leans over her, speechless.

Sarah wipes her hands on her gingham apron. "I reckon we'd better fetch Gabriel."

Rusty grabs his heavy coat. "Don't do anything till I get back."

"Don't trip over the kindling you dropped," Sarah tells him.

Marie has the sense of confusion and noise all around her. Calvin is trying to pick up the wood, and Sarah is shouting at him. "Let that go! Get the fire started! I never saw such goings on. And Marie about to have her child."

Marie gives another cry. More sounds, a door slamming. Hurried footsteps. Suddenly Gabriel is there, squeezing her hand—her favorite brother, his shock of black hair falling over his forehead.

"I knew you'd come," she gasps. "Can—can Jess be here too?"

"We'll send Rusty up and see if she'll leave J. J. with Turah for a little while."

Something crashes in the kitchen. Gabriel tramps to the doorway. "Let's keep the noise down." It is a command, not to be argued with. "Build up that fire. We'll need hot water."

Order is restored. She marvels at the simplicity of it. He takes a seat by her bedside. This time his voice is gentle. "Take deep breaths. Grip my hand it if gets bad."

She looks into his eyes. "Are things going to be all right?"

"So far, they are. Just relax, if you can."

She begins to feel reassured. This, after all, is her own wonderful brother, closer to her than any of her other siblings. The one who introduced her to Rusty, and rescued her from a life of spinsterhood in the dying French section of Gallipolis. Now here she is, actually giving birth to their first child.

The pains are coming in a regular rhythm now. Although she has been given nothing to dull the hurting, she feels as if she is in some drug-induced state where the pains have taken on color and sound. The biggest pains are dark purple, with a tinge of brown. The sounds are like a low violin or cello—not unpleasant, but insistent. She tries to tell Gabriel about them.

"Don't try to talk. You're doing fine."

Her legs are being lifted up, and someone is spreading towels under her. Turah is there.

"Momma said she be comin' soon as she can. Leavin' J. J. with my father."

Gabriel's voice. "He can probably handle that. Alone with his infant son for the first time."

Turah sits beside the bed. "I finished that book you lent me."

"Thomas Paine? *The Age of Reason*? That's hard reading. You know, Brother Strang has a fine library. Books about any subject you care to mention. He says we can borrow any of them, and I've already told him about you. I reckon he'll help us plan what to read next."

"I like to read," Turah says. "Almost as much as I like making pictures."

Their voices sound far away. The brown-tinged purple and the low sounds are everywhere; nothing else is important. The sounds reach a crescendo, and she can hear something beating, racing like mad—her own heart, in the midst of the sounds and the strange color, the purple that is now so tinged with brown that it is downright ugly.

"Push now!" Gabriel's voice. She is feeling faint; she no longer knows what is happening. The sound is deafening—harsh and demanding. The brown-purple color fills her world. Just before she loses consciousness, she has the sense of being in a dark tunnel, pushed along toward an opening above her and some distance away. She is aware of someone screaming. *Herself?* Then there is nothing.

A strange sound. A little gurgling cry. It comes again and again—a baby's cry. She opens her eyes, incredulous.

Sarah is holding something in a towel. It is red, the head misshapen, the eyes little slits. The mouth trembles as it opens. Then Gabriel is leaning over her.

"You have a beautiful baby girl."

Marie can only gasp. "It's over?"

"What's over?" Gabriel says. "It's just beginning. Sarah's going to wash her now."

"She's cute as a button." Jess is sitting beside her. Marie has not even known she was there. She takes Jess' hand and holds it.

When Sarah finally brings her the child, Marie sees that she is indeed beautiful. She is a rosy pink, no longer red, the features perfectly formed—small mouth, upturned nose, the eyes blue and wide apart. "What a sweet face." Marie, looking at her daughter, marvels at the sudden, protective emotion, the sense that she is in love with this tiny being for life. "She will live, won't she?"

Gabriel smiles. "Well, she's living now. Let's see if she'll nurse. First, let's prop you up, and Sarah will bring you some broth. Or maybe a little cider."

After a few moments, both Marie and the baby are eating. The child seems to nurse purposefully, as if she knows just what to do.

"You be doing fine," Jess says. "J. J. had some trouble, figuring it out."

"But then, he was a lot smaller," Gabriel says.

"How come she's bald?" Marie asks. "J. J. had a full head of hair."

Gabriel gives a shrug. "So? Babies are different. She won't be bald forever."

"Oh, this is wonderful," Marie says. "I'm so happy. The only thing is—I wish—oh, I wish Corey could be here. She did love babies."

Suddenly Gabriel's smile fades. He winces, as if he is in pain. Then a change comes into his face, like a shadow passing over it. And Marie knows. Not only does he miss Corey, he loved her.

Marie is about to blurt out an apology, but Jess touches her arm. "She be across Iowa by this time, I reckon. And when yer nursing, it's best not to talk. Helps things go better. I learned that when Turah was born."

Then Rusty is in the room. Jess moves so he can sit by the bed. He sits down, too overcome to remove his coat. "Well, I'll be dad-burned."

Calvin comes in to see his granddaughter. By this time, Gabriel has recovered. He looks tired in the fading light. As Marie glances at the window, she sees that the day has gone; it is almost candlelight. Already Turah and Sarah are setting out the supper dishes.

Marie closes her eyes. A long day for everyone. She hears Jess getting ready to leave, and go back to her own baby.

"Here. Take a dish of these potatoes back with you." Sarah's voice. "And here's ham to go with it. Turah, help your momma."

Marie is hungry. She leans back, cradling her daughter, knowing that both of them will be cherished and cared for. Time to rest. Time to ponder the fact that Gabriel, their leader, gave up a greater happiness in order to guide and protect them all. For Corey would have gone away with him, she was sure. All he needed to do was ask.

Sarah is saying, "Here, Gabriel. There's a plate for you. I don't reckon you'll get much supper if you go home now."

"Like as not, you're right." Gabriel's voice had a note of resignation.

"Eat with us, and we'll give you a plate to take home for her."

She hears them talking in low tones, and finally Sarah brings a tray to her. "Baby's asleep. Let's put her in the cradle."

"Aren't you glad we got it built?" Rusty says.

There is the sound of utensils scraping on china plates. Gabriel says, "And aren't you glad we didn't make a big fuss about things and get ourselves excommunicated like those others? What would we do, with two newborns and two new mothers?"

"You mean, we'd have to leave?" Rusty asks.

"Well, I reckon. Go somewheres else. Into Burlington, with John C. Bennett for a neighbor."

"Oh, you men," Sarah says. "Always suggesting things. I never saw the like."

Manon Louise. That was the name they finally decided on, after the two older sisters of Marie and Gabriel who had married and left for Kentucky. There was some discussion as to whether it should be Louise Manon, but it didn't sound good with the last name Manning.

Another subject of discussion was the christening. Gabriel and Rusty both assured her that little children were considered alive in Christ, and had no need for baptism. Loving and trusting both of them, she finally agreed—a blessing would do just as well, until the child was old enough to decide for herself. Since little Louise had no notion of what was happening, the blessing would take the place of a formal christening.

As Marie accepted this decision, she wondered if she had taken the first steps toward becoming a Mormon. Whatever it was, she felt content—reasonable that the child should be able to choose baptism at the age of eight instead of having it forced upon her before she had any concept of it.

A few weeks later, Sarah paused in her work of straightening up the house. She looked out the window by Marie's bed.

"Looks downright frosty out there. And gray. I reckon we'll have snow this very night."

Marie, nursing her child, only nodded. Sarah went on. "Well, I vow. There's the doctor himself. Just come from the Wanfield cabin. The way he looks after you two, he might as well live here."

But Gabriel hadn't come to look in on Marie and Louise. He had news.

"A feast, you say?" Sarah's tone sounded doubtful.

"A feast to end all feasts." Gabriel gestured in his excitement. "A wonderful celebration, set for New Year's Day. It's to celebrate and dedicate Brother James' new cabin. It's not much bigger than mine, but a lot of folks helped build it. And we're all invited."

"The babies too?" Marie asked.

"Of course, the babies. If it's not too cold."

Marie hoped it wouldn't be. A treat, to walk outside in her good clothes and join a festive gathering. She'd been confined inside too long. No wonder they called it a confinement. She smiled at Gabriel, thinking of the good times they would have.

But Gabriel did not smile; his dark eyebrows drew together in a troubled expression. "It's just the faithful that are invited. The pseudos—them that made all the trouble—well, they won't be there." Then he brightened. "With luck, I'll take Bethia, and she'll enjoy herself. But—" He looked at Sarah. "Maybe you'd better tell her about it, so she won't think it's something I made up. She doesn't trust anything I say, it seems like."

"I'm sorry to hear that," Sarah replied. "I'll do what I can with her."

"I'd be much beholden."

Sarah paused. "I reckon we do have a lot to celebrate."

"We do, indeed. We be in good health, for the most part. We have warm, snug cabins, and a good shop, though it could be bigger. Enough to eat. But—"

"But what?" Sarah asked.

"*Eh bien.* If I could change anything, I'd have different counselors for the prophet than William Smith and George Adams. And John C. Bennett would be back raising chickens."

4

IN ALL, ONE HUNDRED and thirty people attended, with two new houses being dedicated, that of Strang and another family.

"A most sumptuous feast," Eb said as they gathered in the blacksmith shop two days later. "That's what they be sayin', anyway."

"It were a mighty good dinner." Rusty licked his lips, remembering. He piled wood on the fire. "I reckon I could eat one like that most every week."

"I reckon you could, too." Eb shook his head. "'Course the weather coulda been better. Jess had to leave early on account of she wanted to get J. J. home."

"You hear 'bout the meeting at that new house?" Charley said. "A crowd of people—maybe twenty-four or so. Some Illuminati doings, is what it was."

"What about it?" Eb asked.

"Why, ain't you heard? Brother Strang anointed some of them with oil, and darned if they didn't glow in the dark like they had halos."

"I'll be!" Eb exclaimed. "Can you beat that?"

Rusty stood in awe, thinking about it. *Could such things be possible?* Then Gabe spoke.

"*Tiens.* Before we start believing completely, let's think of all the other possibilities. It was a dry, cold evening, right? There's all sorts of ways to make things glow like that."

"Like what?" Eb asked.

"Static electricity, maybe. Something mixed with the oil, like phosphorus. Calvin said the oil smelled strange."

"In other words," Charley said, nodding. "You don't reckon it were a manifestation of the spirit, like the early apostles."

"If Bennett had anything to do with it, I don't believe it was anything but fraudulent."

"You wasn't even there," Eb said.

Gabe waved his hand as he gestured. "No. But Calvin was. Just ask him." His voice sounded happy, more relaxed than usual. Rusty recalled that Bethia had attended the feast and had seemed to enjoy it.

A few days later, Gabe's mood had changed. He grew annoyed at each little thing—the fire not hot enough, the wood-box almost empty. Finally Eb said, "Hang it all, Gabe! You worse than a bear that's sat on a porcupine."

"Am I that bad? I like to see things done right, is all."

There were sounds from outside, horses nickering. A knock at the door. Eb opened it.

A young man stood on the step, his hat in his hand. He looked too thin, his light jacket in tatters. "The doctor here?"

"Right here." Gabe motioned for him to come inside. "What can I do for you?"

"Oh, sir—I live t'other side of the hill, there. My mother's feelin' poorly—coughs all the time. And now she doesn't want to eat."

"Let me fetch my knapsack, and we'll go see her."

When Gabe had gone, Eb closed the door. "Look like another charity case to me. That boy be scrawny as a starved chicken."

Rusty said, "I hope the doctor's nicer to the sick folks than he is to us."

Eb looked at him. "I reckon he is. And I reckon I know what he be frettin' about."

"It be Bethia," Rusty's father said. "He be havin' trouble at home—more trouble than he knows what to do with."

Rusty thought of the conversation with his father and Sarah over dinner the previous day—how, as soon as Marie felt strong enough, it might be a good plan to settle Gabe and Bethia in the large house with Sarah and his father, and let Marie, Louise, and himself have the smaller cabin.

"That way, I can help take care of Bethia," Sarah had said. "Lord knows, she seems to need it. And the doctor might get fed more often."

"But we have to be careful, like," his father had said. "We can't let Bethia know it's because of her. She'd be upset with all of us."

"We can say *we* want it," Rusty had said. "Marie and I need a place of our own."

Remembering, he looked up in surprise when Eb spoke. "Hang it all. It's not that at all. He be bothered about something else."

"What is it, then?" Rusty's father asked.

"Don't you 'member that letter Uriah Nickerson got? The one from Winter Quarters, that place in Iowa where the Brigham Young folks stopped for the winter?"

"By gum!" Rusty exclaimed. "That's right. The 'Camp of Israel.' They read it right out when the bunch of folks was gathered at that new cabin. It told how Uriah's father died of exposure, and his mother—a sixty-six-year-old woman—had to sleep out on the open prairie in the snow—"

"So?" his father said. "We knew there was going to be terrible trials on that journey. Gabe even said so."

Eb laid down the hammer. "No. You don't understand. I reckon Corey and her father and sister was with that bunch. It's them he's frettin' about."

Rusty's father looked puzzled. "I—I see."

Rusty tried to remember. "Why—why, come to think of it—when that was read, Gabe got real quiet. Then he excused himself and went outside—I thought he looked right pale. I figured he'd eaten some victuals that didn't set right or something."

"He look like he been punched in the stomach," Eb said.

They were silent. Then Rusty's father shrugged. "If'n that's the trouble, I reckon he be over it in a few days."

Rusty chose his words carefully, not wanting to invite a disagreement with Eb. He decided not to mention Corey by name. "He sure did set store on that family. They was all his patients."

His father spoke again. "I reckon we're right lucky to be here, and not freezin' out on that prairie."

The rest grunted in agreement, and Rusty took the tongs to lift another piece of hot metal onto the anvil.

"That's what they be telling me." Charley took aim with the ax and split the standing bit of log down the middle. "He had this vision the summer of forty-six—a land amidst great waters, like he said. Covered with heavy timber, with a deep bay one side of the land. And all that business about the air being pure and the setting all serene, with hills and valleys."

"Go on." From his seat on the wood pile, Gabriel watched as Charley swung the ax. More wood tumbled to the ground.

"Well, like I was sayin'—Brother Strang had the promise that he would see this wonderful place 'afore he returned to Voree. And darned if there warn't a storm on the way home from them eastern states, and the boat had to seek shelter inside the harbor. And there it was—the promised land, just like in the vision. The fellers that was with him, they said how they walked around that harbor and saw some of the island. Brother Strang couldn't praise it enough."

Gabriel stood and began gathering up the wood. "So what do we know about this island?"

"It be called 'Big Beaver Island.' There's about ten of these islands, kind of like a string of 'em, way to the north out there in Lake Michigan. This be the biggest, about thirteen miles long, they're saying. All this fertile land, full of timber. And that water—why, they say it be full of fish—lake trout, whitefish—"

Gabriel began to laugh. "They oughta hire you to promote it."

Charley leaned on the ax. "Well, all I can say is, it's a safe refuge for boats. And I reckon, for people, too. Who's gonna bother anyone, up there in the middle of Lake Michigan?"

"*Eh bien*." Gabriel took a deep breath. "What kind of timber? Pine, I suppose."

"They're saying pine, birch and maple inland. Cedar in the swamps. And there's seven lakes on the island."

"Seven!" Gabriel stacked the wood pieces on the pile. "Must be some island."

"Not only that. They say it be the prettiest place you'd ever want to see."

"I suppose there's a lot of beaver," Gabriel remarked.

"No beaver. Leastways, no one seen any. There's just animals that come across on the ice."

"Then why do they call it Beaver Island?"

"Adriel says it's supposed to look like a beaver—upside down, that is. That's what the Ojibwes and them all thought. So they named it that. I hear that sailors be calling the harbor 'Paradise Bay.'"

Gabriel sighed. "Paradise. A pretty place. Safe for folks like us. Where have I heard that before?"

Charley gave him a long, intent look. "I don't know how many times *you* heard it. But I reckon this time they found it."

Gabriel stacked the last of the wood. Then he stood, his hands in the pockets of his thick jacket. "I left my copy of *Zion's Reveille* up in the cabin. Wanted to study it some. I hear it tells something about the island."

Charley put the ax over his shoulder. They walked toward the rear of the building which housed the smithy. "One more thing to study on. I hear the federal government's aimin' to sell land for a dollar twenty-five an acre. Compare that to fifty dollars per acre in Voree."

"I—see your point."

"What I'm tryin' to tell you—I'd like to get up there. Me and Adriel—we could do right well in a place like that. With the fishin' and the lumberin'—Farmin's good too, so they say."

Gabriel stopped. An idea was forming in his mind. "It'd get us away from Bennett and the Illuminati. All that ritual business—signing pledges and the like. But why do we have to travel so far to find this— this place of peace and safety?"

Charley shrugged. "Don't ask me."

"I mean, why can't we do it right here in Voree?"

43

"I reckon some of us can. But it be a lot cheaper up there. And there's something else."

Gabriel waited. "What?"

Charley frowned, then pressed his lips together, as if the next part were difficult to say. "You see—I lived a lot of places. Been up and down the Mississippi, and on the Great Lakes. Adriel—he was born up in the north country. And once you see them lakes—why, they're like inland seas. There's no place like them. Seas of sweet water. They sort of get into yer blood, like, so you'd do most anything to get a sight of them again."

Gabriel, who had only heard about the lakes, felt moved and intrigued by this aspect of Charley which he had never known. "If they're that special, I reckon I'd like to see 'em too."

"I hear Brother Strang's fixin' to go up there again when the lakes are open in the spring. I know some fellers who are goin' with him."

"*Tiens,*" Gabriel said. "Let's wait and see what happens. We don't want to do anything too hasty, like. Let's see what they find out."

⊂⊰⊱⊃

Bethia stands at the pine table kneading bread in the large earthenware bowl. She pulls the ends of the dough into the middle and presses down. Time and again she does this, adding flour or water, depending on the consistency of the dough. On the table, covered with bits of flour, lies the copy of *Zion's Reveille* and the description of the island.

What to do about the island? She has heard Gabriel and Rusty talking about the lumber and the fishing, about the opportunities Charley says are there for the taking. *Charley, indeed.* She shudders. If Charley said they should all jump in the river, Gabriel would probably do it. She gives the dough a last angry shove and covers it with a towel. She is just putting it to rise in the warm place by the hearth when she hears the knock on the door.

Someone for the doctor, most like. She tries to wipe the dough from her hands. Sighing, she pulls back the wooden latch. The door, fashioned of pine logs, swings open.

Sarah and Marie stand there, Sarah carrying a basket of food and Marie with Louise in her arms.

"We came to visit you," Sarah says. "My, that smells good."

Bethia moves back and they enter. Sarah reaches to close the door behind her. "I'll vow. We picked a good time, I reckon. Nothing smells better than baking day. Here." She holds out the basket. "I brought you some squash bread. Tastes right good with cheese."

Betha takes the basket and leans forward as Sarah hugs her. At the same time she is wondering what they want. "Would you care to sit?"

"Land's sakes, yes. These old bones'll sit most anytime. I'll sit here, and Marie can take the rocker. Louise will like that."

"I reckon she's due to sleep for a spell," Marie says. They sit close to the fire, and Marie rocks back and forth cradling the baby.

Bethia wonders if she is about to be treated to a litany of what the baby is doing, how she is eating and sleeping. She braces herself. Instead Sarah says, "We came to get away from all the talk about Beaver Island."

Marie laughs pleasantly. "Seems like that's all they do. How many lakes on the island, how many swamps and stands of hardwood."

Sarah settles back in a chair by the hearth. Bethia moves one of the kitchen chairs closer to them. "I've just been reading. The pseudos be saying that Brother Strang aims to abandon Voree. Get everybody up to that island."

Sarah leans forward. "Why, honey. That just ain't true. Abandon Voree, with the temple started and all the other things? That just don't make sense."

Bethia looks at her aunt, feeling less sure in the presence of such certainty. "Well—that's what they be saying. The pseudos, I mean."

"And how far you gonna trust them?"

Bethia looks down at her apron, crusted with dough. "I only hear what I hear. And Gabriel—he doesn't say much about the island at all."

Sarah gives a laugh. "You oughta hear him over at our place. It sounds like him and Charley be rarin' to get up there."

Bethia draws in her breath. Anger rushes over her—it couldn't be true. Gabriel to go up to the island? "He's never mentioned any such thing. And he knows I wouldn't go to any place like that."

Sarah answers quickly. "Not to stay there, of course. It sounds like he just wants to see it."

Marie's voice is gentle. "It's all just talk. But they say it's beautiful. A lovely, safe place. Bounded by water—who would bother us?"

Bethia glares at her. "Well, you can go if you want. But no one's gonna get *me* on a boat." And Gabriel hasn't mentioned it to her. As if she is not worth consulting. Not wanting to weep in front of them, she wonders how to make them leave.

"Bethia, honey," Sarah is saying. "We didn't come to bother you with talk of the island. We all figured we'll stay right here, leastways for some time. But we were thinkin' that it might be good if you and Gabriel came over and lived with us. He could see patients in that little extra room, and you could help me with the cooking and such. I be gettin' old, and I could use the extra help."

Bethia blinks, puzzled. "But—but what about Marie and Rusty?"

Marie waits before she speaks, which is not like her. "Why, we'd take your cabin. That way, we'd have the privacy we need."

Bethia considers it, unsure. Sarah says, "Why, I have to tell you. Gabe spends most of his time over at our place anyway. So I figured he might as well live there."

Bethia's mind is working. She knows she is missing out on a lot of things, discussions about their future and happenings in the community. Perhaps if she is on the scene, closer to the various activities, she can forestall any talk of moving to the island. Maybe she doesn't need a house of her own after all. As for the cabin, she is tired of it. Isolated and cold—Marie is welcome to it. Finally she sighs. "I reckon that's a good idea. I be willing—let's go ahead."

Do Marie and Sarah exchange a significant look? In her confusion, Bethia can not be sure. At any rate, she is satisfied with the decision. "What about Gabriel? Maybe he won't like it."

Sarah smiles. "Well, we'll let him work it out."

Bethia likes that. If he didn't approve of it, that would be just too bad. She begins to feel excited about the move, planning how to go about it. Something to think about besides that island.

To her surprise, Gabriel made no objection. He even looked relieved, and agreed so readily that she grew suspicious—this man who disliked giving up any part of his independence. As if sensing her confusion, he put an arm about her.

"That way, you'll be a great help to Sarah. Both she and Calvin be getting along in years. Now we can make it a mite easier for them."

She didn't point out that Rusty and Marie could have done it just as well. If Gabriel had thought of that, perhaps he would've considered the move unnecessary. And she wanted to move; she was ready.

Another amazing thing was how quickly the change was accomplished, and how many people were eager to help—Rusty, Eb and Gabriel carting boxes, dishes, bundles of clothing and bedding between the houses, the women carrying precious household items like her earthenware bread bowl. Adriel and Charley helped with the transfer of furniture. Finally her own bedstead stood in the room Marie and Rusty had occupied, and her clothes hung in the pine wardrobe. Her few dishes sat in the kitchen cupboard, next to Sarah's. Before she knew it, Sarah was calling her to share in a dish of stew, brought by a neighbor who knew about the move.

"There. Isn't this cozy?" Sarah exclaimed as Calvin and Gabriel gathered with them around the table. Bethia, still recovering from the speed of it, tried to smile. But sudden change was not to her liking; she had thought it would have taken more planning and discussion. When she said as much, Sarah patted her hand.

"To tell the truth, child, none of us have that much to move. And the sooner it's done, the better."

One thing she didn't anticipate was that Charley and Adriel would eat at least three meals a week with them.

"They be good workers," Sarah said. "Got to keep them fed."

Bethia tried to conceal her dislike of them. As she had suspected, the house of Sarah and Calvin proved to be a gathering place and discussion center for the little community of friends. She began to learn things she had not realized—for instance, that Adriel and Charley were planning to go up to Beaver Island.

"What on earth for?" she demanded of Gabriel when they were alone.

"*Eh bien.* Brother James be going up there soon with a few other folks. Come summer, Charley and Adriel be wanting to get up there."

"But why?"

"To see the island, I suppose, and see if it would be a good place for people to settle."

"Well—you'll never get *me* on a boat."

"Oh, I think we would, if we had to. 'Specially if folks were chasing us."

She stamped her foot. "I'm simply not going."

He laughed then. "No one's asking you to. Most of us be staying here, for now. For myself, I'd like to see the place. No—I'm not going with them. But someday, I'll see it. And don't close your mind completely. Let's see what Charley and Adriel learn."

When she made other objections, he simply looked at her, then shrugged and walked back to the keeping room with the others. She fumed, furious.

To make matters worse, Marie had taken over her little cabin and transformed it into a place of delight and beauty. With what little they had, she had hung colorful curtains at the windows, braided a bright rug for the floor, and arranged the furniture to look inviting and comfortable. She had even hung some of Turah's drawings on the wall— pictures of the river and trees, with the hills beyond. Whenever Bethia and Sarah walked over to visit, they found Louise happily crawling on the rug, and wonderful aromas coming from the kettle over the fire.

"A French custom," Marie explained. "There's always a bit of soup for anyone who stops by."

Bethia didn't like to admit her jealousy. All this, and a baby too. Instead of the dark cabin she'd lived in, it was now a place of loveliness and warmth. She felt crushed—why couldn't *she* have done that? But she hadn't, and now she had to watch while Marie made it into a home where people wanted to gather. Even Gabriel seemed to spend as much time there as he could.

"Just seeing that the baby's all right."

"Well, after all," Sarah said when Bethia complained. "She *is* his sister. Part of his own family. It's not like she's some stranger."

What bothered Bethia most was the wine. In spite of the ban on 'spirituous liquor,' Rusty managed to buy bottles of wine in Burlington, and this they drank with their meals.

"I suppose that's a French custom too," Bethia said to Gabriel.

"*Mais oui.* But that's not spirituous liquor—it's just wine. No harm in that."

Most likely he was over there drinking it too. She wondered if Brother Strang would think it completely harmless—she debated telling him. Then she relented. No sense in getting them all in trouble. Or worse—driving them away from Voree and up to that island. She sighed, and decided to hold her tongue.

⤜⧓⤛

Chopping wood. Swinging the ax. Remembering how Charley had split logs while he talked about the lakes, and going up to Beaver Island. Now it was early summer and Charley had left; he and Adriel were on the island with a small number of settlers who planned to stay the winter.

Gabriel missed them more than he could say, especially Charley and his bits of wisdom. For one thing, it meant that the rest of them had to do more work, with two of their comrades gone. And Rusty, absorbed in his family, wasn't much help.

Still, they were fortunate, with everything considered. Bethia was being cared for, looked after by Sarah. No more worries on that score. Her depression had lifted, in the company of her aunt. And between them, the two women produced wonderful meals. The aroma of fresh-baked bread filled the whole neighborhood on baking day.

He took aim at a standing bit of log and split it down the middle. Not bad, for the second-best ax. Charley had taken the best one with him, plus several other tools which would come in handy. As he gathered up the wood, he thought of the plans they had made.

First, Adriel and Charley would go to the island. Brother Strang and four others had stopped there in the spring; they had put up a cabin and left two men on the island. The rest returned to Voree with glowing reports of what they had found: clean air and fresh water. Two gentile trading posts, whose proprietors were not exactly thrilled to see the five strangers. Other smaller islands close by, some of which they had explored.

Depending on what Adriel and Charley learned, and with plenty of advance preparations, Gabriel envisioned sending the community to the island in stages. Next, Rusty and his family, Calvin and Sarah, and Bethia, with enough household items and staples to make a start in the new place. Then, he would follow with Eb and his family, the rest of the tools and the livestock. If everything went as planned, they could all be on the island by the summer of forty-nine.

Except—there was Bethia. Dead set against the idea. As if determined not to see how much better it would be for all of them. What had happened to her? Was it the countless moves, the threats of persecution? He sighed. Hopefully, Sarah could help persuade her. There was plenty of time.

As he walked toward the house carrying the firewood, his mind did a strange thing. Like a shaft of sunlight, an image of Corey rose before him, smiling, looking at him in her steadfast way. A little ache stirred in his chest, as if he were reminded of an idyllic period in the past, some incredibly romantic time which had never really existed. He shook his head, and the memory faded. Clutching the split logs to him with one hand, he thrust open the door and carried them inside.

5

Rusty preparing for work. Never eager to leave his cabin. He embraced Marie and held her close, then picked up Louise and kissed her. He handed her to her mother. *"Au revoir, ma petite."*

Marie sighed. "Oh, Rusty. You keep forgetting. And you promised."

"Oh, that's right. I'm sorry." In order to insure that Louise grew up bi-lingual, they had decided that Marie and Gabriel would speak only French to her, and Rusty would speak English. He stepped toward the door.

"Don't forget your scarf," Marie said. "It's still cold out."

She had made him the scarf with blue and white yarn from a worn-out sweater. He put it dutifully around his neck.

Outside, he took deep breaths of the pine air. The end of March already. Louise almost fourteen months old. He shook his head, amazed at how fast the time had gone. Soon the little community would have to make a decision about the island. For his part, he was eager for the move—the best thing to do. He remembered Charley's return last August; he'd left Adriel on the island and taken a ship for Racine. Rusty had walked up to the big cabin looking for Gabe. Then in his mind he is back on that day, knocking on the large pine door.

"*Entrez!*" Gabe's voice.

Charley is sitting at the long table with Gabe. Rusty's father is standing by the hearth, and Sarah and Bethia are serving bowls of soup.

"Come in, Rusty!" Gabe waves his arms. "You're just in time for a bit of food."

Always ready to eat, he needs no further invitation. But what Charley has to say makes him forget about the food.

"That air is pure. I never breathed such fresh air. It's the lake water, you see. Keeps things clean—them beaches are a sight to see. And the fish. Them waters have more fish than you could shake a stick at. No one would ever starve."

Bethia has a strange expression on her face, tight-lipped. Charley goes on. "And it's a healthy place. No marsh fevers, like in Nauvoo. In fact, no one was sick that whole summer."

"What about the winters?" Rusty's father says.

"From all reports, no worse than these parts. Maybe a mite colder. Adriel, now—he's set to stay the winter. Some folks came back here. But there's about five families planning to stay. We got us a snug little cabin built—and it wouldn't be that much work to put up others."

"What about you?" Gabe asks. "You fixin' to stay here?"

Charley takes a spoonful of soup. "This is good. I did miss the cookin' and the fancy meals. I be leavin' before winter sets it. That's my home now. Got to get back before the lakes freeze over." He pauses a moment. "Truth to tell, I be a bit homesick already. We found us a little canoe—in fact, we traded for it with some of the Indians. Gave 'em a blanket and some trinkets. Being out on that water—there's nothing like it."

"Brother Strang did say there was lots of Indians," Rusty's father says.

"At least two villages at one end of the island. And some on the smaller islands."

Rusty's father speaks again, eagerness in his voice. "I hear tell there's supposed to be an Indian mission there—according to revelation. Voree will continue, of course—one of the stakes of Zion. But that mission on Beaver Island is gonna be the great corner stake of Zion."

Charley nods. "If Brother James said it, like as not, it'll happen. It'll take some work."

Gabe is staring at the wall above Charley's head, and Rusty knows he is deep in thought. Most likely planning a way to get them all up there. Rusty speaks. "Well, it all sounds very exciting. As for where I stand, I believe I'll have a little more of that potato soup."

A wind rustles in the pines. A crow cries. And Rusty comes back to the present, the March day seven months later. At the same time, he thought of Gabriel and the incidents at Voree which had troubled all of them. First, the business about John C. Bennett and William Smith. They were indeed engaged in the very activities which had led to their undoing in Nauvoo. Adultery and spiritual wifery. Brother Strang had finally had enough. Last October, Bennett had been excommunicated. Rusty remembered the wording: 'apostasy, conspiracy to establish a stake by falsehood, deception, and various immoralities.' William Smith was excommunicated the next day.

"'Adultery and apostasy,'" Gabe had declared. Both Bennett and Smith had left Voree by that time and did not attend their trials. Gabe seemed satisfied with the proceedings, and because of his optimism, the faith in the prophetic office of Brother Strang took a great leap forward among the community members. That made it possible for them to persuade Bethia. Sarah's voice speaks in his mind.

"Lands sakes, honey. The man's a true prophet. If he says it would be good to gather on the island, I vow, it's the thing to do."

Rusty's father: "I heard tell of one woman who said she was too sick to go to the island. Well, finally she said she'd make the move. And she was healed from that day."

"Can you beat that?" Eb's eyes glitter as he gestures. "I'll go tell that one to Jess."

Finally Bethia agreed. The rest of them began to plan the move.

"Brother Strang says we should take provisions for a year," Rusty's father said. "Two barrels of flour, one barrel of meat, and I don't know what all."

Gabe nodded. "It says in the *Gospel Herald*—here, I'll read it. 'An honest, industrious man who is able to take himself and family to Beaver with one month's provisions has nothing to fear, and may be sure of as much labor as he ever needs, in an excellent country.'"

"That's it!" Eb declared. "When do we leave?"

Gabe laughed then. "As soon's we have everything in order. We have property to sell, and tools to pack."

Then, just as a measure of peace had settled over the little group, Gabe came into the shop with more news.

"The what?" Rusty remembered how he'd put down the hammer.

"An equality association. They be calling it the 'Associated and United Order of Enoch.' According to the paper, it's supposed to 'put an end to inequality among the people of God.'" Gabe is moving around, gesturing, almost sputtering as he explains. Then Rusty is back in the shop on that day, listening open-mouthed. His father and Eb abandon what they are doing and move closer.

"Folks are supposed to 'become one in their temporal things.' I heard twelve people have joined already—the Wrights, Finley Page, Francis Cooper and a bunch of others. Promised to consecrate everything they have—"

"Consecrate it to whom?" Rusty's father asks.

"Why, to God. So that rich and poor will share alike."

"What's wrong with that?" Eb asks.

Gabe waves his hands. "There's more. They're pledging to make their families into one huge household, with Brother Strang as the presiding officer. They be having meetings to run the organization, and they promise to live by certain rules. They'll own all their possessions in common, they can't take on any debt, and luxuries are out—no sugar, spices, or dried fruit. And of course, no coffee, tea, tobacco or alcohol."

Rusty's father shrugs. "Well, most of us do that anyway."

"They're talkin' about dressing a certain way, too," Gabe says. "'Uniform style, without needless material or ornamentation.' Women are to make dresses out of drillen—"

"You mean, like for work clothes?" Rusty asks.

"—and aprons out of a fabric with check-prints. The men are gonna wear clothes made of sheep jersey and homemade flannel—that's in winter. Drillen and factory material in the summer. I mean, it's all regulated—even the boots and shoes—"

"No fancy stuff?" Rusty's father raises his eyebrows. "I reckon it'll save money."

Gabe's voice rises. "But—don't you see? When you dedicate your property, you don't own it anymore. It's not yours, to sell or to take."

"Now, calm down," Rusty's father says. "Hang on a minute. Did anyone say you *had* to join this order?"

There is a silence. Gabe looks at him. "Well, no. I reckon not. *I* sure don't aim to."

"All right, then." Rusty's father folds his arms across his chest and strokes his chin. "What if we just wait and see what happens?"

Rusty picks up the hammer again. Gabe says, "That's it. We don't do anything, and we don't sign any pledge. And we try to get up to the island soon as possible." He stares off into space for a moment, chewing his upper lip. "I think it's best if we don't speak out against this thing, no matter how we feel. Just go about your business as if nothing was wrong."

"Well, nothing's wrong yet," Rusty's father says. "Everybody's healthy, and we got enough to eat."

"We come through this winter," Eb says. "And the babies is fine. J. J. be perkier than ever."

"*Eh bien.*" Gabe gives a final wave of his hand. "Let's get to work."

One of their customers brought the news about the land for sale.

"Yes, sir. They say the survey of the island is now complete, and the lands will be formally opened for sale come summer."

"Well, what're we waitin' for?" Eb set the tongs down. "Let's go get us some land. A dollar twenty-five an acre sounds mighty good to me."

"Not so fast." Gabe held up his hand. "That's for the folks already living there—according to the Pre-emption Act, they got first choice. That price is for them, and they can buy up to a hundred and sixty acres if they want."

Eb eyed him. "Well, what about us?"

Gabe shrugged. "We have to go and take our chances like most everybody else. But we'll get something."

"We got to get there first."

"I been studyin' on that. Brother Strang is leading a group up there next spring. And the way I'm figuring, some of us are gonna be part of it."

⸻⊷⊷⊶⊶⸻

Water. Marie had never seen so much water in her life. It stretched before her, grayish white, the wave edges a darker gray. She sat staring, open-mouthed, even while Gabriel unloaded the two trunks from the wagon and Rusty lifted down Louise. Gabriel helped Bethia down to solid ground. Calvin and Sarah had already climbed down.

"Tell me," she began as Rusty took her hand. *"Dites-moi que ce n'est pas le mer."*

"C'est le lac Michigan." Then he laughed. "They don't call 'em the Great Lakes for nothing."

He helped her down, and she took Louise by the hand. Three years old, her baby was now—a sturdy, dark-eyed girl with hair as black as her own, more serious in nature than she had ever been. She hadn't told anyone, but she was almost certain that another child was on the way. She was in that early stage of pregnancy where everything, even sights and sounds, made her feel queasy. Wondering if she should've told Gabriel. Wanting to be sure. Afraid he would make her stay behind if he knew.

But it was only a day's voyage on the propeller ship 'Troy,' on which they had booked passage—for them, hopefully, an overnight journey. Gabriel secured the oxen, and he and Calvin each took an end of one of the trunks. They carried it out on the nearest one of two piers extending on either side of the river's mouth.

"The Root River," Rusty said in answer to Marie's questioning look.

"Root River." She tasted the words on her tongue.

"Wind's picking up," Calvin said.

"Storm somewhere, I reckon." Gabriel spoke out of the side of his mouth.

"Storm?" Bethia gave a little cry. "Did you say 'storm?'"

"Somewheres else," Gabriel told her. "Not here. Why, that sun's lookin' to break through the clouds any minute."

56

She did not look comforted. A group of people stood midway down the pier, their belongings piled on the wooden boards. A man detached himself from the group and walked toward them. Marie saw that it was their leader himself, James Strang.

"There's been a delay," he said to Gabriel and Calvin. "The ship's held up in Milwaukee—bad weather. We been waiting a day now. They say the winds aren't favorable."

"Should be along any time, don't you reckon?" Calvin set his end of the trunk down on the pier.

"I would imagine."

"I'll be getting along, then," Gabriel said. "Lots to do, with packing up the shop. Let's go get the other trunk."

They said good-bye to him on the dock. He hugged each one in turn, except for Bethia who was too upset to let her husband touch her. Gabriel gripped Rusty's shoulders.

"Well, lad. It's up to you. They're in your hands."

Even then, Marie wanted to run to Gabriel and tell him of her condition. But she held back. Surely everything would be all right.

"*Au revoir.*" He walked off the pier. She watched as he climbed into the wagon and urged the oxen forward. He guided them in the turn back toward Burlington, and she kept her eyes on him till he was out of sight.

Bethia was whimpering. "Oh, why did he leave us here? Going off like nothing was happening."

"Nothing is," Marie told her. "We're going to be just fine."

But it was like talking to a child. Bethia turned away and began complaining to Sarah.

Three days of wind. Turning colder. They slept huddled in the harbor waiting room, hardly more than a shed. Marie and Rusty slept on the floor with Louise between them, their cloaks close around them. Each night, before Marie dozed off, she could hear Bethia crying, Sarah whispering words of comfort.

More people joined them. At last there were thirty-eight Strangites waiting for the ship, still delayed because of weather. Marie grew tired of Rusty's explanations to Louise about the docking maneuvers. "See, the water's real shallow here, about five feet deep. The ships come in, and they load them till they're almost touching bottom. Then they back up till the water's deeper, and they take on the rest of their cargo."

And the boats: "Now, that one? That's a schooner. A sailing ship. See the masts? And here comes a scow. Let's see what it's carrying."

Finally Brother Strang lost what patience he had left. He spoke to the ticket agent and announced to the group that they would be sailing immediately for Milwaukee on the 'Lady of the Lake,' a smaller boat which would deliver them to the 'Troy.' "I've already had the agent telegraph the 'Troy' to expect us."

Encouraged by the news, they picked up their belongings and stepped on board the small propeller boat. Marie felt the boat lurch under her feet as she climbed aboard. She held Louise close to her with one hand and reached to grab the rail with the other. The child's arms crept up around her neck. Just behind her, Rusty and Calvin carried one of the trunks.

She didn't mention it, but the wind had a sound in it that she had never heard before, like a high whine. She glanced at Rusty to see if he noticed it too. But he didn't look at her; he turned to go back for the other trunk.

Bethia needed help boarding, of course. Marie watched with a mixture of pity and contempt as Sarah took Bethia by the arm. "There, now, dear. Now the other foot."

Finally they were all on deck with their belongings. The crewmen loosed the lines, and they rocked away from the dock. After about five minutes of rocking, Marie knew this voyage would be one she wanted to forget. She handed Louise to Rusty, then ran to the rail and gripped it. When the spasm of sickness had passed, she straightened up, embarrassed. Was she the only one? Then she saw others at the rail, sensed a presence beside her. She turned. Brother Strang stood looking at her, his face unusually pale. In fact, she would have said he looked green.

"A rough voyage," he said.

"I reckon so."

"This ship isn't steady, like the bigger ones. A small propeller, is what it is."

She didn't reply. He said, "I understand you're not a member of our church."

"No, sir. That is, not yet. I was raised Catholic, and I reckon I still am."

"If you like, we can arrange to baptize you when we reach the island."

She thought a moment. "I'll give it some study. I'm not sure I'm ready, just yet."

The boat gave a violent lurch. He leaned over the rail, and Marie hoped that what happened next was not a critical comment on her reply. She waited till he had recovered, then spoke quietly. "When I'm ready to join, I'll let you know right quick."

He seemed to accept her words. He nodded, then retired to a place over beside the cabin. She moved on unsteady legs to her place beside Rusty and Louise.

"It's my turn." Rusty hurried over to a group of people huddled at the rail. She could see Bethia leaning on the rail, Sarah with one arm around her. Rusty returned.

"Everyone's seasick," he said. "Don't feel alone. I bet even if ol' Gabe was here, he'd be clutching that rail with the best of 'em."

"What—"

"And Bethia. Madder than a wet hen. If she ever sees Gabe again, she's like to bounce a frying pan off his head. And not just any pan. One of them cast iron jobs, with legs."

"But it's not his fault!"

"Try tellin' her. Now, the truth is, it's not that far to Milwaukee. So if we just hunker down—let's make a little bed on deck, with our cloaks—see, like the others are doing? We may be better off lying down. Anyway, it's time to get some rest."

They curled up together with Louise between them. Marie lay listening to the creak of boards, the shifting of the lines. Something tore loose and began knocking, a constant rhythm, wood on wood. She could hear the waves crashing against the bow, and always the wind, with its high whine. She felt it ruffling her cloak, her hair. A cold wind. And no fire allowed on deck. She shivered and drew closer to Rusty, who lay trying to protect them from the full force of the wind.

The boat lurched; spray filled the air. He said, "If anything should happen—I mean, if we don't make it—remember that I love you."

She hadn't thought of that aspect. Of course people drowned at sea; would they join that ghostly crew? She kissed him and clung tighter to him. Louise, between them, slept as if nothing were happening.

More noise. Scraping of wood on wood. Violent motion. Then one of the crew stepped over them. "Sorry, ma'am. You'll have to move, now." He ran to the rail, and Marie heard him fumbling with the lines. With the torrent of swearing that followed, she was glad Louise was still asleep. The crew members were fighting, tugging at the lines, wrapping them around a pier piling. They had reached the harbor.

"Milwaukee, I hope," Rusty said. "Not the pearly gates."

"What time is it?" someone asked.

"Just before midnight." Brother Strang's voice.

Somehow they made it from the boat onto the extended pier, all tired, cold, and seasick. A northeast wind swept across the lake. Solid ground again. But the wind sent water gushing up between the boards of the pier. "So, where's our ship?"

The 'Troy' had already left. To make matters worse, the captain of the 'Lady of the Lake' had augmented the fares before they were able to disembark, a not uncommon practice. Rusty went to learn what was happening, then returned with the news.

"We've engaged passage on the 'Sciota,' another prop boat. A larger one. It's due any time."

The men retrieved the trunks and other baggage from the 'Lady of the Lake.' By torchlight they prepared to make beds on the wharf, for the price of $8.75 which they haggled down to four dollars. Exhausted, Marie slept this time. When she awoke, the water on the dock had turned to ice.

"Watch how you step," someone said. "The ship's here."

The sun had not yet risen when they struggled up and tried to begin the day. Marie fed cut-up apples and bread to Louise, then tried to eat some herself. Her fingers ached with the cold. Rusty got their belongings together, and took one end of the trunk with Calvin at the other end. "Let's get aboard."

In the rough seas, it seemed to take forever to get everyone on board with their trunks, barrels, and other gear. Marie guided Louise carefully around the patches of ice and stepped onto the ship. It didn't lurch as wildly as the smaller one had. She was beginning to think they might have a smoother voyage. She took a place by the rail, just in case, and watched as the rest came aboard.

Rusty and Calvin boarded with the second trunk, which they placed beside the first. Bethia didn't want to get on the ship. Sarah took her arm, apparently consoling her, urging her forward.

"I'm not getting on that thing."

"Come on!" Marie called. "It's not that bad."

"I'm not getting on a boat ever again."

You stupid fool, Marie thought. *You want to spend the rest of your life on a wharf in Milwaukee? Or, worse yet, send for Gabriel to come fetch you? Haven't you given him enough trouble?* Marie saw then how Sarah acted, so patiently and gently. Explaining again and again to Bethia what they needed to do. Suddenly someone spoke, just behind Marie.

"Come along, Sister Romain. They be almost ready to cast off."

It was a kind voice, yet stern, full of authority. Bethia looked up and saw their leader, Strang himself, beckoning to her. Marie wondered briefly what her sister-in-law would do now. Would she still refuse to board?

A helpless, resigned expression went over Bethia's face. She clutched Sarah's arm, and together they moved toward the gangplank. Watching, Marie suddenly realized how wrong it was to be unkind to Bethia, or even think unkind thoughts—like kicking an old, sick dog. She wanted to weep then, and wished she could repent of her attitude the way people in Rusty's church did. As it was, she would have to confess to a priest.

At the same time she wondered at the kindness in Brother Strang's voice. Was this the same man who had denounced them all for failing to join the Order of Enoch? She knew that as of January, only about one hundred and fifty persons had joined, which had caused the prophet to call the Voree Saints "stiff-necked and rebellious."

When they were underway, she talked with Rusty about her feelings concerning Bethia. He smiled. "You don't need a priest. *I'm* a priest, and you've just confessed. Simply be nice to her—courteous. That's all."

"But—"

"As for managing her, let Sarah do that. Or Gabriel. Or Brother Strang, if the situation calls for it."

As the ship sped north into Lake Michigan, the winds seemed to grow less intense. It was as if a voice had declared, "Peace! Be still!" Finally there was a calm, and fog everywhere; she could no longer see the Wisconsin shore.

"Quite a relief, I must say," Rusty remarked. They sat together on a bench in a sheltered space, with Louise on Rusty's lap.

"Charley was right," Marie said. "There's this sense of freedom—of leaving all the unpleasant things behind."

Rusty smiled. "Oh, there'll still be hard work ahead. Everything we did before. But I reckon it'll be different. No more United Order. Last I heard, they was offering rewards for folks to join, and pay tithes and help build the temple and the Tower of Zion and such-like. But not a lot of people responded."

Marie even managed to smile at Bethia, who sat behind them and over to the right with Calvin and Sarah. Bethia had a resigned, dazed expression; she did not smile back. Then, in spite of the calm, Marie had to get up and rush to the rail anyway, leaving Rusty looking puzzled and troubled.

"I be fine," she said, in answer to his look. He raised his eyebrows. "Is it more than just seasickness?"

"I don't know."

He took her hand. They sat in silence, listening to the cries of gulls in the mist.

Almost dark. The fog lifted, and a black line appeared on the horizon. "There it is!" A voice rang out. "Big Beaver Island!"

Most of them were on deck by this time, gazing over the water at their new home. The lake and sky were still light, the sky a grayish pink with the afterglow of sunset, and the land stood out against it like a giant vessel riding on the waves. The ship turned and ran the length of the island. The wind picked up again as they approached the head of the island. As they neared the harbor, they could see the outlines of trees dark against the skyline, and the glimmer of lights from buildings on shore.

Then they were drawing up at the pier, making fast, and people were getting off the ship. "Take Louise and go with Sarah and them," Rusty said. "Don't trip, now. I'll get the trunks."

A familiar figure appeared before her—Charley, who gave her a bear hug. "Here, now. Let me take the little one." He escorted them off the ship, then went back to help with the trunks. Adriel stepped out of the shadows, gripping Calvin by the hand, turning and doing the same thing to Rusty.

"Hang it all. We be right glad to see you."

"Wait'll you see," Charley shouted from the rear of the first trunk. "We got one first class cabin built. So snug you won't believe it. No winter wind's gonna come through *them* walls. And it's two stories!"

Adriel grunted. "We got another cabin started. Be up in no time. And a start on a blacksmith shop, up close to the harbor."

"Gabe and Eb be comin' with all the tools," Rusty said. "Soon's they get packed. And the animals. Maybe by mid-summer."

"Sooner than that." Rusty set down his end of the trunk. "It don't take that long to pack what they got."

Calvin gave a cough. "They got to sell some stuff, too."

"Well, let's show you the cabin." Charley jerked his head to the left. "Just up this way. I reckon we got places for everyone, even Louise."

6

"To tell the truth, Rusty likes to eat. But he doesn't like to work all that much."

These words, spoken by Gabe over lunch, stung him to the quick. He leaned on his ax as he stood now on a little hill, looking over a sea of dune grass and sand to the lake beyond. Hog and Garden Islands, smaller than Big Beaver, rode in the far distance, a dark green. The water shone a light grayish-green, with the outline of little waves dark against it. Farther out, where the small islands were, he could see a streak of lighter green. *Storm before sunset. Maybe even sooner.*

Above him, masses of gray clouds moved toward the land. Thunder sounded, still distant. Even as he watched, the wind picked up. He felt it in his face, blowing back his hair, saw it ruffling the leaves and the shore grasses. How many storms had they weathered, this tiny group of friends? And what weather lay ahead?

He thought about the strange things that seemed to be happening too fast, the rumors, whispered but never discussed. Gabe, with Eb and his family, the animals and tools, had arrived in mid-summer, just in time for a church conference on the island. Many of the church leaders had attended, crowding into the little harbor town, now called the City of James. There were nearly fifty families settled here now, and so many coming that some steamboat captains were reportedly trying to dissuade them from landing on the island. But somehow they managed to get here and clear their land, plant crops and put up their two-storied houses of squared logs, whitewashed inside and out.

Calvin and Sarah had one of the largest log houses, which they shared with Gabe and Bethia. It had one room set aside for Gabe to use as a doctor, but there were so few sick people that it was seldom employed except as a study.

"It's those lake breezes," Gabe had said. "Fresh air. Healthy living for everybody."

Eb and his family had a smaller cabin, not far from the big one, and Rusty and Marie had one beside it. Theirs was indeed a snug house, as Charley had said, one of the first on the island. Charley and Adriel had given it to Rusty and then had gone to live behind the blacksmith shop, close to the harbor.

Now more and more Mormons were buying land in the harbor area. The headquarters was beginning its move to Beaver Island. And there were rumors that some disaffected Mormons were leaving Winter Quarters in Iowa, where most of the western contingent had stopped, and were heading east. On the whole, Rusty had every reason to be pleased and content. Marie and Jess spent their spare moments in each other's company, and the two little ones, now toddlers, played happily together. Marie was indeed expecting another child, not due till December, according to Gabe. With all the cordwood to chop at fifty cents a cord, a week's chopping gave you sixty pounds of flour and a good chunk of pork. And the waters teemed with lake trout and whitefish.

Why, then, did the shadow of uneasiness hang over him like the coming storm? Was it not in his nature to be completely happy? Some flaw in himself, perhaps.

For one thing, there were more rumors flying around than a cloud of gnats. He'd heard there were only three or four hundred people left in the Voree area. Baptisms for the dead had been initiated in the White River in August, the same ritual that they'd had back in Nauvoo. And on the island, two men had been brought to trial and cut off from the church for claiming to be prophets—that is, one of them was designated a prophet and the other 'the lion to come out of the thicket' and destroy the Gentiles, or anyone who was not Mormon. Shaw, the would-be prophet, had predicted an Indian uprising. Finally the local stake officials had stepped in and put a stop to the whole thing.

But the most troubling rumor of all was that James Strang had abandoned his ideal of monogamy and had actually taken a second wife. Right here on the island, they whispered—married in a secret ceremony with two apostles as witnesses. There was even talk of a honeymoon up at Sault Ste. Marie, with lots of drinking and wild behavior.

Rusty knew that wasn't possible, of course. The church leaders were staunchly against the very idea of polygamy. Wasn't Strang even now engaged in a mission to the east, accompanied by his nephew and secretary Charley Douglass?

Thunder sounded close at hand. Rusty jumped. He'd better finish cutting his cord or they'd say he was lazy for sure. He shouldered his ax and hurried to the nearest thicket, where he began working on a felled tree.

⌁

November already. Rusty and Gabe were opening up the shop.

"A frosty morning." Gabe shook the hair out of his eyes. "Let's have some more wood."

Rusty went back to the subject at hand. "Well, suppose he really *did* take a second wife?"

"*Eh bien.* We don't know for sure. I reckon you haven't heard about his first marriage. How Mary has not done well by him, according to my sources. How she even refused to have anything more to do with him."

"I hadn't heard."

Gabe shrugged. "Well, if it's true, it's hard for any man. And him a prophet, a leader? What's he supposed to do? Give up any hope of a normal life? Find a mistress? Marry someone secretly? What would *you* do?"

At a loss, Rusty blinked. "I—I don't know."

"Well, we don't know that he's done anything yet. There's nothing but rumors."

"But—the conference—"

"Which one? The one in New York?" Gabe picked up the tongs and the hammer.

Rusty tried to think. The last conference on the island had been in early September. Then there were the meetings held after that, in New York. In the first one, a black man, Moore Walker, had been ordained to the office of elder.

"What's important is what Brother Strang said," Gabe had reported. "He had no intention of courting the favor of emancipationists. He held that the revelations of God, not the devices of men, were the foundation of all national freedom."

"Amen," Eb had said.

The second conference, nine days later, had disturbing accusations from Lorenzo Dow Hickey and Brother Increase Van Dusen. According to the account in the *Gospel Herald*, Hickey had charged the prophet with being 'a liar, an imposter, a false prophet and dangerously wicked man,' saying he had letters from his wife on Beaver Island which would prove it.

"He's been accused of fornication, adultery, spiritual wifery, and all the 'abominations which ever existed in Nauvoo,'" Rusty said.

"Well, then they couldn't find the letters. You have to wonder if Brother Hickey really has all his oars in the water," Gabe replied.

"You're saying he's crazy?"

"'Misinformed' might be a better word. He's saying things based on rumor, I would imagine."

"But—"

"As it was, the church agreed to withdraw all confidence and fellowship from him. He's no longer one of the Twelve—they've suspended him for slander. As for Brother Van Dusen, they excommunicated him."

Rusty drew a deep breath and looked at Gabe. "But suppose—just suppose—"

"Suppose he's right? What then? We're here now; we can't just leave. Everything we have is on this island. I suggest we go on about our business, and do the best we can. Let's get to work on those spears, so we can fish through the ice when it freezes over."

Rusty handed him the bar of metal. "I—I just don't feel right about it, is all."

"You're not the one who's doing it. And we have no proof yet. Mind the door, now. Here comes Adriel."

As it turned out, Brother Hickey was so distraught that he ended up in a mental institution, repentant and desolate, where George Adams found him in December. The two of them petitioned Strang for forgiveness, which he freely gave.

"It shows wonderful compassion on his part," Gabe observed.

As the weeks passed, the rumors grew more insistent.

"They be sayin' Charley Douglass has curves like a woman," one of their customers said. "And derned if someone didn't say he had a skirt. That's what my friends in Philadelphia be writin' to me."

"When do you think Brother Strang'll be comin' back?" Gabe asked.

"That's anybody's guess. Like as not, he's havin' too much fun with his secretary to come back here."

"It's supposed to be his nephew," Gabe said.

"Nephew, my eyeball! If'n you ask me—"

Then Rusty had something more to worry about. Turah brought the news to them at the shop. "Marie be having her pains since mid-morning. She wants you and Dr. Gabriel to come right away."

Gabe looked at Rusty. "It be a mite earlier than I figured."

They left the shop in charge of Adriel and Eb. Gabe closed the pine door behind them. "Turah, if you can spare your mother, we'll get her over there too."

"I reckon she's there already. And Sarah too."

Gabe and Rusty entered the little cabin. Rusty marveled at how Gabe was able to take charge as soon as he was in the room. First he told Sarah to hang a pot of water over the fire. "Rusty, get some more wood in here. Now, Turah, I want you to take the little ones—J. J. and Louise. Get 'em over to your cabin, and look after 'em there."

Then he moved to Marie's bedside and stayed there, saying things to her in a low, reassuring voice. Rusty knew they were speaking French; he tried to listen. Gabe looked at him.

"Make sure we have enough wood. We don't want that fire to go out."

Rusty assumed they would send him away for the actual birth, but things happened so fast that they apparently didn't think of it. He remembered Marie screaming and screaming, and Gabe doing something at the end of the bed. Rusty was afraid he would begin screaming himself if Marie did any more of it. He drew in his breath. Sarah looked over and saw him. That was it. They would send him out now.

Then Gabe held up a tiny red creature the size of a small cat. He shook it, then slapped it on the buttocks; it made no sound. He laid it on the bed and went to work on it, wiping its face, the inside of its mouth. He turned it over. Finally there was a faint, gurgling cry.

"It's a boy." Gabe seemed to speak with an effort, as if he were exhausted. Sarah scooped up the baby in a towel and prepared to wash it.

"Be careful," Gabe told her. "There's trouble with the breathing—something not quite right." He turned back to Marie, who was now too sleepy to make any more noise. Rusty, watching, had an uneasy feeling that things were not as they should be. When Gabe had finished with Marie, he looked at Sarah. "Let her sleep now."

Sarah shook her head. "What about this little one? I never seed one so tiny."

"Keep him warm, is all we can do."

As he washed his hands, Rusty moved over to him. "What's wrong?"

Gabe sighed and spoke gently. "Well, son. I wouldn't name him just yet. You see—all I can say is that he came too soon. Born too soon. I mean, before everything had a chance to develop. Sometimes these things happen. And we don't know why."

"But—but he's breathing."

"He is now. We'll watch him carefully. But—"

"You don't think he'll make it?"

Gabe looked at him intently, then shook his head. "We'll do the best we can for him. But don't get your hopes up."

Rusty couldn't believe his child would not live. He checked on the baby every hour. Marie slept as if she were drugged. Louise spent a fretful night, with Rusty trying to comfort her. By the time Gabe and Sarah arrived with the morning light, he felt exhausted, unsteady on his feet. Gabe looked at him.

"Yer not workin' today. Go get some sleep. We'll take care of things here."

He felt too tired to sleep. He could hear their voices as he lay beside Marie. "Gettin' him to eat is out of the question."

"What about a clean rag soaked in milk?" Sarah asked.

"We can try it."

Rusty didn't know how many days the child lingered. It couldn't have been very long. He was the one who found it lifeless in the cradle. He stood in the half-light of early morning, wondering how to tell Marie. Fortunately Gabe tapped on the door at that point. Rusty indicated the cradle, and Gabe looked. After a while his eyes met Rusty's. He drew a deep breath. "I'm so very sorry. You know we did everything we could possibly do. We just don't know enough, is all. How to keep a baby alive when it's born too soon."

"Is it something I did? Did we do something wrong?"

"Not that I can see. It's just—one of these things that happens. Most women have lost children. Look at Hannah—one of them stillborn. And Emma Smith. She lost at least three. And no one knows why."

It didn't help to know how many others had lost babies. Rusty felt desolate, inconsolable. Gabe stayed with Marie all that morning, and Rusty's father knocked together a tiny coffin out of pine boards.

"We were fixin' to name him Paul Gerard," Rusty said. "After Marie's father."

Gabe nodded. "You can maybe save the name for another time."

Rusty felt as if he were moving in a fog, barely conscious of the others coming and going. The members of the little community brought food and good wishes. Even Bethia came by and sat beside Marie for a brief time. They had a little service, which Rusty could scarcely remember, and buried the coffin out in the woods.

"Under a maple tree," Gabe said. "He'll be covered with red leaves in the fall."

The next morning Gabe knocked on the door. "All right, Rusty. Time for work. Sarah be staying with Marie and Louise today."

He didn't feel like it, but he went to the shop with Gabe anyway. As he worked, the voices around him seemed muted, as if they came from a far distance.

"Them gentiles be spreading themselves all over the island. I'll vow, they be cutting off all the valuable timber."

"Maybe Brother Strang can do something about it when he returns."

"You heard what happened last week?" a customer said. "About young Spaulding Lewis?"

"What?" Gabe asked.

"Well, a bunch of Mormons was cuttin' down trees, and darned if they warn't attacked by some men from Whiskey Point. A large group of fellers, it was. Well, they beat young Lewis on account of he refused to quit cuttin' wood."

"How's the young man?" Gabe asked.

"Spaulding? He's doing some better. But he was beaten pretty bad."

Gabe laid down his hammer. "*Ma foi!* It sounds like Nauvoo all over again."

"Don't say that," Rusty's father said. "It's only one incident."

When the customer had gone, Eb said, "You heard about that settlement they call Troy? I hear they went and formed a branch of the Order of Enoch. They be conducting business as if they was one family."

"I hear they're trying to keep it secret till Brother Strang gets back," Adriel replied. "Then they can ask for his approval or disapproval."

"Of all the things we don't need," Gabe remarked. "The Order of Enoch."

"Well, no one says *you* have to join."

Charley opened the door and stamped in. "Hey, boys. Here's good news. Now that we're locked in by ice, we're gonna have us a dancing frolic. Over at old Mack's place—he's got a big cabin."

"More like a barn," someone said.

Rusty tried to join in the conversation, but he felt dead inside. And Marie was no longer her vivacious self. He began to worry more about her than his own state of being.

"Just keep close to her," Gabe said. "Talk to her about everything—what Louise is doing, what Eb and Jess are up to. I'll go see her tonight."

But nothing seemed to make much difference. She acted listless, as if she no longer cared about anything.

He wrote to his sister Hannah in mid-February.

City of James
Beaver Island, Michigan

My dear Hannah;

> *I know it's been a while since I thought to write to you. I don't know how much News other people have sent you, but we are all on Beaver Island now, with comfortable cabins and a Blacksmith shop. Our prophet and leader, Brother Strang, is traveling in the east now and trying to win more converts to the Church. Many people have come to the island already, but the Ice will have to melt before any more can join us.*

> *Father is in charge of the farming; we have a plot of land and two oxen to plow it and haul Wood. We still have the three Horses, which we ride into the interior of the island. Some work is being done there building Roads.*

> *Lake Michigan is full of fish. We also have chickens. One of our neighbors has a cow, so we have Milk for the children.*

> *There are now two Children. We have a girl, Louise, almost three and a half. Jess and Eb have a Boy the same age—his name is James Joseph.*

> *We had a second Child, a boy born early in December, but he died soon after. Gabe said he was born too soon.*

Marie I think is still grieving for him, and I feel sad about it too.

Otherwise everyone is healthy, and our little Louise is a delight. Our father and Sarah are in good health, although both are getting older. I hope you are all well. My fond wish is to see you again, but I don't know when that will ever be.

Your devoted brother,
Russell Manning

Montrose, Iowa
April 29, 1850

My dear Rusty,

I was so pleased to hear from you and to know that you are well. How I would love to see little Louise and James, and to see all of you.

Nat and I are in good health, and our children as well. Jody is fifteen now and taller than any of us. He loves the animals, and when he is not in school he helps his father around the farm.

The mean old mule Pete has calmed down some, and seems to be especially fond of Jody. He waits and looks for Jody every morning. Our little dog Nell died this past winter; she was very old. I'm surprised she made it through so many years with us.

Our daughter Gaby is eleven and loves music. She sings all the hymns and leads us when we sing in meetings. We have a younger daughter now, Elizabeth, born in 1848.

She has a cheerful way about her—I am minded of our mother and her sunny disposition.

Be sure and tell Marie that her sweet babe has gone back to be with his Creator and is experiencing joy in His presence. That we will someday see our precious ones again is my continual hope and assurance.

May the One who keeps us all, bless and protect you and your family up there on your island. That is my prayer every day for you.

Hug those children for me.

Love from your sister,
Hannah Givens

Rusty finished reading the letter aloud and looked over at Marie. She smiled as she sat in the rocker with Louise on her lap. "That's a right good letter. Read it to me again."

When he had finished, she sat awhile. Then she drew Louise closer to her. "I reckon we have to treasure the ones who are here, and not fret about things that are past."

"I reckon so." He waited before he spoke again. "There's one of those dancing frolics over at Mack's cabin, come Saturday. They have musicians and all. You want to go?"

She thought a moment. "You reckon it's safe?" He knew she was thinking about the party on New Year's Day, and the reports that the gentiles had invaded the place and beaten up two Mormon men.

"Safe as anything. No one knows about it 'cept us, so no one else'll be there."

Then she nodded, and for a moment she looked like her old, lively self. "Yes, let's go. We'll get Sarah to watch Louise, and if'n the weather's good, we'll walk on over there."

7

IT STARTED INNOCENTLY ENOUGH. Folks having fun at the expense of the Mormons. First, the ox-pulled wagons rumbling by the place of meeting on Saturday mornings, milk cans clanking. Then, actual disruptions of meetings, like the invasion of the debating school. The proceedings had been interrupted by rude conduct and threats of more to come. In addition, there were the beatings of the two Mormon men at the New Year's party.

"They just be high spirited, I reckon," Calvin had said. "Maybe things'll settle down, come planting time."

Gabriel thought of their past history and wondered. The ones perpetrating the abuse seemed not to know that the victims were a persecuted people, robbed and plundered, driven out of previous settlements in Ohio, Missouri, and Illinois. Now, Mormons were having trouble collecting their mail from Whiskey Point, the site of the post office. From all reports, some were beaten, others had their letters taken from them even before they left the post office. Mormon immigrants were being met at the wharf with threats of violence. Some of the new arrivals had feared further persecution, and had turned back.

"What's to be done?" Rusty had asked.

For a while the Saints had practiced strict non-violence. But as the incidents escalated, they decided to take a stand. In the late spring of 1850, with a growing Mormon population on the island, they announced publically that they would return "blow for blow" and punish any man who "insulted or intruded" upon them.

"So there you have it," Gabriel said to Rusty.

"We're in the middle of another war? On an island, with no place to go?"

"No. Come on. It's not a war. A show of force is the thing to do. Those rowdies'll back off now."

In the summer they made plans for the conference at St. James.

"A very special conference," Gabriel reminded the others. "Starting July 1st. That eighth day, we're fixin' to commemorate the fourth anniversary of when Brother James received the commandment to organize the church. That's what they be saying, anyway. They're gonna have all of the apostles there, and all sorts of doings."

To prepare for the event, everyone was invited to take the oath of the covenant.

"That's the Illuminati thing, isn't it?" Eb asked.

"I reckon," Gabriel replied. "I figured we left that back in Voree."

The oath consisted of laying their hands on a cross which was placed on a Bible, then swearing allegiance to Strang, "the Imperial Primate and actual Sovereign Lord and King on earth"...their "true and lawful Sovereign wheresoever and whatever kingdom, state, or Domain" they happened to live. This was "in preference to the laws, commandments and persons of any other Kings, Potentates, or States."

"Would you believe it?" Gabriel told the others. "We're supposed to 'yield obedience to the revelations he shall give...and the decrees he shall make, as the supreme Law, above and superseding all laws, obligations and mandates of any other person, authority or power whatsoever.'"

"So," Rusty said. "You gonna take that pledge?"

"I don't know."

In the end, most of them did. Gabriel heard that one Hiram Beckwith had taken his hand off the cross when it came to the part about acknowledging Strang as king, and had refused to sign the document. Gabriel also refused to sign, and Rusty followed his lead.

"I don't see what the fuss is about," Calvin declared. "King of the Kingdom of God—not an earthly king. We're voicing our support, is all. What's wrong with that?"

"If you can pledge to such a thing, that's fine," Gabriel answered. "I can't."

"It makes for a show of unity," Calvin responded. "And I'm afraid we're gonna need it."

Charley sidled up to Gabriel later. "Adriel and I ain't signin' that thing either. 'Course, Adriel can't sign—he never learned how to write. And I'm not about to do it for him. You know as well as I do, we're loyal and all. We just don't aim to sign any such paper as that."

Living in such a beautiful place, one never knew when trouble was just around the corner. Charley came in with the news just as Gabriel and Rusty were cleaning up the shop at the end of the day.

"Them gentiles is planning an all-fired, bang-up Fourth of July. Adriel and I was just down fishing—he's puttin' the boat to rights. Here's what we heard. They're fixin' to celebrate, all right. And the main event is expelling us from the island."

Gabriel couldn't believe it. "You can't be serious."

"Maybe not. But *they* sure are. They aim to gather a bunch of men and guns on small boats from Mackinac Island. They be arriving at Whiskey Point the night of July 3rd. The next morning, they plan to come to our meeting in small groups and start fighting during the service. They'll scatter the people, and kill our leaders before folks can do anything. Then they'll violate the women and burn our houses."

Gabriel tried to remain calm. "*Eh bien.* That'd do the job, all right. I don't reckon anyone would want to stay after that."

"So what do we do?" Rusty's eyes were wide.

"Nothing," Gabriel told him. "We got some time yet. Charley, I'm hopin' you'll go down to the wharf and see how the land lies."

By evening the members of the little community could talk of nothing else. Over dinner, Gabriel told them, "Charley's out there learning everything he can. He can sneak around and fit in most anywhere."

"I'll wager they think he's one of them," Calvin declared. "The way he looks."

Gabriel laughed. "Like a pirate king. I'd rather have him on my side than anybody."

Bethia threw down her napkin and began to cry. "Oh, how can you sit there and laugh like that? Here we're about to be attacked."

Gabriel sought to reassure her. "Come on, my dear. We haven't been through all of those persecutions for nothing. We'll figure out something. And we're safe for the moment—in fact, it's right peaceful."

But she was too upset to listen. Sarah had to help her into the bedroom and calm her down. When Sarah finally emerged, she tore into Gabriel. "Shame on you—worrying her like that. Don't you have any more sense?"

"Well, should we be prepared or not?" Gabriel raised his hands in a gesture of hopelessness.

"Let's see what Brother Strang says to do," Calvin suggested.

In the next few days, Charley discovered some interesting tidbits of information.

"We're fixin' on some tactics of our own," he told Gabriel and Rusty. "But it's secret stuff. Don't tell anyone. We're calling on men from distant places for reinforcements. We're stashing weapons. We got ourselves a real cannon, with other guns and ammunition. We're gonna have a schooner anchored out there in the harbor, with armed men on it. And we're havin' drills off in the woods there, in a secret place, in case we need to protect ourselves."

"I reckon if they just shoot that cannon off once or twice, it'd do the trick," Gabriel remarked.

"Remember—not a word to anyone. We're all supposed to be in that meeting on July 3rd—that's Tuesday—with our families and everybody."

⌘

Rusty walked toward the unfinished tabernacle building with Louise in his arms, Marie beside him. They stood in line with the people making their way in. Gabe was standing off to the side, waiting as Rusty's father and Sarah went inside with Bethia. Rusty moved up beside him.

"What's going on at Whiskey Point?"

"According to Charley, they be a-gathering. Our schooner's anchored out there in the harbor, but nobody knows there's men inside, waiting below decks."

"Do you reckon—"

"Go on in, now. Not a word to anybody. And be prepared. We may need you later."

Wondering, Rusty took his place with his family. They sat close by his father and the rest of their group of friends. Jess, with J. J. in her arms, moved in to sit next to Marie. Turah and her father took places behind them. Rusty could see Adriel at the end of the row, but not Charley. Out reconnoitering, no doubt.

The thought made him tremble. This was not an ordinary meeting. They were gathered, under siege, unsure of what awaited them on the Fourth. After statements by some of the other leaders, Brother Strang arose and addressed the congregation, speaking in a high, fast voice. "I have been much pleased by the remarks of my brethren in relation to mobs."

He went on to threaten death against those of his enemies who would put up a mob. Rusty, listening, did not feel reassured. He looked at Marie, knowing that he had tried to share his fears and uncertainties with her. At least she would be prepared.

In the evening meeting, George Adams spoke to the assembly about the mob and their intention to drive the Saints from the island. "We wish all persons to understand us…We will not be the aggressors. We will not go out of our way to avoid the threats of those who made them, and we give this warning that men may know what to expect at our hands…"

The women and children were instructed to stay in the tabernacle that night and not return to their homes. Marie looked at Rusty, her eyebrows raised. He put an arm around her.

"It's best," he whispered. "You'll be safe here."

She nodded. Suddenly Gabe tapped him on the shoulder, motioning him to get up. Rusty kissed Marie briefly and handed Louise to her. He made his way to the end of the row and followed Gabe outside. Eb joined them.

"We have a little job to do," Gabe whispered. "Both of you be as quiet as you've ever been. We're going to follow Brother Strang down to the trading post. And the first one who makes a sound has to answer to me."

"We've just threatened our enemies with death," Rusty said. "I hope that's not—"

"Did you hear what I said? You want to go back in there with the women-folks? Or do you want to do some useful work?"

Rusty clamped his jaws together, almost biting his tongue in the process. Whatever their mission was, Gabe was taking it with extreme seriousness. Rusty began to worry that it might involve murder.

Strang was waiting by the corner of the building with a small group of men. He motioned them forward. They started down the hill toward the harbor, moving stealthily in groups of two or three. Rusty followed behind Gabe and Eb. As they reached the buildings around the harbor, they walked single file. The water lay before them, calm, with tiny ripples washing ashore. Four Indian canoes floated near shore, bobbing a little with the waves. A few people were sleeping in them; Rusty saw a blanket move.

Light came from the windows of the trading post. Rusty could hear voices inside. He caught snatches of a song he couldn't recognize, and loud laughter. Brother Strang motioned them to follow him around behind the building. Suddenly Charley appeared, whispering, making gestures of his own.

In the rear of the trading post, barrels stood against the wall. Gabe put his hands on the nearest one.

"Gunpowder," he whispered. "Help me dump it."

"Where?" Rusty asked.

"In the harbor. Where do you think?"

"Here." Eb grasped the top of the barrel, and he and Gabe set it on its side. They began to roll it down toward the wharf. Rusty moved to the other side and helped them roll.

"Easy, now." Gabe looked behind them. "No noise." Between the three of them, they got it onto the dock, pried off the lid, and poured the contents into the water.

Gabe was panting. "Now let's put it back. Same way we found it."

They rolled it back and fumbled to replace the lid. "Now, the next one," Gabe whispered. "No—that's already empty. The one after that."

A loud noise from inside. A door slamming. Then Charley slapped him on the back. "Everyone away!" he said in a low, hoarse voice. "Quickly!"

They started to run back the way they had come. "Quiet, now." Brother Strang's voice. They weaved around the rows of cabins and hurried up the little hill. Bits of gravel fell as they climbed. Rusty's shoe hit a rock; he heard it bouncing down the slope. At last he joined the group gathered in the shadow of the tabernacle. He leaned his hand against the logs, breathing fast.

Charley wiped his sleeve across his forehead. "We found their whiskey supply. Managed to dump tobaccy in one of them barrels. If'n they get into that, they'll all be hog-whimperin' drunk before sun-up."

"Good work, boys," Strang said. "I don't know what more we coulda done."

Dawn. A beautiful, still morning.

"Happy Fourth of July, boys," Brother Strang said. "Let's fire off a 'national salute' for our friends in the harbor."

Rusty helped roll out the cannon. They aimed it at Whiskey Point and began firing. Men rushed out of the trading post and stood looking dazed, as Charley reported. "They done everything 'cept scratch their heads. And I reckon they done some of that, too. Never did they think we would have a cannon."

The people assembled in their tabernacle that morning. Gabe and Eb hurried to join their families inside. Rusty stayed outside with the armed guard of eight men and the twelve who kept the cannon ready and the cannon balls heated.

"Keep an eye out for them, now," Strang said. Then he went inside to speak to the assembly.

Rusty figured there were enough folks to man the cannon and keep watch, so he stepped into the hall just in time to hear Brother Strang's account of last night's "scrape." As Rusty found his seat, Brother Strang was saying, "They think they can kill the church by killing me. But I tell you that though they kill me…they cannot kill the work or church. It depends on God only."

Rusty, sitting with his family, sensed he'd heard the words before. *From Joseph Smith, maybe.* A chill went through him. He tried to concentrate on what was being done up front. But he thought he had never endured a more tension-filled service. From the grim expressions around him, he knew that others felt the same. At least no one slept through the scriptures and homilies.

Before nightfall, they knew their day of extermination had been postponed.

"Them companies didn't arrive on time," Charley said over dinner at Sarah's house. "And the ones that was there—why, they was scared of all the artillery. Afraid that we'd fight back. They just scattered and went about their business."

"Oh, God be praised." Sarah put a handkerchief up to her eyes. "God be protecting us. Keeping us safe from our enemies."

"I knew the cannon would do it," Gabe said. "It puts me in mind of what Napoleon once said. 'God is on the side of the biggest battalions.'"

"Oh, you." Sarah shook her handkerchief. "Bethia's right. You're simply impossible."

Gabriel, sitting in the rear of the tabernacle, knew he should have expected it. All the signs were there. First, the taking of the covenant *en masse*, with fifty or sixty simultaneously swearing their oath of allegiance. Then, the procession, with Brother James in the lead, dressed in a robe of red flannel, floor-length, trimmed with white flannel dotted with black specks. He wore a large metal star on his chest, and had on his head a miter ornamented with more stars. Reminiscent, Gabriel learned later, of what was worn by the Jewish high priests.

Following in the procession came the council, then twelve elders, the seventy and other quorums. They filled the space up front, leaving room for the audience in the rear. Gabriel remembered that it was about ten o'clock in the morning. Something was happening with a closed curtain up front, hanging over a newly-erected platform.

Gabriel glanced at Rusty, who sat beside him, mouth open, his face deathly pale. Gabriel jostled him.

"Hey. It's pure theatre. Didn't you know that ol' George Adams was a Shakespearean actor?"

"I—I didn't expect this."

"I figured you didn't. Relax. Enjoy the spectacle."

Gabriel had time to look at the cloth panels on either side of the stage. One had a flag with a life-sized figure of a man wearing a crown and holding a scepter.

"The King's flag," someone exclaimed behind him. "I helped paint that."

The opposite panel depicted a man holding a cross and a trumpet. Painted drapery hid the joists of the building.

Then the curtains parted. Gabriel had a glimpse of the stage covered with carpet, and in the background, canvas and cloth panels with pillars painted on them to represent the interior of a palace. And there, seated in a large chair, was Brother Strang in all his finery, with a scepter in his hand.

After the opening prayer, Strang revealed to the congregation that he was a Jew, a descendent of the House of David, and that he had inherited the throne of Israel through the lineage of David.

"That's news to me," Gabriel whispered. "I thought he was French." Rusty, apparently in a state of shock, did not reply.

George Adams, who was six feet tall and towered over most people there, took charge. He called upon the president of the apostles, Samuel Graham, to "bring forth the royal diadem." Adams placed the star-studded crown on Strang's head, declaring him the "king of earth and heaven." While James the Anointed waved his royal scepter, the congregation, with raised hands, covenanted with God to "be His people and to keep His laws and statutes."

As the coronation ceremony continued, Gabriel began to worry about Rusty. Marie had stayed home that morning, since Louise had developed a cold and was fussy. Bethia and Sarah had elected to stay home as well. Sarah's comment echoed in his mind: "I've had enough excitement for a while."

Now, here he was, the leader of their little group, responsible in a sense for getting them to Voree and up to the island in the first place. He hadn't anticipated the crowning of a king, and he didn't think it was that great an idea. But, clearly, it was done now, and the main worry was what their gentile enemies would make of it. Was he responsible for his relatives' spiritual welfare as well?

Apparently so. He sighed, folded his arms, and said *"Ma foi"* under his breath several times. Then he whispered to Rusty, "It be warm in here. Let's go get us some fresh air."

Rusty nodded, looking as if he were seasick. They got up and made their way outside.

They walked out past the lone guard at the door. Gabriel put a hand on Rusty's elbow and led him gently to a little knoll just behind the tabernacle. He stopped then and they looked out over the bright waters of the harbor. Gabriel waited, then drew a long breath.

"So, there you have it. *Le Roi James*, it is."

Rusty didn't reply. Gabriel looked at him. "If you have anything to say, tell it to me now. Otherwise, I advise you to keep silent."

Rusty burst out, "Crowned himself king! I still can't believe it!"

"You saw it. We were part of it. And I have to remind you, he didn't crown himself. George Adams crowned him, with the approval of everyone there."

"It's just that—"

"I reckon you know that Joseph Smith was crowned in a similar way—I would hope, without all the theatrics. Crowned by the Council of Fifty, back in Nauvoo."

Rusty looked on the verge of tears. "That was a private ceremony. Very few people knew about it. But this—"

"So there's a difference? Think of it more as a title—like 'pope.' Or 'archbishop.'"

Rusty gestured. "But—but it doesn't seem right. Where have we gone wrong? Where—where is the spirit that we used to have in the services? The spirit that was with us at first?"

"You mean, in Nauvoo?"

"Yes. And—and Far West. Kirtland. The earliest days."

"The Holy Spirit?"

"Yes. It was there, in the meetings. And in this coronation, I didn't sense it at all."

Gabriel paused. This was a tough one. "*Eh bien.* The Holy Spirit is supposed to be everywhere. It's with us all the time, *n'est-ce pas?*"

"Well, I'm not feeling it. It's like we chased it away."

Gabriel watched a single seagull flying above the line of trees. "I reckon you're on familiar terms with this Spirit."

"I know it when I feel it. Sometimes I just reach out with my mind, and it's right there. Today, it wasn't."

Gabriel waited a long time before he spoke. "Since you seem to be an expert on the Holy Spirit, I'd better tell you something. You're talking about a subjective thing—like poetry, for instance. Not everyone reacts to the same poem in the same way. I have to tell you, there be folks in there who'll swear the good Spirit was there all through that ceremony. Don't look so shocked. And there's nothing you can say that'll make 'em feel otherwise." He gave a little cough and went on.

"As for the spirit that was in the early church—this isn't the early church. How can it be? Too much has happened." He paused, then shook his head. "What I'm trying to say. We can't bring back those early days. The only thing we have is right here. Maybe it could be different, but it's not. I reckon we better accept what we have, and try to make the best of it."

"You mean—"

"I mean, here we are, on this island. With plenty to eat and enough work to keep us busy. We're safe, we're healthy. That king business is just a title. *King in Zion.* So, where's Zion? I figure it's somewhere back in Missouri. Now, if someone—say, one of us—makes a big fuss and we get thrown off the island—where do we go?"

"Back to Nauvoo, I reckon. Montrose, where Nat and Hannah are."

"Think a minute, Rusty. It's a far piece back there, with all our children and older people. Bethia, who needs more care then we can give, sometimes. And, you must remember. The policy now is not to let folks take away the things they once consecrated to the community.

Our oxen, our horses and tools—we'd most likely lose them all. Not to mention our household possessions."

Rusty met his eyes, then nodded. "I—I hadn't thought of that."

"I reckon you hadn't."

A blast ripped from the cannon; the ground shook.

"A salute for the new monarch," Gabriel remarked. The cannon roared again. The acrid smell of gunpowder filled the air. After a few moments, the doors of the tabernacle opened and people began emerging. Eb and Jess walked out looking uncertain, blinking as the sunlight hit their eyes. Eb's face brightened as he saw Gabriel and Rusty.

"Remember," Gabriel said to Rusty in an undertone. "Be mighty watchful what you say to folks. These be strange times, and we don't want to call up more trouble than we got."

"I'll be careful." Rusty's voice sounded listless; he didn't look at Gabriel. "I promise." He seemed to be staring at something on the ground, and even when Eb and Jess reached them, he didn't lift his head.

8

Marie couldn't get Rusty to tell her about the coronation. She had to learn the details from her friend Jess.

"Oh, my glory! A red robe, down to the floor, trimmed with white! And a crown with stars!"

Turah, she learned later, had helped with the decorations. With her artistic gifts, Turah had helped paint columns on canvas for the throne room.

"And I had no idea!" Marie exclaimed.

"She didn't, either," Jess replied. "She thought it was just for some dramatic piece that Brother Adams was planning."

When Marie pressed Rusty on the subject of the coronation, he acted embarrassed, as if he were ashamed. She tried to understand his attitude—after all, *he* hadn't done anything. A king was not that big a deal, in her mind. Hadn't the king of France been the 'defender of the faith?'

Knowing that Rusty seemed downcast—possibly about having a king—she got Charley to buy her a bottle of wine from the trading post. She served it with roast chicken that evening. Charley and Adriel joined them in the festive meal, and by the time the banquet ended, Rusty was smiling and joking again.

"Any time you want a bottle, just let me know," Charley told her.

She smiled. "*Merci.* We don't want to bend the rules too much."

"With what else is going on, I wouldn't worry none about a little wine," Charley answered.

'What else' no doubt referred to the new king and Elvira, the young woman now living with his family. No longer masquerading as Charley Douglass, she appeared openly with the prophet. They were seen together, strolling arm and arm on the pathways between the cabins.

"You reckon he's gone and married her?" Marie asked Jess.

"That's what they be a-sayin'. 'Course there's nothin' official yet."

Marie nodded. "He'd have to tell the first wife sometime. And I don't figure that's been done."

"If it was my husband, he'd have to be wearin' full body armor when he did it. That is, if'n he wanted to get out of the room in one piece."

Marie learned from Charley that a priest made periodic visits to the Indian population on the island and held mass for them. Charley told her when the next visit was expected. Not wanting to walk out to the Indian villages alone, she asked Turah to go with her. Turah accepted, and they started out on a Sunday morning in late July.

They walked through the settlement of St. James and out beyond to where the native villages stood. The wind ruffled the trees, the sunlight shifted, and Marie noticed with a sudden pang how beautiful her companion was. Turah, sixteen now, looked in the full bloom of youth, with a glow about her face and eyes. She was taller than her mother and moved with the natural, confident manner of a young person just becoming aware of her own abilities and strengths. *So soon*, Marie thought. So soon we grow old, and the ones we thought of as youngsters become mature adults.

A young man stood at the entrance of a small log house. He straightened up when he saw them, and Marie asked him where she could find the priest.

"The Black Robe? In here. Very soon."

As he answered, Marie saw that he was thin, so tall that he tended to slouch. He had black eyebrows and straight black hair tied at the back of his neck, and his complexion was almost as dark as Turah's. *Tanned by the sun*, Marie surmised. *A fisherman*. He wore pants and vest made out of some animal hide, most likely deerskin, and moccasins from the same material. His hands looked large and clumsy, and he moved them as if he weren't sure what to do with them. He appeared to be not much older than Turah.

"We wait together." He ushered them into the log house.

For chairs, there were up-ended logs, and dark animal skins spread on the dirt floor. She and Turah sat on the logs, and the young man took a place on the floor beside Turah. The aroma of fresh-cut wood filled the air and mingled with the scent of pine and crushed ferns from outside. Marie found it pleasant and refreshing. Then she saw the young man looking intently at Turah. She began to feel uneasy.

The room filled with people, mostly Indian men and women with their children, and a lone white man. As far as Marie could tell, she was the only white woman there, and Turah the only black one. The priest came in, a small, short figure in his dark robe, and the service began.

After the mass, Marie decided she'd had enough of the young Indian lad. She tried to get Turah to go up to the front of the room with her and meet the priest. But the priest moved over to her, and Marie found herself having to converse with him while Turah and the young man talked in low voices behind her.

The priest knew a little English, but he had been born in France. *"Je m'appelle Père Antoine. Et vous, madame?"*

She told him who she was, a Catholic married to a Mormon, and that her husband worked at farming, blacksmithing, and cutting wood. He nodded. Then he asked if she'd heard the news. No, she hadn't; what news?

"Le président Zachary Taylor est mort."

His death had occurred on July 9 from some stomach disorder, after only sixteen months in office. By the time she had finished expressing her shock and surprise, she became aware of what was happening behind her. The young man was speaking in a halting, uncertain voice.

"Kenturah. A pretty name."

"And you?"

"I am *Ma'iingan*." His voice no longer unsure.

"Min—mingan?"

"Means 'Wolf.' Call me 'Gray Wolf.' Most folks do."

"That's a right good name. And you speak English well."

He sighed. "I cannot read it or write it. The Black Robe tried to teach me. But he went too fast, and I did not understand."

"I can do it! I helped teach my momma, and I can teach you."

"Where do you live?" Gray Wolf asked.

Marie thought it best to intervene at this point. "We have to leave now."

Turah and the young man looked at each other. He nodded unsmiling, accepting the fact. Marie hurried her out of the log house. "We must tell the others. There's big news. President Taylor has died."

Turah raised her eyebrows. "I reckon they already know. There be a big commotion down by the harbor, early this morning."

Turah was right. Charley had already told them. A group of the men had gathered in Marie's keeping room.

"Ol' Rough and Ready," Gabriel said. "That means Millard Fillmore's our president."

"That's not much better," Eb remarked. "At least he don't own slaves like Taylor did."

Charley grunted. "What it means is, if Brother Strang wants us to have Beaver Island for ourselves, he's gonna have to deal with another president."

They all knew that Brother Strang had wanted the federal government to set aside the Beaver Island chain for the Saints, and had in fact composed a 'memorial' asking President Taylor and Congress for the right to settle and occupy the islands. The official answer was that they should buy what they wanted. Since the group did not have enough money to purchase the whole island, they had to be content with what land they could afford.

"He wanted a lighthouse, too," Eb said.

Charley shook his head. "A right good idea. But it'll have to wait."

Gabriel gestured excitedly with both hands. "That would be something, I reckon. A lighthouse down at that southern end." Just then Adriel appeared outside at the one tiny window of the cabin. Charley opened the door for him. Adriel stepped in and glanced around.

"Found a young feller from the Ojibwe village just out by yer place. Anyone know of any trouble with the Indians?"

"Why, no." Rusty looked puzzled. "What did he want?"

"He didn't rightly say."

Marie looked around for Turah, but she had slipped outside as Adriel was speaking. Marie glanced out the window. No sign of her.

Eh bien. What was the harm, anyway? A simple friendship between two very young people. She shrugged and said nothing.

After that, she saw them frequently at the edge of the woods, or seated on the rocks down by the sand and dune grass. Once she got close enough to see what they were doing; they were sketching, each with a piece of paper and a bit of charcoal. She caught a glimpse of one of the drawings—either a mallard or a loon, she wasn't sure which. Whatever it was, the sketch was not yet complete.

Drawing for each other. She smiled to herself. When she questioned Turah later, the girl replied, "I'm teaching him to read. And he's showing me about all the birds which visit the island. And how to make baskets out of pine needles."

Once, before Mass, he brought her a pair of moccasins. "My sister made these. See how she did the beading? These much better than the white man's shoes."

Periodically the Indian population would leave to go harvest wild rice on the mainland. Then Turah would be alone. Marie would see her standing amid the dune grass and looking out over the water, always with the sketchbook under her arm.

How have the mighty fallen. The words echoed in Rusty's mind as he swung the ax to complete his cord of wood. *In such a short time.* George Adams had left on a mission only a few weeks after the coronation. His wife Louisa had stayed behind, on the island.

"It's true," Charley had told the others at the blacksmith shop. "There's letters comin' from church members in the east. Louisa ain't his wife at all. He took his real wife, Caroline, to some person's house in New Jersey, figurin' she was gonna die any minute. But the thing is, she didn't die. And here he'd already taken off with Louisa. If they did get married, it sure warn't legal. 'Cause Caroline was still living when he remarried, and didn't die till months later."

"If that don't beat all," Eb had said.

Charley held up his hand. "Wait. There's more. Turns out she warn't a rich widow at all, but a—let's say, a 'lady of the night.' And what she's done is make a bunch of trouble for Brother James. Accusing him of making eyes at a young girl, one of Johnson's daughters. At least, I think that's what the fuss was about. Now he's madder than all get-out. Tellin' her to git off the island if she knows what's good fer her."

Gabe was examining the bellows. "I hear she pulled out a bowie knife and said she'd put it into his heart if'n she had the chance."

Rusty remembered how his father gave a laugh. "Well, at least you can't say life is dull in these parts."

George Adams had returned in early fall. There were rumors that he had apostatized, but apparently anything that had happened between himself and Brother Strang had been resolved; he was censored and forgiven. But he claimed not to like how Louisa had been treated in his absence.

Then, at the church conference on October 13, the new Mrs. Adams was excommunicated.

"I'll be dad-burned if they both didn't up and leave," Charley said.

"And—get this," Rusty's father declared. "They vowed an 'eternal war and a war of extermination.' Then they went off to Mackinac Island, where you can bet they be spreading all sorts of rumors."

"Lies and filth," Gabe said. "Who's gonna believe them?"

Eb shrugged. "You'd be surprised what folks'll believe."

Gabe finished the last few strokes on a hinge. "I happen to know Dr. McCulloch—she hated him worse than anybody. All because he didn't treat her like royalty. He told it like it was."

"They jest dint get along from the beginning," Eb said. "Why, when he first seed her, he said—"

"Let's have a little more fire, Rusty," Gabe said. "Grab the bellows."

Rusty never did learn what the doctor had said to Louisa Adams. Dr. McCulloch, a surgeon, had arrived on the island last spring. Coming from Baltimore after being baptized by George Adams, he most likely knew more than George wanted known. Rusty knew how Mary, Brother James' wife, had become ill in the midst of her theatrical performance in early October. Too ill to be moved, she had stayed in the tabernacle all night with Brother Strang at her side. Dr. McCulloch had examined her the next morning and had proclaimed her "feeble, low, and in an extremely critical state."

Now it was rumored that Mary wanted to leave the island. Had she finally learned about her husband and his liaison with Elvira? Or had she known all along? At any rate, it was said that she disliked island living and no longer wanted to stay.

"A bit late, to leave now," Gabe had remarked. "Winter be settin' in. Better to wait till spring."

That fall, Adams brought a number of legal actions against Strang. He was charged with threatening the lives of both George and Louisa, and of stealing the stage props used for the coronation. Strang saw the inside of the jail on Mackinac several times. While he was away answering the charges, the islanders struggled with accusations against them by their non-Mormon neighbors.

"They say we be stealin' and murderin'," Charley said.

"They're the ones who be stealin'," Rusty declared. "Takin' our letters. Putting marks into wood what belongs to us. Stealing staves from the barrel makers."

Adriel waved his hands. "Don't forget the illegal voting." Everyone knew that the majority of the elected officers for Peaine Township were now Mormon. Some people were declaring that the vote was illegal. "And now they say we be counterfeiting. Storing bogus money—hiding it somewhere."

Gabe gave a laugh. "I wish I knew where. I'd go get me some."

Charley shook his head. "I do recall about George Adams trying to get up mobs against us. Even said they should burn our houses and steal our property. That's when he was really riled—before he left the island for good."

"If that don't beat all," Eb remarked. "I be minded of when he said we should go down and burn out the trading post on Whiskey Point.

'Ruthlessly destroy'—his very words. On account of them stealin' our mail and beating us and all."

"And you can be sure Brother Strang put a stop to that," Gabe said.

"As he should have." Rusty's father's voice was like an echo.

Charley took a seat on an up-ended log. "I'll tell you the one to watch out fer. Eri Moore, that's who."

"That trader feller?" Gabe asked.

"The one that joined the church and even married one of our women."

"He didn't stay in the church very long," Gabe remarked.

Charley waited, then went on. "Well, I heard from someone that Moore wrote to the governor complainin' about us."

"*Us?*" Rusty's voice rose in surprise.

"About how we be doing all these illegal things, counterfeiting and the like. Said we be threatening peoples' lives—"

"Like Louisa Adams, most like," Adriel interjected.

Charley got to his feet. "Then, in a second letter, he said about how Brother Strang ordered us to go out and burn houses, kill any folks that tried to stop us, and get hold of all the guns and ammunition we possibly can."

"I'll be blasted," Eb said. "I reckon he be thinkin' of the coronation, and the cannon and all."

Charley gestured. "Said we was all doin' the counterfeiting. He wanted the governor to send men and take us all into custody. Says they should usher us out of the state or send us to prison before we start burnin' cities."

Gabe put down his hammer. *"Eh bien.* How do you know all this?"

"You should know by this time. I have my ways."

The group of men looked at Gabe. "Lies," Rusty's father was saying. "Senseless lies."

"Oh, there's things going on," Charley said. "It's just that most of us aren't doing them."

"What do we do now?" Rusty voiced the question on all their minds.

Gabe shrugged. His dark brows drew together, and his mouth

formed a grim line. Then he shook his head, and his shock of black hair fell over his forehead. "Why, nothing. We go on about our business. And we try to keep out of trouble. Rusty, we need more wood."

As he started out the door, Rusty recalled a dream he'd had recently. In the dream, searching for his favorite hammer, he'd found it in pieces, the handle broken. The sense of loss still lingered in his mind, the feeling of something precious destroyed beyond repair.

"All right, boys." Gabe gave a cough. "We got work to do. Let's get some of these items ready to sell."

Ordinarily Bethia wouldn't have welcomed Charley into her house so readily. But she felt different these days, elated, light in spirit. Gabriel's words rang in her mind: "I reckon you're going to be a mother." Now the family members treated her with deference and respect, Sarah insisting that she remain seated while Gabriel opened the door for Charley. And even while Charley expounded on the sale of alcohol to the Indians, and how the traders were all doing it, Bethia sat silent and thought of what Gabriel had said. "In the fall, most likely. A good time to be born."

"They be makin' tons of money," Charley was saying. "'Indian Whiskey,' is what they be callin' it. You get two gallons of alcohol and dilute it with, say, thirty gallons of water. Then you add red pepper and tobaccy enough to make it intoxicating, and man, you got yourselves a drink. Now you sell it for fifty cents a gallon if'n it's in a cask, or twenty-five cents a bottle. A single drink sells for six cents. Something that only costs you five cents a gallon to produce."

"*Eh bien*. Someone's making money," Gabriel remarked.

Charley waved his hand. "You can say that again. And the Indians love it. But, as Brother Strang says, it's not that good for them. All their resources—their annuities from the government and what they get for fishing—it's all going to the traders."

Gabriel nodded. "I can see why Brother Strang would be upset. It's not right. In fact, it's despicable. But what can we do?"

Charley leaned back in the chair, balancing himself on the two back legs. "Well, there's this new law just been passed. Traders are supposed to post a bond before they sell the stuff. But none of 'em here can afford it."

Gabriel gave a shrug. "So?"

"So there's been trouble already. Adriel got hisself right in the thick of it. They heard that ol' Eri Moore was over on Garden Island sellin' whiskey to the Indians. The Mormon sheriff took along a posse of eleven men to go git 'em, and darned if Adriel didn't go with 'em."

"It took that many?"

"They figured the Indians would try to hide him, most like, or even defend him."

"So what happened?" Gabriel asked.

"Well, darned if they didn't get over there and found he'd already left. He took his dog sled off to Mackinac to get some supplies and to deliver the mail. Seems he had his wife in the sled with him, and some other men. Some Indians and even a postal carrier. Well, the Mormon fellers who had gone over to arrest him were starting back when they saw Moore and them others comin' back to Garden Island. The story was, they'd found some broken ice and figured they couldn't get through to Mackinac. So darned if the posse didn't start chasin' after Moore, runnin' over the ice and all. Climbin' through the snow."

"They get him?" Gabriel asked.

"Naw. He went off into the woods. No one could find hide nor hair of him. They figured the white men and Indians there helped 'em escape."

"Adriel get back all right?"

"He lived to tell the tale. They all got home safe and sound."

"I'll be blamed. That's quite a story, Charley." Gabriel got to his feet. "Let's have a little apple cider—it's fresh-made. Want some, dear?" He looked at Bethia.

A wave of queasiness rushed over her. "Uh, no. Not just now, thank you."

Gabriel poured some in a mug and handed it to Charley. "Ol' Eri

Moore. Causin' more trouble than he's worth. Selling that rot-gut to the Indians."

⬳⬳⬲

It turned out that Moore was furious. As soon as the break-up of ice permitted travel on Lake Michigan, Moore went to Mackinac and obtained warrants against thirty-nine Strangites. He accused them of putting him "in fear of danger" and charged them with robbery, arson, and burglary. Gabriel learned later that he even brought the sheriff of Mackinac, Henry Granger, to Beaver Island to execute the warrants.

That morning, Gabriel and Calvin walked to the shop, skirting the patches of melting snow. Calvin opened the door. "Rusty won't be coming. He's gone over to Hog Island with a bunch of fellers."

"What're they doing over there?"

"There's a report of some yawl trapped in the ice. They be gone to see if they can rescue her and bring her back here."

They got the fire going and began work. In mid-morning, Adriel threw open the door and rushed in. He stood panting, his eyes wide; for someone who seldom got upset, this was unusual. *Something not right.* Gabriel laid down his hammer. "What is it?"

"I just been down to get the mail. They told me the sheriff was looking for a bunch of us. Most of the ones he wanted was off on Hog Island rescuing a boat. Brother Strang and about eleven others. So the sheriff's gone off with something like forty men. A well-armed posse, to bring 'em in. And—"

Gabriel and Calvin exchanged glances. All the color left Calvin's face. Adriel went on.

"Charley went over to help with the boat. He's with those fellers who're—"

"Rusty, too." Calvin's voice sounded weak. "They'll both be arrested—along with all the others."

Gabriel paused as the words sunk in, then looked at them. "Well, hang it all. They haven't done anything wrong. If they arrest them, they'll have to let them go."

Adriel shook his head and looked down. "You don't understand. Things aren't fair. It don't matter what they've done or haven't done. And Charley's done a lot. Always gettin' someone mad at him."

Gabriel tried to think what to say. "Well, don't be givin' up yet. Charley—he's pretty smart. And Rusty. Seems like he's just dratted lucky. Burglary and arson? Rusty just plain wouldn't know how to go about either of those things."

Calvin shrugged, and the faint hint of a smile crossed his face. Adriel turned to fetch another armful of wood, his eyes no longer wide. They set to work. Gabriel looked straight ahead, not wanting to admit that he felt uneasy about both Rusty and Charley.

⌘

First, the cold. Bone-chilling. Worse in the dark. Past midnight. Camped in the interior of the island, huddled in a close circle. Flickering light, casting strange shadows on the faces of Charley and the others as they cluster around the fire. Brother Strang already asleep, wrapped in his coat, his head on a piece of log.

Rusty, stretched out beside him, is beginning to feel at peace. A full day's work. Home in the morning. From where he lies, he can see Charley still sitting and staring into the fire. Very little wind; off in the woods Rusty can hear stirrings, rustlings in the dry leaves. He wonders what kinds of wild creatures are out there.

He sees Charley reaching down to take off his boots. Charley pauses, his head up as if he hears something. Then a war whoop rings out. Another whoop. Shouting. Dark figures rushing in from the forest.

'All right, men! On your feet!" Charley yells.

The others spring up. They flee in all directions. Rusty runs after Charley, panting, his feet sinking into wet snow. He curses himself for removing his own boots and putting them close to the fire to dry.

They stumble down to the shore, where they left their boat. The boat is gone.

"It's like they chipped it to pieces," Charley mutters.

"We can't stay here," someone says, panic in his voice.

Rusty follows Charley as he dives into the woods. Others follow close behind. They struggle through the underbrush in the dark. Then Rusty feels the cold water swirling around his feet. They wade across a deep swamp. From the groans, Rusty knows he is not the only one without boots.

Finally they stop on the other side of the island. "My feet be right frozen," Rusty says to Charley.

"Let that be a lesson to you, son. Never take yer boots off. I almost made that mistake."

They gather on the shore. Everyone is there except one. David Bates.

"Poor lad. He always wuz slow," someone says.

"We can't go back for 'em now."

"Men." Brother Strang's voice. "There's an old fishing boat just down the way. Full of ice and snow. Spotted it when I came out of the woods."

They set to work scooping snow out of the boat. There is no line to tie the boat with, no means of repairing it, and all they can find are three oars.

"Most unsuitable," Strang remarks.

"Hey, it's better than nothing." Charley replies.

"The ice in it'll keep those holes filled, most like," someone else says.

Charley nods. "Let's launch her and take our chances."

Cold. Icy water around their feet. Lake Michigan lies before them, dark, full of drifting ice. While others man the three oars, Charley takes each of Rusty's feet and rubs them briskly. Then he wraps them in cloths torn from his own shirt.

Hard to tell how long they are out on the water, going around neighboring islands to remain unseen. At least twenty-four hours—the next day and part of the night—struggling with the waves and the wind, trying to avoid pieces of ice.

"Gull Island don't have anyone on it. They all be gone for the winter."

They land on Gull Island. They beach the boat on the shore furthest from Beaver Island and prepare to make camp. In the semi-darkness, Rusty sees that Charley's face is so swollen from exposure that he looks like a stranger. The others, too, have red noses and cheeks burned by the sun and frost. Then Charley looks at him.

"Great balls of fire, lad! I hardly know you."

Brother Strang calls, "This way, men. There's a fish shanty just ahead."

The abandoned shanty, cramped and smelling of damp wood, serves as a shelter. More welcome than even a grand palace. They find provisions, among them frozen potatoes. They tear down nearby shanties to make wood for a fire. But as they gather around their fire, Rusty senses their worries ascending into the air with the smoke. First, the concern for their lost companion. And then, the greatest fear of all—that the gentiles have attacked Beaver Island.

They make repairs on the boat, using wood and rusted tools from the shanties. Rusty marvels at their resourcefulness, and above all, the patience and resoluteness of Brother Strang. His presence a comfort to them. Hard to believe that he is leading his people into plural marriage. Maybe, Rusty thinks, they are all mistaken.

Five days later. They make ready to launch the boat. "I figure the sheriff's given up and gone off by this time," someone says.

They return to Hog Island to look for their missing man. To their joy, they find him.

"I been eatin' rawhide, what they make straps out of. And potatoes. If'n I see one more frozen potato, I'm like to—well, never mind."

The sheriff and his party have left, but not before taking tools, provisions, blankets and cooking utensils as "spoils of war."

"They even took my chest of joiner's tools," Rufus Tucker laments.

Later, the sheriff claimed that it was a "box of burglar's tools."

They made the return trip to Beaver Island to find their families and houses still intact. The sheriff managed to hunt down twenty of the thirty-nine wanted men. They were arrested and taken off to see the inside of the Mackinac jail. Charley and Rusty were not among them.

"Well, I hope you learned something," Gabe said to Rusty. "Don't be in such an all-fired hurry to go off and rescue a boat."

The changes against the men were later dropped. Strang, who

had escaped arrest, now had a price on his head; the sheriff solicited donations for the reward money, set at twenty-fine dollars at first and then raised to three hundred dollars. For the next month, Strang had to deal with bands of armed men, Indians, and half-breeds, all seeking to earn the reward money.

"I reckon they think they would be justified in killing him," Calvin remarked.

"Well, don't say that to the women," Gabe replied. "Let's assume he's gonna be all right."

Rusty, listening, felt a cold touch on the back of his neck, as if a chill wind were blowing. But when he looked, no window or door was open.

9

How long? Five years now? Gabriel tried to remember. *The spring of 1846, when he'd last seen Corey, when he'd said adieu to her on the banks of the Mississippi. So long ago.*

Why, then, did he still have the dreams, the waking to the sense of loss and terrible sorrow? Here he had family and friends, a wife expecting her first child—and letting everybody know it. Enough to eat, if you liked fish, and work enough for everyone to earn a living. Especially if you didn't mind hard labor, and the chance that gentiles would seize the wood you'd just cut and claim it was theirs.

It was not as if Corey were still living on the same street, like in Nauvoo, or even in the same county. For all he knew, she was in Salt Lake City by this time, or somewhere on the prairie, or even dead. Or married, with children of her own. He could only hope that, wherever she was, she had good care and the support of people who loved her.

Shame on him. Living in the past, grieving for something that could not possibly have happened. Here he had more pressing issues to confront.

First, the growing knowledge that their leader, whom they had faithfully followed, had in a sense betrayed them. Staunch in their rejection of plural marriage, they now had to accept the fact that not only was Elvira the second wife of James Strang; she had just given birth to their first child, a son. The two had named him Charles, after the name Charley Douglass, which his mother had used when she was posing as her husband's nephew and secretary.

The child had entered the world on April 6, a significant date, since Joseph Smith had organized the original church on April 6, 1830.

"If that don't beat all," Eb had said. "And it's almost nine months since that coronation."

Gabriel had stared at him. "So, what are you saying? God approves of all of this?"

"I'm not sayin' that at all. But some folks be thinkin' it means God is pleased with how things are going."

"*Eh bien*. If that's the case, I wish he'd do something about all these persecutions we have to worry about."

Lurking in Gabriel's mind was the feeling that he was responsible for putting his community of friends in their present position. He had led them to this place, had persuaded them to leave life on the mainland and build up their homes and business on the island. And he was not so naïve as to believe that they could depart and take all their possessions with them.

Calvin's words rang in his mind. "Some others have tried to leave. The ones that did, had to leave everything behind."

In other words, they were stuck on Beaver Island, unless they decided to abandon everything they had built up. Even as he accepted this turn of events, he worried for his brother-in-law. *Rusty*. The young man put on a brave front, but Gabriel sensed that part of him was crushed inside. *Expecting things to be perfect, or at least ideal.* Gabriel kept a close watch on him, wondering what to do or say to make the situation more tolerable. They could simply leave the island. But where would they go, what would they do, with no possessions, no means of livelihood? Especially with the little children and old people to provide for. And Bethia about to give birth.

The men were in the shop when the news came. Charley rushed in, panting. As usual, he had ways of gathering information.

"The steamer *Michigan's* out there in the harbor. And Brother Strang's on it."

Sure enough. When they looked toward the water, there at anchor rode the "iron ship" itself, with its three masts and two paddlewheels. They learned later that under orders from President Fillmore, the steamer had stopped at Mackinac, forcibly picked up James Grieg, a Beaver Island Mormon and judge of the county court, and headed for Beaver Island. Arriving in the early morning hours, the federal officials, along with Brother Grieg, had persuaded Strang to come on board the *Michigan*. Once there, he had been charged with trespassing on federal lands and other crimes. Thirty-eight other men were also charged; Strang had asked for a list of the men and promised that they would turn themselves in within two hours if he contacted them.

"So they're all going aboard," Charley said. "All of them that's here on the island. And it seems like I'm one of them."

"Oh, no, Charley—" Gabriel began.

"I got two hours. Don't worry—I ain't done nothin'. Tell Adriel for me, all right?"

They embraced him in turn and shook his hand. Gabriel gasped, trying to hold back tears. Charley patted his back. "Don't worry none. I'll be back before you know it."

He left, the door banging shut behind him. Gabriel looked at Calvin. "Maybe it's time to leave. The President. The federal government's after us, for God's sake. For doing nothing."

To his surprise, Rusty spoke up. "Let's wait and see what happens to Charley. And the prophet. They can't hang him for trespassing on federal lands. They'd have to hang everybody—the gentiles too."

Strang and twenty-three others were detained for going out armed and obstructing the United States mail.

"That'd be the fiasco on Garden Island," Calvin said.

Rusty nodded. "Brother Strang's also charged with counterfeiting."

Strang and three others were taken to Detroit to await further judicial proceedings. Charley and the others were left on the island for the time being. As soon as Strang had left the island, the persecutions increased to an alarming degree.

"Reckon we better close up shop for a spell," Calvin said.

"I don't know," Eb muttered. "They be plundering other fellers' property—them that be gone off to jail."

"Maybe it's harder to plunder something when someone's there," Rusty remarked.

Gabriel thought a moment. "Well, let's be prepared. We better keep a shotgun handy, just in case."

The usual harassment consisted of accusing a Mormon man of some offense, then having him arrested and taken off to the Mackinac jail.

"Then they rob his property," Calvin said. "They're figuring that when Brother Strang's found guilty, they can chase the rest of us off the island."

"I hear Hezekiah McCulloch got robbed of one hundred cords of wood," Adriel declared.

"One hundred cords!" Rusty exclaimed.

Adriel went on. "Other folks has lost lumber—not as much. They was gonna use it for houses and docks."

Along with other rumors came the news that Strang had banished his first wife, Mary Perce, from the island.

"Whatever has happened between them, it's too bad," Gabriel remarked. "And curious, too. Here she was just made a member of the governing council."

"Of the island?" Eb asked.

"No—the church."

Calvin ran his hand through his shock of gray hair. "I heard from someone that they think she tried to kill Elvira's child. That's what they're saying, anyhow."

Eb shook his head. "Jess says Mary's been wanting to visit her brother down in Illinois. I reckon that's where she be heading. Leastways, I would, if I was her."

❦

Sunlight dancing on the water. Charley's boat, a reddish-brown skiff, cast a broken reflection as it bobbed near shore. Even the anchor line continued on after it met the water, a wriggly thread. Rusty, on the beach, watched as the little waves rippled in.

"Not much of a wind," Adriel remarked from the stern of the boat.

"Jump in, Rusty." Charley hauled on the anchor line. "There's fish waitin' to be caught."

To be out on the water. Rusty would have liked nothing better. He shook his head. "I have to go work in the shop today. Gabe's already sayin' I be lazy."

Adriel shrugged. "Too bad."

"That makes more fish for the two of us, I reckon." Charley pulled up the anchor. Rusty waved and began to walk along the shore. *He wasn't lazy about fishing, just working in the shop.* Closer to the harbor he could see an array of nets and wooden floats glistening in the sun. He sighed and turned to walk up to the smithy.

The thing about living on the island was that you had so much beauty close at hand. Hard to work when there was always another enchanting view. Vistas of calm water, turbulent water, cloud shapes, with sky and water so intensely blue that the sight was like a jolt to the senses. The hue of the water changing with the passing hours and the wind action, so that every time you looked, it was new and different. Add the dune grass, the sand and the shore birds, the feeling of wildness when you took deep breaths of the fresh air, and Rusty felt he was indeed in a northern paradise.

Of course you had to deal with the winters, the cold weather, the storms, the lakes icing over. With foresight and enough wood, they could keep warm and snug in their cabins. After the hardships of winter, the Michigan spring seemed beautiful beyond belief. Trailing arbutus and trillium blooming in the deep woods, the scent of pine and green growing things everywhere. *A shadow, a movement ahead.* He looked up.

Two men he didn't know were walking toward him on the path. He started to step aside so they could pass. One of them, burly and broad-shouldered, scowled at him.

"Get out of here, you blasted Mormon."

Rusty said nothing. The other man, thin to the point of gauntness, gave a cough. "Oh, let 'em alone, Sam. He's just a kid."

"I know Mormons when I see 'em. And he's one for sure."

"Aw, lay off 'em. The trading post's right ahead."

They passed, and Rusty, shrugging, hurried to the smithy. One more encounter where it was best to make no aggressive move.

"Good thing we got the corn in the ground." Gabriel, always practical, greeted him at the shop door.

"We're gonna need more wood, Rusty," his father called.

Rusty tramped around to the side of the shop, where the woodpile stood. Selecting pieces of firewood, he thought how the island would be an ideal place to live if it weren't for the non-Mormons. *We're here, and we'd better make the most of it.* Gabe's words nchoed in his mind. In spite of what their leader was doing, in spite of persecutions, they would try to stay the course. *Hope for better days.* As he walked with the armful of wood, the various accusations against his people seemed to swarm around him like gnats. *Counterfeiting. Passing bogus money. Interfering with the mail. Trespassing on public lands. Cutting lumber on public lands. Stealing. Treason.*

Eb rushed in while Rusty was stacking wood by the forge. "You hear the latest?"

"No." Gabe sounded tired. "What's happened now?"

"Well, if this don't beat all. Ol' Samuel Graham went down to Whiskey Point to consult with Sheriff Granger. And derned if two men didn't set upon him with a cane—two fellers he hadn't even spoke to. Completely unprovoked, is what they be saying."

"So what happened to Brother Graham?" Gabe asked.

"A broken arm and a fractured skull. And he hadn't said one word to these fellers."

Rusty felt his sense of justice overcoming any attitude of non-violence. Clearly, the Quaker-like practice was not working. "So, I hope they've arrested them."

Eb paused. "Well, that's it. Two Mormon judges issued the warrant. Richard O'Donnell and James Hoy—they was the ones who did the beating. But ol' Sheriff Granger—he wouldn't arrest them or allow anyone else to help. They be sayin' he even protected them."

"So where are they now?" Rusty asked.

"Folks say they escaped to the fisheries."

Rusty kicked at a stray piece of wood. He tried to keep his voice from trembling. "Well, that's just too much. Now they're beating up innocent citizens. Bad enough to accuse them of false charges and put 'em in jail."

"They jest plain don't want us here," Eb said.

Gabe gave a short laugh. "You do get that impression."

"The thing is," Eb began. "We been chased out of too many places. Where do they want us to go? Lake Michigan?"

"Build up the fire," Gabe said grimly. "We got work to do."

The next they knew, the prosecuting attorney had traveled to Beaver Island with a warrant for the arrest of the two men. He gave the warrant to William Chambers, a Mormon constable. When the constable started for the fishing grounds to carry out the arrest, he had to pass by the home of Thomas and Samuel Bennett.

"Derned if they didn't stop him at gunpoint and drive him away," Eb told the group at the shop.

"That's it!" Rusty exclaimed. "We can't allow that."

"Well, be mighty careful 'bout what you can and can't allow," Gabe said. "Mr. Strang isn't here to enforce our rights."

Rusty looked at him. "Then we'll have to enforce our own."

Brother Chambers returned with warrants to arrest both Bennett brothers for resisting an officer who was discharging his official duties. This time, a posse of thirty or forty men accompanied him. Rusty and Charley marched with them.

"I don't look for any trouble," Charley told him. "The sheer numbers'll convince 'em."

Looking back, Rusty couldn't be completely sure about what happened next. From most accounts, the brothers refused to surrender.

"They're runnin' back to their house," Charley said.

Then shots rang out. Chambers fell, wounded in the head. The posse fired back. Rusty, in the rear, strained to see. He followed Charley toward the Bennett house. Thomas Bennett lay dead. Samuel Bennett's hand had been almost shot away. The members of the posse drew back.

Rusty felt Charley's hand on his shoulder. "Come on, son. Let's leave before they start shooting again."

Men were running from all directions, neighbors from the next cabins, fishermen and shopkeepers from the town. "They fired on us first," one of the Mormons was saying.

"That don't matter," Charley said. "Let's just get out of here."

Charley had a way of making himself scarce. When Rusty turned to look, Charley had disappeared. Stumbling over rocks, his feet finding every tree root in the path, Rusty managed to make his way back to the shop. Charley was there leaning against the logs, breathing fast, telling Gabe and Eb what had happened.

"And as far as I can tell, they fired first. On a posse."

"That don't matter none," Eb said. "Not to them."

It didn't take long for "all hell to break loose," as Eb described it. Reports tumbled in.

"They be sayin' it's most atrocious murder."

"They say the Bennetts was unarmed. Standing up against Mormon law. Whatever that is."

"Newspapers all over the state be writin' these things. And worse."

The result was that Samuel Bennett pressed charges against most of the men on Beaver Island for his brother's murder. The knock on the shop door came in mid-morning. Rusty was taken into custody by two men and marched toward the harbor, while Eb and Gabe looked on amazed. On the boat bound for Mackinac, he found Charley, who'd been picked up in the fisheries.

"Don't fret none," Charley told him. "They be takin' us to the finest accommodations in Michigan. Why, that jail—it's a sight to see. Built into the side of a hill, it is—a log building about eleven feet square. Two rooms—one of them's a lavatory. The other—well, it's cold and damp, like an outdoor cellar. And there ain't no beds or chairs. Not even benches or tables."

"But—but what do folks do?"

"Oh, we have to imagine 'em. We'll pretend it's like a king's palace. Don't worry. The two of us, we'll help each other."

"But—our families. The women—the people we left on Beaver."

"I told you not to worry none. Why, there's so many men bein' arrested, the women be doin' most of the work. Haulin' wood, takin' care of the crops. Besides, Gabe won't let nuthin' happen to Marie. He and Eb'll manage jest fine. Less'n they get arrested too."

The jail was everything Charley said it was. Fourteen of the prisoners were kept to await the convening of a grand jury. To Rusty's dismay, he and Charley were among them.

"Why, son," Charley said the first night. "Let's just say we've been 'specially picked to suffer for the sake of justice. Might make it easier, like."

Worse than the rigors of any jail was the pain of being separated from Marie and Louise.

"If this is suffering for justice, then I reckon I don't want to do it again."

"I know, son. Let's make things as good as we can. Spread out your coat, there, and we'll use mine for a blanket."

"You reckon they'll kill us?" asked someone else.

"They sure can't kill us all," Charley answered. "I 'speck they just want to make an example of us. Lock us up for a spell."

"How will this Bennett business affect Brother Strang and the doings in Detroit?"

That was the question on everyone's mind. Even Charley agreed that, with this latest happening, Strang's trial in Detroit had hit a new obstacle. "All we can do's wait and see."

"Wouldn't hurt none to pray, either."

Rusty lay at night worrying about his family on Beaver Island, wondering if they were still safe. When he mentioned it to Charley, Charley looked at the stone ceiling and sighed.

"I reckon Brother Strang be worried about that very thing. His family's all on the island, too. Like as not, he's written letters to the state officials about it."

Rusty tried to adjust to life in jail, the close, dark quarters, the bad air. He thought of spring on the island, the delicate ferns and flowers in the deep woods, the scent of pine and cedar. All lost to him, along with his wife and child, as the days lengthened into weeks. Then Charley had an idea.

"I mentioned to Sheriff Granger that if we was allowed to go out and work around town for wages, we'd give 'em to him for our board and such."

Someone said, "Are you crazy? Our board's being paid by the county anyway."

"At least it'd get us some fresh air," someone else declared.

So they were allowed out during the day to do odd jobs around the town. On one occasion they were asked to serve on a posse. They performed jury duty at an inquest, and two of them gave appraisals on some pieces of property.

"Pretty good for a bunch of men held for murder," Charley remarked.

After ten weeks, the grand jury found no reason to hold them. Discharged, they boarded the boat for Beaver Island. As they watched the island appear on the horizon, Rusty said, "I don't figure on leaving it ever again. Soon's I git home, I'm staying put."

Charley gave a cough. "You want to lay low, the way I try to do. It don't always work, as you know."

"Well, I'll do anything. I'm never leaving my family again."

Charley's dark brows drew together. "I dunno, son. Let's hope you don't have to."

"Bethia, honey." Aunt Sarah's voice, calling her back from the depths of nothingness.

Then Gabriel's voice. "Still groggy. Best to let her sleep, long as she can."

Waking. Waking from deep sleep. No more pain. No more stabs of agony in her midsection. Yet she was still alive—in her bed by the small window. Outside, she saw bright sunshine, blue sky, and a pine tree trunk with the light upon it. So clear and beautiful were the shadows and patterns on the bark that she wondered if she'd truly seen a pine tree before. Or looked at one.

Then she remembered. *Her child.* The pains had begun suddenly, as she was standing over the wash tub. Crying out, she'd grasped her swollen belly. Sarah, ever watchful, had helped her to the bed,

"I'll send Turah down to fetch Gabriel."

After that, she could recall nothing but pain, and the blackness, like a dark fog all around her. Conscious of Gabriel doing something, moving around the bed, and Jess—she supposed it was Jess—patting her forehead with a damp towel. Then her mind had drifted away somewhere; she couldn't remember anything more. Except—

"My child," she managed to say. "Where is my baby?"

Gabriel leaned over her. "Bethia—we're so very sorry. The baby— she came too soon, in the first place. Not fully developed. She was born dead. She never—she never drew breath."

"What? What are you saying?"

Again he tried to explain. "The cord, you see. It was around her neck. And when we finally got to her, it was too late to help her. She—"

Bethia began to cry. Her sobs, like anguished shrieks, filled the room. Sarah sat on the pillow beside her and tried to hold her. Jess kept hold of her hand. Gabriel stood looking tired, shaking his head.

"We did everything we knew. Sometimes these things happen, and we don't know why."

She stopped and took a breath. "It's your fault. You're supposed to know everything. You're supposed to fix things."

"You know I don't know everything." He sounded on the verge of tears himself.

She began to cry again, louder than ever. Sarah said, "Honey, try to relax. It's rest you need now. And the doctor, too. Look at him. Plumb worn out."

Between sobs she said, "Can I see the baby?"

"No." Gabriel was adamant. "There were other things—Bethia, she was deformed. She would not have lived long, in any case."

But she would not be comforted. She began a series of hiccupping, choking sobs, her face turned to the wall. After a while, Jess let go of her hand. Sarah stayed at the head of the bed, making soothing noises; she felt Sarah's hands smoothing back her hair.

"Bethia—" Gabriel bent over her again. "If you can carry one child almost to term, you can have another—one that's healthy, I know—"

"Go away," she told him. "It's your fault. I never want to see you again."

Gabriel looked down and shrugged, tightening his lips together. He straightened up then and walked over to the basin of hot water.

"Where's the baby?" she said.

"Calvin be making the coffin now," Sarah replied. "You don't want to see it. Believe me."

Jess nodded. "You'll just be grieving more."

Bethia didn't think that was possible. A pain throbbed in her chest, an actual ache, even worse than the birth pangs. After a while she felt herself sinking into nothingness again. She heard little whimpering noises. Then she realized she was doing the whimpering. She tried to be still, tried to listen to what the others were saying.

"It's better if she sleeps now." Sarah's voice.

"I don't know what else we can do." This from Jess.

A door banging, far away. Rusty's voice, in the next room. "Gabe. We got news."

Gabriel's steps on the wooden floorboards as he walked into the main room. Calvin's voice. "Wait'll you hear."

Then Gabriel, sounding less tired. "Let's have it. I need some good news."

Rusty said, "Brother Strang's free, and so are the others. The jury found 'em not guilty of obstructing the U. S. mail."

"That *is* good news," Gabriel said. "What about the counterfeiting and the trespassing on federal lands?"

"All the other charges was dropped," Rusty said. "What do you make of that?"

"We got friends somewhere," Gabriel remarked. "I reckon, down in Detroit."

"What's the matter? You're looking pale. All tuckered out?" Rusty's voice, too loud.

"It's nothing," Gabriel replied. "I'll be all right."

Nothing, was it? Bethia's eyes flew open. *His own child born dead, and it was nothing?*

Then Calvin murmured something. They whispered in hushed

tones, and Bethia knew they were talking about her. She strained to hear. They walked outside and shut the front door. Then she heard Calvin talking outside her window.

"The thing of it is, when Peter McKinley went to testify, he said he sent the same mail on a vessel owned and run by the same folks he accused of stealing it. That dog sled? There warn't even any mail on it at all."

"If that don't beat all," Rusty said.

"Brother James be on his way up to the island. And the others with him." This from Calvin.

Then Gabriel spoke. "Maybe now the persecutions will stop."

Bethia closed her eyes, hurt beyond imagining. Then fury took hold of her. That they could talk of trials and mail on such a day as this—her day of supreme loss. She began to weep again. How could Gabriel dare to look her in the eye after such behavior? She didn't know exactly what she would do about it, but he would be sorry. She'd see to that.

10

Fall already. Crops being gathered. The blacksmith shop left with only Rusty and Adriel while the rest attended to the harvest. Gabriel walks amid falling leaves to look in on the shop before he joins the others in the fields.

Bethia still hasn't forgiven him. She lets him sleep beside her in the bed, but that is all. Touching her is forbidden. As he tramps between the piles of red and yellow leaves, he feels a sorrow too deep for tears. A grief for something that never was. Surely Corey would not treat him this way. He should've married Corey when he had the chance. But he was betrothed to Bethia at that time, and could only imagine the hurt he would've caused if he'd broken it off.

His main trouble. Never wanting to hurt anyone. Now he is stuck in this crazy marriage, on this island where leaving is well nigh impossible. He thinks of Brother Graham, the one beaten by the Bennett brothers. Brother Graham had had enough, and had written Brother Strang to advise him of it. Samuel Graham, who had worked tirelessly as an apostle and friend to the prophet, even helping him for two months with writing and translating on board the steamer 'Lexington' last winter. Now this valuable friend and counselor had left the island, and rumor had it that he'd advised the whole church to do likewise. Most people consider him a traitor and apostate. Gabriel is not one of them.

His own troubles swirl around him like mosquitoes. *Three days ago.* Calvin speaks in his mind as they prepare the fire in the shop.

"She's still mad at you? After this long?"

"I reckon so."

"Well, if she don't come around pretty soon, there sure ain't gonna be any more children."

Gabriel shrugged. "Try tellin' *her* that."

Calvin paused. "Maybe I will. I'll have Sarah do it."

"On second thought, wait a bit. I have another idea."

Back to the present. He reaches the shop and opens the main door. Rusty and Adriel are stacking the wood.

"Everything's fine," Rusty says. "'Cept that Adriel got harassed just goin' down to the store."

"What?" Gabriel stands in the doorway, looking at Adriel.

"They threatened to beat the tar out of me, is all. Two of 'em, with bullwhips. But I got away. I can run like the devil was after me, and that's what I did."

"They say anything?"

"Said I was a dirty stinking Mormon, and shouldn't be allowed to live."

"Oh," Gabriel says with a laugh. "Is that all?"

"All for now," Rusty says.

"You fellers stay out of trouble, now. And don't go places alone."

That night he tells Bethia, "I be thinking of taking me a second wife. There's a widow over in Troy who's been mighty good to me. Lots of folks are talking about plural marriage, and I figure I might as well try it out. I'll go see her tomorrow. That all right with you?"

Amid tears, she rages, then begs his forgiveness. After that, he is admitted to her bed with full privileges. Still, he hates to have to lie to accomplish what should have happened naturally.

The old question—one that had plagued them from the beginning, back in 1830. Should they accept the harassment and persecutions, Quaker-like, and respond in a non-violent way?

Nathaniel, their old leader and friend whom they'd left in Missouri, had been raised among the Shakers and would have advocated this position.

Or should they return harassment with harassment, violence with violence, hoping to end it once and for all?

116

Rusty said, "If we are truly Christians, we're supposed to turn the other cheek."

"I've plumb run out of cheeks," Calvin replied.

They were seated around the table in Calvin's house. Gabriel reached for an ear of corn. "*Eh bien.* I thought that when Brother James arrived back on the island, these troubles would stop."

"Obviously, they haven't." Charley passed him the butter. "In fact, it be getting worse. Now, we can't all up and leave, like we done before. Some are leaving, to be sure. But I think we have to take a stand."

"The thing is, what kind of stand do we take?" Gabriel bit into the sweet corn, and for a brief moment he didn't care what stand anyone took. "This be mighty good."

Adriel spoke from the other end of the table. "It sure ain't right, what they do. Git folks arrested and jailed on some pretext, and then rob their property."

"No. 'Course it ain't," Eb said. "But what can any of us do?"

Sarah brought another platter of corn to the table. Calvin reached for one. "Ouch! It's hot!"

"You bet it's hot," Sarah retorted. "Ain't you got sense enough to wait till it cools off some?"

Calvin ignored her and took the ear of corn anyway. "I reckon we oughter pay some mind to what happened with Brother McCulloch."

Hezekiah McCulloch, repeatedly jailed for minor offenses during the past winter, had been facing arrest on yet another charge. But Strang and some of his followers, anticipating the move, had rushed out of a meeting to stop the arrest.

"By gum, they surrounded that sheriff." Calvin waved the ear of corn for emphasis. "They said they would not allow him to take one more person."

"That's good!" Eb exclaimed. "It's about time."

"So what finally happened?" Rusty added one more empty cob to the pile on his plate.

"Why, the sheriff, he backed right off." Calvin licked his fingers. "He cited Brother Strang for helping McCulloch escape, but didn't arrest him. And Brother Strang is still walking around, unarrested, making boat trips to Mackinac and such like."

Then Charley spoke. "So, they're afraid. We stood up to them, and they backed down. There's yer answer. When they harass us, we harass them right back. Follow the example of Brother Strang, and maybe it's them that'll want to leave the island, and not us."

"I don't know—" Gabriel began. He was aware of Bethia looking at him in a strange way. He was reaching for another ear of corn when she spoke.

"Well, Gabriel shouldn't have any trouble following Brother Strang's example. He's already talking of taking a second wife, just like the prophet."

A shocked silence. Gabriel tried to think what to say. He shrugged. There was a clatter as Marie dropped her knife on her plate. "Oh, that's nonsense and you know it. Of all the things—"

"Bethia, we've been all through this before." Calvin's voice was stern. "Gabriel has never shown any tendency to do that."

Gabriel gave a sigh. "Oh, I did speak of it once. But it was in jest."

"Well, shame on you," Sarah said. "Don't you know you don't make jokes in front of certain people?"

"My mistake." Gabriel wondered if Bethia would now ban him from her bed permanently. She looked as if she were about to burst into tears. Sarah flicked her napkin.

"Oh, you men. You're all impossible, if you ask me. All this talk of leaving the island. Harassing the gentiles. Most of you couldn't harass anybody even if they paid you do to it. As for the likes of you—" She glared at Gabriel.

Eb pushed his chair back and stood up. "Gabe, I need to show you something in my cabin. Need yer advice."

Gabriel stood up and threw his napkin down beside his plate. "Good corn. Excuse us, now." He didn't look at Bethia or Sarah as he followed Eb out the door.

"So what've we got?" he asked Eb.

"Nuthin'. I jest wanted to get you outa there. Seems they was all gangin' up on you."

Gabriel laughed. "Thanks, anyway. Fresh air is mighty welcome."

"They say we can't harass anyone. Let's go find someone and harass them."

"I've eaten too much to do that. Let's go over to your place and think about it for awhile."

Eb clapped him on the shoulder. "That's really what I had in mind."

"She's right, you know." Rusty took a flat piece of wood and turned one of the fish. He and Adriel were drying whitefish on a rock over a fire, while Eb looked on.

"Who?" Adriel asked.

"Why, Sarah. We aren't cut out to harass people. Look at Gabe. He's just too nice. Goin' out of his way to be generous and help folks—it don't matter if they be Mormon or not."

Eb shook his head. "Well, maybe there's others that be better at it than us. It may not take much."

A voice spoke behind them. "It won't take much at all, now that Brother Strang be justice of the peace."

It was Charley. He strode forward and surveyed the rows of fish. "That one needs turning."

Rusty obeyed. The smell of slowly roasting fish filled the air.

"How so?" Adriel poked at the fire with a stick.

Charley shrugged. "Well, when these trouble-makers are brought before him, and he administers justice—why, they aren't gonna like it one bit. It might get so uncomfortable for them that they might all up and leave."

Rusty sat back. "Wouldn't that be something? We'd have the whole island all to ourselves."

Charley nodded. "Already they're outnumbered, for sure. Might take 'em a while to figure it out."

"That election were a surprise," Eb remarked.

Charley laughed. "That shows how clever Brother Strang is. You see, they had this reapportionment of voting districts, and Emmet

County—that's our county—was reapportioned to the Newago district instead of to Mackinac. Well, a lot of folks didn't even know this. So when Brother Strang was nominated to run for the state representative, he didn't put his name in till just before the election. Well, you can believe how surprised them folks was when they learned that Beaver Island was indeed part of their district, and James Strang was their new representative. All legal. He be going down to Lansing, to be a member of the state legislature."

"I hope no one tries to stop him," Rusty said.

Charley grunted. "They won't. He's pretty smart."

"It be gettin' cold." Eb rubbed his upper arms through his thin jacket.

Adriel poked at the fire. "I reckon we won't be out here dryin' fish much longer."

Charley agreed. "Fishin's mostly finished for the year. That blacksmith shop'll be nice and warm, I reckon."

"Seems to me there was more fish when we first came here," Adriel remarked.

"Maybe so," Charley said. "But there's still a lot left. Mackinac, now. They're really in trouble up there. Wondering where all the fish have gone."

Marie sits by the fire, her knitting in her hands. She has just finished a sweater for Gabriel, and now she is at work on a pair of warm socks for Rusty. She is tired; Louise is asleep at last in the loft upstairs. Just for a moment, she rests, her head leaning back against the rocker.

A warm contentment steals over her. Outside, a winter storm is raging. But inside, the fire dances, the firelight flickering on the cabin logs. In the chair opposite her, Rusty sits reading by the light of a small candle. He turns pages, half-smiling as he reads.

She looks at his tousled red hair, his brows drawing together in intense concentration, and thinks how much she loves him. They fit together, he and she, in a bond stronger than mere physical attraction.

She thinks how lucky she is to have found him, and what a strange path they have trod together. To end up on an island in the middle of an inland sea, while the wind howls and the snow swirls around them.

Gabriel says her husband is lazy. But he has not seen how Rusty reads late into the night and studies. He borrows books from Brother Strang's library and shares them with anyone who will listen. He mentions how he would like to get Brother Strang off alone sometime and ask questions about what he has read. But the prophet is much too busy with his legislative duties and the responsibilities of leadership.

Right now Rusty is reading *The Book of the Law of the Lord*. He has told her that it is supposed to be a translation of an ancient work called the 'Plates of Laban.' Kept in the ark of the covenant, it was considered too sacred to go into the hands of strangers. It was lost to the Jewish nation at the time that they were conquered by foreign powers. Now it had come forth once more and had been translated by Brother Strang.

What was in the ancient writings?

"Well, the Decalogue, for one thing," Rusty told her. "And comments about it, and how the Sabbath should be observed on the seventh day. And other things we should do."

Rusty looks up. He catches her eye and smiles. "Here's something interesting. It's about the conservation of forests and such. It says how groves of trees should be maintained on each farm, and in each village and town. Farms and cities without trees are required to have them planted, and to establish parklands so that 'the aged and the young may go there to rest and to play.'"

"What about polygamy?" she asks. "Is that in there?"

He laughs. "Apparently you may take another wife only if you can afford it. And the first wife has to give her permission."

He goes back to his reading. She gazes at the fire and thinks of the last time she attended mass. There was another priest now, Father Francis, from Harbor Springs. During the previous winter, the Mormons had aided twenty-seven Indian families on Garden Island. The priest told his flock that if they had any difficulties or anyone tried to sell them whiskey, they should go to Strang for help, but that they should not go to hear him preach.

She thinks of Turah and Gray Wolf, still friends, and how he waits for her before the mass begins. She knows they meet at other times; she's seen them in the woods together, walking and holding hands. She wonders if Jess and Eb know—perhaps she should tell them. Would they worry, or would they think it was a good idea?

A knock at the door. She starts up, almost dropping her knitting.

"I'll go." Rusty gets to his feet and puts the pamphlet on the chair. He pulls back the bolt and opens the door. Gabriel comes in shedding snow. Rusty draws in his breath. "What are you doing out in this weather?"

"I had to see a patient. Old Sister Gilmore is down with the grippe. Poor lady—she may not make it."

"Come sit down," Marie says. "Get yourself warm. I'll heat up some cider."

"Don't trouble yourself." Gabriel removes his coat and brings it close to the hearth to dry. "I'll only stay a while." He looks at Rusty. "You hear the news?"

"What news?"

"Brother Strang has taken a third wife. He's gone and married Betsy McNutt, and brought her to live with Elvira."

"Betsy McNutt?" Rusty asks.

"From all reports, she's thirty-two years old, an old maid in anyone's book. Not very attractive. She told someone she would only consider marrying one man, and when Brother James heard about it, he sent someone to ask her. She accepted, and now they be married."

Rusty gives a slow smile. "So that's how it's done."

"Don't get any ideas," Marie tells him.

"Of all the things you have to worry about, that's not one of them," he says.

"I should hope not," Gabriel murmurs.

They sit close to the fire, Marie and two non-polygamous Mormons in a world that is turning upside down. As Rusty picks up his pamphlet, his expression is one of pained resignation.

"Some good news," Gabriel says. "I heard from Charley that there's only about twenty gentile families left on the island."

"I reckon that's something," Rusty answers.

"They're leaving, one by one. And Brother Strang's buyin' up land. He already owns his new home and the tabernacle we haven't finished yet. We'd be in good shape, if it weren't for this plural marriage business."

Rusty is silent, gazing into the fire.

Gabriel runs his hands through his hair, says "*Tiens,*" a few times, and sighs. Marie wonders what she can say to them. She can't think of anything that might help. Best to keep still, for the moment.

Late spring. Marie works in the garden that spreads all around the front door of their cabin. With the help of Louise, she tends and weeds, and adds new plantings, flowers she finds in the woods. In the back grow iris—a patch of Blue Flag, and close to it, Dwarf Lake. She names the plants for Louise's benefit.

"*Fleur de Lis.* And here we have Yellow Lady Slipper. And Jack-in-the-Pulpit."

Later in the year, her daisies and Indian Paintbrush will bloom. Along the little fence at the side of the cabin, bean vines grow, their scarlet blossoms nodding in the breeze.

"Soon we'll have us some beans," Marie tells Louise.

"Beans," the girl says. Bethia emerges from her large cabin next door. Marie waves to her, but Bethia only stares and heads back inside. Marie shrugs. *Some neighbor.* She sits a moment feeling sorry for Gabriel, then thinks of how she tried to tell Jess about Turah and the boy from the Ojibwe village.

"Oh, yes." Jess' words ring in her mind. "Gray Wolf. He's harmless. They're both interested in art—drawing and such. She's taught him to read, so I hear."

"I think there's more to it than that. I've seen them in the woods, walking hand in hand."

"Well, I wouldn't pay it no mind. They're both so young."

"Jess, she's eighteen!"

"Well—what's she gonna do? Run off with him? I don't reckon so. She's got some sense. Besides, where would they run to? Garden Island?"

When Marie mentioned it to Gabriel, he acted mildly surprised.

"It's a good thing she has a friend. There're not that many young people here for her." He paused, then said, "So soon, they grow up. She's always been such a help. Willing to work, to make things easier for her folks. I wouldn't worry none. I don't see any trouble."

"She's so gifted," Marie said. "She's spoken of going to school— maybe college."

"So she has. With all our troubles, we've been neglecting her. *Eh bien*. I reckon we can find a school for her. There's Oberlin, down in Ohio. I'll look into it."

"You don't think we should separate them? Forbid her to see him?"

He thought a long moment before he replied. "I reckon it'd be a mistake. In the first place, I don't think it would work. Besides, who are we, to decide whom she can see or not see? I mean, how do we know that it might not work out for them, if that's what they want? But I think, in time, they'll just forget about each other. 'Specially if no one makes a big fuss about it."

Marie looks at her garden and sighs.

"What's the matter, mama?" Louise touches her on the cheek.

"Nothing, dear. Let's go bake little cakes for when Papa comes home."

<hr />

Time to help clear some more land for farming. Rusty made the short trip inland with his father and Eb. For once they let Rusty ride Freedom, Gabriel's prized spotted gelding. Calvin and Eb rode the two older horses.

What they rode to participate in was called a 'rolling bee.' Most of the timber was cut to sell as cordwood for the steamers docking at the harbor. Some of the wood proved too hard to split, and these logs were cut into lengths to be burned. It took at least four or five men to pull and lift the logs onto the pile, then one to stay and tend the fire until the logs were burned. With neighbors helping each other, going from farm to farm, they accomplished the final clearing of the land.

The three turned their horses out in a pasture and joined the rest of the group. Together they made a crew of seven. Rusty looked at the logs with the long, hard spikes at each end, used for transporting them. He had seen such spikes being made at the blacksmith shop. He remembered wondering why anyone would need such long spikes.

"All right, men." The one in charge, a large, burly man with black hair and beard, laid his hands on one of the spikes. "Let's go." Eb assisted at the other end, and then Rusty and his father helped hoist the log into place. They labored with the sweet scent of fresh-cut wood all around them. As they worked, they talked.

"There's more leaving every week, it seems like," someone said.

"I reckon the harassment tactics are working," Rusty remarked.

"It's what they done to us," the burly man declared. "It's what most of 'em deserved."

"'Course some of it's pretty bad." A voice spoke from the other side of the pile. "Burnin' homes, destroying their business so they won't come back."

"And this so-called township tax," Rusty's father said. "A good excuse for taking the property of them that's leaving."

"I say they had it coming," the burly one declared. "We got the upper hand now, and it looks like we can do anything we want."

"It's about time," someone else said.

At the third farm, they left Rusty and Eb to oversee the burning pile. Calvin elected to stay with them. "I be plumb tuckered out."

"That's all right," the burly one said. "We got enough to finish up. Just one more farm, and we'll get the owner to help us."

As they poked at the logs, Eb looked at Calvin. "What's this township tax all about?"

"Well, you know," Calvin began. "They organized us into a township—Peaine, to be exact—in April. So, we got Mr. Strang as town supervisor, Brother McCulloch as clerk and health officer, and George Miller as secretary. And a whole bunch of others—assessors, school inspectors, folks in charge of highways, constables. Even a keeper of the pound."

"Pound?" Eb asked.

"Yes, for stray animals. If, say, you own a dog, he has to be licensed and wear a collar with the owner's name on it at all times. Or else you get fined. No animals can roam around wherever they want."

Rusty nodded. "I reckon that's a good idea. No more lost dogs."

His father grunted. "Yeah. Well, my favorite is about the rotting fish."

"Rotting fish?" Eb's eyes grew wide.

"It's to do away with the smell. Fish must be cleaned inland—not in the harbor. The leftovers are to be buried within twenty-four hours in a—let's see, what did they say? A trench at least one foot deep, and ten feet from any dwelling."

Rusty looked at his father. "That oughta improve the atmosphere a little."

Calvin smiled. "That's what it's for."

Laws. Rules for everything. Rusty tried to remember as he rode Freedom home that afternoon.

The observance of the Sabbath, on the seventh day. If you weren't in church on Saturday, you'd better have a good reason why not. Their church services were held at 11:00 a.m. and 2:00 p.m., with classes at 9:00 a.m. On Thursday and Saturday evenings there were prayer meetings. One tenth of all they earned, raised or received was to go into a public fund, used for taking care of the poor, making improvements to roads and such, and paying state, county—and now, township—taxes.

All to the good—schools were organized and doing very well, the printing office was producing any tracts, pamphlets, papers or books that the church needed. A hospital was kept open and in readiness. Every Thursday during navigation season, the weekly newspaper, the *Northern Islander*, was published.

No betting or gaming was permitted, and of course, no tobacco or alcohol. Instead of wine, Marie now used cider in her cooking. But if you wanted amusements, there were plenty to be found. Social gatherings, dinners, a debate club, a thespian group, all kinds of music. Piano lessons, lessons in the German language, and an educational society—The School of the Prophets. Brother Strang had an excellent library, which he was willing to share with anyone. *Something for everyone.*

In fact, Rusty concluded as he dismounted and led his horse into the stable, they had everything they needed to make themselves useful and wise. As long as the fishing was good, no one would starve. *God has made us a kingdom.* Brother Strang's own words. No call to feel uneasy or afraid any longer.

But as Rusty removed the saddle from Freedom, he felt a chill wind on the back of his neck. He shivered as he hung up the bridle, and when he stepped outside, he saw the lake waters all gray and angry with whitecaps, and dark clouds down near the horizon.

11

Rusty thought it strange that a group of people, once staunchly against the whole idea of plural marriage, now seemed to accept it with very little difficulty. To be sure, the ones engaged in the practice were not that many. Strang, with his three wives, had more than any of the others.

"Oh, they're some opposed." Gabe was sweeping out the shop. "But they're not sayin' much."

"And neither will you, if you know what's good for you," Charley remarked.

They talked about the plans for new settlements on the island. Charley had a copy of the *Northern Islander*. "They be settling down at the southern end. And they're thinking of going over to High Island and the one called Fox, and living there."

Gabe raised his eyebrows. "I reckon, if you did it right, you could have a wife living on each island."

"Oh, be serious," Charley said. "This article be sayin' that Benjamin Wright and a bunch of families are preparing to settle at Cables Bay— that's south—and others be going to Lake Watonesa—"

"That's on the west," Adriel said.

Gabe gave a shrug. "So, what are you saying? We should re-locate?"

Charley shook his head. "I don't reckon it would matter. The harassments have pretty much stopped."

"The government's busy moving against the saints in Utah." Gabe looked at Rusty. "We need more wood. So maybe they'll forget about us for a while."

"Derned if Mr. Strang didn't come out and defend them." Charley dug into his jacket pocket and fished out a piece of newspaper. "Listen to this:

> Polygamy is not forbidden as common law. It is not forbidden in the Bible, and the Brighamites, the citizens of Utah will not make a law against it, and for want of something else to make a fuss about, the judges have come home with this as the great complaint against the citizens of Utah. Had it been found that the Territory was overrun with brothels, as every city in the US is, with free quarters for public officers, no complaint would have been heard for such offenses.
>
> But when they are found regularly marrying wives, taking them home and providing for them and their children, as Jacob, David, Solomon and the Prophets and Patriarchs generally did, in this Christian land they are charged with immorality and crime, and a public outcry is raised against, and, an excuse got up for persecuting them."

"Charley, most of us have read that." Gabe picked up the hammer. "I dunno if it was wise or not, but the paper's gone and printed it. Rusty, are you gonna fetch that wood or not?"

Charley folded up the newspaper. "I just wanted to make sure you knew. This's what all the gentiles and enemies and such be reading."

Rusty hurried out the door. Behind him, Gabe was saying, "And they aren't here to do anything about it. So why should we worry?"

"I'm just sayin'."

Outside, Rusty grabbed wood from the pile. Hot for June. He selected five good pieces and tramped around to the front door. He wished he could be out on the lake fishing instead of inside the shop. Or back in the cabin where Marie no doubt sat fanning herself.

In truth, hot as it was, she and the other women were most likely preparing for the holidays, the Fourth of July and then King's Day, the church conference and ceremony to celebrate the second anniversary of the coronation. Rusty's mouth watered as he thought of the special feast planned for mid-day—all the foods he liked—spread out in his mind and lined up for him to eat. He knew that Gabe had arranged to buy a lamb from a neighbor who raised sheep, and this would be offered, along with others, at the 'most solemn sacrifice' at sunrise. It sounded like a good day, if you weren't one of the sacrificial animals.

"Ninety-five families," Charley remarked later. "That was how many that presented animals for the sacrifice. All killed, cooked, and dismembered without cutting or breaking a bone."

The feast proved to be all that Rusty had hoped for. He heard later that four hundred and eighty-eight people had partaken of the numerous roast meats and other dishes at one o'clock that afternoon. After that, the celebration continued, with sermons and a baptismal service at Font Lake. In the group of on-lookers, Rusty saw Turah and her Ojibwe friend. Strange how similar they looked, as if the friendship had changed both of them.

Of course. It hit him like a lightning strike. *They were a couple.* He wondered briefly if Marie and the others knew. Maybe they could make a Mormon out of him yet.

He was about to mention it in the shop that next week, but Charley had other news.

"They do be sayin' that the Mormons have driven residents off the island. They be callin' 'em refugees now, and sayin' they're destitute."

"Oh, you mean like us after they drove us outa Missouri?" Eb asked.

"That's about what Mr. Strang says in this article—let's see, now—" Charley brought out a folded-up newspaper from his jacket pocket.

"Charley, we got work to do." Gabe picked up a glove. "They want more spikes to move logs with."

But in the weeks to come, more accusations poured in.

"They say most robberies and crimes and such are being done

by—get this. 'Desperadoes from the Beaver Islands.' Meaning us. So—which of us has been stealing?" Gabe struck the heated steel with his hammer.

Charley put down the bellows. "Brother Strang wrote how them 'desperadoes' stole about twenty barrels of pork and lard from one of our stores. Derned if they didn't find the stuff buried in the sand two years later. Where? At the front door of one of our enemies."

"And that boat," Adriel said. "'Member the boat that was stolen from that lighthouse on Isle-le-Galet? Why, they swore up and down we done it. Then they found it over on Hog Island with all the provisions and such still in it."

Charley hauled out his *Northern Islander*. "The thing is, there really *are* pirates. Folks stealin' stuff all over the Great Lakes. But it's not us." He began to read. "'The people have itching ears to hear something against the Mormons. No matter what occurs, if it is ill done it is laid to them.' Now, that's Brother Strang writing."

"They might as well blame us for everything," Rusty declared.

"Yeah, and get it over with," Eb said.

On the way home, Rusty caught sight of two oddly-dressed women out between the cabins—Marie and Jess in the new bloomer outfits. Their pantalets were made of calico, long loose trousers gathered at the ankles. The trousers were covered to the knee by a skirt of the same material. The calico overdress hung straight from the shoulders, without a waistline. It was made, as Marie had told him, with no "tuck, ruffle or puff."

Rusty knew that Marie liked the outfit.

"No more dragging long skirts in the mud and snow and such. So convenient. Now I know why Jeanne d'Arc wore soldier's clothes."

But others, Sarah among them, hated the idea of pants and a shortened skirt. "I never thought I'd see anything like it, in all my born days."

She wore hers anyway, and others did so out of loyalty 'to the king.' "What's next?" she asked. "Wearin' our night clothes to meeting?"

The sight of women in their Strang-devised outfits, with their hair slicked back and tightly braided, both amused and offended the gentiles. Rusty had heard that one writer had called the outfits 'hideous.' He shrugged and hurried to embrace Marie in her calico finery. "You look like you're ready to conquer the world."

"Ready to do housework is all. There's soup over the fire, and bread cooling on the table."

Rusty stepped inside. Louise ran to meet him and he scooped her up in his arms.

"Papa, Mama and Aunt Jess are sewing trousers for me, just like they have. And Mama wants a cooking stove."

"She does, does she?" He knew kitchen stoves were offered for sale down at Franklin Johnson's store, which also had fresh goods, dry goods, groceries, fishing tackle, and most anything else one would want. All this, and at 'Buffalo and Detroit prices.'

He smiled. "Well, we'll see. Let's have some of that fresh bread. Don't know why she wants a stove, when she can turn out things this good on a hearth."

"That's the way of it," his father said later. "You give one of 'em a stove, and they all be wanting one. As if these new-fangled clothes aren't bad enough. I don't know why they can't be happy with what they've got."

"If it means more and better food, I'm all for it," Rusty replied.

"Yeah, well, it's all your fault," Eb said. "Marie's got her stove, and now Jess be agitatin' for one."

As the winter set in, they discovered that the stoves made the cabins even warmer.

"Good idea, that stove," his father remarked. "We shoulda thought of it soomer."

Gabe managed to have some sort of talk with Gray Wolf, and came back full of excitement about the native American use of white pine. "They make an infusion from the needles and inner bark, and they can treat colds and stomach ailments. They use the pitch to extract slivers, and also the poison from boils. The needles make nice little baskets. And there's nothing like a bed of pine boughs—I knew that already."

"So, what did you say about Turah?" Eb asked.

"Blame it!" He clapped his hand to his head. "I plumb forgot. We talked about these other things. He's still learning English, but he speaks French right well."

Eb turned away, shaking his head. "If that don't beat all."

Reports came back that James Strang had taken his seat as a member of the Michigan Legislature, in spite of attempts to prevent it. He evaded an ambush set up for him on the way by taking a different route. He arrived to find his certificate of election mysteriously missing from the Secretary of State's files, but he had brought his own copy.

"I tole you he was smart," Charley said.

Gabe nodded. "They say he's really making an impression. Once folks get to know him, they see he's not such a monster after all."

Charley had his usual pieces of newspaper. "This's from the *Detroit Advertiser.* '...I take pleasure in stating that throughout this session he has conducted himself with a degree of decorum and propriety which have been equaled by his industry, sagacity, good temper, apparent regard for the true interests of the people, and the obligation of his official oath.'"

"That do sound good," Eb said. "This is Brother James they're talkin' about?"

Gabe smiled. "It means he hasn't made any of 'em mad at him yet."

Charley shook his head. "'Cept that, all over Mackinac, they be plenty mad and gettin' madder."

In fact, the Mackinac people became agitated enough to hold a meeting at the Mackinac Island courthouse to discuss how they could protect their property from the Mormons.

"May sixth, it were. And here's their resolution." Charley unfolded his *Northern Islander.* "'The high-handed pretensions and immoral courses of the people called Mormons are inimical—' whatever that means—'to our republican institutions, subversive of the good order of society, and destruction of all security to person and property.'"

Gabe ran a hand through his thick black hair. "It means that whatever we're for, they're against it."

Rusty's father shook his head. "I reckon they're mad mainly because of how this part of Michigan was organized. Why, just look at Emmet County. All the area north of Grand Traverse Bay, Charlevoix Township, Beaver and the other islands, with the exception of Mackinac. Now, with all them newly-elected officials in these other places, Mackinac no longer has the power it once did. Nor all the fish, for that matter."

Charley waved his newspaper. "Emmet now has the main fishing grounds of Lake Michigan. Now, if that warn't cleverly done, I don't know what was."

"Brother James did all that?" Eb's eyes were wide.

Charley laughed. "Well the Legislature did. And I reckon he must've helped them."

Rusty said, "I know Beaver has two townships now. Peaine in the north, and Galilee in the south."

Charley folded up the newspaper. "They're mad about the fishing— that's one thing. But the main grievance is about the new law sayin' that anyone selling alcohol has to have a license. Sheriff George Miller, now—you heard how he went and vowed he'd arrest any trader or fisherman selling alcohol on Lake Michigan. 'Cause you know none of them's gonna bother with a license. And they're all fit to be tied."

"So they're sayin' we're robbing them," Rusty said.

Charley nodded. "Not only that, but whenever they break the law, we can try them in our own courts here on Beaver Island."

"You could say the worm has turned," Eb declared. "The Lord be praised."

The Battle of Pine River. That's what they called it later. A real shooting war, on the Michigan mainland. The first Rusty heard of anything amiss was when Adriel appeared at the shop just after they opened.

Adriel looked around quickly, his eyes wide. "Charley not here?"

"No." Gabe leaned the broom against the wall. "Adriel—what's wrong?"

Adriel drew a little breath, then shook his head. "He's not been home all night. His boats's still at anchor. And none of the horses is gone."

Gabe thought a moment. "Maybe he be over workin' on the King's Highway." This was the road they had all helped build, the main route to the interior of the island.

Adriel shook his head. Gabe frowned. "*Eh bien.* Where did he go yesterday?"

"I begged him to stay put. A bunch of them was going with the sheriff over to Pine River. They needed some fellers for jury duty, and they all be living there at Pine River."

Gabe raised his eyebrows. "Well, maybe they had so much fun over there, they decided to stay the night. I wouldn't worry none—you know how smart Charley is."

Adriel stayed to work with them. He sighed at intervals, and Rusty sensed his distraction. He wondered if Adriel should even be working around a hot forge. Just before noon, Rusty's father appeared in the doorway.

Gabe looked up. "Mornin', Calvin. You're just in time to fetch us some more wood."

"Hang the wood," Calvin replied. "We need you back at the house."

"What's Bethia done now?" Gabe asked.

"It's Charley. Dr. McCulloch just brought him in. His shoulder's shot up pretty bad. There's been some sort of shooting over in Pine River."

Adriel pushed past Calvin in his haste to leave. Gabe, Rusty, and his father left Eb to deal with the fire.

"Just let it go out and close up the shop," Gabe told him.

When they reached the largest cabin, Adriel was already there, on the settle next to Charley. Charley sat looking angry, his left shoulder bandaged, his arm in a sling.

"I did the best I could for 'em," Dr. McCulloch was saying. "I got the message before dawn—fourteen or fifteen of 'em, down in the Galilee harbor. Two boats, one of the oars so shot up it'd make a better sieve than something to row with. He'll tell you all about it."

Rusty tried to listen while Dr. McCulloch talked with Gabe. Something about two bullets just missing the shoulder joint.

"He's one lucky cuss. I'm surprised none of 'em died. I have to go take three other fellers to their homes. Had to borrow a wagon to get 'em all up here."

Dr. McCulloch left. Gabe closed the door and pulled up a chair next to Charley. Rusty and his father sat around the table. Sarah stood beside her cherished stove, a ladle in her hand, with Bethia watching from the doorway.

Gabe gave a little cough. "Now, then, Charley. Are you ready to tell us what happened?"

"Am I ready? Why, them low-down dirty, stinkin', mud-eating sons of varmints—"

"Remember," Gabe reminded him. "There's ladies present."

"Oh, so there is." Charley drew a deep breath. "All right. Well, Sheriff Miller had to go over to Pine River and summon three more fellers for jury duty, with the circuit court meeting comin' up at St. James and all. I said I'd go with him. Well, he had me and about four other men in the boat with him, but he got wind that there might be some trouble. So he stopped at Galilee and picked up a second boat and nine other fellers. Let's see, there was Jonathan Pierce, and Franklin Johnson, and Brother Hickey—"

Gabe gestured impatiently. "Well, never mind that. What happened?"

"All right. So we rowed over there. It were getting on to about two o'clock in the afternoon, and we could see armed men running up and down the beach. They was firing shots, I reckon to warn the other folks there. We figured they thought we'd come to arrest some of 'em, and things'd calm down once they knew it was just jurors we needed. So we beached the boats just south of the river.

"Now, a bunch of folks was gathering on the beach, fishermen and what not. I was mighty glad we'd brought our guns—four of them, hidden under our coats in one of the boats. But when we got out and went toward that crowd, we was unarmed. The sheriff began to read out the summons for jury duty. I reckon maybe they thought it sounded more like a warrant. Someone in the crowd said that no one would be taken, and told us to leave immediately.

"Well, about that time we could see armed men moving around up on the bluff. A few fellers had been lookin' in our boats, and when they came back to the crowd I heard one of them say, 'They have no guns.' We headed back to our boats. And derned if these fellers, about thirty of them, didn't file down through the trees and stand there on the beach, all lined up. And every last man of 'em carried a gun.

"Well, with that many guns, one of 'em's bound to go off. It got someone in the crowd. He fell, and there was all kind of yellin' and what not. In all the confusion, we tried to shove off. The last man was just climbing into the boat when all hell broke loose. They was firing at us from the beach and the bluff. And we had to stand up in the middle of this—this barrage—to push off with our oars. Balls was just raining like hailstones. Folks was yellin'. There was wounded men all around me. I swear, some of them fishermen was acting like we was target practice.

"Well, you can bet we rowed like crazy. One feller was rowin' with one arm, 'cause t'other was hangin' useless. Another one got hit in the shoulder. We got out of range, and then they began to chase us. They had one of them heavy fishing boats, with about twenty-five men in it. Then there was two smaller boats. We had a good lead—them smaller boats was about a mile back. But that larger one was gainin' on us—it had eight oars, and the ones we had was bullet-ridden by that time.

"I tell you, if ever I prayed, it was then. One of our men had collapsed already. Our boat was full of blood—water and blood all over the bottom of the boat. It was obvious—we was outgunned. And certainly outnumbered.

"Then we spotted it—a ship lying becalmed. Turned out it were the bark *Morgan*, on her way to Chicago. We pulled for her as hard as we could, those of us who could still row. When the folks from Pine River saw what we was aimin' to do, they started firing at us.

"It was nigh onto dinner time, and the captain was having dinner in his cabin when he heard the shots. We came within hailing distance, and one of us—someone in the other boat—begged him to take us on board and offer us protection—we was being chased and we had reached the end of our strength. Well, he saved us. When we was securing our boats on the protected side of the *Morgan*, one of our fellers grabbed a rifle and said, 'Now we'll give it to them!' But Captain Stone, he forbade it, and took all our guns.

"Them varmints from Pine River, they stopped firing. They was about fifty yards away, laying on their oars. They yelled at the captain, saying he must not receive any cursed Mormons on board. Said we was all pirates, we deserved death and should die. They threatened to fire at the bark if the captain offered us protection. Meanwhile, we showed the captain that none of our guns had been fired. We were not the aggressors. The captain, well, he was as calm a man as I've ever seen. Told them not to come any closer in their excited state.

"Well, they waited off there for a while. Then they decided to head back to Pine River. Our wounds were dressed, and we was given dinner on board the *Morgan*. Along about midnight, they took us closer to the island. We managed to row our own boats, blood-spattered and bullet-ridden as they was, back to Galilee harbor. But I never saw the like, and I hope I never do again."

Gabe shook his head. "Those fellers are lucky to be alive."

"Some of them warn't even hit. Sheriff Miller, now—he's fine. And Lorenzo Hickey and Brother Johnson—they're all right. But them boats—how we made it home in one piece—it's a bloody miracle."

"When did you get hit?"

Charley rubbed his nose with his right hand. "I don't rightly know. It were twice—it happened at different times. I think the first one happened right away. 'Cause my shoulder hurt the whole time."

Gabe got to his feet. "Well, Charley, you deserve a good rest. Let's get you something to eat—I know we have soup on the stove. Then I'll have a look at that shoulder for myself."

A day later, Charley felt well enough to walk into the shop. In his free hand he held the broadsheet extra published by the *Northern Islander*. He showed them the headline: MURDEROUS ASSAULT—ATTACK ON SHERIFFF MILLER—SIX MEN WOUNDED.

Then he read aloud, "'…measures are being taken to bring them to justice. There would be no difficulty in fitting out a party from here who would make the Pine River settlement as bare as the palm of a man's hand; but the moral effect of sending a half dozen to State Prison is worth more than the death of them all. Legal remedies are better than violent ones.'"

At the circuit court session in St. James, indictments were issued against those who had shot at the sheriff. When an officer went to Pine River to make arrests, he found the place deserted.

"They all be gone off," Rusty's father said. "Some to Little Traverse Bay, some to Grand Traverse. I hear some fled to Washington Island, over near Green Bay. Even the fishermen on Gull Island are gone."

"The dirty, lily-livered cowards," Charley muttered.

"Can you beat that?" Eb said. 'Looks like you fellers lost the battle, but won the war."

Gabe laughed. "They actually thought we were going to attack them."

Charley grunted. "I don't reckon any of 'em'll ever be arrested now."

12

OCTOBER. **THE SKY A** deep blue, with dazzling white clouds near the skyline. Still warm, even though the harvest is done. And a wonderful harvest it is, with potatoes, squashes, corn and pumpkins, rutabagas, cabbage and turnips. From where she sits, on the log bench just outside the cabin, Bethia can see the lake waters stretching away to the islands and the horizon beyond. She wonders how she could have ever wanted to live anywhere else. All that fuss about boarding the boat that was to bring them here.

A lot of trouble she has caused them. And she is sorry, especially for Gabriel who has tried so hard. Still trying, even now—coming home exhausted from the shop or from seeing to patients. Working now on a new frame house to replace the main cabin—she can hear the pounding of hammers from a distance. She hates to add one more burden to those he carries already. In fact, she is determined not to. So she sits quietly in the warm sun, trying to relax, trying to still the pounding in her chest.

For Bethia has a terrible secret. Most every morning now, she wakes with a heaviness in her chest, a feeling of something being squeezed. Sometimes it goes away. But sometimes it stays for what seems like hours, a pain like grief or sorrow. At first she thought it was sorrow, after her baby's death. But with the passing of time, it has grown worse.

Should she tell Gabriel? What can he do? For one thing, she is afraid he will say that she should not have a child. And that, she cannot face. As long as he doesn't know, there is still hope.

So she keeps her secret, hiding it even from her aunt Sarah, who steps out into the yard carrying a pan and a basket of green beans.

"Here, honey. How 'bout helping me with this mess?"

Sarah puts the pan on the bench between them. They sit together stringing the beans. "I declare, this is a good crop. Firm and good-tasting. And the men'll be hungry tonight, I'll vow. Workin' on that new house."

With Gabriel, Calvin and Eb putting up the house, that left Rusty, Charley and Adriel to tend to the shop. The pounding of hammers seems to increase in intensity, more pounds per moment. The energy of it makes her feel tired. But Gabriel has assured her that the new place will have plenty of room for children.

"Think it'll be done by winter?" Bethia asks.

"Like as not, if they keep workin' steady-like. But there's always something to distract them, seems like."

Bethia doesn't answer. Sarah pauses in her stringing. "Just think how it'll look. All nice and white-washed inside. And with our stove— why, we'll be snug as bugs, come winter. Or whenever they get it done."

<hr>

With neighbors helping, the frame house stood ready before the coldest weather set in. As Rusty walked home from the shop, he marveled to see it rising behind the old cabin. Its shingles, new from the cedar swamp, shone with the frost upon them.

"Maybe in time, we'll have us a house like that," he told Marie.

"That's mighty fine," she replied, embracing him. "But I reckon I fancy our cabin."

"It be gettin' old. The chinks be needing repair. Besides, you deserve better."

She kissed him. "But we've been so happy in this little place.'"

"I reckon we'll be happy wherever we are, long as we be together."

Rusty worked with his father and the others to finish up a house for one of his neighbors. He hoisted a board into place while Gabe wielded the hammer.

"I hear tell the population is really increasing." A neighbor, a man with a gruff, gravelly voice, handed him another board. "On the island, I mean."

"And there ain't no paupers among us," someone else said.

"There be schools for all the children," Rusty's father remarked.

The man with the gravelly voice picked up the bucket of nails. "And look at us. We been workin' fer two hours, and there ain't no cussin' or foul language."

"Well, I wouldn't push *that* one too far," Gabe said. "If my finger gets between the nail and a hammer, you're like to hear some words that'll curl yer hair."

Rusty gave a laugh. "In French, most like. So you won't even know he's swearing."

"Even the Indians," the gravelly-voiced man continued. "King James says they be superior in morals to any others in the state."

One of the neighbors picked up the ladder and laid it against the side of the house. "I reckon we be mighty lucky. We got wonderful breezes, good grass, pure water—"

"—inland lakes full of fish," another said.

"—cedar swamps for shingles and fencing. Streams for cattle to drink, and to run sawmills and such."

They spoke of the work awaiting them that winter, the cordwood which they would cut and haul to the docks to await the steamboats when the ice had gone.

"Seventy-five cents per cord!" someone said. "You can't beat that."

All these blessings. Combined with the love of Marie and their child, Rusty felt he indeed lived in paradise.

In the spring, there was talk of Mormon settlements on the mainland. Brother Strang mentioned Pine River, now deserted, as having excellent farmland and connections to the water. Drummond Island and other islands in Lake Michigan and Huron offered good places for colonists.

"Things be going well here, too," Charley declared. "Why, according to the newspaper, we all be prospering."

"That's good to know." Gabe put a large log on the fire. "Most of what I hear is how much our fellow citizens dislike us."

"They say we be destroying fish shanties." Rusty bent to straighten up the wood pile. "And stealin' boats and nets from gentile fishermen."

"Why should we steal their boats and nets when we got our own?" Eb asked.

"Why, to make trouble fer 'em, I reckon." Charley rubbed his left shoulder, the one that had been injured. "The truth is, the fishing around Mackinac has fallen off. So they be comin' down here to get the fish."

"*Our* fish." Adriel waved a stick of wood.

Charley went on. "And there be fewer steamships stopping at Mackinac. 'Cause they've cut down a good part of the timber on the island."

"Which leaves *us*." Gabe took the tongs and grabbed a piece of hot metal. "We be selling our wood to most of the ships now. A handy position to be in."

Rusty had a recurring dream, one that he recalled having at least three times. Whenever he experienced it, he had the sense that it had happened before. The dream was about climbing a mountain—strange, because there were no mountains on Beaver Island or the mainland, only small hills. His family climbed with him in the dream—Marie and nine-year-old Louise, and the other members of his community— Eb and Jess, with J. J., Gabe, his father Calvin and Sarah. He could not remember Charley or Adriel as part of the group, and Bethia was decidedly absent.

The most striking part had to do with their leader, who was climbing just a little way ahead of them. For it was not Brother Strang, but their old friend Nat Givens, who had helped them escape the persecutions in northern Missouri. Nat, who still lived just west of Nauvoo on the Mississippi—Nat himself climbed before them, bearded now, with gray specks in his black hair, forty-five by this time, an age considered old on the frontier. Yet he was leading them, beckoning them on, urging them to the top of the mountain. They never reached the summit in the dream; the greatest emphasis seemed to be on the fact that Nat was leading them, and that they should trust him.

"Passing strange," Rusty said aloud.

"What, dear?" Marie stirred beside him. "What's so strange?"

He kissed her as she snuggled into the crook of his arm. When he tried to describe parts of the dream to her, she laughed.

"You've had us on wagons and boats, on carriages, and now we're to climb mountains too?"

"I know. It's silly—just a dream."

But was it? He'd heard of spiritual dreams, intimations of things to come. "Maybe it wasn't a real mountain," he murmured.

"I should hope not. Go to sleep, now. It'll be daylight soon, and you have to be in the shop early."

⬲⬲⬲

Bethia can hardly wait to share the news. She knows that what she has to say will top most anything else the rest of them are doing. So she fidgets, rocking by the fireplace, while Sarah sets out plates for bread and jam and dried blueberries, picked a month before. Little mugs for cider complete the arrangements.

A knock at the door, a trill of laughter. Then Marie pushes open the door and walks in, followed by Jess.

Sarah looks at them. "Where are the young'lins?"

"Playing in the mud," Jess answers. "I swear, gettin' them both cleaned up and presentable is too much for me."

"They'll be fine." Marie sinks into the chair across from Bethia and smoothes down the short calico dress she wore over her trousers. "They're just around in back. I'm glad to have me a bit of rest."

Jess takes a seat on the settle. "I declare, they be sayin' children are a blessing. But at times they be more trouble than they're worth, seems like."

Now is the time. Bethia opens her mouth to speak. Marie says, "Jess, you might as well tell them. They're bound to find out, sooner or later."

Sarah pauses, her hand on the table. "Find out what?"

Jess gives a sigh. "Oh, it's Turah. She's fixin' to run off with that young feller. Gray Wolf."

144

"But they be married," Marie says. "According to her, they went to the priest—Father Francis—and he married them."

Sarah pauses. "But is that a real wedding? If'n you be married by one of our priesthood, with the proper words and all, it's for eternity. Theirs is for time only."

Marie gives her a surprised look. "Well, it was good enough for Rusty and me."

Sarah speaks quickly. "Of course—I was forgetting. I'm sorry."

"Legally, they be married." Jess speaks in a toneless voice, as if she is still shocked at the thought. "What's done is done. But how's he gonna support her? Fishing full-time? Eb offered to help him build a cabin. But he's making her a canoe instead."

"A canoe?" Bethia asks. She tries to keep the disappointment out of her voice. No news of hers can equal this.

"One of those big, family-sized ones," Jess replies. "Big enough to sleep in."

Sarah gives a little laugh. "So they're fixin' to live in a canoe?"

Jess sighs. "I think the plan is to go over to Arbre Croche and live there. There's a bunch of Christian Indians living there, and the priest is there most of the time."

Marie nods, looking into the fire. "It's not as if it's a sudden thing. They been friends for a long time. I think they'll be fine."

Jess rolls her eyes. "That's all right for *you* to say. Where's all this talk about how talented she was, with the writing and the art and all? How she was maybe going to college to study and learn helpful things?"

Marie shrugs. "Maybe she can still do something like that. There's lots of time."

"Sounds like she's made her choice." Sarah pulls back once of the chairs. "Let's gather 'round and have a little something to eat. Here, Bethia—you sit here."

Bethia feels a sudden lurch in her chest as she walks to the table. Better tell her news now, before her heart starts racing again. "I'd like—"

"And as if I don't have enough trouble, it seems I'm expecting another child." Jess waves her hands in a little excited motion. She and Marie take the chairs opposite from Bethia.

"That's wonderful." Marie hugs her. "J. J. will have a younger brother. Or sister."

"This calls for a celebration." Sarah unfolds her napkin. "Let's pause for a blessing on the food."

Her heart is pounding now. As soon as the "amen" is said, she speaks, too rapidly. "I'm—I be expecting too."

"Well, that's wonderful news," Marie says. But no one jumps up to hug her. "You and Gabriel should be very happy."

"Oh—we are," Bethia manages to say.

Sarah counts on her fingers. "If our reckoning be right, both these babies should be born sometime next June. Or July."

"Just in time for King's Day." Marie reaches for the blueberries.

Sarah slices four pieces from the loaf of bread. "This be baked fresh this morning."

They spread butter and peach sauce on the bread. "It be right good," Jess says.

After a pause, Marie wipes her fingers. "News of new life. I reckon it'll help us not worry about Turah so much."

Jess lays down her knife. "I'm done worryin'. I had such high hopes for that girl. Born a slave, and now free. And what does she do? Takes up with the first Injun she can find. Doesn't listen to a thing I say. Comes and goes as she pleases. Wild as a deer, that one. Half-savage, herself."

"Wait a minute." Marie holds up her hand. "You can't call Gray Wolf a savage. He speaks French good as anyone. And she's teaching him English."

"Maybe so." Jess reaches for another piece of bread. "It's not what I would have chose for her, is all."

Marie nods. "I don't reckon any of us have gone the way our folks would have chosen. Gabriel was supposed to become a priest, and he chose something way different. A blacksmith and doctor, on an island as far from Gallipolis as you can get. And I figure I was expected to keep house for my brother Étienne all my life. But I went with Rusty instead."

Sarah nods and cuts some more bread. "Let's just praise God that we're here, and we be in good health. Eat up, now. Remember, yer eatin' fer two."

But as Bethia reaches for the bread, she feels the tightening in her chest again.

Gabriel helped Calvin ready the shop for the morning's work while Rusty brought in wood.

"They say some folks be sneakin' back to the island," Calvin remarked. "Stray fishermen and such."

Gabriel had his mind full of the patient he had to see that morning—a man with a weakness on one side of his body. "*Eh bien.* If they get caught, they're like to be mighty sorry."

They'd heard stories of intruders being pushed out to sea in boats without oars. Gabriel had never witnessed such a thing, and he hoped he didn't have to. But there were no good feelings between those who had fled the island and those who remained.

"We can't be too careful," Calvin went on. "'Specially now that you have two women in the family way at the same time."

"*Pardon?*" Gabriel gave a laugh. "Would you mind rephrasing that? If our customers hear you, they'll think I'm the king."

"Oh, of course not." Calvin's face reddened. "I only meant—well, two in the same household. The same group. You know what I mean."

Rusty straightened up from stacking the wood. "And now they're three."

"Three?" Calvin looked puzzled.

"Three women expecting. We can add Marie."

Gabriel found himself slipping into French. "*C'est vrai?*" At the same time, Calvin said, "Well, I'll be—"

"You'll be a grandfather." Rusty stood smiling. "Again."

Gabriel nodded, his mind racing. "At least they won't be all at the same time. Bethia and Jess'll be first, I reckon, sometime in the summer. Then Marie."

"All the more reason for us to be careful." Calvin spoke softly, as if talking to himself. "All we need is strangers comin' back on the island."

A customer walked in, and the talk turned to the happenings in Lansing.

"I hear Brother Strang's there with Mary." The customer leaned against the wall, his arms folded. "The first wife. And their little daughter—how old is Harriet now?"

"I reckon she'd be about six." Calvin brought down the bucket of nails and fished out three of them.

"They must be gettin' along pretty good, if'n she's there with him," the customer said.

Gabriel gave a little cough before he spoke. "I reckon. What's important is what he's doing there."

The customer nodded. "I hear he be serving on the Indian Affairs Committee."

"Maybe he can help them some," Gabriel said. "Did you know he denounced the Fugitive Slave Law?"

Eb spoke up. "I'm right proud of that. He be opposed to slavery in any form."

Gabriel waved his hands, getting into the subject. "And—and we hear he helped pass a rights and liberties law that provides protection for fugitive slaves."

"Folks is refusin' to turn in them that might be escaped slaves," Calvin said. "At least, I heard up in New England, some are refusin'."

The customer shrugged. "They say the legislature's tryin' to separate the mainland portions of Emmet County from the Beaver Islands. Something about a new county, with just the islands. Brother Strang wants to call it 'Manitue,' or something like that."

Gabriel thought a moment. "Manitou. That's what the Indians call the Great Spirit. A good name." Then he handed the hammer and tongs to Calvin. "I have to go and see a patient. Here're the gloves." He opened the door and stepped outside.

"That's not a good idea," the customer was saying. "We'll no longer have the power we held as part of Emmet County."

"That's probably the idea," Calvin replied. "I don't think Brother Strang approved of it. Most like, he had no choice."

Changes coming. How would a decision made in faraway Lansing affect them? Gabriel tried not to think about it; he needed to concentrate on the matter at hand. *His patient, and what could be done for him.* He hurried the short distance to his patient's house and turned up the gravel walkway.

Shrouds of fog all around the island. Like a white curtain. The smaller islands all hidden in the mist. Marie, gathering her cloak around her, wondered if it were wise to walk alone down to the Indian village. It wasn't that far. But Turah was nowhere to be found. No doubt she was off somewhere with Gray Wolf; they would most likely appear for Mass later that morning.

Charley had scratched on her front door just as she was preparing breakfast for Rusty and Louise.

"Father Francis be on the island. Thought you'd like to know."

She invited him in, but he declined. "Have to do some work in the shop."

"I'll be along in a while," Rusty called.

Marie had sent Louise over to stay with Jess and J. J. The dress she planned to wear had a spot on the front of it; she'd not taken time to clean it. The only thing she had to wear was her bloomer outfit. If she kept her cloak wrapped around her, perhaps no one would notice.

In the place of gathering, she found Turah and Gray Wolf. Turah took her hand and held it; they sat together on the up-ended logs.

"Why haven't you been to see us?" Marie asked. "We been missing you. Your mother—she misses you something terrible."

Turah kept holding her hand. "Haven't you heard? Papa wants me to leave the island and go to college. Without Gray Wolf. When I told him it was out of the question, he said that he would get Brother Strang to persuade me. And, I suppose, enforce his wishes. So I thought it was best to stay away."

149

"I reckon you're right," Marie replied. "I'm real sorry. We miss you all the same." She sat in silence, wondering why folks were so misguided in the treatment of their own children. Wise or not, Turah had chosen for herself.

After the service, Turah whispered, "I'll be over to see Momma and J. J. sometime this week. When Papa's at the shop."

She squeezed Turah's hand. Just then Marie noticed the three white men. They wore boots and work clothes; she sensed them looking intently at her and talking among themselves.

"Who be those?" she asked.

"Some of the fishermen—I reckon they just happen to be on the island."

"Do you know them?"

"We've seen 'em a few times. I don't know their names." Turah turned to follow Gray Wolf outside.

Strange, to have white men there. Usually the ones attending Mass were Indians and their families, a few children. Things were changing. Marie wrapped her cloak around her and started to walk back toward St. James and the harbor.

A portion of the trail wound through tall grass toward a place where the trees grew thick, crowding almost to the edge of the path. The fog was lifting; there were dark shadows on the path. Marie stepped over the stones. Did something move in the woods? She couldn't think of any wild creatures on the island that would be a threat to her.

Suddenly someone grabbed her from behind. Before she could cry out, a hand clapped over her mouth. At the same time, she saw a figure rush out of the woods. She recognized one of the men she had seen at the service. Tall and broad-shouldered, he hurried toward her with a limping gait. Injured somehow, she reckoned.

"Don't make a sound, now." The voice spoke from behind her.

She shook her head. The hand slipped away. Struggling, she heard herself say, "What is the meaning of this?"

"Shut up," the voice said. She managed to turn; the man, another who had been at the service, was grasping her by the shoulders. This one was shorter, and from his girth, she surmised he had not missed many meals in his life.

The tall one laughed. "She's a little spitfire, she is. Like the girls back in County Derry."

Marie was terrified now. "Let me go. Please. *Je vous en prie—je suis—je suis enceinte.*"

"Oh, it's a French one," the plump man said. "All the better."

She gave a mighty push. He fell back. She started to move forward. Then the tall one grabbed her. "Come on, lass. We can fight all afternoon. Or you can make this easy. You can be home in time for the noonday meal."

"Why are you doing this to me?" she cried. "Didn't you see me at the service?"

"Yer nothin' but a Mormon," the tall one replied.

"I'm not! I was at Mass. Didn't you—"

"Yer wearin' Mormon clothes. Bloomers, and the like."

"My husband is Mormon. I'm not."

"Yer husband be Mormon? Well, ain't that too bad? He ain't here to help you none."

They began to fling her back and forth between them. As if she were nothing but a toy, and it was all a game to them. *Scream,* her mind shouted. But if she angered them, and they started to beat her, they would harm the child she carried. She felt them tumbling her to the ground. Sobbing, she tried to fight them off. Between breaths, she pleaded. "Don't do this. I'm—I'm with child."

They didn't seem to understand English or French. Or else they didn't care. She kicked and fought. Wearing a hollow in the earth around her. Loose stones flew in the air as she flailed. Her strength was waning. She knew she couldn't keep it up for very long.

The tall one caught her arms and pinned them to the ground above her head. With one hand he grasped both her wrists. With the other he began to pull at the pantaloons. *Never,* Marie thought. *I will never attend Mass again anywhere, if this is how they behave toward helpless women.*

She felt his hands creeping on her bare skin, up toward her breast.

Submit, the voice in her mind said. *You might still save your child. Especially if they finished their work quickly.* But would Rusty even want her now, after this? "Please," she begged. "Let me go."

Suddenly a voice spoke from the woods. "Stand up, or I'll blow your head off."

Charley! He moved out of the woods and she saw him standing to the right of them with his shotgun aimed at her attacker. The plump one took a step back.

"You move once more, and yer a dead man," Charley told him. "As for you, get up real slow, like."

The tall one scrambled to his feet, reaching to tuck in his shirt.

"Git yer hands up," Charley said. "Both of you." The two complied. Charley looked at her. "Get up, Marie. You all right?"

She managed to stand up. Stunned, in shock, she felt the ground unsteady under her feet. Charley repeated his question.

"Uh—yes. Yes, I reckon I'm all right." The baby—she felt it move in her body. She put her hands up to her face, wet with tears. Her wrists were bruised where the man had grasped them.

"It's a good thing she's all right, like she says," Charley declared. "'Cause if she weren't, both of you scummy varmints'd be meetin' yer Maker about this time. Now, turn around."

Marie moved to stand beside Charley as the two attackers turned around to face the woods, their hands in the air.

"Two of you, and a helpless woman," Charley said. "What a sorry pair. Why, I oughter blow you both to Kingdom Come."

One of them started to speak. The other said, "Shut up."

"Start walkin'," Charley intoned. "Real slow, like. That way. Toward the harbor."

They started to walk, their hands up. Charley continued. "And once you git there, I advise you to git the first boat outa here. 'Cause if I see you around here again, yer good as dead."

They walked, stepping cautiously, the plump one pushing ahead of the other as the path narrowed. When they were out of sight, Marie pressed Charley's arm. Still breathing hard. "How—how can we ever thank you?"

"Well, now, ma'am. I say you'd thanked us plenty, jest fer bein' friends with the likes of Adriel and me. I don't know where else we'd find a group of folks like this, that welcomed us and helped us like we was family."

They walked to the blacksmith shop, Charley moving slowly with Marie clutching his arm.

"I reckon it's best if you don't wander these parts by yourself no more. You can't tell what kinds of scoundrels be about."

Marie gave a sniff. "No need to worry about me going over to the Indian village ever again."

"Well, now. It ain't the Indians so much. Adriel and me—we be part Ojibwe. It's them fellers comin' over from Mackinac and the mainland—them's what you have to watch out fer. I was lucky I happened to be up on that trail—lost my good knife somewheres up there."

"I hope you find it." Marie dabbed at her eyes.

"T'were stolen, most like."

Inside the shop, she rushed over to Rusty. He put down his ax when he saw her face. "Marie. *Qu'est-ce que c'est?*"

She drew a deep breath. "Rusty, I—I want to be baptized into the church. Right away."

"Uh—what?"

"Right away," Marie insisted. "No waiting."

"Well, uh—"

Gabriel moved away from the anvil, the hammer still in his hand. "I can give your name to Brother Strang. And then any of us can baptize you, in a proper service in Font Lake—Calvin, or Rusty. Or myself. But—*tiens*. Let's wait and talk about it some. You want to be sure—"

"I'm sure," she declared. "I've waited long enough."

Rusty finally found his voice. "Charley? How did you convert my wife?"

Charley gave a shrug, and a smile spread over his rough features. "I didn't do nuthin'. Just found her in the woods, is all." He paused, then nodded. "I reckon she'll tell you about it someday. But it's not what you think."

13

Jess had her baby in early July, a girl. As Marie had predicted, the little one arrived just in time for King's Day. Marie, close to Jess all through the birth, watched as Jess held the baby for the first time.

"Look at those hands," Jess murmured. "Those fingers—so tiny. She puts me in mind of Turah when she was born."

"And she's a bit bigger than J. J. was," Gabriel remarked. "All to the good."

The door opened. Eb hurried in, followed by Rusty. Sarah said, "I tole 'em they could cone in now."

Eb bent over his new daughter, his eyes alight. Jess held his hand. "I reckon I'd like to call her Cinda Rae. I had a friend back in Virginy, name of that."

"'Course you did." Eb nodded. "I 'member Cinda—she helped us when Gabe and I went to find you. That's a right good name."

Rusty moved over beside Marie and began saying something. It took a few seconds for her mind to jump from the baby to what he was saying—something about a picnic on the mainland.

"It's gonna be the best frolic you ever saw—we're gonna cross over in fishing boats. Charley's already promised us places in his boat. We're gonna camp, have ourselves a conference, and a picnic to end all picnics. And do you know where? Right there at Pine River, where we was attacked two years ago. Ain't nobody gonna attack us now."

"Now, hold on a moment." Gabe's voice sounded weary. "You're gonna be taking Marie, who's expecting a child, over to Pine River in a fishing boat?"

"Charley's boat. Lord knows, it be safe as any. Hasn't capsized yet. And the child isn't due for another three months. Right?"

"Oh, please, Gabriel." Marie clapped her hands in her excitement. "Couldn't I go?"

Gabriel paused, his black brows drawing together. Then he drew a deep breath.

"Well, you can do what you've a mind to. I'll not stop you. And I reckon it'll do you good—the fresh air and such. But just be careful. No falls and such-like. No sudden jolts."

"I'll watch her," Rusty said.

"I wish I could go," Jess murmured.

"Absolutely not," Gabriel replied. "Eb can go if he wants. But you're staying here."

"I'm not leaving here." Eb spoke firmly. "But J. J. would enjoy it."

Rusty waved his hands. "We'll take both him and Louise."

"And it goes without saying, I'll be here," Gabriel said. "With Bethia about to deliver at any minute, I don't dare leave."

"And I'm staying right here with you," Sarah declared. "Calvin might want to go."

As the day of departure dawned, Calvin decided he would join the expedition. He helped as Rusty loaded baskets of food on the boat, then took his place with Rusty, Marie, the young ones Louise and J. J., and Charley and Adriel.

"Leavin' Gabe with all those women," Charley remarked as they pushed off. "The poor cuss."

"He's been through worse," Adriel said. "Like the time them bears almost came through the tents back in Wisconsin."

"You sure that was worse?" Charley laughed. "All those women, back in that cabin. Tellin' him what to do?"

"If he c'n frighten off bears, I reckon he'll deal with them," Calvin said.

Marie leaned forward, intent on what she was hearing. "I never knew about any bears."

"Well, 'course not," Charley said. "We wasn't about to frighten you with such things as that. 'Specially with you in the family way and all."

Marie shook her head. "Well, we never knew."

"You know what they say." Rusty raised his eyebrows. "What you don't know won't hurt you none."

"Well, you coulda told me later."

Rusty smiled. "This *is* later."

"And there's worse than bears to be scared of," Charley remarked. "But not today."

The sun sparkled on the water as the boat sped toward the mainland. The dark blue water had gentle swells which lifted their craft and set it down again. The wind filled the sail. Marie felt a sense of freedom, of wild abandon—all troubles left behind, scattered by the wind blowing in her face.

"Good breeze today," Adriel said.

They began to talk of the recent conference, and what had happened.

"Two of them," Calvin was saying. "Removed from office. Two of the top leaders—Samuel Bacon, and Franklin Bevier, of all people. Accused of 'corrupting themselves—going among enemies of the church.' Why, Warren Post even said that Brother Bacon had denied that the work being done was the inspiration of God. He called it 'human invention.'"

"Can you beat that?" Charley said.

Marie noticed that Rusty said nothing, but a strange expression came over his face. A trick of the light, she thought. His knuckles were white as he gripped the side of the boat.

"We got five new apostles," Adriel said. "Some good men."

"We still got three vacancies," Calvin replied.

"That's enough talk about that." Charley hauled the sail a bit tighter. "Let's think about what we're gonna do on the mainland."

Rusty brightened. "Why, we'll have us a picnic that'll top all other picnics. Wait and see."

Marie was not impressed with what they finally did. For one thing, she began to feel unwell—tired, and queasy after the voyage. She tried to keep up with the young ones, Louise and J. J. No sense in letting them get into trouble. But it was hard for her to breathe; she had to keep stopping to catch a good breath. Finally Rusty took her arm.

"Let's just set a spell." He guided her to a fallen tree trunk. "I be a bit winded myself. We'll catch up with the others later."

What they did was to camp on an island, which they named Holy Island. To get to the island, they traveled up Pine River and through a lake which they renamed 'Lake Mormon.' Here they prepared to hold a conference. Many other Mormons, settlers in the Pine River area, came over to join the group.

After the conference, everybody gathered at the mouth of Pine River. With timber they had towed from the island, they erected a gallows where they hung in effigy the ones who had made the assault on the two boatloads of Mormons two years ago. The *Northern Islander* later described it as a "murderous attack," and commented, "Had the men been in hand instead of the effigies, they would have doubtless shared the same fate."

The picnic was everything Rusty could have hoped for, with roast chicken, other meats, breads, rolls, baked potatoes, and fruits of all kinds, all washed down with cider. Marie did not eat that much; she still felt unwell. Perhaps she should have listened to Gabriel and stayed home. The troubles she'd left on the island gathered around her again. She didn't feel that anything was physically wrong. But there seemed to be a shadow over the proceedings, as if the gayety were somehow muted.

As they prepared to sail back to Beaver Island, they learned that their prophet had taken a fourth wife, seventeen-year-old Sarah Wright. Rusty shrugged and made no comment.

Marie, stepping into the boat, tried to remember the good things about the voyage—the picnic, and the synagogue they had put up to use for future worship. On the voyage home, she leaned close to Rusty. He put his cheek on the top of her hair, and they rode, rocked by the waves. A journey of rare beauty and closeness, with blue water and bright sunlight—yet she sensed something amiss. Had the island been attacked in their absence? No—there it was, riding like a jewel on the lake's surface. She glanced over at Louise and J. J. They seemed at ease, talking with Charley and Calvin. Nothing wrong there.

Charley steadied the boat, one hand on the pier boards, as Rusty helped her onto the dock. She walked toward shore as Rusty and Calvin gathered baskets with leftover food, and blankets they had used for bedding.

"Here." Rusty handed baskets to J. J. and Louise. "Carry some of this up to the cabin."

A little crowd had gathered at the foot of the dock, people watching as the boats came in. Marie, glancing around, saw Eb in the crowd. He moved toward her, but when she flashed him a smile, he only shook his head. No smile from him. That's when she knew. *Something not right.*

"J.J.'s fine," she told him. "He and Louise had a good time."

"That's good to know." Again, no smile. His eyes met hers. "Let's— let's wait for the others."

"Eb, what's wrong? Jess—is she all right? The baby?"

"They both be fine." He drew a breath.

"Gabriel? He's all right?"

"Gabriel? I reckon. Let's wait a bit. J. J.? Come on over here. You, too, Louise."

The young people drew close, casting questioning glances at each other. Rusty and his father joined them, and finally Charley and Adriel gathered around. "What is it?" Charley asked. "We have to take the boat back to its mooring. That is, Adriel will take it back, and I'll go pick him up in the canoe." Then he looked at Eb's face and stopped.

Eb tried several times to speak. Then he said, "It be Bethia. She— she's dead."

"Dead!" Marie cried. Rusty put an arm around her.

"The pains—they started two mornings ago. Everything went as it should—leastways, that's what Gabe said. Along about mid-afternoon, the baby was born. A big, healthy boy. Gabe, he was holding him up, showing him to Sarah. All of a sudden, like, Bethia makes a little sound. They turn around, and she has her hands to her chest, like this. Gabe did all he could, but she was gone in a very short time. So Sarah says. Jest too tired, or something."

"But—" Marie was still trying to understand.

"The child," Calvin said. "How—"

Eb sighed. "The Lord does provide. Right now, Jess be feeding two babies."

Calvin drew away. "I'd best get up there right away. Sarah be grieving for sure."

Eb looked at him. "Sarah ain't the only one. Gabe, he be acting like it's his fault—he missed something. I—I wanted you all to know. Don't be makin' a lot of noise, goin' up there." He eyed the two young people.

"We'll be quiet as mice," Louise said.

Eb sniffed. "Well, I don't know about that. Jest be respectful."

Calvin was already on his way toward the cluster of homes. Marie hurried to keep up with him, feeling stunned, not able to believe what she'd just heard. Rusty and the youngsters followed behind with Eb.

"How could such a thing have happened?" she said out loud. That was a silly thing to say, she knew. More women died in childbirth than from any other cause. But Gabriel was so knowledgeable and careful. "How terrible he must feel."

She didn't enter her own cabin, but went straight to the new big house. She tried the door; it swung open. Gabriel sat at the dining room table staring out at the garden. Sarah turned from stirring the pot of soup on the stove.

"Well, glory be," she declared. "About time you got home."

The normalcy in her tone disturbed Marie even more. Gabriel looked around then. As she hurried toward him, he stood up. His face was drained of color, his eyes blinking as if he needed sleep. His tousled black hair looked more disheveled than usual. She put her arms around him and he hugged her back. They stood wordless; Marie was aware of Calvin walking in and embracing Sarah. Rusty came in just behind him and stood with his hat in his hand.

Marie whispered to her brother in French about how sorry she was. Finally he released her and stepped back.

"So glad you're here. You don't know how glad. But, *tiens*. Enough of this. Come see my son, and your nephew."

She followed him past the little study where the box of pine boards rested beside the desk. "I have some work to do on the coffin," Gabriel told Calvin.

Calvin gave a little cough. "I'll finish it up."

They followed Gabriel to the cabin next door, where Eb stood in the doorway. Soon they were all inside. Jess, resting in bed, held her baby girl close to her. "I just got Jacob to sleep."

"Jacob?" Marie asked.

Gabriel smiled. "I figured I'd name him after Bethia's uncle, who died back in Kirtland. Jacob Paige Romain. Sarah likes that too, since he was her first husband."

Gabriel bent over the cradle. The baby slept with a look of purpose on his face.

"He looks like you," Marie whispered. "Look. He's even got the hair."

The infant already had a mop of black hair. "Like as not, it won't stay," Gabriel remarked. "But it'll come back."

A figure straightened up from the hearth. To her surprise, it was Turah.

"Momma needs me now," she said in answer to Marie's startled look. "I've made potato soup. Would you like some?"

"No, my dear," Gabriel replied. "*Merci.* But see that your mother has plenty."

As they walked back to the big house, Gabriel put an arm around Marie. He spoke slowly. "Life is strange. All she ever wanted was a healthy child. And now we have the child. But not her."

Marie said nothing. He held the door for her, and they went inside.

⚔

Rusty happened to be in the shop when one of their customers declared, "I swear, they be accusin' us of stealin' horses all over Michigan. And stealin' wheat—why, we ain't even got a grist mill on the island. Why would we steal wheat?"

"And don't forget the children," Charley said. "Why, they say we been stealin' children on account of this prank some of the Injuns played over in Grand Traverse. Why, even Brother Strang said it was a mere joke, and later they caught some young fellers tryin' to steal watermelons from a neighbor."

"And murder." The customer waved his hands. "They say we be plunderin' and stealin' and murderin', and I don't know what all."

Gabe gave a little laugh. "Well, Pete. Just keep yer nose clean, and I reckon we'll all be all right."

The others began to relax, and Charley even teased him. "Yeah, Pete. Better git home 'afore they figure yer the one that did it."

Rusty looked at his father, unsure and shaken by what he'd heard. Calvin gave him a wink and then turned away.

"*Eh bien.*" Gabe shook his head. "If they're gonna think we're pirates, we might as well look the part. I'll get me an eye patch, and I'll make me a wooden leg."

Charley said something else, and Gabe laughed again. Then Rusty caught his breath, realizing it had been weeks since he'd heard his brother-in-law laugh. Was Gabe coming out of his shock and grief at last? If so, they should all rejoice.

"I'll help you with that wooden leg," he said.

"I reckon I don't need any help."

Charley grunted. "It do be a strange turn of events. I mean, first it seems we be on top, and in control of things. Then more and more enemy folks—I mean, them that don't wish us well—be coming to the island and—and nearby places. Gettin' themselves elected to positions of authority and such. And it don't seem we can do anything about it."

"It puts me in mind of Far West," Rusty's father said. "Or Nauvoo." *Both settlements where the Mormons had been chased out.*

Rusty looked at Gabe, still their leader. Gabe snorted and threw down his hammer. "Now, that's nonsense. Best not to think about it. That's not gonna happen here."

The next day they had something else to think about. Marie's pains started early in the morning. Rusty sent Louise to fetch Gabe in mid-morning. He arrived right away, his expression tight-lipped and determined. Rusty felt a surge of relief. Gabe was not about to lose either mother or child this time, if he could help it.

"Go fetch Turah," Gabe told Louise. "Or Sarah. Whichever one is available."

"Turah be taking care of Jess and the babies," the girl said.

"Sarah, then."

From the bed, Marie called, "Jess. I want Jess."

Gabe looked at Lousie. "See what can be done."

Jess came to sit beside the bedside, leaving Turah to look after Cinda and Jacob. Rusty bent anxiously over Marie; she lay still, breathing fast, her face drained of color. Then he heard Gabe say to Louise, "Go tell your grampa to come fetch his son and take him down to Charley's. Charley'll know what to do."

In his stunned, bewildered state, Rusty wondered what Charley would know how to do. Calvin appeared in a very short time—Rusty wondered if his father had actually run—and soon he was being led out the door. "Come on, son," his father murmured. "It's best if you're not here."

Louise left to go stay with Turah and the babies. Rusty's father took him over to the old cabin which his father and Sarah had vacated for the new frame house. Now Charley and Adriel lived together in the cabin. Adriel and Eb were down in the shop, but Charley acted as if he'd been expecting the father and son.

"Come in and have a seat. You do look poorly. Right peaked, I'd say."

"Oh, he'll come through all right," his father said. "It's right tough, becoming a father."

"I wouldn't know." Charley poured something into a glass. "Here. Drink this."

"What is it?" Rusty took the glass.

"Somethin' Brother Strang doesn't need to know about. It's fer times like this. Drink it down."

"I c'n use a snort too," his father said. Soon they were sitting on the wooden benches, drinking something that burned as Rusty swallowed it.

"It's not what they sell to the Injuns," Charley explained. "No rotgut, that's fer certain. This's high grade stuff."

Rusty wiped his mouth on his sleeve and looked around the cabin.

No sign of refinement here. Two painted buoys leaned against the rough pine wall, and beside them lay fishing nets dried and stored for the winter. A pair of wooden oars, both of which had lost any sign of paint, leaned side by side in the corner. Just above the fish nets hung a furry black bearskin.

"One of them Injuns traded it to me for some nets," Charley said. "We had extra ones."

There was a wild, woodsy smell about the place, and a faint odor of fish. Rusty began to feel more and more at home, drowsy from whatever it was he was drinking. He left the talking to his father, with short answers from Charley.

His father's voice: "So what if we do everything we're supposed to do. Really worked to appease those mainland folks. And they persecute us anyway. What do we do?"

Charley lifted his glass. "I reckon we do what we've always done. Hunker down. Try to weather the storm."

"No. I mean, what if they drive us off he island? That's what they'd like to do, doncher know?"

Charley paused and took another drink. "All right, Calvin. Let me ask you. What would *you* do?"

Rusty's father hesitated. "Well, I reckon—I guess I'd try to head back to Montrose. To my daughter Hannah, and Nat and the children. Try to be a farmer again."

"You reckon it's safe in those parts? Across the river from Nauvoo?"

"Well, how safe is it here? He's got lots of cabins scattered in those woods, back in Ioway."

Charley put down his glass. "I don't figure on going back there. I don't know. Adriel and I, we've spent too much time on these lakes— they get in your blood, seems like."

Rusty's father waited before he spoke. "Well, supposin' you couldn't stay here."

Charley leaned back. "I reckon we'd look for a place—maybe Grand Traverse. We'd be strangers—no one would know our religion. We'd be on the water, and we could fish for a living."

"So you'd just go off alone?"

"Well, it sure beats stayin' here and gettin' killed. If it came to that."

Rusty managed to speak. "Don't let Sarah hear you talkin' that way. She'll get after you with a fryin' pan, for sure."

Charley gave a laugh. "I reckon I c'n handle the likes of her."

His father sighed. "Let's hope none of that ever happens. About havin' to leave and all."

Charley snorted. "It's happened before. You think it can't happen again?"

"'Course it could. Let's hope it won't."

Rusty was beginning to think that a nap would be a good idea. Even the wooden bench had a softness he hadn't noticed before. He leaned back against the wall.

The next thing he knew, Sarah herself was standing over him. "Of all the— I never saw the like. Here your wife be laborin' all afternoon, right next door. And you over here, sleepin' on a wood bench."

Rusty struggled, feeling like a swimmer coming from deep under water. By this time, Rusty's father was on his feet. "What's the news? He be wakin' up."

"The news? You've got a new grandson. And he's got a pair of lungs that'll wake the dead."

"It's a boy?" Rusty asked. "I have a son?"

"Yes. It's a son." Sarah shook her head. "And let's hope he's not as lazy as his old man."

"Oh, let up on the lad, Sarah." Rusty's father handed his glass back to Charley. "We gave him a little somethin' to relax him. 'Cause he was mighty riled up."

"Can we go see 'em now?" Rusty stood up slowly.

Sarah looked at him, her eyes narrowed. "Well, I reckon. You better hurry, afore Marie goes to sleep herself. I must say, she deserves to sleep for a week."

By the time Rusty reached his cabin, Marie was sitting up in bed nursing the newborn.

"That's him?" Rusty exclaimed. "He sure is red."

Gabe smiled. "Yes, and what hair he has is red, too."

"He looks like he's been boiled or something."

"Well, he's just been born. Give him a few hours, and he'll look just fine."

Rusty leaned over to kiss his wife. The baby gave a fretful little moan.

"Don't get him started," Gabe said. "He's got a cry that can shatter glass."

Rusty sat at the foot of the bed, looking at Marie and the newcomer. Her black hair hung down around her neck in ringlets, and her lovely French face with her wide apart eyes seemed the picture of peace and repose. At that moment he felt he had never loved her more. Aware of someone watching him, he looked over to meet the eyes of Jess, who sat beside Marie. Jess smiled her approval. Gabe moved closer to the little group, and for a brief time Rusty felt that they were all caught up in a rare cloud of enchantment and beauty.

Then Sarah came in, followed by Rusty's father. "If that doesn't beat everything!" Sarah exclaimed.

"What?" Gabe asked.

Rusty's father shrugged. "Oh, Brother Strang has gone and got himself another wife. This one be Phoebe, the cousin to the last wife. Sarah Wright. She's the one he married at the time of the last conference."

"So, this be number five?" Jess asked.

Calvin nodded. "If'n you c'n keep 'em straight. The trouble is, plural marriage is no longer a secret. All sorts of folks be talkin' about it now—all our enemies."

The spell of contentment was broken. Rusty's father moved closer. "So, there's the little tyke. Looks healthy enough."

"How'd you find out?" Rusty asked. "I mean about the fifth wife?"

"Adriel came home and told Charley. I reckon everybody on the island knows by this time."

14

IN THE EARLY WINTER evenings, Gabriel liked nothing better than to sit in front of the fire with Eb and Jess. Gabriel held his own sturdy son on his lap while Jess rocked her little girl Cinda. Sometimes Gabriel sang in French to the children, songs from his own childhood.

Il était une bergère
 Et ron ron ron, petit patapon,
Il était une bergère
 Qui gardait ses moutons, ron ron
  Qui gardait ses moutons.

Finally Gabriel felt Jacob relax completely in his arms, felt the tousled head on his shoulder. "He's sleeping now." At such times, Gabriel became aware of how fragile and dependent the child was, and how he, Gabriel, was all the family that Jacob really had. He felt compassion and determination rushing over him, resolving to be the best single parent his son could have. But how could he be both mother and father too?

When Marie was able to have more company, he would bundle Jacob up and carry him over to sit beside Marie's hearth. Rusty sat reading while Marie and Gabriel sang songs to Jacob and little Paul Gerard. Later he would take Jacob over to Jess' cabin for a last feeding, then carry him back to the frame house, where his cradle waited beside Gabriel's own bed.

At times he missed Bethia, wondering how things could have

gone so amiss. His fault—not talking with her enough, not knowing something was terribly wrong. When he said as much to Sarah, she shook her head.

"None of us knew. And I knew her better than anybody. Whatever was wrong, she hid it pretty well. And I reckon she knows, wherever she is. She knows you did the best for her, and she be watchin' over that child."

As he held Jacob, both of them half-asleep beside the fire, he was able in his mind to see Bethia as a whole person, as if he could glimpse all of her life at once. He could see her compassionate nature, her love for both children and animals, her desire for a child of her own. Then it seemed that the more troublesome parts of their relationship receded, and what emerged was the gentle, pleasant person he had first known.

It grew colder. One day, just before noon, he returned from visiting a patient and sat holding his son in his arms in front of Jess's fireplace. Snow before long. He marveled at the passage of time—it seemed just a few weeks since Jacob was newborn. Now he was a hefty five months old, and Bethia had been gone that long. Some said it was time to look for another wife—to find a mother for his son. Sarah had even hinted as much.

"I thought you knew a widow over in Troy."

"There never was a widow in Troy. Leastways, not one I'd care to marry."

In truth, he knew that if he ever remarried, it would only be to Corey. And she was long gone. He had half a mind to go look for her, to seek her out and learn what she was doing now—if she was happy. But that would mean leaving his son, and that he couldn't bear.

"I reckon I'll stay put for now."

"Uh?" The child looked at him, then struggled to get down. Gabriel put him on the floor facing away from the fire. Immediately the boy pulled himself up, then sat back down again.

Gabriel stayed in front of the fire while Jess picked up Jacob and carried him off to his midday meal. Jacob and Cinda were eating applesauce now, and tiny pieces of bread. Gabriel knew he should probably go down to the shop and see what was happening there. But he felt tired, and he knew a cold wind was blowing outside. Then he heard voices—Marie and Sarah coming in to see Jess. They gathered around the table, Marie with Paul bundled up in her arms.

Gabriel's eyelids fell; he half-dozed, listening to the rise and fall of their voices. First, Sarah:

"I vow, she be all of twenty years younger than him. Everybody's talkin' 'bout it. Like marryin' yer own daughter."

That would be the prophet's youngest wife, Gabriel surmised. Well, it was none of his business. But for a lot of the church members, it was difficult to accept.

Marie spoke in a gentler tone. "They do say he is a good, loving husband to all of them, and a kind father."

Sarah again: "Oh, you'd defend the devil hisself. Always looking at the other side."

Jess gave a sigh. "You all be forgettin' something. If'n you get caught with more than one wife, the state of Michigan can fine you five hundred dollars. Or put you in prison for up to five years."

"He does have a right pretty house," Marie said. "All wood-frame, and whitewashed. It's got a view of the lake, and that thick grove of trees all around. And the tabernacle just behind it."

Sarah spoke again. "Did you hear? That fourth wife's been called to the ministry—to be a teacher."

"She's right smart," Jess said. "All his wives are."

"And they all have their specific duties," Marie remarked. "One does the cooking, one looks after the children. Elvira—she's the secretary. And Mary, the first wife—she goes with him to Lansing—"

"Dr. Gabriel!" Jess called. "Come have something to eat."

An offer he can't refuse. He rose from his chair and walked over to join them.

The extreme cold weather continued.

"We gonna be settin' a record," Calvin complained. "Goin' down in the history books."

"I hear tell it's like this all over," Charley said. "Even in places where it don't get this cold."

The community spent eight days feasting between Christmas and New Year's Day, much to Rusty's delight. Everyone else seemed to enjoy it too. The ice froze two and a half feet thick in the harbor, and finally they heard that the lake was frozen over for forty miles around.

"If that don't beat all," Eb said.

There was an ice bridge between the island and the mainland, the way marked by evergreen boughs and piles of brush. Calvin waved his hands. "Why, we can take the horses and sleigh right over to Pine River. I mean, when we need supplies and such-like."

The ice bridge lasted more than seven weeks. Gabriel thought he had never known a more beautiful winter. The mornings were misty, the tree limbs encased in ice, and icicles hung like sparkling crystal from fences and out-buildings. The horses' hooves made a crunching sound in the deep snow, and the northern air had a crispness about it, a scent of crushed pine needles. The lesser islands rode like dark shapes on the icy expanse of lake, and the shadows were blue on the mounds of snow. The center of town looked like a Christmas village, lights glittering amid the world of white.

They bundled up the children, down to the smallest of the babies, and took them riding in the horse-drawn sleigh. They crowded together in the sleigh, Marie, Rusty, Jess and Sarah, with Calvin riding beside Gabriel as he drove. Gabriel thought of how Bethia would have enjoyed the snow, the beauty of it, especially with her hardy young son beside her. Then he sighed and shook his head. Well, maybe somehow she did know—perhaps even more lovely sights were now hers. And—blessed thought—perhaps she had found healing at last.

Somehow, everyone got a chance to ride in the sleigh, even Eb, Charley and Adriel.

"It sure be right pretty," Charley remarked. "I told you, them lakes is special."

"Every view is magnificent," Rusty exclaimed. "'Specially with the sun on that ice."

"It be all covered with snow," Adriel told him. "You can't even see no ice."

"Well, when the wind blows it off, you can."

Mr. Strang spent the first part of the year in Lansing, serving his second term in the Legislature. The men talked about it in the blacksmith shop.

"Sounds like trouble. This idea of dividing Emmet County," Charley said. "Isolating us to Beaver, Fox and Manitou. Just them islands. Them fellers from Macknac, they say that's gonna fix us fer good."

"It sure ain't gonna help us none," Calvin remarked. "Politically, I mean. More and more gentiles gettin' elected to things."

"I wouldn't worry none." Gabriel picked up his glove and hammer. "We're safe for a while, all locked in with ice. No boats for a long time. And no one's gonna come over to bother us in dog sleds."

Calvin grunted. "I reckon yer right. Spring's on the calendar, but there's no open water."

Spring finally arrived. The weather broke, and the ice started to melt, leaving patches of open water. Mr. Strang, back on the island, had ideas of producing a daily paper. *The Northern Islander* came out every Thursday during shipping season. Now, with the opening of navigation, a *Daily Northern Islander* would start publication.

Charley, as always, liked to talk about what was in the paper. "Do you know what he wants in the way of new settlers? A bookbinder, some boat builders, a handful of journeymen. Oh, yes, and a painter, and some printers. And schoolteachers—qualified ones."

"Don't forget the furniture makers, and a baker," Adriel said. "And someone to make cedar pails and tubs and such—wooden dishes. And a brick maker, and brick and stone masons and plasterers."

"I reckon he'll get all them folks." Calvin reached for his apron. "People are looking to come here. And Pine River—that bunch over there be doin' well. They've even made a start on a sawmill, and the local Injuns are acting right friendly."

With the spring, Turah had left her family's house and gone back to Gray Wolf and the Ojibwe village. Gabriel wondered if she still feared that Eb would separate them, with the help of Strang, and send her off to school. At any rate, she was gone before the start of the shipping season.

In May, more people arrived on the island, led by missionaries. There was even a reception for the returning missionaries and their converts.

"It were sure a glorious frolic," Charley remarked after the event. "Some of the newcomers couldn't figure out how you could have such a good time without drinking and swearing and such-like."

"They'll get used to it, I reckon," Calvin said.

Work resumed on the unfinished tabernacle, and the people began the project of whitewashing the buildings in the downtown area. There was talk of supplying wood to the railroads, the transportation of the future, and also the possibility of settling as a larger body in a place like Texas or Canada. With the growing fears of a civil war in the states, Beaver Island was still considered the safest location for the population of Mormons.

Calvin nodded. "Best we stay put."

⬳⬲

Rusty was accustomed to rumors about how Brother Strang's life had been threatened. "Why, land's sakes," he told Marie. "At least once a week you hear of another plot to do him in. But he's well protected—people all around him. I wouldn't worry none." As he worked sweeping out the shop, he heard the others talking behind him.

His father was inspecting the bellows. "Well, the trouble started way last year, when them women started refusing to wear the bloomer outfit."

"What women?" Gabe's voice sounded weary, as if he were tired of hearing about difficult people.

"Why, Ruth Ann Bedford and them. Tom Bedford's wife. And there was all that talk about them serving alcohol to a bunch of young folks at a party."

"I thought they settled all that," Charley said. "Strang warn't too happy about it, but they moved on."

His father again: "Well, the main trouble was his drinking. As Strang said, he 'drank more than a teetotaler would sanction.'"

Gabe sighed. "But—thirty-nine lashes. That seems a harsh punishment, just for imbibing."

Rusty's father grunted. "They say it were for lying and tale-bearing, inciting to mischief and crime. I reckon he opened his mouth once too often."

Charley folded up his newspaper. "Well, Sarah Wright said it were because his fishing partner came home and found Tom in bed with the partner's wife. When he was supposed to be out fishing."

Rusty looked at the pile of wood, then went outside to fetch some more. Tom Bedford had been taken out and whipped by a mob of men around the first of March. The implication was that Strang had ordered the whipping, but no one could prove it. Bedford had vowed vengeance since that time. Rusty selected four pieces of firewood and carried them back into the shop.

"There's other folks hatin' him," his father was saying. "Hezekiah McCulloch, now. Everybody knows he's drunk as a skunk half the time. It warn't no surprise they dumped him from the Quorum of the Twelve Apostles. And you know about his defrauding folks about the amount of wood they placed on his dock. That's why he's no longer County Clerk."

"His main trouble is the boats," Charley said. "The boats that serve liquor. You go into any one of them docked here, and you'll find him and his drinking buddy. Why—"

Gabe held up his hand. "That's enough. I think it's better if we don't speak of such things. We're like to get in trouble ourselves. Who wants to receive 'forty stripes save one?' Not me. We'd all just better keep our mouths shut and our eyes open."

After a morning's fishing, Rusty was on his way home with Charley and Adriel. A foggy morning; the water stretched before them, a placid gray. The island appeared suddenly out of the mists as they approached the harbor. Then Rusty remembered. "Gabe wants us to work in the shop this afternoon. He has to see patients."

"Fishin' ain't that good anyways," Adriel remarked. "Too early in the season."

"Water's still pretty cold." Charley began hauling in the grayish canvas sail. "Hardly enough wind to ghost in. We'll take 'er down now and row into the harbor."

Adriel stowed the nets and put what few fish they had into the hold. Then he manned the oars while Charley finished stowing the sail. Charley looked up. "I'll vow, there's a big ship in the harbor. Look! It's the steamer *Michigan*."

"There's a lot of folks out on the dock," Rusty said.

"I can't see a thing," Adriel complained.

"Jest keep rowing." Charley shook his head. "I reckon there's a bunch of 'em waitin' to complain to the captain about conditions on the island, and how they been treated. Folks like McCulloch, and Tom Bedford. Oh, they'll do it secretly, of course. Brother Strang won't hear a thing."

"You sure smart, Charley," Rusty said.

"I get around. Like Gabe says, I keep my ears open and my mouth shut."

Rusty blinked as the sunlight hit his eyes. "So what's the captain gonna do? He can't change things."

"He c'n tell the governor, is what he can do. It be a United States vessel, after all, making its usual rounds. Like as not, nothin' will come of it. Pull on the left one, Adriel. More to port. That's it."

They tied up at the mooring and transferred themselves and fish into the waiting canoe. Charley looked at the fish—three whitefish, five large perch. "Enough to feed our families."

Rusty's thoughts were all on a fish dinner cooked by Marie as he helped haul the canoe up on the beach. Dimly he noticed the bulk of the steamer and the men gathered on the dock. Then he followed his friends up toward the houses, Charley carrying the fish strung through the gills.

A few days after the *Michigan* had departed, Rusty was working in the shop with his father, Eb, and Gabe.

"I reckon Adriel and Charley be gone fishing," his father remarked.

Gabe straightened up, the hammer in his hand. "*Eh bien.* We could sure use them today. We've got to get this job done by tomorrow afternoon."

"Did I tell you Turah came back to us?" Eb put another small log on the fire.

Gabe gave a little cough. "Did she, now?"

"She said she'd heard things from the Ojibwe—her husband's people. She told us we should get out now—pack up our things and go."

"Some families be doin' just that," Gabe said. "But there's folks doin' it all the time. One feller said he was moving over to Pine River. He was allowed to take his possessions, on account of he was planning to settle over there. Well, he left completely. No one's seen 'em since."

Rusty's father stepped closer. "So, what are we lookin' at? An Indian uprising?"

Eb shook his head. "No. Most of 'em seem to like us. So Turah says. But they hear things, and they know things that we don't."

"What'd you tell her?" Gabe asked.

"I said we figured we was safe enough. But she cried and took on even more, beggin' us to leave, soon as we got the chance. Finally she said good-bye. Said she and Gray Wolf was packin' up their canoe. Goin' over to Arbre Croche for a spell."

Rusty's father grunted. "I reckon they'll be safe enough there."

Gabe stood for a moment, his eyebrows knitting together in a frown. Then he sighed. "I reckon I'll go pay a visit to that village before they leave. I want to talk to Gray Wolf and find out what they know."

"Right now?" Rusty's father asked.

"Well, no. We'll finish this up first. In the next couple of days."

"I'd be right pleased if'n I could go with you," Eb said. "See my girl fer one last time."

"Fine. We'll plan on it."

A noise at the door. Charley came in, looking grim and puzzled at the same time. Adriel stepped in just behind him.

"What's the matter, Charley?" Gabe put down his hammer.

"The steamer *Michigan* be back. It's down in the harbor. And a whole bunch of folks is wondering why. Seein' it just left and all. Folks is millin' around in front of Johnson's store, down by McCulloch's dock. In fact, a lot of 'em are in the store."

"Let's go over and see what's up," Rusty said.

Gabe looked at him. "We need to finish what we're doing. Oh, what the heck. You and Charley go on over. But, Adriel, you stay here—we need you."

"Sure enough," Adriel replied.

"And you two get back soon as you can."

Rusty hurried alongside Charley as they made their way toward the harbor. Charley rubbed his stubble of a beard. "No need to rush. That ship'll be here fer at least another day. It takes a heap of folks to cast her off and back her up away from the dock."

"Thanks for gettin' me out of workin' fer a spell."

"Don't thank me. It's him that decided. Gabe. I reckon he figured that outside news was better than everybody workin' all day."

Rusty looked at the dock, laden with stacks of cordwood. An aisle led between the piles of wood to the ship at the end of the dock. "What d'you suppose is goin' on?"

"Hanged if I know." Charley and Rusty joined the group at the foot of the pier. Charley leaned close to one of the men. "What's up?"

The man gave him a funny look. "Can't say fer certain. There's a bunch of marines on the dock here, and in the store. Sailors from the *Michigan*. Folks be wondering why she came back so soon."

Someone nearby said, "They just sent an officer from the ship to go find Brother Strang. That feller—what's his name—"

"Alexander St. Bernard. He's been here before," another one said. "He's a civilian pilot—been on these lakes a long time. Mr. Strang knows 'em. They get along."

Rusty had a feeling it was almost supper time. Marie would be waiting for him, back in the cabin. He turned to speak to Charley, thinking he would excuse himself and go home. But Charley was talking to an older, whiskered man.

"He were headin' for the tabernacle," the whiskered man said. "But Strang ain't there. He be home with his family by this time."

Then they saw Brother Strang walking toward the harbor, arm

in arm with the pilot Alexander St. Bernard. They were apparently exchanging stories and jokes; Strang was laughing. The crowd of men watched as they reached the foot of the dock. The two started to make their way toward the ship, with cords of wood stacked on either side of them.

Tom Bedford stepped out of the crowd and walked along behind them. Alexander Wentworth walked with him. Others followed, curious to see what the captain wanted with Brother Strang. Charley took a step forward. Rusty stayed at his side, figuring that supper would wait until Strang was aboard the ship.

Then a shot rang out. Rusty's heart gave a lurch. Two other shots followed, echoing through the harbor. Rusty heard at least three, but there might have been more. The men at the foot of the dock rushed to make their way through the passageway. Rusty and Charley were swept along by the crowd.

Rusty saw Strang clinging to St. Bernard's arm, blood streaming from his head. Wentworth ran up the gangplank to safety. Bedford leaned over Strang. Then Rusty saw he was beating Strang in the face with his horse pistol. The pistol broke, and Bedford rushed into the ship. Strang fell onto the gangplank leading to the ship.

By the time the crowd had reached Strang, the deck hands had lifted the gangplank. Strang's body slid back onto the dock. St. Bernard, covered in blood by this time, helped several other crew members carry Strang off the dock. Rusty stepped back to make way for them, too stunned to speak. Dizziness rushed over him; he felt sick to his stomach. Charley put a hand on his arm.

Wingfield Watson had witnessed the event from the roof of the tabernacle where he had been working. He raced to his fallen prophet and held his finger on Strang's head wound to stop the bleeding. Rusty learned later that he did this for the next seven hours.

In a short time—Rusty couldn't say how long—a mob of men, women and children had rushed to the scene. The air was filled with the howls and cries from the people as they hurried in from all over town. Rusty felt himself being jostled; he tried to stay close to Charley. But the horror of what had happened, the shrieks and the sight of blood, made him feel faint. He had the fear his legs would no longer support him. All thought of supper had vanished; he didn't think he could ever eat again.

"Let's get him out of here," a voice shouted. "Where's the nearest house?"

"There's the Prindle house. Let's take 'em there."

"Hold on, now. Give 'em space to breathe."

Charley said, "Let's find Dr. Gabriel. He's needed here."

Someone said, "The surgeon from the *Michigan* is coming."

Charley said, "Well, then I guess they don't need Dr. Gabe after all."

"Those cowards," someone said. "They're safe aboard the ship. They be afraid to come back and face us."

In the confusion, Rusty wasn't sure what was happening next. They heard that the ship's surgeon had told Strang that his wounds were mortal, and that he would not recover.

He remembered someone telling Alexander St. Bernard that he should seek safety before folks thought he'd been involved.

"I reckon I'm safe enough," he answered. As far as Rusty knew, the mob did not turn on him.

"Now, Rusty," Charley said in his ear. "Go home and stay there. Before anyone thinks you had anything to do with this. I aim to hang around and see what I can find out. I'll come to you later. Go tell the others, if they don't know by this time."

"You think there's gonna be trouble?"

"Son, we already got trouble. Big trouble. Make yourself scarce, now."

Rusty managed what he thought was a clever exit from the crowd and headed up toward the cabins. He wondered if he should stop at the smithy and tell the others. No—they most likely knew by this time. They would've heard the shots and the noise for sure.

He passed several people hurrying toward the harbor. He entered the woods and took the short cut to his cabin. How could he tell Marie that he felt he would never eat again?

Later, the group of friends gathered in Rusty's father's keeping room. Charley told them how the sheriff had asked the captain of the *Michigan*, Charles H. McBlair, to turn over custody of the shooters and anyone who was an accessory to the crime. The captain had refused—they were to be delivered to the civil authorities on Mackinac.

"Then—" Charley said. "Then they sent soldiers to round up the shooters' families, and anyone else who'd had a hand in it. They're all down at McCulloch's house, with guards to protect them."

The *Michigan* left the next morning, with the families and friends of the assassins. From all reports, the captain had paid one last visit to Strang. Conscious now, Strang demanded that the perpetrators be turned over to the officials on Beaver Island. The captain refused.

Much later, they learned how the two assailants had been hailed as heroes on Mackinac Island. After a mock trial, the two were discharged.

15

"THE BEST THING IS to get him off the island," Rusty's father said.

"Why?" Rusty reached for his glove. "He be in his own home now. And they say he be getting some better."

His father shrugged. "Well, you know, there's been more trouble. Enemies hanging around and such. So they held this council—the leading men on the island. They're afraid them fellers'll come over from the mainland and kill him first thing. Best if him and all the leaders is off the island."

"But—but we'll fight to protect him."

"He says not to fight." Gabe picked up the bellows. "Not to resist. His very words."

"Oh." Rusty stood in a shaft of sunlight, his mind in a turmoil. First, the horror and shock that their leader lay wounded, close to death. *In dreams he still heard the shots echoing over the harbor, saw the blood-soaked body falling on the gangplank.* Second, the question of what they would do next. *Would he and Marie be able to continue their lives as usual, with the children, the fishing, and the work in the shop?*

"Best if we all go somewheres else," his father said.

"I reckon you're right," Gabe replied. "Let's see what we can do."

Charley came in with the news. "They be puttin' him on board the prop boat *Louisville*. Takin' him back to Voree. Others are goin' with him—some of his family, and a few leaders. The apostles George Miller and Benjamin Wright be going. And Lorenzo Dow Hickey."

Gabe gave a sharp intake of breath. "We'll be left leaderless."

Charley nodded. "They think it's for the best. The rest of us are advised to follow. Soon as we can pack up, and the ships come in."

Gate shook his head. "We have no protection left. None."

Adriel entered the shop. "That ship be settin' off in bad weather. The lake is mighty riled."

"*Eh bien.*" Gabe gave a harsh laugh. "If it's that bad, they can't come after us yet, *n'est-ce pas?* We have a few days."

Rusty did not feel comforted as he walked home with the sound of waves crashing on the shore.

⬿⬾

When Gabriel hiked down to the Indian village on the north end of the island, he took Eb and Adriel with him. French he could manage, but Adriel spoke Ojibwe. Between them, they might have a clearer idea of just what the villagers knew.

"That water be still as glass," Eb remarked.

"Just a few ripples," Gabriel replied. "You wouldn't think it ever stormed. Well—here we are."

Adriel asked one of the men where they could find Gray Wolf. The man looked at them, held up a hand, and disappeared into one of the bark-covered wigwams.

"He says to wait," Adriel told them.

They waited. Gabriel looked at the latticed patterns of sunlight on the forest floor, and the small dwellings, dome-shaped, that dotted the clearing. The scent of woodsmoke and crushed pine needles hung in the air. Close by the nearest wigwam lay an overturned birchbark canoe. He wondered if it was the one Gray Wolf had made.

A figure emerged from one of the structures and walked slowly toward them. Gabriel saw that he was thin and bent, possibly one of the oldest persons they had ever met. His face was wrinkled; he had deep-set, dark eyes, and a grayish braid down each side of his face. His clothes looked old and ragged. Three strings of colored beads hung around his neck. He gave the impression of fragility, yet he moved with purpose and dignity.

180

"I think this is their chief," Adriel whispered.

The old man carried a blanket similar to one Gabriel had seen in Eb's cabin. He had something else in his hand; Gabriel couldn't tell what it was. The man stopped in front of them and spoke without smiling.

Adriel said, "He bids us welcome, yet he greets us with great sorrow."

Again there was an exchange in the Ojibwe language. Adriel winced, then began the translation.

"You seek Gray Wolf and his woman. They started for the east country some days ago, before the storm. The bad weather hit them in mid-journey. They—" Here Adriel's voice broke.

"They found the canoe just off the mainland. No one was in it. The one who brought the news, found these things in the canoe. A blanket, and—"

Then Eb saw what the chief held in his other hand. Eb burst into tears just as Gabriel recognized the object. A perfect deerskin moccasin with beadwork in a precise pattern—Gray Wolf's gift to Turah.

"That's hers," Eb exclaimed through his sobs. "I seen it a million times. I'd know it anywhere."

The chief spoke again. Gabriel tried to hear the words, but Eb was gasping and wiping his eyes. Gabriel put a hand on his friend's shoulder. Eb trembled as if he were in a cold rainstorm. Adriel gave the translation.

"We are bowed down with sorrow. The big sea water is full of treachery. Even the most skilled warrior cannot survive such a storm."

The chief paused, then spoke one more time. Adriel waited, then translated. "We have all lost, my friends. Gray Wolf—my grandson."

Gabriel stepped forward and put his hand on the chief's arm. The old man drew back, and Gabriel withdrew his hand, afraid he had made some cultural error. He said in French how sorry they were, and thanked the chief for telling them.

The man responded in his own language. Adriel quickly said, "He doesn't know French very well, but he accepts your sympathy. He gives you the blanket and the moccasin."

Gabriel took the items. He looked at Adriel. "Ask him what he knows about our enemies coming to the island."

Adriel shook his head. "It's not the right time to ask such a thing. He's in mourning."

The chief spoke for the last time, then turned away. Adriel translated. "We know you are followers of the big man. You must leave the island immediately. Many men come, many canoes. Even now, they come, to parts of the island you do not know."

The old man was moving slowly, back toward the cluster of dwellings.

"That's it?" Gabriel asked. "No more information?"

Adriel shrugged. "Not from him. What more do you want? Our fears are confirmed. And—" He looked sadly at the blanket in Gabriel's hands.

Gabriel followed his glance. "You're right. We should be getting home. We need to tell Jess and the others. Come on, Eb."

There was a fresh outburst from Eb; he stood sobbing, rubbing his eyes. Gabriel passed the blanket to Adriel, then took Eb by the arm. They walked back the way they had come, moving in and out of the latticed pools of light which Gabriel had noticed before.

"What about the canoe?" Gabriel asked. "Was that it, the one we saw?"

"No," Adriel replied. "There's no way for them to get it back. Most like, it sank soon after they found it. Close to the mainland? That's more than thirty miles of open water."

Gabriel nodded. "I reckon they're lucky they found it."

"Most often, folks disappear and no one ever knows."

They had just left Eb's cabin after giving Jess the news. "It's a blessing, in a way, that we know what happened. I'll go back and stay with them, soon's I tell the others," Gabriel said. "Or I'll send Marie. Someone has to take care of the children."

Adriel turned to go to his own cabin. Gabriel put a hand on his shoulder. "Thanks, Adriel, I'm mighty glad you were there. You were a great help."

"Gabe, what are we gonna do?"

"I think we keep right on with what we're doing. But just be aware we may have to leave."

Gabriel waited until Adriel had gone. Then he hurried down to the shop, empty now. He went in through the back door. On one of the shelves stood an old cast-iron bean pot. He hauled it down. Inside lay a leather pouch with a drawstring, and inside the pouch he kept the proceeds from the shop. He had already shared the week's earnings with the others; what was left was his. He drew the pouch tight. Around his neck he wore a brown leather strap attached to a metal clip he had fashioned in the blacksmith shop. He clipped the pouch securely to the strap and thrust it under his shirt. Then he began the walk up to the cabins.

∞

"It seemed to me like he was prophesying, like," Adriel was saying. "Or he saw something in vision."

Rusty was in Charley's cabin watching Charley repair a net. Charley looked up from his work. "You mean, the chief? Gray Wolf's grandfather?"

Adriel nodded. "I warn't sure if it was happening now, or in the future."

Charley resumed his work. "It's hard to tell. 'Specially if he be as old as you say he is. Like as not, he was confused. And, as you say, he be grieving. I don't figure anyone knows what's gonna happen."

Adriel looked out into space for a moment. "You reckon we got time to go out and rescue that skiff?"

Charley raised his eyebrows. "It'd sure bring us some money. And Lord knows we might need it."

As Rusty understood the story, someone had abandoned a skiff on the far side of Gull Island. Charley had heard about it from other fishermen, and someone else had offered good money to anyone who would rescue it and bring it back.

"I say, let's do it." Charley put down the net.

Rusty got to his feet. "Count me in."

Charley grunted. "Let's make tracks, then. They say it be stuck on a sandbar. I'll get the shovel and some rope from the shop. We'll meet down at McCulloch's dock."

Another adventure. Rusty rubbed his hands together. He was frankly bored with packing up and waiting around the cluster of houses for some ship to come in. This would get his mind off of Brother Strang and the things which had happened. He rushed over to his cabin and told Marie what they were about.

"Sounds like a good idea," she said. "We're almost all packed here, anyway. Mostly baby things, and not too many of them."

He kissed her and hurried down to the dock to meet the others. They pushed off in the canoe, found their own boat, and hoisted sail. Gull Island lay fourteen miles to the west. As they left St. James and the harbor, Charley looked back. "There be a heap of boats comin' in. Like as not, they couldn't catch nothin'."

"Some days the fish just aren't there," Adriel replied.

They rounded Whiskey Point and headed to the west. Rusty could make out High Island just to the north of them. The water was choppy, with a brisk wind blowing. As far as he could see, whitecaps crested and disappeared.

"If this wind keeps up, we'll be there in no time." Charley held the tiller firmly while Adriel clutched the sheet to the mainsail.

Rusty said, "You think we should've told Gabe where we were going?"

Charley gave a shrug. "Naw. He be mighty jumpy anyway. Don't know what's got into him."

By the time they reached Gull Island, the whitecaps formed continuous lines. The wind came at them, sweeping across the full expanse of the lake.

"It's really makin' up," Adriel said.

Charley grunted. "I reckon it's usually rough out in these parts."

"Must be almost thirty knots now."

They found the abandoned skiff. Rusty and Charley worked to free it from the sandbar while Adriel hovered close by in their own boat.

Rusty felt the cold lake water swirling around him. He pushed, and Charley attacked the sand with the shovel.

"Hold up a spell," Charley said. "My foot's stuck."

A great wave broke over them and the boat floated free. Charley grabbed its painter. They were on the lee side of the sandbar. Charley brandished the shovel. "Let's take 'er into shore."

They beached the boats side by side in the sand. Then Charley inspected the rescued craft. "She don't leak. A good sign. In fact, she'll do right well. If'n we can get her back in one piece."

Rusty wasn't sure how much time had passed. He stood looking out to the west. It wouldn't take long for their clothes to dry, in this wind. Whitecaps stretched as far as he could see. Adriel moved up beside him.

"Rough out there," Rusty remarked.

"The water tiger be riled today," Adriel replied.

"The what? Oh—that's right." The native people believed that a monster lay beneath the waves, in this case a huge cat or water tiger, and at a moment's notice it could become angry enough to destroy ships. Rusty shrugged. "Well, I don't reckon we should rile it any further."

Charley was looking too, squinting into the sun as his eyes swept the horizon. "Like as not, we'd wreck 'er for sure if we tried to tow her back now."

The three of them stood silent, and Rusty suspected they were all thinking of Turah and the overturned canoe. Rusty spoke first.

"They say it's an easy death, drowning is."

"Well, we're not gonna risk it," Charley replied. "Adriel, let's break out the victuals."

They sat on overturned logs just out of the wind, eating crackers and dried whitefish. Charley talked about refitting the skiff. "I reckon with a new mast and sail, she'll do just fine. Any longer where she was, and she'd be dashed to pieces. Why, if we stay on Beaver, I wouldn't mind keeping 'er myself."

Darkness settled around them. They made the boats fast to trees on shore. Charley brought Ojibwe blankets from the hold of their boat, then instructed Rusty to sleep in the rescued boat.

"You'll be protected from the wind and such."

Charley and Adriel bedded down in their own boat. Rusty dozed off to the sound of waves slapping on the hull, and the memory of his young son Paul. *What would Paul look like in five or six years? Would his hair be red, or dark like Marie's? Would he love the water and the north country the way Rusty did?* Images played in his brain…*teaching an older Paul to fish, to sail a boat.* Then the sound of the waves washed everything away, and he slept.

⬥⬥⬥

Just before candlelight, a furious knocking on the door. Gabriel, with Jacob in his arms, rose from the table to answer it. But Calvin got there first.

"Be careful," Sarah whispered.

Calvin pulled back the bolt and opened the door. From where he stood, Gabriel saw one man with a torch, and others crowding behind him. The man raised the torch, and his eyes looked wild in the light. *Too much whiskey,* Gabriel was thinking. *Not one of our people.* Then he became aware of faint cries and shouts from the area of the town, and the scent of burning wood.

"You got twenty-four hours to get out of here. Pack up and git ready. This is yer first warning."

A woman screamed, close at hand. *Jess,* Gabriel thought. *Or Marie. Both with babies.* He felt a sickness in the pit of his stomach.

Calvin stood, looking pale. Gabriel stepped forward. "We be packing."

"See that you do."

Sarah opened her mouth. Gabriel silenced her with a look, a shake of his head. Someone in the crowd yelled, "We gonna burn this place or not?"

The man with the torch gave a shrug. "Let 'em be. Jest some old folks and a kid, is all. And they're not fightin' us." He nodded, and the crowd moved on.

Calvin closed the door and started to bolt it.

"Don't lock it all the way," Gabriel said, when he could finally speak. "We may have to leave in a hurry."

Sarah found her voice. "Why, those low-down—why didn't you let me tell them what I think of them?"

Gabriel handed Jacob to her. "He's almost ready for bed. Now, listen. I don't know what's going on—*eh bien*, I'm afraid I do. We want to get away safely. Try not to antagonize them."

"What do we do?" Calvin was breathing fast.

"For you, just sit and relax for a spell. If you have anything that isn't packed, finish packing it. I'm going to see if Marie and the others are all right."

"You want a torch?" Calvin gestured toward the hearth.

"No. I intend to be invisible. Now, when I return, I'll give three knocks. Then you can open the door for me."

"But—" Calvin waved his hands in a despairing gesture.

"*Au revoir.*" Gabriel opened the door and slipped out. He heard the wooden *thunk* as it closed behind him.

In the space between the houses, the wind hits him. Gusts shaking the trees. Hard to hear above the sound of the wind. Maybe he has imagined the noises from the harbor area. But as he reaches Marie's door, he hears them again. A faint scream, and rough laughter. He knocks, a little five-knock pattern they'd devised from their childhood. Immediately she opens the door. A lone candle burns on the kitchen table.

"Oh, Gabriel. They were just here—these strangers—"

"I know." He puts his arms around her. "Just—just try to stay calm. The children asleep?"

"Louise is right here. Paul is sleeping."

"And where's Rusty? Not out somewhere, I hope."

She gives a little intake of breath. Her eyes fill with tears. "He went with Charley and Adriel—something about rescuing a boat on Gull Island."

"Oh, great." *Of all the—* He tries not to betray his uneasiness. "*Eh bien*. With this wind, they be slow getting back, I reckon."

Marie begins to cry. He gives her a little shake. "Now, stop that.

We have to keep our heads. Do you want to come over and stay with us—you and Louise, and the baby?"

She looks at him, wide-eyed. "Oh, no. If we're not here, Rusty won't know where we are."

"All right, then. Bar your door. Don't let anyone in but him." He glances around. "I see your trunk's ready to go. Calvin will help Rusty carry it down in the morning. Tell Rusty I'll need his help with the animals. I've got their feed, and the wagon and carriage all ready. We'll just take everything down to the harbor with the first light."

Marie looks hesitant. He gives her a little shove. "This be one of the adventures we talked about when we were little. *Souviens-toi?*"

"Some adventure."

He hugs her one last time. "I have to see if Eb and Jess are all right."

"Do you need a light?"

"No."

The door swings shut behind him. *Curse Rusty—why would he do such a stupid thing? Now, of all times. Bad enough to have Eb and Jess still grieving over the loss of Turah.* Eb has been very little help packing up the blacksmith tools. Fortunately, with Calvin's help, most of them are packed in wooden crates, ready to be carried down.

Lights, down at the end of the row of houses. Torches. Gabriel freezes. He waits, then slips into the shadows. Moving silently now, the way he did when he used to rescue escaped slaves coming across the Ohio River. He reaches Eb's cabin. No light inside. He stands for a moment, resting his hand on one of the logs. Then he moves to the large pine door and raps.

No answer. Strange, that they should sleep through all the commotion. Maybe the torch-bearers simply passed them by. Should he let them sleep? He draws in his breath, then knocks again. No noise from inside the house.

Waiting. On impulse he tries the door. It opens.

"Eb? Jess?" He hurries from room to room. Now he wishes he'd brought a light. He feels in the bed. Nothing. Cinda's cradle is empty.

He stands just inside the front door, wondering what to do. Where would they go? Inland, most likely—maybe up by the stables. He thinks of walking up there. Risky, in the dark. Besides, if he runs into trouble or is taken by the mob, there will be no one to help the family he has here. Then he decides. He will stay with them—Calvin and Sarah, with Jacob. Marie and her children. If Eb and his family are in the stables, he will find them at first light.

He hurries back to the frame house and gives three knocks on the door. Calvin opens it. Gabriel tries to keep his voice steady.

"Marie and her children are waiting for Rusty."

Calvin shakes his head. "He's not there?"

"He's out somewhere with Charley and Adriel. Rescuing another boat."

Sarah begins to sob. Gabriel puts a hand on her arm. "Now, stop that. You want to get Jacob all upset? We have to be strong, for the sake of the young ones. And I reckon Rusty'll turn up—he always does."

"But—but—"

Gabriel looks at her. "The best thing we can do right now is get some sleep. Soon as it's light, we'll get our belongings down to the harbor."

Up at first light. Leaving Sarah to dress and feed Jacob, who is still asleep. After a brief breakfast, Gabriel and Calvin prepare to carry the trunk and the two wooden crates, full of tools from the shop, down to the harbor. Gabriel gives last minute instructions to Sarah.

"Don't forget your knapsack. Put some clothes in it for the baby, and some food. Who knows when we'll eat again."

Gabriel has seen that all of them have knapsacks. He and Calvin are both wearing theirs. Sarah says, "Most of the clothes be in the trunk."

"Keep a few with you," Gabriel tells her. "And be prepared to leave the house and get down to the harbor."

They knock on Marie's door. She opens it, her face tear-streaked. Gabriel looks at her.

"Rusty never showed?" It is an observation, more than a question.

She rubs her eyes. "Oh, Gabriel. What do we do?"

"Well, I reckon we do anything they say. Get dressed, get ready. Louise? Help your mother. Pack those knapsacks and get over to the big house."

"But, what—"

"*Now!* Don't argue. Go stay with Sarah till we get back. We'll come fetch yer trunk. If they tell you to get to the harbor, do it! We're going to get the animals ready."

Gabriel and Calvin carry the trunk and tool boxes down to the dock. "Here's a likely place," Gabriel remarks. There is very little activity on the beach. In the dim light, Gabriel cannot see any sign of a large ship.

"I don't see no boat," Calvin says.

"I reckon she's out in the mist, just off shore. Let's fetch the livestock."

Feeding the horses and oxen. A measure of oats for each horse, fresh straw for the oxen. As they are harnessing the animals, Gabriel realizes that Eb and his family are not in the stables.

"I'm wondering where Eb and them are."

"Can't stop to look fer 'em now," Calvin muttered.

Gabriel hitches up Jeb and Jenny to the carriage, packed with saddles, riding gear, and sacks of oats. Freedom is tied to the back of the carriage. Just behind them, the two oxen pull the wagon, with Calvin in the driver's seat. They make their way down to the water front, and Gabriel puts the trunk and tools in the wagon.

All around them now are other piles of goods, trunks, bedding, farm implements. Other men are bringing what belongings they have, and placing them where they can be loaded on the ship.

"It beats me how they're gonna get all this on one ship," Calvin says.

"We're one of the first, so I reckon we'll get on." Gabriel runs his eyes over the harbor. A little wind is ruffling the lake surface, sending wavelets shoreward. If they have to leave, it is not the worst day for a voyage. Smaller boats are coming in. Maybe Rusty is in one of them, with Charley and Adriel. No—they would be towing a second boat, the rescued craft. None of the boats look familiar.

The man next to them has a cow and four sheep, all tethered together. He looks at Gabriel. "She be expecting a calf most any day now. I hate to put her through this move. But I can't just leave 'er."

The air is full of animal noises, cattle bawling, goats bleating. One woman has five geese in a wooden pen, their heads sticking out between the bars. They are squawking. Somewhere a dog barks, a high, anguished yelping. Then Gabriel sees a bunch of men tramping up from the harbor. Most are armed with rifles and pistols. A sinking feeling creeps into the pit of his stomach.

"Quick," he says to Calvin. "Go fetch the women before these scoundrels do it. We'll have to get Marie's trunk, too. I'll see to the loading of the livestock."

Calvin hurries in the direction of the cabins. More and more people are coming down to the harbor, women with babies in their arms and older children clinging to their skirts. Most of them are escorted by groups of the strangers. An older man stumbles as he reaches the foot of the dock. One of the invaders pushes the old man as he struggles to stay on his feet. "Hurry up, Grandpa. Your ship'll be here soon enough."

Gabriel itches to rush over and confront the stranger. The old man's companion, an elderly woman, takes his hand. They move out onto the dock. "Faster!" the stranger cries. "You can move quicker than that!"

Marie and Sarah, each carrying one of the babies, walk down the hill and wait side by side near the carriage. Gabriel watches as Marie's eyes sweep the crowd for a sight of Rusty. *Drat the lad. Where is he?*

Toward evening, the ship comes in. It docks at the end of McCulloch's pier.

A commotion to his left—they are telling the owner of the cow and sheep to get aboard.

"I can't," he protests. "I have to stay with my animals. My Bossy, she—"

One of the strangers, a red-haired man with a front tooth missing, gives a harsh laugh. "I got news fer you. Yer leavin' right now. Yer animals be stayin' here."

"No," he says. "They're all ready to board."

The red-haired man claps him on the side of the head. "Get up there, you blasted Mormon. Next time I'll take a rock to you."

Gabriel cannot tell if the man is crying or not. The man reaches out a hand and touches his cow on the side of her face. Then they pull him away.

Other people are being separated from their belongings and livestock. Gabriel has only seconds to realize that they must leave everything behind, even the animals and the tools. He blinks. How can he tell the others? He sees Calvin and Louise making their way down the hill with Marie's trunk.

"Where shall I put it?" Calvin asks.

"I don't reckon it matters much. In the wagon, I suppose."

"What're you talking about?"

"*Eh bien.* Just look around."

Calvin is standing, open-mouthed. Gabriel moves over beside Marie. She is crying, cradling her baby. "Rusty—" she begins.

"Where's your knapsack? Turn around."

She does. Gabriel unhooks his pouch of money and thrusts it deep into the knapsack, under diapers and whatever else is in there. "Whatever you do, don't lose it."

She says, "I don't see what—Oh, Gabriel. Rusty's not here. I—I have to wait for him."

"Rusty's not stupid. He can look after himself. You have to come with us."

Someone screams. A woman is being dragged to the gangplank by two of the strangers. She cries out, "My father! My father's in the barn!"

"Shut up and git on the boat," one of the strangers says.

"Let me go back and find him!"

The other stranger speaks. "You ain't gittin' back on this island fer nothing. Only place yer goin' is on board!"

Gabriel glances around for Eb but does not see him. Instead he sees a swarm of people, all being herded toward the ship. A smaller ship has entered the harbor and is preparing to dock.

"All right. Come on." Someone gives Gabriel a shove from behind. He tries one last time, but he senses it is futile.

"My animals—I need to board my horses and oxen."

"You ain't boardin' nothin'. Them is all stayin' behind. Understand? In fact, that's a right handsome team. Them horses. I'm takin' 'em fer myself. And the oxen, too."

Gabriel shrugs then. "Well—treat them well."

"Shut up and git moving."

Gabriel looks at Marie and motions with his head for her to follow. He begins to move forward. She hesitates, then walks just behind him to the left. She is crying, clutching little Paul to her chest, her shoulders shaking. Sarah and Louise walk beside her, Sarah carrying Jacob. Calvin has not moved fast enough; someone pushes him from behind. He stumbles, then regains his footing. He looks dazed, older than Gabriel has ever seen him. Shouts and cries echo around them, mingled with animal noises. Their footsteps make a hollow clumping on the wooden planks of the dock. They reach the gangplank.

"On you git," the red-haired man says. "Oh—and I'll just take this." He reaches over and grabs the leather strap from around Gabriel's neck. He hauls it out and looks at it. "I thought sure you had some money on it."

"No," Gabriel says. "Just a strap."

The red-haired man looks puzzled. Gabriel says, "See—it's a little clip. You just press—"

"Git on." The man gives him a shove. Then he flings the strap into the lake. Gabriel watches impassively as it sinks. He shrugs and climbs the gangplank, his family just behind him.

Another man says, "We'd better search them knapsacks."

"What fer? All we're finding is diapers and such like. Let 'em go."

There are other Mormons already on the boat, people forced on board at Aldrich's dock on the southwest side of Beaver Harbor. "Why didn't we fight?" a young man asks. "We shoulda fought."

An older man coughs. "Strang said not to. Doncha remember?"

Another man says, "And no one's armed. I reckon there ain't even fifty firearms on the island."

Marie is still crying. Paul begins to hiccup and cry too. *What to do?* Gabriel uses his most commanding voice. "All right, everybody. Over by those benches. Marie—sit down. You, too, Sarah. Louise, take Paul for a moment. Calvin, there's space for you, at the end."

Moving close to them, standing in front of them. Making eye contact with all of them. "Listen to me. It's happening, what we all feared. I can't speak for what comes next. But we have to be brave—trust in God, and all that. He will bring us to a safe place. Have courage, for the sake of these children. Now—whatever you do, Marie, don't lose that knapsack."

She gives him a confused look, then nods. He looks at Sarah. "Did you bring any food?"

Sarah frowns. "I have rolls and dried apples. Some dried whitefish."

Marie says, "I have two loaves of bread."

Gabriel smiles. "Ah—loaves and fishes. We won't starve, then. And the children will have enough, till we get to where we're going."

"Where's that?" Calvin asks.

"I aim to find out, soon's we're settled down here."

More people are coming aboard, some weeping, all carrying whatever they have managed to salvage. Gabriel moves to stand beside his family, to make room for the influx of people. A child cries out, "My puppy! I want my puppy!"

"Hush," someone tells him. "We have to leave him here."

"Why? Why can't we take him?"

"They won't let us."

This produces fresh tears from Marie. Sarah is wiping her eyes. Louise sniffs and holds Paul close to her. Paul has stopped crying and is looking around wide-eyed, as if the crowd of refugees is for his amusement.

Gabriel takes Jacob from Sarah and stands holding his son in his arms. He wonders for a brief moment what he has done to deserve the loss of his home, his crops, his tools, his wagon and carriage, and his animals. All his life he will pray for his animals, that they get better care than he fears they will receive. They are valuable—surely they will be fed and cared for, even by hard-hearted masters. He can only hope.

The people. The ones in his care. He tries not to think of Bethia, left forever on the island. Best that she never see what he is witnessing. His efforts, his strength, must be for the living. Two elderly people, one clearly dazed, two infants, a young girl, and a grief-stricken woman. He bows his head, his cheek against Jacob's, while the crowd noises surge around him.

16

THE *BUCKEYE STATE*. THE name of the ship, according to Gabriel. Marie sits huddled on the edge of the bench, Sarah beside her. She leans against Sarah. Louise is standing on the other side of Marie. The girl looks dazed as she holds Paul, who is mercifully asleep. Marie wonders how anyone can sleep through the noises—women crying, children shrieking. A man's voice: "Shut up and git movin'! You ain't goin' nowhere 'cept on board."

"Blasted Mormons," someone else growls. "I reckon we be seein' the last of 'em."

"Naw. There's others left."

Gabriel has gone to search the ship for Rusty and Eb, and any of the others he can find.

"They're casting off," Calvin remarks. The ship lurches. There is the sound of heavy lines, massed together, falling on a wood surface. The smell of something burning hovers in the air.

"They be burning houses," Calvin says in answer to her look. "Just as well we're here and not there."

"If they're burning houses, where will they live?" Louise rocks Paul in her arms. "They took everything we had—I figured they was gonna use the houses for themselves."

Calvin pauses. "Well, I reckon—"

"It's the prophet's house they be burning," Sarah declares.

Calvin nods. "I reckon you're right." He moved to the rail, then returned. "The smoke be comin' from there. The print shop and the tabernacle are all on fire."

From a state of utter shock, Marie feels new uncertainties rising like flotsam to the surface of her mind. *Rusty is gone. Lost…waylaid. Maybe even dead. Whatever it is, her husband is no longer with her. And everything she owns is gone—her clothes, bits of jewelry, her dishes and cooking pots. All she has now are her children, her husband's parents, and her brother Gabriel. Her favorite brother. And her nephew, little Jacob.* Beside her, Louise lifts Paul to one shoulder.

"He's waking up. Oh, *maman*—do you think Uncle Gabriel will come back with J. J.?"

Marie sighs. "I don't know. I'm hoping for more than just J. J."

"*Mais oui.* The others, too. I mean, there're lots of people on the ship."

Marie raises her head. Somehow, the statement gives her hope. Of course—Gabriel will appear with Rusty, and Eb's whole family. For a moment she wonders why she felt downcast at all. "Paul must be hungry. I have some pieces of apple for him." She rummages in the knapsack. "What's this? Oh—here are the apples."

She holds a tiny piece up for Paul. He grasps it in his hand and it goes immediately to his mouth. "Here—let me take him."

Louise hands the baby to her. Marie is calm enough now to marvel at his intense blue eyes, as she has done many times. And the chestnut hair—like his father's. She settles him in her lap and gives him another piece of apple. A shadow falls over her. She looks up.

Gabriel stands there, alone except for Jacob riding astride his neck. The boy's chubby fingers are buried deep in Gabriel's hair.

"No Rusty." Her voice is a statement rather than a question.

"I couldn't find him. Or Eb and his family. No Charley, no Adriel."

"No J. J.," Louise says.

Through a numbed haze, Marie hears the other things Gabriel is saying. How Wingfield Watson, one of the last to board, was forced to carry his newborn daughter for almost six miles while his wife stumbled beside him. How the islanders had been overcome by six squads of men, strangers from all over that part of Michigan. "Mackinac. And Grand Traverse. And even beyond that."

According to his words, they had landed on remote parts of the island and stayed hidden until their reinforcements were complete. He waves his hands. "Then they struck. One of the last on board said they were torching the businesses, the little shops. He says—well—" Gabriel pauses, then continues. "They were shooting Brother Strang's prize chickens, just for sport. And they took out all the books in his library and—and trampled them in the mud."

Silence after that. Louise gives a sniff. Marie thinks of the books they have borrowed from that library, books that Turah and Rusty have read with eagerness and delight. She wants to weep then, but she does not know why. *Weep over books when people are missing.*

"Bunch of ignorant scoundrels," Calvin remarks.

"*Eh bien.* They may be ignorant, but I reckon they've done us in."

The boat is midway down the island now, heading to the south. Calvin shakes his head. "You know where we might be heading?"

Gabriel shrugs. "From what I can gather, it's Chicago. We'll find out right soon enough."

Sarah, huddled against Marie, gives a little cry. "Oh, what's to become of us?"

Gabriel strides over to stand beside Marie. He stoops down in front of Marie and Sarah. "Now, listen. Both of you. You too, Louise. We don't know what's going to happen. But we're together, and we're still alive. This is where faith comes in. Try to be of good cheer. For the sake of the children."

Sarah sniffs and nods. Marie wipes the tears from her cheeks and looks at him. He waits, then speaks again. "Let's have some of that apple for Jacob, here. Then we'll think what else to do."

Early afternoon. A brisk wind blew from the west, and they sailed in a broad reach to the south of High Island.

"Tighten 'er a bit more," Charley said. "The wind's changing."

Adriel pulled on the sheet. Rusty, in charge of managing the boat under tow, tightened his grip on the tow line. Even though the end was made fast to the stern, he had no intention of losing their prize.

"Too bad one of us couldn't sail 'er home," Adriel remarked.

"Not with that rudder like it is," Charley replied. "How's she doin'?"

Rusty turned to answer, and that's when he saw it. A plume of black smoke over St. James harbor.

"Look!" He pointed. The others peered around the edge of the sail.

"I'll be blamed," Charley muttered. He squinted in the bright sunlight.

"What d'you reckon is up?" Adriel asked.

"Beats me." Charley was frowning, chewing his lower lip. "Nothin' good."

The plume hovered, unmistakable now. And there were other, smaller pillars of smoke. Rusty felt a flutter of fear in his chest. "We'd better hurry."

Charley shook his head. "Well, hold on, now. We can't go much faster. Not with a boat under tow. And we'd best be careful 'afore we know what's afoot."

As they got closer to the island, they could see the burned-out shops, the smoke where the nearest settlement had been. The walls of the blacksmith shop gone. Beyond that, up on the little hill, the houses burnt. *His house. His family.* Rusty felt an insane urge to jump overboard and swim to shore.

"Wait, son." Charley put a hand on his arm. "Let's beach the boats a little further down. Near the tabernacle. We won't go into the harbor."

"Somethin's sure wrong," Adriel said. "Look—the tabernacle be burnt."

Charley blinked. "I'll be dad-blamed." He paused, then shook his head. When he spoke, his voice was low. "Here's what we'll do. We'll head in right for that stretch of sand. Right there—south of the bluff. See it?"

"If we c'n miss the rocks," Adriel said.

"We'll miss 'em." He maneuvered the boat closer to the shoreline.

"Keep yer eye on our other boat, there." The process of landing took only a few moments, but to Rusty it seemed like hours.

"Drop the sail," Charley said to Adriel. Adriel did so. "Now, go overboard."

Adriel secured the sail and jumped into the water. "I c'n touch bottom."

"Good. Now, take us in. Let's get the centerboard up. And you—" He looked at Rusty. "Secure the other boat."

Rusty splashed into the lake, feeling the cold water swirling up around him. He untied the line to the other boat. Then he pulled the rescued craft to shore, following Adriel as he hauled their own boat. They beached the boats side by side on the strip of sand.

"Now." Rusty turned to run up toward the cabins.

"Wait!" Charley said. Rusty looked at him. Charley's eyes were sweeping the hillside, the bluff where the ruins of the tabernacle stood. "Take great care, son. Stay in the woods, if you can. Till you know what's happenin'. Stay—"

Rusty raced up the hill without waiting to hear any more. Running. Stumbling, dislodging loose stones. He heard them falling onto the rocks below. Dodging trees, tree roots, veering around boulders. Winded already. Panting. *Stay in the woods.* Charley was crazy. He'd never get to his cabin, at that rate.

Bounding up the little path, pounding on the front door. No response. He pushed frantically at the door. It opened. Rushing from room to room, calling for Marie and Louise. Nothing.

He stood in the main room, his chest heaving. *Think,* he told himself. The trunk was no longer there. Somehow they'd left. Some bedding was missing, packed in the trunk. Most of the baby's things were gone. He stood blinking in the glare from the open door. A strange odor, like something burning. Not the smell of fresh bread and soup simmering, or even the comforting scent of horses. *Animals.* Of course. He would go see if anyone were in the stables. But first he would run over to the frame house where his father lived with Sarah, and Gabriel had his room with Jacob.

He stepped out into the front garden. Along the fence, scarlet bean vines fluttered in the breeze. He thought how Marie had tended and cared for them. He stopped, struck with such pain that he didn't think he could walk any further. *Where was she now? What if he searched the frame house and she wasn't there? How could he find her again?*

He glanced around. To all appearances, the little community lay deserted. The acrid smell of smoke hovered everywhere. He hurried through the gate and up the path to the frame house. The door gaped open. Once inside, he rushed from room to room, calling out their names in turn. The sounds had a hollow, echoing quality. No one answered.

"Marie!" he cried for the last time. An answer came from the keeping room. But it was not her voice.

"She ain't here, son."

A gruff, raspy voice, one he'd never heard before. He took a few steps toward the sound, then stopped. Too late for caution. The owner of the voice appeared in the doorway. A short, stocky man, dark haired, bald on top, looking amused but not sympathetic.

"She ain't here, and none of them others yer yammerin' about."

Rusty found his voice. "They're not—"

"Them are all gone. This be my house now. Everything in it's mine. So what're you doin' in my house?"

Dumfounded. "*Your* house?"

The man looked him in the eye. "That's right. That's how it is."

"Is that so?" Rusty felt his courage returning; he knew he was a lot brawnier than this stranger. "That's a laugh. Because, you see, I helped build it. Every stick of it."

The man shrugged. "Well, I reckon you done a good job. Fine piece of work. I'm gonna like livin' here."

Rusty drew in his breath. "Where are the people that lived here?"

The man looked at him, then smiled. It was the nastiest smile Rusty had even seen—more like a sneer. "Well, now, son. If they was Mormons, they all decided to leave. Real sudden, like. The climate jest dint agree with them no more."

Rusty took a step forward. He tried to keep his voice steady. "What have you scummy varmints done with my family?"

The man raised his eyebrows, sneering. *Wipe that smile off his face.* Rusty lunged at him. His fist slammed into the man's jaw. The man staggered; he managed to give a whistle. "Get 'em, boys!"

A noise behind him. Before he could turn, Rusty felt an arm encircling his neck in a hammer lock. A rough hand grabbed his shoulder. He kicked and threw himself forward. His adversary hit the floor in front of him, crashing into the man with the sneer.

Rusty turned to run, but a third man grabbed him. In an instant the other two sprang up and circled him. The first man raised his hand. Rusty felt the blow even before he saw the punch coming. One to the right side of his face. Another to the nose. Amid the pain, he felt the blood trickling down his face. The second man cuffed him over his left ear. He struggled, kicking out at them. He got one of them in the groin area. The man doubled up in pain. *Touché,* Rusty thought.

Finally they subdued him. One of them pinned his arms to his sides and grabbed both his wrists behind his back in a vice-like grip.

"Now." The first man stood panting. "Yer goin' with us peaceful-like, or we'll break yer neck."

"Just tell me where my family is," Rusty demanded.

The second one, whom Rusty had propelled onto the floor, gave a cough. "How do we know where yer family is?"

"They went on a nice, long cruise," the third one said. "And that's where yer goin'."

"Any more noise, and like as not, you'll go someplace else." The sneering one raised his hand again.

"Don't hit him no more," the third one declared. "We don't wanna have to carry him. That's work."

They marched him down toward the harbor. He felt dazed, but he managed to walk. Whitish mist floated in front of his eyes; he had trouble making out the objects in the harbor. The usual boats and canoes, he figured. He stumbled once. They yanked him to his feet. He became aware of a sharp pain in his right knee. He hoped the leg would support him till they got where they were going.

Boards underfoot. The McCullochs' pier. Trouble seeing now. He heard the sound of their feet on the wooden boards. Something in front of him—a huge, towering shape.

"Up you go, son." They pushed him up an incline. Then he was shoved into some dark place—it felt like a corner. He heard their footsteps going away.

"That one's a fighter," one of them declared. "Most of 'em—they won't lift a hand to defend themselves. Their prophet said not to fight."

A darkness settled over him; he felt his mind blacking out. The next thing he knew, someone was touching his shoulder.

Were they going to hit him again? His eyes flew open. Eb's face, full of concern, filled his field of vision.

"Eb. I sure be glad to see you."

"Hush. Don't talk none. Jess be gone for some water. Then we can clean you up some."

J. J. knelt beside his father, his eyes wide. Eb said, "They really roughed you up."

"You know where Marie is? Or Gabe?"

"Son, we ain't seen 'em. We stayed in the blacksmith shop, thinkin' we be safe there. When they started burning shops, we left. Then they got us and brought us here."

"Where's 'here?'"

"We on a ship, goin' somewhere. Away from the island, is all I know."

Jess came in with a tiny bowl of water. Rusty recognized it as one of the bowls they used for Cinda. "Where's Cinda?" he asked.

"Right here." Jess spoke in a soft, reassuring tone. "She ain't goin' nowhere. And neither are you." She dipped a cloth in the water and began dabbing at his face.

"We be casting off!" someone yelled. Rusty looked around. They were on the deck of a boat, against the wall of the cabin. *Another noise.* Two more men were being hustled up the gangplank by a crowd of the strangers. Rusty squinted in the glare of sunlight. Then he recognized Charley and Adriel.

He started to call to them, but they hurried over immediately.

"Well, look at you." Charley shook his head. "Told you to keep to the woods."

Rusty blinked. "I thought sure you'd get away."

Charley grunted. "They got us when we tried to sneak into our cabin."

"The others are all gone," Rusty said.

Charley nodded. "I reckon so. From what I can see, there's no one left. If you promise to rest, I'll go see if they be on the ship."

"Oh, would you? *Merci.*"

"We be away from the dock, now," Eb said. "We can rest easy."

Rusty looked at him. "What do you mean?"

"A bad thing happened when they found us. One of 'em said, 'I didn't know Mormons had slaves.' And when we said we warn't slaves, they said that maybe they should turn us in as fugitives. That really scared us."

Rusty sighed. "Those scummy varmints."

"We be safe now." Jess washed the blood from the side of his nose. "Jest be quiet, and let us help you."

Rusty, in his state of shock and numbness, willingly submitted to her ministrations. At least he had Eb and his family, and Charley and Adriel. And, like as not, the others were somewhere on the boat. Charley would find them. "I sure do thank you," he murmured.

When Charley returned, he was alone. At first Rusty couldn't believe it. "Why couldn't you find them?"

"Now, don't get yer shirt in a knot. I reckon they be on another boat, is all."

"Another boat?"

Charley gestured, a shrug with his hands spread out. "Well, where else would they be? They sure as heck aren't on the island."

"What boat are we on?" Adriel asked.

"This be a prop boat—I think they said the *Louisville.*"

"Any idea where it's headed?" Rusty asked.

"Well, we be goin' north now, toward Mackinac. I reckon we be goin' to Detroit."

Detroit. Rusty leaned back against the cabin wall and closed his eyes. A dull, sick feeling settled in his stomach. *Would he ever see Marie and the children again?*

"We in this together." Eb's voice. "Don't fret so."

<hr/>

Gabriel sits leaning against the wooden bench, his legs stretched out. He has not slept all night. Jacob is sprawled on the floor with his head on Gabriel's knees. Cradled in his arms, Paul sleeps, thumb in his mouth.

On the bench, Marie is leaning back, her head against the cabin wall. Louise has her head on her mother's lap. Both sleeping now. At the other end of the bench, Sarah is silent, deep in sleep. Calvin sits on the floor beside her. Gabriel worries about them—so old, to be treated this way. Worried about Marie, too. And the children. Here he is, charged with the care of two infants, a mother, a ten-year-old girl, and an elderly couple. Staring out into space, wondering how best to protect them.

Dawn is breaking. The gray water stretches before him, little wavelets rippling the surface. In the group just ahead of him, a woman is sitting up coughing and coughing. If she were his patient, he would tell her to lie down and get some rest. And stay warm. But with what? She didn't bring a coat, and she has no blanket. Gabriel sighs and looks at the horizon.

They are running parallel to a shore now. The Wisconsin shore, most like. A small settlement, there on the bank, a long pier jutting out into the water. He watches as the pier gets closer. Shouts from somewhere. Preparations for a landing.

His family is beginning to stir. The group on the deck ahead of them is already awake. Voices drift to him, one of the men saying, "This boat is overloaded. There be 330 of us on board—I heard 'em say."

A gentler voice, a woman: "Good thing we be safely across."

"I also heard that McCulloch paid for the whole trip. Gettin' us off the island and onto the boat."

"The passage, you mean."

"Yeah. Ain't that a rip? Ol' Hezekiah hisself. And he gets to stay on the island."

Gabriel shakes his head. *Life isn't fair. When you expect it to be fair, you run into trouble.* He watches as the boat docks. The gangplank goes down.

"They be lettin' folks off," Louise says.

Gabriel speaks then. "Don't get off till they put us off. And whatever you do, stay together."

The members of his group listen in silence. The people ahead of them are talking again.

"They went through my knapsack. They took my mother's silver necklace."

"They made us leave anything of value."

Gabriel looks at Marie. "They didn't search your backpack."

She gives him a weak little smile. "I reckon they figured it was nothing but diapers."

He nods. "Just keep it close to you. I got plans."

She sighs. "Oh, what'll we feed the babies? There's no milk."

"You still got apples, don't you?"

"Yes, and cheese. And bread."

Gabriel shrugs. "We got enough. For the moment."

Voices ahead of them. "Somebody said 'Green Bay.'"

"Let's get off."

Louise starts to get up.

"Stay put," Gabriel tells her. She looks at her mother and sits down again. They wait while a large number of people leave the boat. Finally the boat pulls away; Gabriel sees them on the dock, huddled together in little groups.

"Oh, what's to become of us?" Sarah asks.

Gabriel gives a little sigh of exasperation. "Don't lose hope. Just wait. And don't leave the group. 'Specially when they're puttin' folks off the boat."

Over open water, he lets them move around a bit and refresh themselves. The next stop: Milwaukee. An even larger group leaves the boat. Gabriel looks at them on the dock. Women with their dresses in tatters, some still wearing the bloomer outfit, children barefoot. Nothing but the clothes on their backs. He feels a sudden, overwhelming pity for them all. Where was God in all this? Words escape him: "Where is God?"

"Right there," Marie says.

"What?"

"God is right there with those people. Suffering along with them. And with all of us. Don't you feel it?"

He has to admit he doesn't. But he takes Marie's hand and squeezes it.

As they approach the next stop, a crowd of people move out on the dock. Their voices fill the air. "Go away! No Mormons here!"

"We don't want the likes of you!"

Shoguns glisten in the sun. To Gabriel's relief, the ship pulls away. "Well, I reckon we ain't landing there," Calvin remarks.

At Racine, people prepare to disembark. This time there is no welcoming committee on the dock, only one lone man, who climbs aboard when the gangplank is in place. Gabriel recognizes him as Benjamin Wright's son—he can't recall the first name. The man speaks to the people gathered near the gangplank.

A wail rises from the people in front. Gabriel wants to get up, but he has two sleeping children on his lap. "What is it?" he calls to the group ahead. "What's happened?"

One of the men turns. "It's Brother Strang. The prophet. Died early this morning."

Strang dead. By this time, everyone is wailing. Marie, Louise, and Sarah stare open-mouthed, numb with shock. Calvin fishes in his pocket for a handkerchief. *Keep your head*, Gabriel tells himself. But he is breathing fast; he feels faint. *For the sake of the children.*

He takes a deep breath and tries to remain calm. A group of people follow Brother Wright off the boat, stumbling, their eyes red.

Calvin's voice is husky. "This be the closest to Voree. Aren't we getting off?"

Gabriel tries to keep his voice steady. "We're not going to Voree."

Calvin seems to accept this; he shrugs and leans back.

The little boys are awake. Gabriel and Marie feed them apple pieces and bits of bread. Marie looks at him. "What happens when we run out? There's enough for one more meal."

He gave a little cough. "Let me worry about that."

"Well, you can deal with the crying, then."

Jacob wants to walk. Gabriel holds his hand and they walk up and down the deck.

"It be gettin' hot," Sarah says. "That sun is fierce."

The ship approaches a long pier, backs up, then churns forward. Finally it docks. The sailors throw lines to men on the pier.

"Chicago!" someone shouts. "Everyone out!"

The gangplank is lowered. Gabriel picks Jacob up. "All right, folks. Everyone stay together."

They file out with the rest of the passengers, all refugees from Beaver Island. Gabriel estimates there are at least a hundred people who descend the gangplank and stand on the pier looking dazed in the hot sun. Gabriel gathers his little group around him. Some women are fanning themselves. One, red in the face, sits down on the edge of the dock.

Then Gabriel notices the strangers, other people staring at the bedraggled group of Mormons. Someone in the crowd of onlookers begins to laugh. The laughter ripples through the crowd.

"Pay them no mind," Gabriel tells his group. "And stay right with me. Marie, where's your knapsack?"

She shows him the strap, and he nods.

"Oh, I'm so hot," Sarah declares. "I'm like to faint." One of the babies starts to cry.

"There's a large building at the foot of the pier," Gabriel tells them. "Let's make our way toward the shade. And keep together."

Walking unsteadily, stumbling a little, they follow him. The going is slow; there are people in the way, strangers eyeing them. Suddenly an older man, bald with a long nose and receding chin, bursts out of the crowd.

"You blasted sons of varmints! Yer worse than varmints! You oughta be ashamed of yourselves! Makin' these poor folks wait in the hot sun while you make fun of them. Women, and—and little children. Here!" He strides over and shoves apart the doors on the large building. Some sort of warehouse, Gabriel surmises. The man speaks again.

"Here, ladies and gentlemen. Come in here out of the sun, and stay until you find places."

"The first kind words we've heard," Calvin remarks.

Soon they are inside, out of the sun. Sarah sinks down on the floor and begins to weep.

"Now, now, my dear," Calvin says. "Bear up a little longer."

Gabriel gathers his family and draws them into a corner. "Stay here for just a moment. Don't leave till I get back."

He hurries out and finds the man who has opened up the warehouse for them. "Excuse me, sir."

The man turns, annoyance in his face. Gabriel tries to sound authoritative. "You know where I can hire a horse and wagon, and a driver?"

The man hesitates. Gabriel goes on. "I have some people who are feeling poorly. Two babies, a child, an older couple. A young mother." *Not sick now, but they will be if I don't get them some help soon.*

The man's features soften. "There be a livery stable three blocks down. That's all I can suggest."

Three blocks. Even Sarah can walk that far. "Thank you, sir. I'm much obliged."

He fetches the members of his group. "Marie, give me your knapsack. We're walking down this way—three blocks. Calvin, you take Paul. I'll carry Jacob. Come on, Louise. Marie, you help Sarah."

"I don't need no help," Sarah retorts.

"Fine. Show me. This way."

They follow him outside, blinking in the sunlight. Sarah stumbles, then regains her footing. Stooping, Gabriel lifts Jacob and sets the boy astride his neck. Jacob likes this; he laughs and grabs his father's mop of hair. Gabriel straightens up. "Come on. It's not far."

Calvin walks beside him. "What are you aimin' to do?"

"Hire a rig and a driver. We're headin' as far west as he'll take us."

"To the Mississippi?"

Gabriel nods. "Then we find a steamboat."

"Goin' south. That's what I figured. Only—" Calvin gives a sigh. "I hope Rusty knows what we're about."

"He will, if he has any sense. 'Course, it may take him some time."

17

SWIRLS OF MIST. DARKNESS enveloping him. Through waves of pain Rusty struggles to wake up. His nose and the right side of his face feel swollen. He isn't sure if he can even speak. His left ear aches, and his right knee twinges as he moves it.

Eb sits beside him. "My, my. They sure did work you over. Yes, sir. You jest rest up, now."

"They be puttin' some folks off the boat." Jess holds Cinda close to her. "Jest leavin' them off, without nothing to eat, no place to go."

"If they put us off, we stay together," Charley says.

Adriel nods in agreement. "We be good workers. We'll work choppin' wood and such like. Pretty soon we can buy us all some food."

Rusty feels the greater pain rising to the surface of his mind— the loss of Marie and their children. Not to mention his father and stepmother. Like a large piece of himself being ripped away, leaving the rest of him wounded and aching. He tries to concentrate on what Eb is saying.

"Rusty, can you tell us how you feel?"

How could he possibly tell anyone how he felt? He shakes his head. Not familiar with this magnitude of loss, he wonders if it would go on and on. Was there a grief so deep that you didn't recover?

The boat is turning. A little breeze fans their faces and ruffles the edges of their clothing. A voice rings out. "Detroit! Everyone off!"

As they dock, Charley and Adriel help Rusty get to his feet. Charley holds his arm. "Steady, now. Soon's we're off the boat, I'll make you a cane. I still have my knife—they didn't take it."

Eb and his family walk down the gangplank, followed by Rusty with Charley and Adriel supporting him. The man securing one of the lines gives them a brief, disgusted look. As they pass, Rusty hears the words. "Blasted Mormons. Let's get the rest of 'em off the ship."

"It might be well," Charley begins, "if we didn't tell anyone we was Mormon. Or that we was on the island."

"Fine with me," Eb answers. "I ain't sayin' nothin' to nobody."

They try to hurry off the pier to make room for the others. At the foot of the pier, the refugees huddle in little groups. Rusty knows he is not going to be able to walk very far. *What do they do now?*

"Let's get out of the sun, at least," Charley says.

"Cinda be cryin' pretty soon if she don't get somethin' to eat."

"Don't you have some bread?" Eb asks. "Feed her some of that."

"She done ate it all."

"I have some," J. J. says. "I be savin' it. Here."

"There's a good boy," Jess tells him. "Little sister needs it. We'll get somethin' fer us right soon."

But where? They begin to walk along the shore. "We'll do better away from the city, most like," Charley remarks. "We need to find a farm where we c'n work for food."

Rusty feels his leg giving way. "Hold up a second. I have to rest."

Waiting. His friends looking at him with sorrow and concern. *Try,* he tells himself.

Nodding at last. "Let's go."

Ahead of them, a small crowd of people. Two men leaving the crowd and walking toward them. One, a white man who looked to be in his forties, dressed plainly in homespun. He had an upturned nose and blue eyes under blond, bushy eyebrows. He wore a hat like the Quakers wore, dark and wide-brimmed. The second man, young, of African descent—either a freedman or an escaped slave.

"There be one of us," Jess said in a low voice.

"My friends," the white man said. "We know about Beaver Island, and some of what's happened up there."

"You do?" Eb sounded surprised.

"We stand ready to help, and to take thee to a place of safety."

"I'll drink to that," Charley said.

The man looked startled. Eb spoke quickly. "These three are our friends. Where we go, they go."

The man nodded. "I am John Bestertag, and this be Lemuel. We happened to be selling some wood, and we saw the commotion at the wharf. I always keep a lookout for folks who might need help, 'specially people of color. And thee—" he glanced at Jess and Cinda, then at Rusty. "I reckon thee could use some."

"I reckon yer right," Adriel said.

"Lemuel's going to fetch the wagon. We'll wait here—it's not far off."

"I sure do thank you," Eb said. "I'm much beholden. I was wonderin' what we was gonna do."

"Well, we'll do what we can. I reckon thy friend here," —he indicated Rusty— "could use some rest, and time to heal."

"They did rough him up a little," Eb replied.

"Rough him up! I'd say he'd been beaten within an inch of his life. He can hardly walk." He addressed Rusty. "And thee didn't fight back?"

"There was three of them, as far as I can figure," Eb said. "Warn't much he could do—none of us had weapons."

By the time Lemuel arrived with the team of horses and the wagon, they had introduced themselves and were talking freely, except for Rusty who could only nod and mumble. John Bestertag was indeed a Quaker, as they had guessed.

"We have a little settlement, about fifteen miles west of here. A group of folks working the land, taking care of peach and apple trees, and corn. Other vegetables, too. There'll be food waiting when we get there, and a place to rest."

They passed a large farmhouse which had once been painted white. Now its clapboard exterior was faded and cracked. John Bestertag glanced at it and shrugged. "We don't want to call too much attention to it."

"It puts me in mind of stops on the Underground Railroad," Eb remarked.

"Thou sayest," John Bestertag replied.

Rusty found his voice. "You mean it really *is* a stop on the Underground Railroad?"

"Not so loud, son. It's a place of safety. We're about fifteen miles from the Canadian border, and we've helped lots of folks get across. But some have decided they'd stay for a spell and work the land—grow their own produce. Rest up a bit. And that's what Shadrach's Hollow's all about."

Eb grunted. "Shadrach's Hollow, huh?"

"That's right. We're almost there."

Just over the next hill, half-hidden behind thick underbrush, lay a cluster of small cabins; they looked similar to the ones Rusty had helped to build in Voree. Among them stood a larger building, like a meetinghouse. As he gazed at it, he was aware of John Bestertag watching him.

"That's where we'll go first," Mr. Bestertag said. "It's the main kitchen, with tables for eating."

They climbed out of the wagon, and Lemuel led the horses and wagon away. In a short time they were sitting at one of the tables, with vegetable stew and warm cornbread in front of them. In Rusty's opinion, nothing had ever tasted so good.

"There's fresh milk for the children. Have some cider." Mr. Bestertag set a jug and a tray of ceramic mugs on the table. Lemuel came in to join them. Charley and Eb told the story of their forced exodus from Beaver Island. Eb poured more cider in his mug.

"And Rusty here be missin' his wife and children. Most like, they put 'em on another boat."

John Bestertag looked horrified. "That's—that's unspeakable! That they would actually separate families."

"Well, they sure separated his."

Charley spoke up. "But don't worry none. I reckon he'll find 'em again. It's a matter of lookin' in the right place."

Everyone laughed except Rusty and John Bestertag, who shook his head and tightened his lips. When they had eaten, Lemuel escorted Eb and his family to one of the cabins. He showed Rusty, Charley and Adriel to the one next door.

The cabin, made of dark logs, was dark inside except for one tiny window. In the early twilight, they could see that it had three wooden beds, two single and one double, sheets, blankets and pillows for each bed, and a wooden bench by the fireplace. Charley made Rusty sit on the bench while they made up the beds. When the big one was finished, they helped Rusty into it.

He protested. "I should take one of the smaller beds."

Charley sounded firm. "Yer takin' this 'un. And no back talk."

Adriel said, "There be wood for the fire. I don't reckon we need one tonight. Be you cold, Rusty?"

He wasn't. In fact, he felt too warm. Twice during the night, he stirred. Both times, Adriel got up to give him water.

"I sure do thank you," he murmured at one point.

"Stop thankin' us, and just git some sleep. I reckon it's what you need."

Rusty lost track of the days; he wasn't sure how long he stayed in bed or close to it. He knew that Charley and Adriel came and went—he figured they were working somewhere, helping with chores on the farm. They brought him trays of food, and after a few days Charley came in with the news that Brother Strang had died.

"Died in Voree, he did. They thought he was gettin' some better. But he didn't make it. Too badly wounded."

"So, who's taking his place?" Rusty asked.

"What?"

"Who's the successor?"

Charley spread his hands in a gesture of hopelessness. "There ain't one."

Rusty looked at him. "There's got to be. Who's gonna lead the church?"

"He never chose anyone."

"So, what are folks gonna do? What about us?"

Charley sat down on the bench. "Son—right now, yer gonna work at gittin' well. Well enough to travel. Adriel and me—we figure we'll most likely head up north again. No, not to Beaver, or Mackinac either. Maybe the Grand Traverse area, or even further north, to Little

Traverse. No one'll know we was once on Beaver Island. I reckon we can make a go of it fishin', or workin' around the docks. Even workin' as blacksmiths, if it came to that."

He paused. Rusty blinked, trying to understand. *His church was leaderless, and his friends were leaving.* Charley went on.

"See, bein' on the lakes gets into yer blood, so to speak. You don't want to live anywheres else. At least, that's how it is with Adriel and me."

Rusty tried to sound cheerful, but it was a poor attempt. "When are you leaving?"

"Not fer a while. We're not leaving *you*, if that's what yer worried about. We'll see you git 'cross Michigan and over toward the big river."

"But—but where—"

"Where are you going? Why, son, if I was you, I'd head back to Hannah and Nat, in Ioway. That's where yer Pa said he'd go, if we was ever chased off the island."

"Oh." Rusty tried to remember.

"'Course, you could always come north with us. Fishin', workin' around boats. A life so free and wild, you forget about most everything else. Religion, and such like."

"I—I need to find my family."

"All right. We'll help you all we can. You rest, now. Get strong."

Rusty's convalescence gave him plenty of time to think. Still befuddled by the beating and the sudden trip south, he tried to hope that Marie and his family were safe. When he expressed his fears to Charley, his friend only laughed.

"Are you serious? Gabe's with them; you know that. He'll take care of 'em like a mother bear protects her cubs. I wouldn't worry none about their bein' safe."

Then there was the matter of church leadership. Since the prophet had died and left no successor, did that mean the church itself was no more? He remembered the hymn they had sung in Voree:

> *Oh, a church without a prophet*
> *Is not the church for me...*

He wondered where most of his people were now. Scattered up and down the Michigan shoreline. Homeless, with no possessions. Forced to leave everything behind on the island.

Would they attempt to gather again, try to construct another community?

For his part, he was tired of forming communities. What had gone wrong on the island? Declaring oneself a king wasn't the best idea in the world. And he knew the plural marriage had been a mistake. A betrayal of his hopes, and those of others. Was it even possible to organize a religious community without going into polygamy, or some other strange practice? Why couldn't they just adhere to what was in the New Testament? Teach that, and nothing else?

If it were his decision, that's what he would do. He lay, bedridden for the time being, a priest in the church that once was. A minister whose people were dispersed over the whole state of Michigan by now. All their efforts—and for what? Two prophet-leaders dead, the communities now lost in the dust of history—Kirtland, Independence, Far West, Nauvoo, Voree. Add Beaver Island.

He would simply give up on gathering in large groups and being any sort of minister. He would try to see God in all living things, and forget about any formal worship. As he made this decision, a sense of peace settled over him. All his energy, everything he had, would be directed toward finding his family. He thought of the devoted husband and father he would be if he ever found them again. The first thing to do was to heal from the beating. He drifted into sleep.

In a few days he was able to walk outside, using a cane Charley had carved from a pine branch. He found Eb repairing the split-rail fence around the cow pasture. Eb put down the ax.

"Well, looky who's up and about."

"I wish I could be of some help," Rusty said.

"Well, I reckon that'll come. Yer walkin' jest fine. Soon you be splittin' logs with the best of 'em."

Rusty learned that Shadrach's Hollow was a tiny community in itself, its members mostly people escaping from slavery. It had a barn with three horses and five cows, a collection of chickens and ducks, and a few white geese.

"There's even pigs," Eb said. "And dogs and barn cats."

One of the dogs, a small terrier type, came running up as he spoke. The dog, who looked to be around fifteen pounds, sniffed Rusty's shoes and pant legs with great thoroughness. Rusty bent to stroke the animal's head. "But is it safe?"

"This place? Safe as any, I reckon. There's John Bestertag and his family in the frame house just down the road. And on the other side, to the west, there's Mennonite families, a whole bunch of 'em. If anyone come lookin' fer us, we'd have plenty of warning."

"So, what would you do? Hide?"

Eb stood a moment, lost in thought. "I reckon. If things got really bad, we'd go over the border. But, the truth is—we like it here, Jess and me. It's a good place, and there's people like us."

"So, of course you're not going back to Nauvoo. Or Voree."

Eb shook his head. "That be very risky, fer us. We be best off stayin' here."

Sometimes in the evenings, people gathered around a small campfire and talked together. Rusty wondered that they never spoke of slavery, or what had happened to them. But they wore the marks of their oppression. One man had his face so badly beaten with a whip that he'd lost an eye. Rusty saw the marks of the whip on their backs and arms. Several of the men walked with a limp. When there was a lull in the conversation, someone would start up a song.

One evening John Bestertag joined them. He walked over and stood next to Rusty.

"How is thee makin' it, son?"

Rusty smiled. "I'm feeling much better. I reckon that soon I'll be able to start lookin' for my family."

"That's good. Thee wants to start before the cold sets in."

"I hope so, sir. And I sure want to thank you."

"Don't thank me. We do what we can."

The group began singing a song Rusty didn't know.

> *"Follow the drinking gourd,*
>   *Follow the drinking gourd.*
> *For the old man is a'waitin' to carry you to freedom,*
>   *Follow the drinking gourd."*

"Folks think that's just a song," Bestertag said. "But it gives directions on how to get north. That drinking gourd is really the Big Dipper."

Rusty remarked that he hadn't heard them ever talking about their experiences as slaves.

"No. Thee won't hear them talking about that. They know what they went through."

Rusty felt something pressing on his foot. He looked down. It was the same little dog he'd seen before. The dog was licking his shoe.

"He likes thee," John Bestertag said. "Could thee use a dog?"

"I—uh—I don't know."

"He'd be a good traveling companion."

> *"I thought I heard the angels say,*
>   *Follow the drinking gourd.*
> *The stars in the heavens gonna show you the way,*
>   *Follow the drinking gourd."*

Rusty said, "Do you think it'll ever stop?"

Bestertag looked at him. "What? Slavery?"

"Yes. It's such—well, this monstrous evil. The worst I can think of."

Bestertag nodded. "That's the way we see it."

"And there's nothing we can do to change it."

Bestertag paused a moment. "We can't change it right now. But we can help the victims. Even if it means breaking the law. So, as I said—we do what we can."

"Why is it called 'Shadrach's Hollow?'"

"Ol' Shadrach Pierce was the one who received the land grant. For his service in the War of 1812. One of my wife's relatives. Not a Quaker—we don't hold with war."

Rusty said, "We don't, either. We're forbidden to shed blood. But it may take a war to settle this issue."

"Whatever it takes, it has to end. If more and more people see the effects of it, then they will refuse to tolerate it. We can only hope."

Rusty reached down and picked up the little dog. The fur felt rough, more like hair. The dog licked his face. "Back in the early thirties—1832, it was— our prophet Joseph Smith had a revelation about a conflict that would start in South Carolina and involve the whole country. A civil war between the northern and southern states. Many would be killed. And—and the slaves would rise up against their masters."

John Bestertag nodded. "That's interesting. But it doesn't take a prophet to know there's gonna be big trouble. An uprising—I wouldn't be surprised. A war—well, who knows? I'm just gonna keep trying to rescue folks. 'Specially anyone escaping from 'this monstrous evil,' as thee calls it."

"You sure rescued *me*." Rusty felt the dog's head resting on his shoulder. "My people had nothing, and I could barely walk. We're much beholden."

"Just do the same for somebody else."

The dog gave a hiccup. "Does this critter have a name?" Rusty asked.

"They call him 'Rags.' He's about two years old. He's never taken to anyone else. But thee he likes."

In the morning, when Rusty stepped outside, Rags was there. The dog followed him to the dining area and sat waiting as Rusty went inside. Rusty shook his head, puzzled. He had done nothing to earn this kind of devotion.

"He jest likes you, is all," Lemuel said.

"But—but what does he eat? And when?"

"Any time he can, most like. Them little dogs—they keep the varmints out of the barn."

Charley was listening. "I reckon he'll eat anything, right?"

"Scraps and such. Whatever you don't eat," Lemuel replied. "Whatever's left on your plate."

Charley and Adriel began laughing. Charley said, "If'n Rusty had 'em, he'd starve fer sure."

Rusty protested. "Oh, no, he wouldn't. I'd—why, I'd feed 'em."

He was a winsome little thing, Rusty had to admit. He had a short muzzle, a black nose, deep-set eyes, and what looked like a beard. He had a long, shaggy coat, and a stump of a tail which wagged whenever Rusty looked at him.

"Had a longer tail once," Lemuel said. "But it got caught in the stable door. John Bestertag had to chop it off."

Rusty tried not to wince. "Must've hurt."

"Oh, he yelled. But he be fine now."

Wherever Rusty walked on the farm, the dog followed him. Out behind the barn, he found other small dogs, three of them. When they saw Rags, they crowded around wagging their tails.

He inspected the five cows in their pasture—milking time was long over. In the barn, he saw three handsome horses, a bay and two speckled ones, like Freedom. He thought of the animals they'd had to leave on the island, and felt a twinge of sadness. There were also a number of cats—he wasn't sure how many. One orange tabby started to follow him. Rags growled, and the cat retreated.

That night Rusty had the old dream about climbing a mountain, with his brother-in-law and friend Nat Givens as the leader. He assumed the dream had something to do with religion. Strange, since he had forsworn any attempts to help organize a church or community again. Yet he reminded himself that where he was living now was indeed such a community, with people working for the common good and caring about what was best for every member. A good place for Eb and his family. At least for now.

Toward morning, he felt something licking his hand. He reached out and found Rags beside him on the bed. Someone had left the cabin door ajar, or else the dog had pushed it open. Rusty wondered what to do. Then he decided.

"All right, fella." He scratched Rags behind the ears. "You win."

His family was missing, but at least he had a dog. He drifted off into sleep with the dog curled up against him,

Over the next few days, he prepared for the trip west with Charley and Adriel. Charley made knapsacks out of canvas and burlap, with leather straps. In his own, Charley put matches, his knife, and a few apples. On the morning of their departure, John Bestertag gave them cheese and a loaf of bread. Lemuel gave them a canteen for water.

"Mr. Bestertag," Rusty began. "About Rags. I'd sure like to have him. But, you see—"

"Take him. He belongs with thee; that's plain."

"But I have no money to pay for him."

"Then, consider him a gift."

Rusty gestured. "But—don't you need him? To help kill vermin and such like?"

Bestertag began to laugh. "Old Brother Hunsler, just down the hill, has a dog with a litter of pups. Once they grow up, we'll have all the dogs we can handle. So take him. Thee is welcome to him."

They gave him a little porcelain dish for the dog and some dried jerky.

"For the dog—not you," Charley told him.

Out of scraps of leather, Rusty fashioned a small collar and a leash. These he put in his knapsack.

When the time came to say good-bye to Eb and Jess, Rusty rhought he would break down for sure. He hugged each one in turn, ending with J. J. The boy whispered, "When you see Louise, tell her we be fine. And we be free."

Rusty began to sniffle then. Eb clapped him on the shoulder. "Take care of your dog, there. And tell Gabe I sure do think of him."

Charley said, "You know how to write, now. If'n you go 'cross to Canada, write to Nat—tell 'em where you finally settle."

Rusty wiped his eyes. "We'll see you again, most like."

"I hope so, son," Eb replied. "Maybe so."

They started on the road west, walking with the mists of early morning rising from the fields. For a moment Rusty wondered if Rags would really follow him. The day would seem less bright somehow if he had to drag the dog away with the leash. Then he heard a rustle in the grass. When he looked, the dog was trotting along beside him.

18

MARIE SAT IN THE wagon with Paul asleep in her arms. Next to her, Louise held Jacob, who was squirming. On the other side of Louise, Sarah tried to distract him with clucking noises. Sarah waved an oak leaf in front of him.

"Soon's we git to moving, most like, he'll go to sleep."

"Most like, so will I," Marie replied. She was bone-tired—tired of traveling, of jouncing around in wagons, trying to soothe and pacify children when all she wanted to do was sleep. Not even time enough to mourn the absence of Rusty, whom she missed more than she could put into words.

Gabriel walked beside the wagon, grim-faced, a smudge of grime on his forehead. Positioned above his left eyebrow, it gave him a rakish air. Calvin trudged along on the other side. Their driver, a surly, silent fellow, looked straight ahead. Every once in a while he flicked a whip over the flanks of the two bay horses. She thought of the first driver they'd had, and what had happened that first evening. They'd stopped at a farmhouse, as was the custom, to ask lodging for the night. She remembered the person who had answered the door, a paunchy, well-fed man clad in denim overalls.

"We're seeking shelter for the night," Gabriel told him. "We have two women-folk, a girl, and two babies."

"Well—" the householder began.

"We come from Chicago," Gabriel said. "A far piece."

"That far?" the man asked.

Sarah broke in. "Further than that. Northern Michigan. We be Mormons—outcasts from Beaver Island. Our leader James Strang was assassinated, up on the island."

"Is that so?" The man started to close the door. "We ain't takin' in no Mormons."

"But we're refugees!" Sarah's voice rose to a desperate pitch.

"I don't keer. We don't have room for the likes of you."

The man's wife was standing behind him. "But, dear. They have little children. Babies—look! If we take them for one night, no one will know."

"No. And that's final." Then he paused. "Old Jeremiah lives just down the way. He'll take in anyone."

The door closed. Gabriel turned to help them get back in the wagon. But the driver said, "Ye dint tell me yer was Mormons. I wouldn't've had anything to do with you if I'd known."

Gabriel grasped the side of the wagon with one hand and gestured with the other. "But—we're peaceful. We've done nothing wrong."

"Pay me what you owe. I'm pullin' out right now."

Gabriel looked tried in the fading light. They were all exhausted from the day's travel. Paul was beginning to fuss. Marie tired to soothe him. Gabriel paid the man, and they watched as the horses and wagon disappeared into the dusk.

"What do we do now?" Louise asked.

Gabriel sighed. "Let's go find Jeremiah, who'll take in anybody." He led the way, in the direction the man had pointed. As the lights of the next farmhouse flickered through the trees, Gabriel turned and looked at Sarah. His voice was not gentle.

"If anyone mentions 'Strang' or 'Mormon' or 'Beaver Island' one more time, I will personally see that they *walk* all the way to the Mississippi."

"Well, my heavens," Sarah declared. "I didn't know."

"You do now."

They found lodging and comfort at the house of old Jeremiah, who didn't look much older than Calvin. In the morning, the old man directed them toward the nearest public stable. It took most of the morning before they found someone willing to drive them west.

They finally located a man with a team, who agreed to take them as far as the big river. The man spoke out of the side of his mouth. "My horses are good and fresh. Strong, too. Won the horse pull at the fair last spring. They c'n haul most anything."

Gabriel nodded. "Well, then, I reckon they can pull Sarah. Get in."

Sarah gave him a furious look, then burst into coughing. The women and Louise took their places in the wagon, and the men handed the babies up to them.

Marie tried to remember—how long had they been on the road? Too tired to think. A week? More than that? One day seemed to fade into another, a succession of trees crowding close to the road, fields full of corn and wheat, farmhouses where they were sheltered and fed, stables and barns spreading their shadows on the meadow grass. Tangled forests, woods so thick you could not see through them, places where the ruts of the road disappeared into the underbrush.

Then, the next day, a light, misty rain. Marie managed to shield the babies with her shawl. Finally she made a place for Paul under the wooden seat. There was room for Jacob too, but he didn't want to lie still. Louise had to hold him on her lap.

Gabriel took off his jacket and put it over the heads of Marie and Sarah. "That'll keep you dry for a spell."

"But, what about you?" Marie asked.

"Don't worry about me none. I'm fine." He returned to his place beside the wagon.

In the late afternoon, Sarah began the coughing. Gabriel came back, grasping the side of the wagon, and looked at her. She shook her head and sneezed. The rain increased.

Gabriel shouted to the driver. "We'll stop at the next inn."

"We have enough money for an inn?" Marie asked.

"I hope so." He didn't look at her. Sarah sneezed again.

Marie put an arm around Louise and drew her head under the jacket. The girl snuggled against her, and for a brief time, all three children dozed. The only sound was the dripping of the rain, and the horses' hooves clopping in the mud. Then Sarah started coughing and couldn't stop.

Paul wailed from under the seat. Louise stirred against her, and Jacob, who always woke up fretful, began crying. One of the horses neighed.

"My goodness." Sarah's whole body shook. "I'm sorry."

"For what?" Gabriel was looking over the side of the wagon. The public house loomed before them, the lights from the windows misty in the rain. The horses pawed at the ground.

Between sobs, Sarah managed to say, "For—for sayin' we was Mormon, and up on the island with Mr. Strang—" She began coughing again.

Gabriel gripped the side of the wagon. "Listen. Don't try to talk any more. And try to keep from coughing, at least till we get rooms. All right?"

She nodded, sniffing. Gabriel looked at Marie. "Stay dry, now. Back in a moment."

Then he was gone. They waited, Marie trying to soothe both babies. Louise took Jacob and began talking to him. "Look at the woods. You might see a deer. We saw some two days ago. Remember, in the meadow?"

Deer were a novelty, since there weren't any on Beaver Island. Jacob stopped crying and peered out at the trees surrounding the building. Suddenly the driver turned around.

"Be you Mormons?"

Sarah drew in her breath. Marie was too astonished to reply. Was he about to dump them all out into the rain?

"We're actually refugees," she managed to say. "We're trying to get back to our home, in Iowa."

The driver nodded. "Me cousin joined up with the Mormons. Went west with Brigham Young, he did."

Marie made no comment; she couldn't think of any. The driver turned away from them. Then Gabriel appeared, followed by an older man, apparently the inn-keeper.

"They have two rooms in the back for us. So give me Jacob, and we'll get everyone inside."

He took both babies, and Calvin helped the women out of the wagon. Marie reached for her knapsack.

"Why, where's yer luggage?" the inn-keeper asked. "This all you got?"

"We—uh—travel light," Gabriel replied.

The man shrugged. "Follow me."

They followed him around to the rear of the building, where the two rooms awaited them.

∞≫≪∞

"I'll have a fire going in a few minutes." The inn-keeper, a short man with white hair and chin whiskers, looked about the same age as Calvin. Gabriel noticed that he favored his left leg. "It's already lit in t'other room."

"We thank you, sir," Gabriel replied. "We're much obliged."

The man limped over to the fireplace. "Did you fall, sir?" Gabriel asked.

"Fell off me horse last week. He threw me, but I don't like to admit it."

"Have you seen a doctor?"

"Can't afford it."

Gabriel smiled. "Well, *I'm* a doctor, and you can afford me. I don't have any of my medical things with me, but I can examine you and see if I can help."

The man considered, then nodded. "I'd appreciate that. More than I can say."

"I'll get them settled here. Then I'll be in to see you."

While the man built up the fire, Gabriel looked over the rooms. The first one was already warmed by the fire. In it he put Sarah and Calvin.

"See that she keeps warm," he said to Calvin. "We'll get her some hot food, soon as we can."

Marie, Louise, and the babies would have the second room. He would stay in there too, close by in case he was needed for Sarah. Later,

226

after everyone had eaten, he remembered about the driver. He hurried out into the rain. He found the man and his team in the stable.

"Do you want me to get you a room for the night?" Gabriel asked.

"No. I'm happy here. I c'n keep an eye on the horses, and they keep me right warm."

"Let me get you something to eat, at least."

The man got to his feet, brushing bits of straw from his clothes. "I hear tell yer a doctor."

"I am."

"I got a misery in my foot. Hurts to walk. Stepped wrong going over some rocks last week."

"Come inside, and I'll have a look."

Later they sat together in the public house, sharing a pitcher of cider.

"Like I said, it's bruised, is all," Gabriel told him. "Just rest it all you can. No ten-mile hikes for a while."

The man raised his glass. "I'll drink to that."

Gabriel took a sip of cider. "How far do you reckon we are from the river?"

"'Bout one day."

"One day? That's good." Gabriel took another drink. "We have a chance of gettin' there sooner than I figured."

"What d'you plan to do when you get there?"

Gabriel thought a moment. "I'm gonna get everyone on a steamboat. Heading south."

"Nauvoo?"

Gabriel nodded. "My sister's sister-in-law lives in Montrose. That's where we're headed."

One day. Gabriel's enthusiasm was short-lived. The next morning, Sarah felt too ill to travel. They waited three days, then four. Gabriel and Calvin started doing odd jobs around the inn, to earn their keep. Gabriel grew anxious about having enough money left for the steamboat passage. Maybe he and Calvin could walk, and the others could take the boat. Or he could go on with Marie and the children, and Calvin and Sarah could stay at the inn until she was well enough to travel.

Meanwhile, he worried that one of the others—Marie or the children—would come down with the illness.

On the fifth day, Sarah felt stronger. Gabriel decided to resume the journey.

"I sure do thank you for staying with us," he told their driver.

"Doc, after what you done fer me, I'd do most anything. I feel some better already."

They loaded everyone into the wagon. The inn-keeper, whose limp was less noticeable now, came out to say good-bye. They set off once more. Gabriel took his place beside the wagon, walking close to where Marie sat so that he could see Jacob. At one point he reached for Jacob and put the boy astride his neck.

"Hold on, now."

He felt Jacob's hands gripping his hair.

"Don't tire yourself," Marie told him. "That boy is heavy."

Gabriel nodded. "He's grown some since we left."

Marie looked tired, more tired than Gabriel had ever seen her. Her eyes had a dull, glazed-over expression, as if she realized she no longer had control over her life, and what was happening to them. He knew she grieved for Rusty as if he were dead. They had no way of knowing whether he'd made it off the island safely or not.

Worried about Sarah and Calvin too. At their age, they couldn't take much more exposure to extreme heat, then cold and rain. And the babies. Not to mention Louise. All three youngsters in good shape now, but for how long?

He thought of all the suffering he'd witnessed as a physician, the scenes of persecution on the island, the way his people had been treated. The death of their leader James Strang. The drowning of Turah and her young husband. The suffering and death of his own Bethia. Now, Marie's grieving, Sarah's bout with illness, the troubles of the inn-keeper and their driver. Underlying all these happenings was the idea that if God knew about them and couldn't stop them, then He was either powerless or He didn't care. Or He didn't consider such things important. To Gabriel, they were very important, and he wondered, as he had in the past, if there were something wrong with God. Perhaps the Supreme Being was a bit deranged. As an elder, a minister, he knew he had to come up with some answers for himself. What if someone else needed to know, and he couldn't tell them?

Why all this suffering? The loss of homes and possessions, being forced to wander, to seek shelter, to endure physical pain in the process? He sighed, and stared glumly ahead to where the trees made dark shadows on the road.

"Let me take Jacob," Marie said. "He looks sleepy."

He handed the child up to her. On the other side of the wagon, Calvin stumbled. They felt the wagon lurch as he caught the side of it. Alarmed, Gabriel hurried around the back and joined Calvin on the other side.

"My foot hit a root or something," the older man said.

"You all right now?"

Calvin gave a short laugh. "Oh, my, yes. I've come through worse than this, and I'll make it now."

Gabriel began to walk on the other side of Calvin, nearest the side of the road. He spoke in an undertone. "It's sure something, all the things we been through. Not just the physical sufferings—that's enough in itself. But being driven off the island—that part makes no sense."

"It do seem strange. Like it coulda been stopped, somehow."

"Well, then, here's a question for you. If we're supposed to be God's people, then why didn't He stop it?"

"You mean, why did God let it happen?"

Gabriel paused, then gestured with his hands. "I reckon that's what I'm wondering. For us, especially—trying to live peaceable-like and not bother anybody."

Calvin said, "Seems no matter where you go, there's always someone that gets bothered."

"But all we did was to seek a place of peace. Where we could live and raise our families, take care of our livestock—"

Calvin grunted. "We just haven't found the right place yet. The land of promise, the Peaceable Kingdom."

"*Eh bien.* Voree sure wasn't it. And Beaver Island didn't work out, either."

Calvin went on. "Remember that letter of appointment? The one Brother Strang had from Joseph Smith? It said he was to take the people to a place of safety. Now, it didn't mention being safe forever, or even for a long time. But, you see, that's what he did. We was safe at Voree, and for a time on the island. It wasn't till they shot him that we was driven out."

Gabriel paused a moment. "And we're left still seeking. That place, that golden city."

"We may be seeking it fer a long time. Maybe all our lives. I remember what Nat said. You even told me. He said, 'Maybe we be a better people, for all the seeking.'"

"That's true. He did say that." Gabriel fell silent, and for a time the only sound was the horses' hooves on the dirt road, and the creaking of the wagon.

Then Calvin said, "As for me, I reckon nothing's been as terrible as the loss of my first wife. Rusty's mother, and Hannah's too. She was the love of my life. After that, none of these other things has been as bad."

Gabriel looked at him, startled. Something about Calvin he had never realized. Stupid of him—he should've known. He swallowed, then nodded. "Loving someone like that is a fearsome thing."

"Well, not everyone takes it as hard as I did. But you go on, somehow. And it gets less with time." He paused. "Sometimes it seems she's still with me, in a way. I can't explain it, or put it into words. But at certain times, I feel it."

Gabriel stepped around a puddle in the road. He walked on, imagining Calvin with the spirit of his beloved hovering close to him. Was such a thing possible? He had not felt the presence of Bethia, but then she had not been the one he had truly loved. Like Calvin, he carried a secret grief. He thought of Corey then, and suddenly it was as if she were walking beside him, the actual presence and personality he had remembered.

Was she dead, then? Why else would he feel her spirit so close to him? He had thought vaguely of trying to find her, to seek her out and learn what had happened to her. After all, ten years had passed. But now—perhaps he would be like Calvin, hiding the sorrow that had changed his life, trying to be helpful and kind anyway. *Eh bien*. If Calvin could do it, so could he.

"Mud ahead," the driver called.

In a matter of minutes they were in it, the horses' hooves and wagon wheels splattering mud everywhere. Gabriel sprang to the side of the road, and Calvin followed him, crashing through the sea of ferns and underbrush. They made their way to the top of a little hill. The driver brought the horses to a halt. Gabriel and Calvin, their clothes mud-stained, walked up alongside the horses and stopped.

The driver waved his free hand. A wide ribbon of silver shone through the trees. "We be about there. There's yer river."

19

R USTY SITS CROSS-LEGGED IN the clearing and watches as Adriel pokes at the bacon with a flat stick. They have managed to buy a small three-legged skillet, called a spider, and now it is warming over a little fire while Charley slices potatoes. Finally he adds them to the bacon, which is already simmering. Hardly a gourmet meal. But the odor that fills the air is tantalizing.

"Smells good enough to eat," Rusty remarks. At the sound of his voice, the dog stands up and wags his stump of a tail.

Charley gives a short laugh. "Waal, look who else is ready to eat."

"He looks a bit thin," Rusty says. "You think we be feeding 'em enough?"

"That dog's fine," Adriel says. 'Stop frettin 'bout him and think about yerself. You got a bit of ground to cover afore you see Hannah and them."

Rusty sighs and nods. He has become used to the routine of walking all day, sleeping wherever they can at night, sometimes burrowing into haystacks or sneaking into barns. Every few days they approach a farmhouse and offer to cut wood in exchange for food, or the rare cash payment. He senses he is gaining new strength with each day's work. But the idea of continuing on without his two friends leaves him feeling uneasy and vulnerable.

"I reckon we be somewheres south of Chicago by now," Charley says. "You got about two hundred miles to go, if I figure rightly. Maybe less, by this time."

Adriel stirs the potatoes. "Jest keep goin' west, till you hit the river. If you can get across the water, you'll run right into Montrose."

"How do we get across?" Rusty asks.

Adriel raises his eyebrows. "Why, hang it. Anyway you can. Find some cuss with a skiff, offer to row. You'll think of something."

Charley gives a little cough. "Don't try walkin' on the water. It didn't work on Lake Michigan, and it won't work here."

They laugh, Charley slapping his knees. Rags gives a soft 'woof.'

"I reckon we're about ready here." Charley produces two wooden spoons from his knapsack and hands one to Rusty. "Let's dig in."

They gather around the skillet and take spoonfuls of potatoes and bacon. Adriel serves himself with the stick he has used for stirring. Rusty saves a little for Rags, and sets the porcelain bowl down for him.

"If that don't beat all," Adriel says. "The dog gets to eat out of a dish, and we don't git nothin'."

Rusty gives a shrug. "They gave it to me for the dog. You c'n eat off it if you have a mind to."

"No, thanks."

Charley says, "That were a pretty good set-up, come to think of it. That little group, with John B. and them other folks lookin' after it."

Rusty nods. "I hope they'll be safe there."

"I reckon they got a good chance. As good as any. They can leave right quick if anyone gets after them."

Adriel stirs what is left in the skillet. "Eb, he's pretty smart. I figure he'll take care of that family right well. If the time comes to make tracks, he'll get 'em all across to Canada."

Charley looks at Rusty. "And now, we come to you. It's almost time for you to head west alone. You and Rags. Don't travel due west. Cut south a little bit."

"I see." Rusty speaks slowly, trying not to let the consternation show in his voice. "I—I reckon it's about time."

"Adriel and me—we be headin' north in the morning. If'n we're lucky, we can maybe catch one of the big steamers. Find work on her."

Rusty nods. He tries to listen to what they are saying. "We be leavin' you the spider. And some cheese and apples and such. One of them spoons. And some matches. Don't let 'em git wet, or you'll be up the creek."

Rusty nods again. They talk of other things, how autumn was in the air, and how with luck he could find fresh apples most of the way home.

Charley clears his throat. "Don't get shot by some farmer thinkin' yer stealin' apples. And—Oh, yes. I'm givin' you my knife."

Adriel looks startled. Charley says, "We got the hatchet. That'll do fer us."

A warm evening, with no rain. Another piece of luck. They make beds of pine boughs, in a clearing away from the trail. Rusty curls up with the dog lying beside him, and stares out into the darkness. *On his own, tomorrow. No one but him and Rags.* Through the trees, the stars of the Big Dipper gleam. He remembers how his friend Nat could tell time by the stars. He wishes he had listened more carefully when Nat was trying to teach him. The moon is rising. The dog gives a long sigh, and that is the last thing Rusty remembers.

Morning. Mists rising from the clearing where they have camped. Adriel started down to the creek with the tin container they used for water. Rusty struggled to his feet, the dog licking his face in the process. Then it hit him. His friends were leaving, and he would have to find his way alone.

He tried to keep up a cheerful appearance as they prepared breakfast—bacon, and johnnycake soaked in bacon fat. Adriel went to wash the utensils in the creek, and Charley readied the backpacks.

"This'un's yours. I c'n tell 'cause the dog chawed the strap here."

Rusty nodded. He must have sighed, for Charley said, "You can always come north with us, you know. You don't have to go back to Nauvoo."

Rusty shook his head. "There's a chance they might be there. My family."

"There's a right smart chance. Don't be afeard, and don't take any sass off anyone. And I wouldn't go around sayin' I was Mormon. This ain't the time fer preachin'."

"Oh, I know."

The time came for the parting. Both Charley and Adriel thumped him on the back and shook his hand.

"Godspeed," Adriel said.

Charley gave a little cough. "Good luck, now. 'Member what I said."

"I'll do fine," Rusty replied. "Thanks for everything."

"You'll make it," Charley said. "Say hello to Nat and Gabe fer us."

Then they turned, heading in a northerly direction. Rags started after them, then stopped. The dog sat down in a little patch of grass, looking from Rusty to the two that were departing. For a moment Rusty feared that the dog would follow them. He gave a whistle and started to walk in the opposite direction. In a moment the dog was trotting beside him.

When he looked again, there was no trace of his traveling companions. They had disappeared as silently as if they were two deer. He drew a deep breath and began to follow the little creek toward the southwest.

He reached a place where the creek took a turn toward the east. He crossed the creek, Rags splashing behind him. A little trail led off to the southwest. He decided to follow it, but first he got on his knees to fill the old canteen Charley had put into his pack. Made of metal, it had a covering of coarse, brown cloth. As he dipped it into the stream, he saw his face reflected in the water. He blinked. A stranger's face stared back at him, the skin bronzed from the sun, the red hair long and unkempt. He had a growth of beard hiding the lower half of his face, and his eyes had a wild, haunted look.

Like someone who'd lived in the woods all his life. That can't be me. Marie would never know him now. And even Gabe would have trouble. Shaken, he rose to his feet. They struck out on the trail, which was hardly more than a deer path. Maybe Indians had used it. He heard chickadees chattering high in the trees, and somewhere a jay called. Once there was a rustling off to his left, and a deer leapt across the path. Rags gave chase. Rusty stood, wondering how to get the dog back. He heard something crashing through the underbrush, then faint barking.

He continued on the trail, giving a short series of whistles at intervals. He was ready to give up when suddenly Rags appeared. The dog panted, obviously exhausted. Rusty stopped to rest for awhile. He ate some cheese and leftover potatoes from the previous evening. He fed some to Rags, who twitched his tail. The dog curled up next to him while he finished his meal.

"I reckon that's lunch." He wondered if he'd eaten it too soon. Hard to judge what time it was. They took up the trail again. It led to a real road with wagon ruts. He followed the road; it stretched off to the west. The land changed to rolling fields and isolated clumps of trees. *A farmhouse in the distance.* He attached the leash to the dog's collar; some of the farm dogs might not be too friendly. Subdued, the dog trotted beside him.

Just before sunset, he knew it was time for supper. He ran his fingers through his hair and tied the long ends at the back of his neck with a bit of cord. Then he picked out a prosperous-looking farmhouse and knocked at the front door.

A heavy-set woman opened it. Red-faced and sturdy, she stood looking at him as she wiped her hands on her large white apron.

"'Scuse me, ma'am," Rusty began in his most polite voice. "Could I chop you some wood for a place for the night? And possibly a spot of victuals for myself and my friend here?"

"Oh, it's a little dog," the woman said. "He's right pretty. What's his name?"

"I call him Rags."

"And you are—?"

"Rusty. Russell Manning. We're tryin' to get back to Iowa, where my family is."

She looked at him a moment, as if weighing whether he was honest or not. Then she nodded. "I don't need no wood cut, but I'd be obliged if you carry some logs in. Jest fill up the wood box, by the fireplace.

"I'd be glad to do that."

"And yer welcome to stay the night. I have some leftover beef stew for the dog."

"I reckon he'd love that."

"But he'll have to stay in the barn with the other critters."

Rusty nodded. "You know, I reckon I'll join him in the barn. Most barns are nice and warm. Then he'll settle right down and sleep the night. And so will I."

"Suit yourself. But cone in for supper."

Rusty filled the wood box with split wood from the wood pile. Then he tied the end of the dog's leash to a peg in the barn wall.

"Stay," he commanded. The dog looked at him and sat down. Most likely he was used to barns. Then Rusty joined the family for a meal of fried chicken and corn pudding.

"This is mighty good," he said.

They didn't ask any questions of him, and he didn't volunteer any information. They accepted him, a stranger who needed a place for the night. He took a pan of stew out to Rags and put some in the ceramic dish. Rags gulped it down. Rusty took care to save some for the next morning.

He made himself a bed in the clean straw and sat cross-legged checking the contents of his knapsack. The knife Charley had given him. Food for Rags in the morning. Apples and cheese for himself. Hopefully there would be a good breakfast at the farmhouse to start the day.

Rags crept into his lap. He stroked the dog's head. He thought it strange that Rags' coat was hairy and wiry, not like fur at all. A shadow fell over them. Startled, he glanced up.

One of the girls from the family stood looking down at him. She was a pretty little thing, hardly more than fifteen, with an angelic, heart-shaped face and small, delicate features. He had forgotten her name, although he was sure she had been introduced. He smiled at her, unsure what to say.

She spoke first. "I brung some bones for your dog. Beef bones."

"Well, that's very good of you. I'm sure if he could speak, he'd thank you himself." He stood up, dumping the dog into the straw, and took the package.

Her eyes met his. "Where you headed?"

"I'm going to a place called Montrose, on t'other side of the big river."

"That's a far piece."

"I reckon so. But if I keep traveling, I'll get there afore the cold sets in."

She raised her eyebrows. "It must be lonely, traveling with only a little dog."

"I'm not lonely; he's my true friend. We take care of each other. But it's good to see people once in a while."

She stood on one foot and then the other, reminding him of Turah when she was that age. Suddenly she said, "Take me with you."

"What?"

"Please. Let me go with you when you leave. I'll come out early, and we can leave before my father wakes up."

He felt like he'd been struck in the face. "But—"

"I always wanted to see what was south of here. The Mississippi, and all that. And I'll cook—I can cook fer you, and keep you warm at night."

"Now, wait. Hold on just a minute." Rusty searched for works. "You—why, you don't even know me."

"I don't need to. I know your name's Rusty. I see that you be kind, and—and handsome. And I'll go with you, wherever you go."

Rusty tried to remain calm. "Now, listen. What was your name again?"

"Betsy."

"Well, now, Betsy. In the first place, I be married—I have a family. I'm going to where my wife is."

She looked unconcerned. He went on. "In the second place, I am Mormon. A persecuted people. You don't want to have anything to do with me."

A smile flitted across her face. "I hear tell Mormons can have more than one wife."

"Well, that's some Mormons. And I'm not one of them. Now, in the third place, what do you reckon your father will do, if'n you run off with me?"

"He'd take a shotgun after you. But we'd be long gone afore he's even awake."

Rusty drew a deep breath. "I don't reckon you've thought this through. I'm trying to get back to Ioway. And all I need is someone with a shotgun chasin' me."

She looked at him, breathing fast. She was a lovely youngster; he wondered at her wanting to run away. He said gently, "Betsy, I think you should go back inside now. You don't want to come with me. You want to stay safe, with your family."

"But I don't want to 'stay safe.' I want a more interesting life, with adventure, and new things. Excitement. Passion."

Rusty thought a moment. "Well, I don't reckon you'd want it if'n you knew what it was like."

She nodded, sighing. Then she brightened. "I'll go inside now. But I'll be out, soon's my parents be asleep. I'll come and be with you. Just us, out here. And I reckon you'll change yer mind 'bout us going off early in the morning."

"Now, look here—" he began. But she turned and left before he could finish. He heard her footsteps going toward the house.

He sat back down. *What to do now?* He felt bone-tired; he needed a good night's sleep. It occurred to him that if her father found her in the barn with him, he was as good as dead.

Quickly he packed up his knapsack, including the paper of beef bones. No good breakfast for him. But Rags would have enough.

Candlelight at last. Dusky shadows out in the field. He shouldered the backpack, put the leash on the dog, and made his way stealthily past the farmhouse. A faint light flickered from a window. He snuck past the building and headed for where he remembered the road was. Hard to see in the dark. Once he stumbled on a tree root. Rags gave a "woof."

"Quiet," he whispered. He found the road and started walking. He had hoped to see by the light of stars, but the sky was dark. Far to the west, lightning flashed. All he needed. A storm.

He wondered what Charley or Adriel would have done, in his situation. Much the same thing, most like. Then he began wondering about the girl, and why she seemed so anxious to leave. Was someone hurting her, at the farmhouse? Maybe he should've tried to rescue her. As for taking advantage of her, he was too grief-stricken over Marie to do anything like that.

No. She would have to be rescued by someone else this time. He followed the road toward the storm, wondering where he could find shelter. Too late to bother some farm family. Had he walked far enough to be safe from young Betsy? To say nothing of her father's shotgun.

Once he thought he heard footsteps behind him. He froze, and something pounded in his chest. He looked back. Nothing. Only the wind, rustling the dry leaves by the road's edge. He felt the first drops of rain. Shelter was crucial.

A flash of lightning. He saw two dark shapes off to his left. Haystacks. He stepped off the side of the road into tall grass. The lightning flashed again, and in the brightness he saw a shed standing just beyond the haystacks. Thunder crashed. The dog whined.

"It's all right, fella. Let's see if there's a way in."

He lifted the wooden latch and opened the door. In the lightning flashes he saw piles of straw, a feeding bin, and a large mule with his ears back.

He spoke in a reassuring voice. "All right, fella. It's all right. In fact, it's fine." He pulled the door shut. At the same time he remembered Nat's mule Old Pete, one of the orneriest creatures that side of the Mississippi.

He found a pile of straw as far away from the mule as possible. He and Rags prepared to bed down for the night. With his knapsack as a pillow, he covered himself with straw. The mule snorted and stamped his foot. Rusty considered his choices: a night with a not-too-friendly mule or a drenching. He lay still. Rags crept into the crook of his arm. The rain began to drum on the roof. Lightning flashed, and thunder crashed around them. Rags whined.

The storm, or series of storms, must have lasted most of the night. Rusty woke at least twice to the sound of thunderclaps. One distinct dream he had was of Owen Crawford, Nat's friend, being chased around the pasture by the mule Pete.

The morning brought a steady rain. Good, in a way. It meant that Betsy would probably not try to follow him. He got up with the first light and fed Rags the leftover beef stew. For himself, there was an apple and a piece of cheese. The mule watched with wary eyes. Rusty gave him the better part of an apple. The mule stamped his feet, his tail swishing, and crunched the apple. Rusty had no more fear of him, but kept well away from the hindquarters.

Mid-afternoon. The rain had stopped. Rusty's clothes had dried, but his shoes were encrusted with mud. The road was a sea of mud. Even the dog's legs were mud-stained. Rusty kept walking, wondering where he was going to spend the night.

Noises behind him. He turned to look. A cart creaked slowly down the road, pulled by two oxen. The man in the front seat was short and gray-haired; his drooping moustache reminded Rusty of a walrus.

Rusty stepped aside for the cart to pass, motioning the dog to his side. "Good afternoon."

"Well, good afternoon to you," the man replied. "What're you doin', out here in the middle of nowhere?"

"Just on my way home."

"And where's that?"

Rusty smiled, knowing it sounded ridiculous. "Montrose, Iowa."

"Lands sakes," the man said. "That's—

"—a far piece. I know. But that's where I'm headed."

The man pulled the oxen to a halt. "Well, climb on. The least I c'n do is give you a lift. That's a purty little dog, there."

"I'm much obliged." Rusty picked up the dog and hoisted himself into the place beside the driver. "I was gettin' plumb tuckered."

"I don't wonder. Where'd you come from?"

He started to say "Beaver Island," but thought better of it. "A little place up in Michigan. Near Detroit."

The man squinted, looking at him. "And you come all this way by yerself?"

"Well, no. I had friends with me. But they left to go back up north."

The man clicked to the oxen, and they began plodding through the mud. Rusty wondered how much to tell him. Would he understand about being taken off the island, separated from his family, and left with no money and only the clothes on his back? Even Rusty had trouble understanding it, and he had lived through it. Finally the man said,

"I'm wondering why you didn't take a stagecoach, or one of them new-fangled trains."

"Trains, sir?"

"Well, yes. Don't tell you you ain't heard of the Illinois Central Railroad. It's been bringin' settlers in from all over. People from England and Canada. Places like Vermont and Germany. Ireland. Why, we got scores of folks from Pennsylvania, Ohio, New England and such like."

Rusty tried not to show his surprise. Best not to let it slip about being in the wilds of Wisconsin and on an island for ten years. "I reckon I just didn't have the money for such a thing as that."

"Well, that's a pity. It must be quite something, to take a trip on the railroad."

Rusty nodded, reluctant to admit that the only railroad he knew much about was the underground one. He was getting into the area where it was not safe to express abolitionist sentiments. After a while they stopped at a public house. Rusty tied Rags to a knob on the side of the cart. He went inside with the cart owner and they shared a bowl of stew.

"My name's Jason Harris," the man said. "How 'bout some cider?"

"I'd be much obliged."

Rusty learned that Jason Harris was on his way home, and that he and Rags were welcome to spend the night. As they got into the cart again, Rusty was thinking *What luck*. Suddenly Harris gave a cough.

"Tell you what. Here's what I'll do. If you give me that little dog, I'll see you have enough to get a stage home. Get close enough to the river, and you can get on a steamboat."

Rusty considered, turning it over in his mind. The dog licked his hand. Finally Rusty shook his head. "I reckon I better keep 'em. He's my only friend. Fact is, I never knew an animal could be this devoted. I—" He paused. "See, if'n I git home, and my family's not there, well—he'd be the only family I'd have. So—no. He's not fer sale."

Harris shrugged. "Suit yourself."

Rusty looked at him. "What would you want 'em for."

"He'd keep critters out of the barn. Rats and such."

"He does like to chase things."

Harris nodded. "Well, if you change yer mind, let me know."

Toward sunset, Harris turned the oxen onto a rough, rutted road overrun with weeds. They drove past a weathered farmhouse to a barn which hadn't seen a coat of paint in a decade, Rusty guessed. After the oxen had been fed, and Rags tied up in the barn, Rusty joined the Harris family for a dinner of ham and potatoes. To his relief, there were no young women staring at him, only Jason and his wife. Rusty offered to sleep in the barn with the animals.

"Nonsense," Harris declared. "Here's yer chance for a nice warm bed. A good night's sleep. I reckon you 'bout forgot what it feels like."

So Rusty took some leftovers out to the dog. "Lie down, now. And stay." He saw that the leash was securely tied, and went back to the house.

He hadn't intended to sleep so late. The sun was high when he finally stumbled outside after breakfast. He had some bacon for Rags. Shouldering his backpack, he opened the barn door. No dog. The leash hung from the peg where he'd tied it, the collar still attached.

He whistled. Still no Rags. He picked up the collar and untied the leash. Mr. Harris came upon him still looking at the collar and shaking his head.

"I reckon he slipped his collar," Rusty said.

"Is that so? Mebbee he got hungry and went lookin' fer food."

"I fed him well last night."

The man stood looking at him, blinking in the sunlight. "Well, I dunno, son. Dogs be strange critters."

It was then that Rusty began to suspect something. But what could he do? How could he accuse his host outright? And of what? Stealing a little dog that wasn't worth much except to keep vermin out of a barn.

Rusty looked around the outside of the barn, whistling at intervals. Then he said, "Well, I've got to be on my way. Thanks for everything, if you see Rags, take care of him."

"I'll do that."

Rusty stowed the bacon—he'd eat it later. He tramped out to the rutted road and began walking. Every once in a while he gave a whistle.

Once he thought he heard rustling in the tall grass. But when he looked, there was nothing.

Silly little dog, anyway. He should've sold him and taken the money. At least then he'd have something. He reached the main road and headed west. Bereft of Rags, he found himself missing his family even more. The sorrow lay like a pain in his chest and stomach. Would he ever see any of them again? If only one of them had survived—say, his little son Paul, or daughter Louise. But the one he missed most was Marie.

He thought of the wonderful things she had concocted in the kitchen, even when times were uncertain. A procession of meals ran through his head—*coq au vin*, and fish prepared in endless delicious ways, and always the bread, baked fresh with yeast and honey. *Time to eat.* He found a stretch of woodland, and followed a little path to where he would not be seen from the road. He sat down under a large maple and fished in his backpack for food. He hauled out an apple, a hunk of cheese, and the three pieces of bacon, limp by this time. He sighed and cut up the apple. Better eat the bacon before bugs get it.

He lifted a piece to his mouth. Branches crackled. Suddenly something tore out of the underbrush. He would describe it later as a blur of fur. Terrified, he tried to think what kind of creature he was encountering. A catamount, maybe? No; they were quite shy. Wildcats and lynx kept well hidden. He was halfway to his feet before he recognized the dog.

"Rags! What a fright you gave me! What—?" The dog was dancing around him, giving high squeaks. Rusty interpreted them as squeals of joy. He reached down to pat the dog, but Rags would not stay still. Rusty sat down again. The dog crept into his lap, panting. It was then that Rusty discovered the rope dangling around the dog's neck, the same color as the fur. Rusty removed the rope; it was frayed at the end, where Rags had either pulled it or chewed through it.

Clearly, Harris or someone had tried to steal him. "Well, I won't leave you alone again."

Rags licked Rusty's face and emitted more high squeaks. Rusty gave him the bacon, and for a brief time there were no more squeaks, only crunching noises. Rusty wondered if he would have to use the rope to improvise a collar and leash for the dog. He took a bite of the cheese. A piece fell on his shirt. He reached up to retrieve it, and found the leash with the color attached. He had draped the leash over the back of his neck while he was hunting for the dog.

"I reckon we're having good luck," he told the dog. "If you gettin' almost stolen is good luck. But we'll be more careful now."

Toward sunset, Rusty stopped and offered to work at a public house if they would provide him with a meal. Soon he was busy splitting wood, with Rags tied a short distance away.

At last they stood on the bank of the great river. It was mid-afternoon. The sun cast glints of gold on the water. Just offshore, a bed of water lilies floated, the yellow and white flowers bobbing up and down with the current. Rags waded into the water and sniffed at a piece of log. The opposite shore appeared closer than Rusty had imagined. After the wild expanses of Lake Michigan, this stretch of water seemed tame by comparison. Then he figured that the river hadn't really widened to its full extent; he was still some distance north of Nauvoo.

"Well, Rags. Let's head into town and see if we c'n get a ride across before nightfall. I reckon it'll be yer first ride in a boat."

The dog splashed out of the water and followed. They made their way south through the undergrowth, following the river.

20

MID-MORNING. **GABRIEL SHEPHERDED THEM** off the boat at Fort Madison, on the Iowa side of the river. Marie followed him down the gangplank, Paul in her arms, her knapsack heavy on her shoulders. She noticed with a start that Gabriel's hair—once jet black—had tinges of gray. More than tinges. She wondered if her own hair had grayed also; she was only fourteen months younger than her brother.

"What's the matter, *maman*?" Louise's voice, just behind her.

"Nothing. Watch your step, now."

Still she pondered. Poor Gabriel, grown gray with the rigorous work on the island, the exodus, and now, the care for his family. As for Calvin and Sarah, their hair was almost white. She held Paul close to her and joined the others on the dock.

"*Bon*," Gabriel was saying. "Everyone looks fit." He set Jacob on the dock and kept hold of his hand. "We may have to do some walking. The steward said the livery stable is down in the middle of town. Are we ready?"

He led the way past stacks of boxes and weather-beaten storehouses, to a boardwalk which took them to a line of store fronts. The old wooden buildings, typical of a waterfront town, made her think of Charley and Adriel. *River rats, they'd called themselves. Were they somewhere, even now, with Rusty and the others? Eb and Jess and their children?* Then she began to cry, not able to wipe her eyes because her arms were full.

"Careful," Gabriel was saying. "Watch out for the puddles." Then

246

he was looking at her. "Here. Let me take Paul for a spell. Louise, can you mind Jacob? Don't let go his hand. We be almost there."

"Almost there?" Sarah asked. She was breathing fast.

"Well, Montrose is twelve miles away. Too far for any of us to walk. 'Specially with the young ones. But we'll find us a ride."

They reached the public stable. It took the better part of the morning before they found someone willing to drive them south. Meanwhile, Gabriel managed to buy some bread and rolls from the public house next to the stable. He and Louise carried the food to the family.

"Too bad we ain't got cider to wash it down," Calvin remarked.

Gabriel looked at him. "Come evening, I reckon you c'n have all the cider you want."

"I warn't complaining. No, siree."

Sarah nudged him. "Shut up and eat while you got the chance."

Finally they found a driver, a young boy who looked to be not much older than Louise. He offered to drive them south, and the price was agreed upon.

"I got me a strong mule, and a wagon. First I got to go tell my folks."

He came back with his mule and the wagon, hardly bigger than a cart. But it held the women and children. The boy said his name was Burt, and his mule was Baxter. "Ol' Baxter, he be a right good mule. I reckon he can pull most anything.

Was it her imagination? Marie caught the young lad smiling at Louise, looking at her the way Gray Wolf had first looked at Turah.

"Louise, come on back here." She tried not to sound anxious.

To her consternation, Gabriel actually said, "Oh, you ladies settle in back there. Here, Louise. Get up on the front seat, here." And he handed her up to sit beside Burt.

Marie and Sarah both sat in the rear seat, each with a child on her lap. Gabriel and Calvin began to walk on either side of the cart. Marie had time to see that Burt had wispy straw-colored hair under his cap, a pug nose, and freckles. Too young to look at Louise like that. She strained to hear what he was saying to her. Something about his mule.

"He c'n pull really heavy loads. And he does it on account of he likes me. I never beat him or tease him, like some folks do their animals. He knows I'd never hurt him."

Marie began to relax. What kind of courtship talk was that? Nothing to worry about, there. She took deep breaths of the fresh air, savored the scent of sweet blooming plants mingled with the faint river-smell of fish. Hard to believe they were going home. Back to where she had first lived with Rusty. Only this time, without him. She felt like crying then. She closed her eyes, swaying with the movement of the cart.

Burt was saying, "Mornings, I always bring him a carrot. Or an apple. He's always there at the gate, waitin' for me. Rain or shine."

And Louise's reply. "It must be nice to have an animal like you that much."

Marie didn't hear what Burt said next. The words ran together in her mind; she leaned against Sarah and slept.

When she woke, the tree shadows stretched long across the gravel road. She could see the sun, a golden presence in the trees to the west. They were on the familiar approach to Montrose and the farmlands beyond. She began to marvel at what was new and what she recognized from before. Just over ten years...a lot happens in ten years. New frame houses in the downtown area. New-built store fronts, a log cabin or two on the outskirts. Another barn. More trees down. After a while, she began to wonder if it were the same town. Then she caught Gabriel smiling at her, his hand on the edge of the cart.

"Change happens," he remarked, raising his eyebrows.

She nodded. He reached to pat her on the shoulder. She wondered that he looked a bit sad in the glow of sunset. Tired, most like. Their journey almost over.

Wheels creaking. The mule slowed his pace. "Which way now?" Burt asked.

"This path, to the left." Gabriel moved up beside the mule. "See that house, in that grove of trees? That's where we're going."

They made their way up the slight hill in silence. Sarah, dozing beside her, swayed as the cart turned. Both babies slept. Suddenly Sarah woke up.

"Glory be! Look where we are!"

Paul and Jacob started to cry. Gabriel leaned closer to Burt. "Just take us around in back."

A young man stood on the back step, his hair the color of Rusty's. Marie's heart leapt; for a moment she thought it *was* Rusty. Then he turned, and she saw it was a younger version of him. *Rusty when she first knew him.*

"Who's that?" Sarah asked. "Some stranger, I'll be bound. I reckon Nat done sold off the farm and moved."

"Relax, woman." Calvin shook his head. "That's Jody, Nat's oldest. Don't you 'member?"

Jody, meanwhile, had stepped to the back door. "Mother! Gaby! Get out here! Quick!"

Then Hannah herself appeared on the porch, tall, not as slender, with the same look of openness and independence. She wore her auburn hair done up in a bun. "My family!" she cried. "I don't believe it!"

Then everybody was hugging and exclaiming, quick, questioning phrases. "This is Paul?" "Yes, little Paul." "And Louise! How she's grown!" "That she has." "And where's Rusty? Where's my brother?"

Hannah's father held her in a long embrace while Marie tried to explain about Rusty. "We couldn't find him when they put us off the island."

Hannah held each of the babies and exclaimed over them. "Oh, he has Rusty's eyes."

With all the attention, the babies stopped crying. Hannah spoke to Jody. "Run over and fetch your father. Tell him to drop what he's doing and get down here."

Finally they were all gathered in the large front parlor. Gabriel told Burt to tether his mule; there would be a place in the stable for Baxter later on. Now Burt sat with Louise and her nine-year-old cousin Elizabeth, who looked very much like Hannah. The older daughter, seventeen-year-old Gabrielle, had dark hair like her father Nat; she hovered in the background.

A man stood in the doorway, Nat Givens, who looked the same as Marie remembered except for his full growth of beard. Many men had beards now, Marie had noticed. Strange how fashions changed. He strode over to her and hugged her before she could rise. "We know a little about the doings on Beaver Island. But what happened to Rusty?"

"I—that is—I don't know," she managed to reply.

He embraced each of the others, even Burt. "Yer right welcome here, lad. We'll put you up for the night, and give yer mule a good feed too."

"Much obliged," the boy replied.

Nat looked around, and his bushy eyebrows drew together. "Where's Bethia?"

Gabriel looked paler than usual. "She—uh—died in childbirth. Giving birth to Jacob, here."

"How old is Jacob?" Hannah wanted to know."

"A little more than a year. Fifteen months."

Nat paused, then nodded. "Looks like a good, hefty lad. I'm sorry about Bethia."

Hannah stood up to go into the kitchen area. "Jody. Go up and fetch Auntie. Bid her come right away."

Who was Auntie? Had Nat taken another wife? Not very likely, considering his stand on plural marriage. Someone hired to help, perhaps. Marie bent to sooth Paul, who didn't seem to need it. He looked around with bright eyes, and munched on bits of apple which Hannah had provided.

Hannah and Gabrielle began doing things in the kitchen, setting out plates and glassware on the large table. Marie wondered if she should go help them. She started to get up, still holding Paul.

"Here." Sarah reached for him. "Let me take him."

Just then a figure appeared at the front door. Marie turned to look. She blinked, not believing her eyes. For it was Corey, an older Corey, who walked forward into the room, wiping her hands on her mud-smeared apron.

"Papa and I have been weeding the garden," she said. Then she stopped and put a hand to her face, her mouth open.

By this time Gabriel had risen to his feet. Marie was able to catch the expression of utter shock on his face. He looked deathly pale, as if he'd seen a ghost. Finally he gave a little nervous gesture with his hands. "I—uh—Sister Corey. I—I didn't look to find *you* here."

"Nor I you," she replied, although Marie sensed she was speaking with an effort.

"It's a long story," Nathaniel remarked. "You'll hear it all during dinner. We have a lot to catch up on."

Marie had the presence of mind to hurry and embrace Corey. "So nice to see you again," she murmured. Corey returned the hug, but her eyes were staring beyond, at Gabriel. *What to do?* Marie took Corey's hand. "Come and see my children. That's Louise, over on the bench. And this—" She led Corey over to Sarah. "This is Paul Gerard. Born last fall, he was."

"Oh, he's beautiful." Corey bent to look at him. "He has hair the color of Hannah's." Her eyes fell on Jacob, who was standing, clutching Gabriel's pant leg. "And who is this?"

Gabriel laid a hand on the boy's head. "This is Jacob. My son."

Marie saw Corey accept this news and then glance around the room. "Where's his mother?"

Gabriel opened his mouth and closed it; he seemed incapable of speech. Marie sighed. *How could men be so stupid?* She said quickly, "She died when Jacob was born. She's buried on Beaver Island."

"Oh. I'm sorry." Corey paused a moment, breathing fast. Then she began to cry, wiping at her eyes with her fingers. Marie put a hand on Corey's shoulder. She could feel Corey's body shaking with her sobs.

Gabriel reached down and picked up Jacob. "There's no need to fret so. I reckon she's gone to a better place. And she didn't live to see us thrown off the island. T'would've broke her heart, so see such things as that."

Corey nodded through her tears. But she couldn't seem to stop crying. Marie suspected that wasn't the reason Corey was weeping. But she didn't know how to communicate it to Gabriel.

"Come gather 'round," Hannah called. "After a trip like that, you must be starved."

"I'm hungry as a bear," Louise announced. Marie sighed again. All attempts to teach her manners had failed.

"Come on, then." Nathaniel took Marie by the arm and led her to

251

the table. She saw Gabriel offering his free arm to Corey, who took it, still wiping her eyes.

Set before them were slices of ham, a big dish of applesauce, corn on the cob, and boiled potatoes. A loaf of bread lay on the bread board, ready to be sliced and served. Close by was a dish of butter, and a jug of milk. Hannah invited everyone to sit down, and began pouring out mugs of milk for the children.

Corey took the seat to the left of Marie. "And where's your husband?" she asked as Hannah was getting the children settled.

Now it was Marie's turn to stammer and act confused. Gabriel, on the other side of Corey, tried to answer. "We don't rightly know. We got separated when they were putting us on the boats. We haven't seen him since, or Ed and Jess. Charley and Adriel be missing as well."

Corey patted Marie on the forearm. "I didn't know."

Nathaniel's voice cut across the other noises. "Let's pause for a moment of prayer."

Marie, who'd had her fill of prayer on the island, bowed her head. She should at least go through the motions, if only to keep peace with what was left of her family. Although she privately thought that if God had all power, He would not have allowed the terrible things which had happened on the island. And especially He would not have separated her from Rusty.

To her surprise, Nat's prayer was not pompous at all, but a heart-felt petition for healing after what they had undergone. It even had the feel of prayers she had remembered from the Nauvoo days. It ended with an expression of thanks for the ones who had reached safety, and a plea for help for those still missing.

She didn't like to admit it, but she felt comforted. They ate together, passing the potatoes and corn. Sarah fed Paul bits of food, and Gabriel gave Jacob morsels from his own plate.

"First, the food," Nat said. "Then we'll share our stories."

Another man entered the room and took a place beside Calvin. Marie recognized him just as Gabriel declared, "Why, if it isn't ol' Jubal Langdon himself. My favorite patient."

Corey's father smiled. "Good to see you again, Dr. Gabriel."

"What happened? Didn't you like Salt Lake City?"

"I dunno." Langdon's bushy white eyebrows drew together. "We never got there."

"You never got—" Gabriel began. Nat interrupted him.

"All that's for later. Have some more corn."

"Sorry to be late." Langdon brushed a hand over his thick white moustache. "Weedin' that last patch."

Gabriel leaned closer to Corey and said in a low voice, "I don't see your sister. Where's Casey?"

Corey wiped her lips with the cloth napkin. "We—we left her in western Iowa. The winter was too much for her. She's buried near Kanesville."

"*Eh bien.* I'm sorry to hear that." He nodded. "I reckon winter was hard for a lot of folks."

Finally it was time for the sharing of stories. Paul slept on Sarah's lap, and Jacob curled up, his thumb in his mouth, his head on Gabriel's chest. Nat leaned back in his chair. "All right, Gabriel. You go first."

"Why me? There's Calvin, and Marie and them."

Nat smiled. "Well, if you forget, they'll remind you."

"That's what I'm afraid of."

With all eyes on him, Gabriel began the story of the Voree settlement, the voyage to Beaver Island, and life on the island. In Marie's opinion, he handled the whole thing very well, only stumbling when he came to the shooting of Brother Strang and the confusion afterward. But then, Marie reasoned, he hadn't been an actual witness like Rusty and Charley. Then he described how the people had been forced from their homes and herded together, separated from their animals and possessions. He mentioned the splitting apart of families.

"They didn't care if folks were together or not. I never seen such lack of feeling. So our bunch was put on a boat for Chicago. And where Rusty and the others went, I have no idea."

"Another boat, most like," Calvin said.

"Well, yes. They couldn't stay on the island." He went on to tell of the death of James Strang, and their boat's arrival in Chicago.

"Now, we had some money. We hid it in Marie's bag full of

diapers—under the diapers, I might add. They never thought to check it."

Everyone laughed at that, but it was uneasy, nervous laughter. *The story is too dark*, Marie thought. But it was the truth. How could he change it?

"So, after a few carriage rides, a steamboat, and Burt's cart here, we managed to get back to a familiar place. And it sure is good to be here."

He'd said nothing about the persecutions, the hateful looks, the shoving as their enemies tried to get them on the boat. The heartless remarks, as if they were no better than cattle. And all because of their religion.

"I hope all your troubles are in the past," Nat remarked. "All right. Now for the Langdon family."

Corey seemed to be waiting for her father to speak. Finally he gave a cough and began. "Well, t'were the late summer of '47 that we started off. A wagon and two oxen, driven by the blacksmith Nigel Barrymore and his new wife. I drove some, but my daughters stayed in the back of the wagon, mainly. Oh, Corey helped with the cookin' and all that.

"Well, when we came to the Missouri River, the cold weather was settin' in. A heap of folks camped up and down the river, settlin' in, waitin' fer spring. Some built cabins and such like, to keep the cold off. Some folks took sick with the exposure and all. And I don't know rightly how it happened, but my youngest girl, Casey, came down with something-or-other. A weakness in her lungs. She couldn't stop coughing. And she—" He stopped, then swallowed. "We buried her there, on the prairie."

"Near Kanesville," Corey said.

"It be called Council Bluffs, now." There was silence for a moment. Then Jubal went on. "Now, toward spring, we began hearin' things about doings out in Salt Lake City. Riders comin' back through, on their way to Nauvoo to pick up more people. And what they said was that plural marriage was bein' taught and encouraged; it was an established fact, not just a rumor. I asked myself, did I want my daughter to be someone's plural wife? And I figured I didn't.

"Now, there was other folks feelin' the same way. One family had saved a huge cheese to pay their tithing when they reached Salt Lake.

The father didn't allow anyone to eat that cheese, no matter how hungry they got. But when he heard of the goings-on in the Salt Lake Valley, regarding plural marriage and all, he put his foot down. 'Cut the cheese!' he shouted. 'We are not going!'"

Everyone laughed, an easier, more relaxed laughter this time.

"Well, we found a ride back across the prairie, Corey and me. And the only place we could think to come was here."

"We're mighty glad you did," Nat said.

"I'll second that." Gabriel gave Corey a sideways look. "What about Nigel and his wife? Did they come back?"

Jubal shook his head. "They went on. I reckon they be in the valley by this time. Some folks just stayed where they was, just made their homes there along the river. Planted crops and such. We thought of doin' that. But I figure it was better to turn back."

There was a pause, a lull in the conversation, as if people were thinking about all the events which had been related. Hannah served the applesauce in little dishes. Gabriel took a spoon and began feeding it to Jacob. Corey watched, then said, "Here. Let me do it. If he's agreeable."

"Oh, he'll take food from anybody," Gabriel replied. "I—uh—no offense meant, of course."

She reached for the spoon and offered the applesauce to Jacob. He ate eagerly, looking at her with large, dark eyes.

Nat gave a little cough. "Well, I reckon yer wondering what we've been doing, while you were on your island and in Iowa and such-like."

Gabriel raised his eyebrows. "I figured you were farmin' and tryin' to raise children, like most folks."

Nat's lips moved before he spoke, a habit Marie recalled from past times. "How do you feel about Mr. Strang, now that it's come to an end? Still think he's a prophet?"

Gabriel waited, then said, "He was a very gifted leader, in some respects. Well-read, good at speaking—"

Calvin cleared his throat. "He had his good points and his bad. That plural marriage business was a mistake."

"So he went into polygamy," Nat said. "Why didn't you leave then?"

255

Gabriel gestured with his hands, a sign of agitation. "Maybe we should have. But our possessions were all on the island, and our livelihood was there. With our little children and the older folks, we thought it was best to stay put."

Nat nodded. "I see. Difficult to leave. I can understand."

"Another thing." Gabriel put a hand on his son's head. "It's hard to explain. But he was a friend to me. And a friend to most folks on the island. He wanted the best for us. It's hard to just dismiss him and say he was a false prophet."

Nat leaned forward. "Well, a group of us, and other little groups in this area, have been meeting on a regular basis. Just a bunch of old-time Saints, from Nauvoo and other parts, preachin' and studyin'. And prayin'. Lots's of prayin'"

Gabriel shrugged and smiled. "*Eh bien*. I hope it does something for you."

Nat went on. "Spoken like a true skeptic. Now, about the prayin'. You see, they're hoping that God will send a prophet and leader to them. And they're hoping it will be young Joseph Smith. The Prophet Joseph's oldest son."

Gabriel wiped Jacob's face with the napkin. "Wasn't he—I believe he was twelve when his father and uncle were killed."

"Well, he's grown up now. As a matter of fact, he's studied law. He got married just last spring. And I hear tell he might run fer Justice of the Peace, over in Nauvoo."

"That's a reversal. They're no longer ready to kill us, I take it." Gabriel put Jacob on the floor. The boy stood, clutching his father's knee. "How does the young man feel about leading a church?"

Hannah got up and began to clear the table. Nat put down his spoon. "He hasn't agreed yet. But they just started approaching him. The word was that he wasn't ready."

Gabriel nodded. "I hate to disillusion you. But he may never be ready. Do you realize what an undertaking that would be, to try and fill his father's shoes? Think of his family—what they would go through."

"Bein' a prophet ain't the easiest job in the world," Calvin added.

"That's why we pray," Nat answered. "For him, and for our little groups."

Gabriel made no reply. Nat gave a cough. "Now, I can understand your feelings about it. You've seen two leaders assassinated. Joseph Smith, and your Mr. Strang. So I reckon you're suspicious about one more."

Gabriel shrugged. "Actually, I have no particular feelings. It's an interesting prospect. I would say, he should do what he wants. And if God directs him to such a course, then so be it."

"That's how we look at it," Nat said. "But we pray anyway."

Gabrielle stood up to help her mother. The older children began carrying dishes to the sink. Corey rose from her chair, and Gabriel did likewise. Marie stood up and tapped him on the shoulder.

"I'll put Jacob to bed. Leave him with me; he'll be fine." *How could she signal him, that he should go off alone with Corey?*

It turned out that he didn't need a signal. Hannah took charge. "We'll put the babies down in the guest room. There's plenty of room for them on the big bed. And we'll be right next door."

"You go on," Marie told Gabriel. "Go get you some fresh air."

Gabriel moved closer to Corey. "Well, Corey. Will you come for a walk with me?"

She paused. "I reckon I will."

"We can stroll down to the river." This from someone who had walked beside a cart for most of the day.

Corey was dabbing at her eyes again. "If you like."

"The river!" Louise exclaimed. "Can we come too? Burt and I? I want to see the river. Don't you, Burt?"

"No!" Marie had not meant to sound so stern. "You be helping me in the kitchen, miss. And we have to put the young ones to bed."

"Oh, pig feathers," Louise retorted.

Marie stepped close to her. "Don't speak like that to me. Let your poor uncle alone. I'll tell you why, later."

Louise stomped into the kitchen behind Marie. The girl began rattling cups and plates, to show her mother how displeased she was.

"Watch your manners," Marie told her. "This is not your home."

She set Louise to work washing dishes. When she looked into the dining area, Gabriel and Corey were still there, talking with Nat. She sighed then and gave up. She had done all she could.

⚜

Seeing Corey again had shaken Gabriel to the core. He had managed to partake of the evening meal and feed Jacob, even answering Nat's questions and relating their adventures on the island. But his mind was in turmoil; it was all he could do to keep his composure. His medical training, even his skills and patience as a blacksmith, came to his aid as he tried to control his emotions. Even so, his hand trembled as he reached for the napkin to clean Jacob's face.

He had asked Corey to go walking with him, and she had consented. But Nat waylaid them at the door with more questions about Mr. Strang.

"At what point did you realize that he was not the prophet you envisioned?"

He tried to think of an answer. The last thing he wanted to do right then was to discuss Strang's merits as a leader. "I—I really can't say. I'm not sure what to think, right now."

"Well, you certainly should. After all, you're an elder."

"Well, I—"

Just then Hannah broke in. "Leave him alone for now. He just got here. And you know he must be tired—too tired to debate about who's a prophet and who isn't."

Nat backed away then, and Calvin joined the discussion. "After all, the poor man be dead and in his grave now."

Nat turned to him. "And you were left without a leader?"

This gave Gabriel a chance to get out the door with Corey. Hannah even held it open for them. They crossed the porch and he helped her down the three wooden steps. He sensed that she probably didn't need his help, since she'd been on her own these many years.

The heat of the day had ebbed, and there was a warm, gentle wind blowing from the river. They passed Baxter the mule, tied to a fence post. Then they followed the trail, stepping in and out of the tree shadows. Tall grass rustled on either side, and clumps of ferns turning brown with the change of seasons. Gabriel wasn't sure what to say, but he began.

"I can't tell you what a joy it is to meet up with you again. And a surprise."

She smiled. "Yes. Indeed, a surprise."

"All this time I thought you were in Salt Lake City. Settled down and raising children."

"I reckon not."

He tried to choose his words carefully. "I'm—I'm most sorry about your sister. You must miss her a great deal."

She looked at him, her eyes wide. He had forgotten how blue her eyes were. At first he was afraid she was going to cry some more. She said, "Not so much anymore. But Casey and I were connected, in a way most people didn't understand. I loved her, you see, and cared for her. And I know she loved me. I was all she had. Papa was usually out working, or someplace else during the day. But she and I had a special relationship, perhaps because I was responsible for most of her care. It wasn't something I expected to happen. But it was there, this special bond. It's hard to describe. I felt blessed, in a way."

Gabriel wondered about it as she spoke. How something regarded as a tragic event could turn out to be a blessing. "I understand."

"Do you? That's good. Not many people did."

He impulsively reached for her hand, and she let him take it. He had debated doing it earlier, but didn't want to seem forward or overeager. He still wasn't sure how she felt about him—the sudden appearance of someone from her past.

She said, "You must miss Bethia."

He frowned. "I blame myself for her death. Oh, I didn't kill her, or anything like that. It was just that I didn't know enough. I delivered the baby, and when I turned around to show her, she was gone."

She raised her eyebrows. "You shouldn't blame yourself. I'm sure you did everything you could."

"Well, there was sure something I didn't know. Something I

overlooked. Maybe her health was not what I thought it was." He smiled and shrugged. "Anyway, now I have a son. And I'm trying to be both father and mother to him."

She met his eyes. "That sounds impossible."

"Well, fortunately I have Sarah and Marie to help. Jess nursed him when he was first born. She had one of her own, and she just nursed Jacob along with Cinda."

"Cinda—that's a pretty name."

"She had another child too, a boy. They named him James Joseph—J. J. for short. He was so tiny, I wasn't sure he'd live. But he did."

He didn't feel up to telling her about Turah, and what had happened to her and Gray Wolf. He was wondering how to communicate to her his own feelings, his affection for her which had never stopped. Perhaps it was too soon to say anything. He should do some courting first.

They reached the area of swampy grass at the river's edge. The wind sent ripples rolling in, and made the sea of lily pads rise and fall. There were posts in the water, part of an ancient dock that had long since fallen apart. The last light coated the western edges of the posts with patches of red-gold. Gabriel watched as the reflections of posts and river reeds trembled with the wavelets. Corey spoke in the stillness. "And where are they now?"

"Jess and Eb? I wish I knew. I'm hoping that Charley and Adriel are with them, and Rusty too. Charley has enough smarts to keep them all safe."

She paused, then said, "How old is Jacob now?"

"Almost fifteen months."

"I should think you would have found another wife by this time."

That settled it. He would speak. The loveliness of the setting gave him new courage. "Corey, there's only one person in this world I would want to marry. And she wasn't on the island."

"Oh?" She looked at him, puzzled.

"I once had it in my mind to go looking for her. But I couldn't leave Jacob, you see."

"Of course. May I—will you tell me who it is? Is it someone I know?"

"She's standing right here."

Her mouth opened and her hand—the one he wasn't holding—flew to the side of her face. Before she could say anything, he went on, trying not to speak too fast. "I asked you to come for a walk with me. Now I'm asking you to walk with me forever. I've had feelings for you for a long time—I've always had you in my heart. I—"

Suddenly she burst into tears. Gabriel stopped, stricken; *what had he done?* Then she flung herself into his arms and he was holding her close to him. She seemed to speak with an effort.

"I will, Gabriel. I'm assuming that was a proposal of marriage. And I accept."

He kissed her on the lips, then kissed her tear-stained face. He marveled that they seemed to fit in each others' arms so naturally. He kissed her again and they began to relax and laugh together. He said, "I wasn't sure how you would feel about me, after all this time."

"How can you be so blind? I've always cared for you—I thought it showed in everything I did. Especially tonight. I thought everyone at the table would know."

He chuckled. "I was figuring I'd have to do a heap of courtin' first. Before I actually asked you."

"Well, you can do the courtin' too. Don't stop, just because I said I'd marry you."

"Should I—I reckon I should ask your father. For your hand, that is."

She laughed. "Ask him if you want. He's been tryin' to get me married off for years."

The opposite shore was dark in the deepening twilight. Beneath it, on the water, the rosy hue of sunset was reflected, a streak of soft pink.

"*Eh bien.* I reckon we better go tell the others. Before they all go to bed for the night. I have a feeling that Marie and Hannah will be 'specially pleased. And, as you say, your father. Then I'll walk you to your cabin."

They turned to retrace their journey back to the main house. The trees stood etched against the sunset's afterglow. Gabriel was struck with a heightened awareness of the beauty of it, an intense appreciation of life. He thought it strange that he could feel as happy as he did at that moment, after all that had happened to him. *"Men are, that they might have joy."* He whispered the old quote from the Book of Mormon.

"I think that goes for the women, too."

"I'm sure it does." He tightened his arm about her shoulders, and she nestled against him as they walked.

They passed the fence where the mule had been tied. The mule was gone. Gabriel wondered if he should raise an alarm. Then he saw three figures walking down from the barn: Calvin, Nat, and the boy Burt. He slipped his arm from around her shoulders and took her hand instead, waiting as the three approached.

"Mule's gone," he called.

"No, he's not," Nat replied. "He's settled in for the night. We had to put him on t'other side, with the cows, on account of Ol' Pete woulda kicked the living daylights outa him if'n he had the chance."

Corey whispered, "That's Nat's mule."

"Oh, I know," Gabriel answered. "I remember Ol' Pete. The meanest critter in three counties." In a louder voice, he said, "Nat, I reckon you'd better gather folks together. We got an announcement to make."

21

Misguided. **To think he** could go without food for a day. Now he felt not only lame and footsore, but hungry as well. He had kept a few scraps for Rags, but none for himself. He watched as Rags ate the last few bits of bacon.

He figured he was just north of Fort Madison. If that were true, a day's walking would bring him to the Montrose area. He brushed the straw from his clothes—he'd spent the night in a haystack. Not that bits of straw mattered—the clothes were threadbare. In other words, he looked like a tramp. He ran his hand over his growth of beard. Soon he would resemble his dog more than his former self.

In a short time they were walking on the road leading south. He knew he would have to swing west to avoid the stretch of swamp. Then east and south again. He stopped to pick apples from a farmer's orchard. Three—that should do it. He continued walking, eating apples. It would take more than apples to give him the strength he.needed.

That was why he had not stopped at one of the farmhouses and offered to chop wood last night. He didn't feel he had the strength to do it. Besides that, his feet had begun to ache in a way he'd never experienced before. He figured he'd feel better in the morning.

Around mid-morning he felt his feet simply giving out. And the injured knee was aching again. He picked up a stout stick from the road's edge and used it as a cane. He should have kept the cane Charley had made for him. But he didn't reckon on needing it.

He limped through the town—it was indeed Fort Madison. Then

he knew he had to stop. Maybe rest for a bit. He tried to think what to do. He had no money. He'd given his watch—a gift from Hannah and Marie—to the man who rowed him across the river. His only hope was to rest, maybe even a few days, and then try to look for work. *But where to rest?* There was swampy land on one side, and tangled underbrush, the beginning of forest, on the other. At any rate, he knew he couldn't go much farther.

He whistled for the dog and slowly made his way to the forested side of the road. He found a large maple, its leaves just starting to turn. In fact, one whole branch was a bright orange-red. Just as he was placing his knapsack at the foot of it, he heard the *clip-clop* of horse's hooves on gravel, a large, solitary horse, from the sound of it.

He looked around. It wasn't a horse, but a handsome bay mule, pulling a cart. The driver, hardly more than a boy, pulled up beside him.

"Howdy, sir. You walk like you need a little help. Can I give you a ride?"

Rusty reached for the knapsack. "You sure can. I'd much appreciate it."

He put his knapsack in the back of the cart. Then he picked up Rags and climbed up beside the driver. "Hope you don't mind. The dog goes, too."

"Not at all." The driver had wispy blond hair and a freckled nose. He wore a straw hat that had seen better days. At least it shielded him from the sun. "How far you goin'?"

Rusty ran his fingers over the dog's back. "Just south of Montrose."

"Is that a fact? That's where I'm headed."

"Oh?" Rusty looked at him.

"I got a friend down there—I reckon, a bunch of friends. This girl said I can visit whenever I like."

Rusty smiled. "You seem too young to have a girlfriend."

"Oh, she's not a girlfriend. Just a special, nice friend. One of the nicest folks I ever met. They meet for church in a house nearby. And I been meetin' with them."

"What church is this?" Rusty asked.

"I don't know the name. One person said it was the church of Jesus Christ. But I thought all churches were that."

"And what's so special about this church?" Rusty asked, intrigued.

"I don't know. They talk about Jesus a lot, and how He's comin' back. And there's gonna be a time of love and peace—sort of a golden age."

Rusty smiled. "I reckon you just want to see that girl again."

The boy reddened. "Maybe so. But I do like this church. They're just really kind to each other. Like they care about what each person is doing."

"Maybe you simply caught them on a good day."

"They talk about some prophet who might be their leader someday. Something about the 'seed of Joseph.'"

"Joseph? Joseph Smith?"

"I'm—I'm not sure. A bunch of 'em came from some island up in Michigan."

Rusty sat up straighter. "Beaver Island?"

"I don't rightly know."

Was it possible? A group of Strangites in Iowa? "I think those might be my people. That's where I came from—an island in Michigan."

The boy looked at him, eyes wide. "You walked all that way?"

"Well, no. Half the time I was on a boat, and recovering from a—well, an altercation."

"A beating, you mean." The boy's lips tightened in a hard line.

"You can call it that. But I survived."

The boy shook his head. "No wonder yer havin' trouble walking."

They drove through the town of Montrose. Rusty found it hard to remember what it had looked like ten years ago. The livery stable was still there, the public house on the corner. At the edge of town, the mule hesitated. The cart slowed.

"Ho, Baxter!" the boy shouted. "Giddyup!" The mule broke into a trot. "We been here enough times, I thought he knew the way."

To Rusty's surprise, they started up the road toward the Givens' farmhouse. At the front steps, Rusty said, "I reckon I'll get off here. I can't thank you enough for the ride. I was plumb tuckered."

"That's all right," the boy relied. "I'm taking the cart around in back and tying up my mule."

Rusty jumped down with his knapsack and dog, and stood wondering if his feet would hold out till he reached the front door. He set Rags on the ground. Then he shouldered his pack and climbed the two steps to the door. He knocked. *What if Marie were not there? What would he do—how would he find her?*

The door opened. Nat stood there, tall, broad-shouldered, with a fuller beard than Rusty had remembered. They looked at each other, Nat drawing in his breath.

"Don't tell me you don't recognize me," Rusty began.

"Well, my gracious!" Nat exclaimed. "If it isn't the last of the Strangites!"

Rusty grasped him by the upper arms. "Oh, tell me, please. Don't tease me now. Is she here?"

"Who?"

"Marie. My wife. Don't tell me she's not here."

"Son, there's a whole bunch of folks here. In fact, I reckon yer just in time for a wedding. A few more days, and we'll have the ceremony. Now, you know women—there's all sort of preparations they have to make and such-like."

Noises from the interior of the house. Four women hurried out of the kitchen, all wearing aprons. He recognized Hannah and to his surprise, Corey. One he reckoned must be Gaby, Nat's oldest daughter. Rusty remembered how they'd named her after Gabriel when he delivered her, long ago on the flight from Far West.

Then he heard a shriek, and a rushing sound. Before he could brace himself, Marie flew into his arms, almost sending him back down the steps. He embraced her and held her, not moving, both of them weeping. They stood together until Nat gave a cough. "Come into the room, at least. If'n I don't close the door, we'll have a passel of flies."

Rusty took a few steps into the room. Nat grabbed his arm. "Land's sakes, son. You c'n hardly walk."

"He's injured." Marie took his other arm.

"No, I'm not," he declared. "That is, I was. But I've recovered."

He felt Nat sliding the backpack from his shoulders. "Just sit down, now. Where's Gabriel? Let's get the doctor in here."

"He's over workin' on his cabin." Marie wiped her eyes with the edge of her apron. "The one he and Corey are going to live in."

"So they're the ones gettin' married." Rusty scratched at his beard. "How did he find her? I thought she went with the folks goin' west."

"They started," Nat explained. "But she and her father came back."

Hannah hurried toward them, wiping her hands on her apron. "Don't get up." She leaned over to hug him. "We're so glad you're safe. You'll never know how we worried."

Rusty shook his head. "I did some worryin' myself."

Nat smiled. "I reckon you did."

Hannah straightened up. "Gaby's gone to fetch our father. He's over helpin' Gabriel. And I know you want to see your children. Paul's asleep right now—Sarah's lookin' after him. And Louise—she and Elizabeth are outside with Burt."

"Burt," Rusty repeated. "That's the young feller with the mule?"

"That's right. Oh—you rode in with him."

"He showed up in the nick of time," Rusty replied. "A very helpful young man."

"Isn't he nice? He's been meeting with us Sundays, over at our neighbor's house."

"So I've heard." Rusty felt tiredness creeping over him. He spoke with an effort. "I couldn't have made it without him."

Nat moved toward the door. "I'll go find Gabriel. I think he needs to see you."

There was a scratching noise at the door, then a series of sharp whines.

"That's my dog." Rusty turned his head weakly.

"Your dog?"

"Rags. I got him in southern Michigan. This place outside Detroit, where Eb and Jess are now. Sort of a communal farm."

"You left them there and picked up a dog?" Nat opened the door. Rags rushed in, his stump of a tail wagging. He jumped into Rusty's lap and licked his face.

"My goodness!" Marie exclaimed. "Does he do that often?"

"I'll tell you about Eb and Jess later." Rusty stroked the dog's back. "They're in a safe place. This little fella—he stayed with me all the way from Detroit."

"When did you eat last?" Hannah suddenly asked.

Rusty tried to think. "Two days ago. I had some apples this morning."

"I declare! Let's get you something." She hurried back into the kitchen.

"Why didn't you eat?" Marie asked.

"No money for food. And I felt too weak to chop wood for anyone."

Marie looked ashamed, as if she regretted asking the question. She looked at Rags. "He's a cute little dog. Sort of funny-looking, with that little beard."

"He could use a bath, most like," Rusty said. "And so could I."

"I reckon you'll get all that." Nat glanced out the window. "Here comes Gabriel now. He didn't need for anyone to fetch him."

"Here's some food." Hannah put a plate on the end table. There was a thick slice of bread with butter, and a bit of ham and cheese. She set a mug of cider beside it. "Don't let the dog get it."

"Well, he's hungry, too." Rusty reached for the food.

"I have something for him in the kitchen. Come on—what's his name?"

Rusty's mouth was full of bread. "Wags."

"Here, Wags." Hannah snapped her fingers.

Rusty swallowed. "Rags. Rags."

Even with his proper name, the dog refused to leave Rusty's lap. Finally Hannah brought some scraps of ham in a little bowl. She set it on the floor. The dog jumped down to eat.

"I see he's attached to you. Dogs don't generally eat in the front parlor."

Rusty sighed. "I know. This'll be the last time."

Gabriel opened the front door and entered. "*Qu'est-ce que c'est?* What have we here?"

268

"H'lo, Gabe." Rusty reached to shake his hand. "I'm having trouble walking."

Gabe was smiling. "You are? Well, I see you have no trouble eating. That's good. Don't stop."

"Hey, Gabe. What's this I hear about your gettin' married?"

"That's right. If you can stand on that day, you'll be my best man."

The thought of standing made Rusty groan. Gabe looked at him. "When did you start having pain?"

"It's been comin' on. Both feet, and then my knee. I thought the knee was all healed. I rested up some, back in Detroit. But the last few days, it's been something fierce."

Gabe nodded. After a pause, he spoke. "I reckon you're plumb tired out. I think, with a few days of rest and good food, and Marie's care, you'll be good as new. Fit as a fiddle, as they say."

"Are you sure?"

Gabe laughed. "Well, that's my prescription."

The dog jumped back onto Rusty's lap. Gabe raised his eyebrows. "Who's this?"

"They gave 'em to me in Detroit. He's been with me ever since."

"*Eh bien*. I hope you haven't been lugging *him* around. That'll wear you out faster than anything."

"Oh, no. He walked, mainly. When he wasn't chasing something."

Before long, the rest of the family entered in little groups and greeted Rusty. His father hugged him, tears running down his face, and held his hand a long time. Louise sat on the arm of the chair and laid her head on his forehead. "What a darling dog. Look, Burt. Papa, this is Burt."

Rusty smiled. "We've met."

People sat on the parlor chairs and the settle, and the young ones took places on the floor. Sarah brought Paul in to see his father. Finally, Rags moved over so Paul could sit on Rusty's lap.

"That's a fine thing," Sarah scolded. "Can't hold your own son on account of some old dog."

Rusty shrugged. "There seems to be room for both."

While Hannah and Corey worked in the kitchen, Rusty gave an

account of his travels, and what had happened to Eb and his family. "They're safer than they would be here, from all I've heard. Louise, the last thing J. J. said to me was, 'Tell Louise we be free at last.'"

Then he told about Charley and Adriel, and their decision to return north. "Like as not, they be workin' on one of those steamships, hoping to get back to northern Michigan."

Gabe said, "I hope they have the good sense to write us a letter. As for this farm, Shadrach's Hollow, do you reckon you c'n find it again?"

"Oh, yes. I know right where it is."

"Maybe we can go up there someday and see if we can find Eb."

At this, a look of horror went across Marie's face. Rusty wanted to laugh. Gabe said quickly, "But not too soon."

For the first time in many days, Rusty felt a sense of peace settling over him. Marie was with him at last—she was holding his hand again, kneeling by the side of his chair. And his family was intact. Paul was even now patting the dog and exploring his floppy ears. Rags didn't seem to mind at all.

"All right," Hannah announced. "It's dinner time. I have a cloth to wash Paul's hands. I'm afraid Rags will have to go outside for a bit."

"He won't mind. He'll be fine." Rusty handed Paul to Marie. Then he got to his feet. He managed to reach his seat at the table with a minimum of pain. Everyone gathered around while Hannah gave directions. "Burt, you sit here, next to Elizabeth. Louise, you help Jacob."

They paused while Nat said the blessing on the food. Then they passed around potatoes and corn, sliced tomatoes and fresh-baked bread.

Rusty reached for the bread. "You know, I think I'm going to recover."

Nat gave a laugh. "I was sure of it."

They ate and talked together, the conversation punctuated by whines and scratching from the door. "Your dog needs to be taught some manners," Nat remarked.

"Oh, he'll get used to being outdoors." Rusty waved his napkin. "He was right good company on the journey."

Finally the talk got around to the question of church succession and what was happening to the Strangites.

"Far as I've heard, there's no leader yet," Rusty's father remarked. "Leastways, none that we know about."

Nat mentioned the hope of the little groups meeting in Illinois and Wisconsin—that the oldest son of Joseph Smith would become their leader.

"You people are looking for another prophet?" Rusty lifted the mug of cider. "Well, as Eb would say, here we go again!"

Gabe laughed. "You're right. Eb would say something like that."

"I'm done with man-made leaders," Rusty's father declared. "'Specially self-proclaimed ones."

The people who had been on the island looked tired in the fading light, as if any interest in following another leader was the last thing on their minds. Maybe it was simply his perception, Rusty thought. God knows, he'd felt discouraged and disheartened a number of times. An image flitted through his mind, the dream he'd had, of Nathaniel leading them all to the top of a mountain. The recollection made him pause; he decided not to say anything critical. Then he became aware of Gabe watching him from across the table. Gabe smiled.

"I reckon we all need to rest a spell, and think about getting used to normal life again."

"I be wonderin' if this area could used another blacksmith shop," Rusty's father said.

"Why not?" Gabe speared another potato with his fork. "'Course it'll take a while to buy all the equipment we'd need."

Rusty's father went on. "We got me and Rusty, and Gabe. 'Course, I'm gettin' up in years."

Jody leaned forward. "I'd like to know the trade."

"So would I," Burt said.

Rusty's father laid his napkin down by his plate. "There you go. Young blacksmiths, ready to learn."

Gabe pushed back his chair. "I'll keep an eye out for tools. Well, Corey, my dear. Shall we take a walk before candlelight?"

In a few days Rusty had regained much of his strength. He was able to walk outside and down the path to the barn, Rags trotting behind.

"I swear, that dog," Nat remarked. "He waited outside the door all the while you were resting up."

"He's a good little dog."

"Well, if he can keep the rats outa the barn, and not get kicked by Ol' Pete, he'll be doing well."

Rusty was able to stand up with Gabe the day of the wedding. The ceremony took place in the Givens' front parlor, with Nat officiating and the sunlight streaming through the windows. A crowd of family and neighbors, farming people from the area, sat on chairs carried in from the dining room. After a vocal solo, a simple hymn sung by young Gaby, the two exchanged vows.

Corey appeared radiant, young again, but all Rusty could think of was Marie and how lovely she looked with her dark hair pinned up in a bun and her best clothes—some of the few that she had, since they were in the process of sewing new clothes for all of the travelers. He thought how lucky he was to have her as his own. When he started to walk toward her after the ceremony, her eyes met his, and he marveled that he had come home at last.

22

From the Journal of Elder Russell Manning,
November 20, 1862, Montrose, Iowa

BOTH NAT AND GABE say that when One becomes an Elder, he should keep a Journal. Now, I can't write as Good as they can, so I'm just going to pretend I am Talking (which they say I do Right well). And maybe folks will get the Gist of what I be trying to say.

Now, I should've been writing in it right Along, but being of a Lazy nature (again, according to Nat) and inclined to put things off, I have neglected my Duty. So this is an attempt to make up, so to speak, for all the Writing I should have done.

Let's see, now—where shall I start? Gabe and Corey got married—well, maybe you knew that already. Happened six years back. But what you didn't know is that they set to having children right off—three in Six years. There be Casey, almost five years old by now, and Matthew and Jubal, twins, three-and-a-half. And she be expecting again. I'm not sure Gabe knows what to do with all those Young ones—Marie and I have another, name of Suzanne, who is two. She and Paul Gerard be in there most of the time, with Gabe's family. They all seem healthy and energetic, which keeps Marie and Corey on their toes.

As for Gabe—I've never seen him Happier. He has his medical Work, of course. Him and my father, along with me, have managed to open a Blacksmith shop, and while it doesn't have all the fancy Tools we had on Beaver Island, it seems to answer the needs of Folks in these parts.

Hannah takes care of most of the Cooking, and we all give her a hand. We like to take our Meals together, in the main house. Sometimes it puts me in mind of the early Christians, and how they shared meals with each other. Of course it's probably Noisier than any early Christian gathering, with all the yelling and little ones crying, Rags barking outside, and the mules kicking up a fuss in the pasture. But there's a good feeling about it, if you Know what I mean.

My Louise is all of 16 now, almost as Pretty as her mother. But she has a mind of her own—I reckon her Mother does too.

Burt, the young man with the mule, is learning the blacksmith Trade along with Jody, Nat's boy. He's also paying court to Elizabeth, Jody's young Sister. While I had hopes for Burt as my own son-in-law, it seems to be Elizabeth he's Partial to.

Gaby, Nat's oldest daughter, married a young fellow from a farming family over in Montrose. They be living in Town now.

My own father and Sarah be getting On in years. They seem devoted to each other, though Sarah scolds him a Lot. We all look after them, and he likes to help in the shop.

My son Paul is six and a half now, a sturdy little fellow. He and Jacob, Gabe's oldest, are always together, and the trouble they can get into is Amazing. Last week they disturbed a bee hive, and the bees even chased into the House after them. I be minded of the days when I fancied myself teaching Paul about Boats and fishing, but the only boat he sees now is Nat's old skiff, still Afloat after all these years. My dog Rags is almost eight now, I figure, still following me Most everywhere. He's sleeping now, his head resting on my Boot so he'll know if I move.

Rags went on a Journey with Gabe and me. We went back to southern Michigan, going by Rail, stage, and our own two feet. I made a little valise for Rags, with holes in the sides, and he would jump into it on Command. This served us well for steamboat rides and train travel. He knew to be Mighty quiet. No one even knew we had a Dog.

"Of all things," Gabe said to me. "A dog on a missionary journey. Whoever heard of such a thing?"

We managed to find Shadrach's Hollow—it was still there, flanked by the Mennonite and Quaker settlements. John Bestertag, an old man by this Time, welcomed us with joy. But when Gabe and Eb saw each other—it were an amazing thing. They actually fell into each others' arms and wept, like folks did in the Old Testament. Later, the whole community Listened while Gabe and Eb told how Eb had been rescued, wounded, from the Ohio River and led to safely by Gabe, back in old Gallipolis.

They let us preach, and we told them some about the groups of People uniting into a new church, with the young Joseph Smith III as their president. Sure enough, Eb said "Here we go again." But he listened most attentively with the others while Gabe described the Things which had happened.

I should explain that Young Joseph did indeed feel led to take his place at the head of the church—in fact, he stated that he did so in obedience to a Power not his own. The people accepted him as their leader and prophet—this was back in 1860. In this new Organization, great care has been taken to see that no one individual has absolute power, and that Everyone has a say in the direction and procedures of the church. Common consent is carefully observed. So far it seems to be Working.

I must admit that I had Reservations at first, and came into the movement rather reluctantly, perhaps because of my experience on the island. What Won me over in fact was Joseph Smith's strong views against Slavery and his admiration of Mr. Abraham Lincoln. As I write these Words, it is now two months since the signing of the Emancipation Proclamation, and I can only Rejoice, with tears in my eyes, that my friends Eb and Jess, and others like them, are indeed free People.

With the start of the War and all, we searched our hearts for what to do. We knew this was the conflict that would End slavery, yet we, as ministers and followers of the Lord Jesus, were Forbidden to take life. Now, some of the fellows tried to enlist, but by the time they went over to the recruitment office, they found that the Quota for the area had already been filled. So they were free to Defend their families here at home. A few of our people did join up, and as Far as I know, they are somewhere with the Union Army.

We haven't gone north to find Charley and Adriel yet, but Nat did get a letter from them about a Year ago. They found other Strangite families in Voree and spent some Time there. Then they went to work on one of the lake freighters, and after a couple of voyages, they ended up in the Grand Traverse Area. That's well South of Beaver Island. Every so often, they run into other people, followers of Strang, who had been on the Island. But, as they say, they keep Mighty quiet about it. No one knows; everyone thinks they're just like Ordinary folks, with no memories of violence or persecution. I like to think of those two, out on the big water, fishing and working on Boats—just what they liked to do.

Strange how our past affects us, the good along with the bad. I know that I'm not the same person I was when I left Nauvoo. For Gabe and Marie and all of us, so much has Happened. I think of Brother Strang and his kindness to us, and I think of young Joseph and the words he heard when he was debating whether or not to go to Utah and unite with the People there. He had a spiritual experience in which he was Told not to do so, for "the light in which you stand is greater than theirs." All these things Flash through my mind, and I begin to think that maybe I am in a good spot, the right place for me at the present Time.

Beaver Island. At times I think of it, the way it was When I was there, and I imagine that if I were to return there, I would find the same people I Knew before—Brother Strang with his straw hat and his black-and-white checked trousers, Bethia in the bloom of youth, expecting a child...my own oldest children, infants again, and Marie waiting for me in her bloomer outfit. Eb and Jess are there, and Charley and Adriel, just returned from a fishing trip. Even Turah and Gray Wolf are there, drawing bird pictures for each other.

Now I know this is my own mind doing strange things, for some of those folks are no longer on the Earth. So I tell myself. But sometimes in the early morning, I wake up and hear the sound of the Waves breaking on the shore, the cries of the sea birds. I smell the scent of pine and the fresh water, tinged with the faint scent of fish. I feel the sense of freedom and joy that I felt when I was there, returning along the trail to our group of cabins. And for me, I Rejoice in the life that was mine, the people that I knew and, yes, loved. And I go back to sleep wrapped in the Knowledge that myself, my family, and all those living and dead, whom I knew, are in the hands of an Eternal God.

About the Author

ELAINE STIENON GREW UP in Detroit and began writing fiction at an early age. One of her first short stories appeared in National Scholastic Magazine when she was sixteen years old. She attended the University of Michigan, majoring in English and American literature, and won a Hopwood Award (a prize in creative writing) for a collection of short fiction in her junior year.

Since that time, five of her novels have been published, two by Herald House in Independence, Missouri. She has had short stories published in literary magazines such as Phoenix, South, the Cimarron Review, the Ball State University Forum, The Writer's Journal, and the Bear River Review. A piece of flash fiction, 'Skipping School,' won an award and publication from the Potomac Review.

Children of a Northern Kingdom is the fourth in a series of historical novels dealing with the early Mormons, their efforts to stay together in spite of persecutions, their wanderings, their eventual exodus from Nauvoo, Illinois, their city on the Mississippi, and their dispersion. Two of the novels have won recognition. *In Clouds of Fire* was a Best Books Award Finalist in 2008, and *The Way to the Shining City* was a runner-up in the Los Angeles Book Festival in 2011.

About the Artist

The cover artist is Constance van Rolleghem, who studied drawing, art history, and painting restoration at the Académie Royale des Beaux-Arts in Brussels. Her work has appeared in galleries in New York and Brussels. Her art focuses on the way we express ourselves within a language that we cannot master, playing with the accidental or voluntary mistakes of communication and the completely abstract sense of communication as a sound, gesture or word.

The cover art is from a series of micro-images that capture a moment within the fluid layering of papers, paints, and light. It is a product of the most abstract sense of a message, where what appears is the remnant of a physical trace of an action or gesture.

Currently, she is the Co-chair of the Museum Access Consortium, an organization promoting diversity and inclusion in cultural institutions. She is also a member of the education advisory board for the Rett Clinic at Montefiore Hospital, and was the co-founder of Blue Sky Girls "Reach for the Top," an annual worldwide event to raise awareness of Rett Syndrome.

More of her work is featured on her website: www.artance.com.

Printed in the United States
By Bookmasters

11-2018